MIRROR MAN

MIRROR MAN

William M. Heim

Chapter 1

There were sounds of people all around him. Happy people mostly, chattering incessantly about those events in life that cause one to pump their fists in the air and yell "Yes, Yes" at the top of their lungs. People bursting with anticipation as they waited for the arrival of close friends. They wanted badly to share news of a promotion, or maybe to rave about a new romance. Those celebrating personal triumph were among the faithful gathered here tonight. A team of weekend warriors crowded against the bar, banging together sweaty mugs of sloshing brew to cheer their latest softball victory. Not far away, two tables had been pushed together, and three generations rose to their feet and joyously lifted their crystal champagne flutes to toast the arrival of a first born child. The fourth generation was here. Back further, deep in a quiet nook just far enough away from the kitchen to muffle the stampede of bustling waitresses, a lone couple locked eyes. The man extended his arms across the table, palms up, and the woman placed her palms on his, fingers entwined. They were deep into a ritual as old as the Willow trees for which this town was known and as unpredictable as a Missouri winter. White wines nearly untouched, an exciting chapter of their lives was just beginning.

All these people. He could feel their energy, and almost see the aura they exuded as he watched their animated movements tell a story. There was no need to actually hear their words, he could read their faces and bodies as well as he could read a well-spun tale. He was allowing the forest of emotion and humanity to envelop his very being. He could drink it in just as easily as the softball team's beer bellied part-time left fielder and full-time stockbroker guzzled his Michelob. The hair at the nape of his neck was still wet from the exertions of his play, and a single drop of amber liquid that missed his open lips dribbled down his whiskered chin. It formed a bead that dropped unnoticed onto the bare thigh of his twenty-something full-time secretary and part-time mistress. *They're already shitfaced.* He suspected the stockbroker had left his best game on the field, and his performance in bed would be deadened by the alcohol. *Poor girl.*

He resumed scanning the bar, looking for more amusing vignettes. He sensed movement right beside him, and caught the scent of perfume.

"Ever seen anything like this?" A woman's voice interrupted his thoughts.

He turned toward the voice, and looked up from his stool at the auburn haired woman standing next to him at the bar. She was absolutely breathtaking, even without the alcohol filter that made most of the clientele here at least palatable. He guessed she was around forty, but a less astute observer might have said thirty-three. She was not slim by today's waif-like standards, but she could hold her own with any fashion model he'd ever seen. There was not an inch of flesh on her that was anything less than firm and toned, except maybe for the gentle slopes of her perfumed breasts, which could be seen peeking out of the top of her form fitting jade green dress. The color of her dress complimented her hair and eyes perfectly. This had to be her best *fuck me* outfit. He looked at her shapely legs and dropped his gaze to her feet. A least three inches of heels were strapped to her ankles. He smiled his best smile.

"This is incredible. Who would ever think that there would be a place like this in the middle of a gymnasium."

"Believe me, this is no ordinary gym. I sometimes think that working out is only an afterthought around here. This is a whole social event, every day, every minute. I've belonged here for three years now, and I still discover new wrinkles. It's never boring. I can spend hours just watching what goes on, the parade of studs and starlets alone provides an interesting backdrop. I've never seen you here before. Are you a member?"

"Not yet. Actually I just dropped in to see what it's like. A friend of mine recommended it. I can see why."

"No question about it, it's an experience. Is your . . . your friend meeting you tonight?" She lowered her voice and put on a sultry face as she spoke, and her message was clear. She looked at him with anticipation. *She's mine for the taking,* he thought. *If she only knew.* She seemed to fit his profile. This place was indeed a target rich environment. But tonight, he had different prey in mind. He looked at her with regret, and unlike most of his performances, he was sincere this time.

"Yes," he said finally. "I'm expecting her soon." He paused, unsure if he should be so bold, but after two Manhattans decided he would. "It's nothing permanent. Maybe another time?"

"Maybe," she answered, and let her fingers caress his wrist and arm as she turned and walked away.

Despite the outward appearance of celebration and happiness, he knew this place also harbored those in desperation and decline. As he continued to wait for his "friend," he allowed his dark side to take over. He resumed scanning this crowded menagerie of humanity. Despite its rich leather and wood trappings and its unusual location, it was still just a bar. There were those who came here to drown their sorrows and to drink the liquid courage needed to speak their minds, and it didn't take him long to pick them out. There was a middle aged man and woman seated near the entrance, caught in the din of revelry, but engaged in a muted but heated argument that was anything but happy. They were framed by the neon lights that rimmed the doorway to the lounge, close enough to be bathed by the garish glow. The effect was surreal, like an Andy Warhol painting. And then there was the man seated by himself at the opposite end of the long bar, slumped against the wall. The man's head was bobbing and weaving, like drunks often do before nodding off to a dead sleep. For an instant, their eyes met, although the drunk's were unable to focus. They were empty, devoid of any hope or promise. He thought about seeing his own reflection just a few hours ago, as he shaved and prepared for this meeting tonight. *If the eyes are the windows to the soul*, he thought, *then God help us both.*

Chapter 2

With his rage still seething beneath a calm surface, he sat silently at the bar, hoping there would be no further interruptions. She should be here soon. He had talked her into meeting him for a drink. It was a tough sell, but he did it. He told her that he had some items of hers he wanted to give back, and that he wanted closure. Women liked that word "closure." They needed to wrap things up all nice and neat. *I'm finished with this part of my life. It's over. Final.* So with his best soothing manner he had convinced her to join him, despite her reservations. He had always had a pleasant way about him, and had capitalized on his good looks and salesmanship to permit him entrance to mainstream society. Only a few people knew that this was an act, a performance. In reality, he was a dark and malevolent creature who learned social grace only so he could invade one's private space without notice or alarm. He was a virtual Trojan Horse. He had chosen his seat in the lounge so that he was in position to see her when she entered without her seeing him. He wanted to watch her come in, to see her face and body as she entered, unaware she was being observed. He wanted just a moment to decipher any messages that she was sending by her choice of clothes, or the way she'd styled her hair and applied her makeup. He knew that when she spotted him she would mask her emotions instantly. He'd seen her do it before, and she was good at it. Before that happened, he needed just a moment to look at her and decide on one of two courses of action.

She arrived fifteen minutes late. This was typical for her, one of her little flaws. He remembered waiting for her to arrive at the club in Atlanta on many occasions, feeling frustrated and a bit awkward as he unconsciously checked and rechecked his watch. But he also remembered that she was always worth the wait. Tonight was no different. She was dressed to kill in a fiery red dress, cut low at the neck and high on the thighs. Her blond hair was swept up into an elegant design, perfectly framing her delicate face and exposing the nape of her smooth, sensuous neck. She was even more beautiful than the woman who tried to pick him up. He felt himself stir immediately. Before she turned in his direction, he looked at her intently, taking in her expression, trying to read the thoughts behind her sparkling green eyes. Unfortunately, he didn't see what he'd hoped for, a look of longing, perhaps even desperation. Instead, she looked confident, seeming to indicate her life was okay at least, maybe even better than okay. This was difficult for him to take. No, this was impossible for him to take. He'd thought for a long time what he'd do if this ever happened, and so was prepared for the choice he now made that would change his life....and end hers. So be it.

She had spotted him, and walked toward the bar, her hips swaying with that unique rhythmic motion that was of one her sensual trademarks. He rose to greet her. He smiled his best smile.

He didn't want it to turn out the way it did. Really he didn't. When he first began to watch her, he had none of the thoughts that would lead him to believe he was capable of the horrendous course of events that would soon follow. That kind of behavior was behind him. He had moved on. Sure he was spying on her, but meant no harm. He was simply curious. He had followed her to Highland Park, and innocently watched her from afar for several weeks. Well, maybe it wasn't really so innocent, but his feelings were not strong enough to be labeled an obsession. He had no evil intent. He had no ultimate plan. He just wanted to see what she was doing, to see if she missed him. At first, everything was all right. She seemed content, but not happy. She had a job, and occasionally went shopping. Once, she went to the movies, by herself. No sign of other men, no sign she was doing better without him. This was good, and he was almost satisfied. As long as there was no one else, as long as leaving him didn't make her life better, he could handle it. He had pretty much resigned himself to the fact that *he* would never be happy. He had come to know that a true, intimate relationship was never going to be in his grasp. On those couple of occasions he had come close, it was snatched from him quickly, leaving him broken and depressed. It was safe to say he'd given up hope. He was even planning to leave and return to Atlanta, he was ready to quit and leave her alone.

Then it happened. It was a Friday night, the last time he was going to watch her. He was sitting down the block in a rental car, his fourth in three weeks. He didn't want to set any patterns or be recognized as a frequent intruder in the neighborhood, so he had periodically changed disguises, costumes, and cars. He was accumulating quite a variety of different looks, and was getting pretty good at masking his appearance. Fortunately, she lived in a bustling neighborhood of apartment dwellers and transients, so his frequent comings and goings were not noticed. He had even taken a few walks around the development, learning much about the routines and habits of the occupants. No one even looked twice at him, let alone challenge or question him. Once, he had spent hours in the lobby of one of the larger apartment buildings here, just lounging in a plush chair, watching some TV and reading magazines. He looked as if he belonged, and most of the residents and visitors who saw him took him for a new resident. He enjoyed this juxtaposition of anonymity and acceptance. After all, he was just watching, and gave no reason for concern.

About eight o'clock a silver Lexus pulled up to her apartment. A tall man with short dark hair got out and walked directly to her building. The man was around forty, give or take a couple of years, but looked much younger. The guy was in good shape and was dressed stylishly, which may have contributed to his youthful appearance. He had often thought about her apartment, what it looked like inside. A few times, he had almost been overcome with the desire to break in and see, but had managed to resist. He could picture it in his mind, and imagined a neat, stylishly decorated home filled with her particular taste and her unique touches of femininity. He sniffed the air unconsciously, his mind searching for her scent.

The dark haired man looked at the three doorbells; one for her, one for the old lady who lived in the apartment above her, and one for the even older man who lived on the first floor. He rang the middle bell, and seconds later was buzzed into the common foyer. The man disappeared behind the closing door. He knew from experience that the smoked glass of the door's windowpane prevented anyone from seeing into the foyer. He had tried before, close up, and only saw his own reflection in the glass, like a mirror. Minutes later, two figures emerged. She emerged first, striding quickly in front of the man, turning to smile at something he said, her long hair bobbing rhythmically as she swung her pretty head toward her date. Now the man was smiling too, and he was looking her over appraisingly. He had a smug look on his face, like he already knew how the evening would end, like he already expected that he was going to get laid in a few hours. Instantly, the watcher hated them both. The rage he had been fighting to contain for so long erupted like a volcano, suddenly and with unbridled vengeance. On an unconscious level, despite his silent protestations, he had known it was coming all along.

Jason Coulter walked up the short flight of steps from the locker room to the main floor of the Apex Gym. There was no mistaking the familiar scent that hit him as he entered the room. The sweet and sour combination could be exhilarating one moment, slightly sickening the next. Perfume and sweat. It was the scent of sex, he often thought, and tonight it was exhilarating. Jason looked around the elite health club as he made his way to the free-weight section. The

Apex was the most exclusive club in town, bar none. Not only was it a fully appointed gym and health club, it also contained a resort-like pool, whirlpool, and sauna complex, all surrounded by a series of restaurants and lounges. The lounges contained some of the sexiest little nooks and crannies you could imagine, just right for a little escape from the pressures of your job, or a quiet, discrete drink with a lovely blond you happened to meet doing flys on the incline bench. The main floor contained a comprehensive gym. The largest room was a combination of circuit weight training, various machines designed to work virtually every part of the human anatomy. On the outer perimeter of the room, arranged in a circle behind the muscle building machines, there were at least two dozen lifecycles, treadmills, and stair-steppers. Above all of this were numerous television monitors, tuned to various local and specialty channels. The sound was turned off on every one of them, but this was compensated by the pumped-in music that reverberated throughout the building. Each venue had its own music. There was elevator music for the main floor, rock for the hard-core weightlifting room, and that incessant, head pounding club music for the aerobics room. In the nooks and crannies, it was low volume blues and smooth jazz. Jason spent most of his usual workouts in the hard-core room. He liked doing some heavy lifting, especially bench pressing, and enjoyed the rough and tumble camaraderie in this part of the club. This morning he was going to stay in the big multi-purpose room, which was also the hub of social activity at the Apex.

It wasn't long before Jason spotted Marjorie Jo Propenski working her upper thighs on that tortuous machine Jason never used, or even understood. But Marjorie, or Marjo the Pro as everyone called her, was always there, kicking back and forth for all she was worth. Of course, no one really knew what Marjo was worth, but she was seen on the arm of some of Highland Park's most eligible bachelors. She had also spent some time in the dim recesses of the nooks and crannies with some prominent men who, because of the small gold band they wore around the third finger of their left hand, were *not* so eligible. Marjo was the definition of the brick shithouse, and she was one of the few club members who routinely violated the no thong rule at the Apex. She was a charter member of the Tuesday Club, a group of women who met for an early morning workout and seemed to regale in their ability to hold spellbound even the most hardened Lothario. It was called the Tuesday Club because most of the group was sure to be here, bright and early, every Tuesday morning. They stayed for the whole routine; workout, sauna, shower, massage, and brunch. Brunch was often punctuated with champagne and orange juice served from traditional long-necked crystal flutes.

Actually, the Tuesday Club women covered their backsides with a wisp of cloth over the thong, thus technically complying with the rules on dress. But

11

watching them perform their routines and seeing that wisp of cloth flutter as they kicked and stretched and preened and pranced only accentuated the fact that their bare asses were more frequently flaunted then covered. To be honest, only Marjo the Pro wore a real thong, the others wore outfits with a Brazilian cut, still very brief coverage, and still very alluring. There probably would have been much less reaction if they walked around naked. Today, Marjo was wearing a powder blue bodysuit cut straight across the tops of her breasts. Fastened loosely around her hips was a swath of cream colored material that resembled a type of scarf. She spent just as much time twirling and adjusting this scarf as she did exercising. It reminded Jason of a matador and his red cape, except in this case, men were not drawn away from the main attraction by this swirling distraction. Jason walked over to a machine he wanted to use. A young man about thirty, dressed in a mesh tank top and baggy nylon shorts was leaning against it, mesmerized by Marjo's kicking routine.

"Like what you see?" Jason said, getting the man's attention.

"I'm sorry," the man replied sheepishly, averting his eyes. "Let me get outta your way."

"No problem." Jason smiled. He understood the man's reaction. Marjo was a pretty awesome sight, especially when she swung those long legs into the air. It was poetry in motion. Men's attention was constantly drawn to these women, especially to the Tuesday Club members. And they seemed to enjoy the attention. Jason counted four of them today. Besides Marjo, there were Christine Ballentine Price, the wife of one of Highland Park's wealthiest businessmen, Laura McIntosh, an advertising executive, and Michelle Lee, who described herself as the only "working girl" of the group. Michelle was an elementary school teacher, and unless it was summer recess, she was always the first to leave the club on Tuesdays. The fifth member of this comely crew, Janet Witherspoon, his favorite, was missing this Tuesday.

He remembered the day he'd met Janet. She had approached him at the gym, sidling up as he was just finishing his workout.

"Hi," she said, walking straight up to him as he was curling a set of forty-five pound dumbbells. "Can I talk to you a minute?"

"Sure," Jason replied, trying to make sure his form was perfect as he finished his set. He tried not to exhale too hard as he set the weights back in the rack. "You're Janet aren't you?"

"Yes, how did you know my name? Have we met before?"

"No, not really. But we have a mutual friend. Christine . . . Christine Price."

"Oh sure," she replied, "I think Christine did talk about you a couple of times."

In fact, Janet had asked Christine about the handsome detective on more than one occasion, trying to find out if he was single, and to learn more about him. Usually, police officers were not her type, but this one seemed different, more cultured and refined. She'd watched him for awhile, and had finally gotten the nerve to approach him today.

"You're a cop, aren't you. A detective?"

"True," he replied, "I'm Jason Coulter, and I'm very pleased to meet you. What did you want to talk about?"

"I hate to bother you now, but I've been having some problems with my ex-boyfriend. Nothing violent or anything, just childish stuff, like letting the air out my tires on a Saturday night when he knows I have a date, or damaging some stuff we bought when we were together. Once, I found my apartment had been broken into and my things gone through, but nothing taken. I can't prove anything, but I'm sure it was Robert."

Jason was instantly mesmerized. He saw her mouth move, but didn't hear what she saying. Instead he was focused on the movements of her ruby lips, and the twinkling in her deep blue eyes. Janet was a striking blond, about 30 years old, who worked hard to keep in good shape, and like the other members of the Tuesday Club, was not shy about showing it off. Nonetheless, he had always considered her too high brow for him. He had tried without success to catch her eye during workouts, and he figured by the way she dressed and the newer model Jaguar she drove that she was out of his league, at least financially. He had never been this close to her before, and seeing her like this did *everything* for her looks. She was even more beautiful, unlike many gym rats who only looked fetching from afar. He tried to recover from his boyish reaction and listen to what she was telling him. It was not an easy task, even for a trained interrogator.

"Do you have any advice?" She was waiting for his response, confused by the vacant look in his eyes.

"Oh, yeah, sure. What you're experiencing is pretty typical. A lot of guys fall hard when they're dumped. Most often, these incidents subside quickly. But you can't count on it. I can give you some pointers. Have time for some coffee?"

After this first meeting, they had met a couple more times in the nooks, but never went on a real date. Jason just wasn't sure if she was interested in him that way, and was satisfied with being friends . . . for now. He was usually good at picking up signals people sent, one of the skills he'd picked up as a policeman, but he wasn't sure about Janet, and he didn't want to push it. Maybe someday.

Jason shook off the daydreams, and tackled his workout. He had once been a competitive weightlifter, but had stopped several years ago. Approaching thirty-seven, it was time to concentrate on staying in shape, not how many pounds he could hoist. He soared through his aerobic routine, and tackled his anabolic circuit weight training in workmanlike fashion. It was one of his light days, meaning that he was using low weights and doing lots of reps, so he worked quickly. Forty-five minutes later, feeling slightly fatigued but exhilarated, Jason left the gym floor, showered, and dressed for work. By 8:30 am, he was at his desk in the headquarters of the Highland Park Police Department. Highland Park was a busy suburb of Philadelphia. Bordering the northeast section of Philly, Highland Park was a balanced mix of residential, commercial and light industrial buildings. About 55,000 people called it home, and some of these left everyday for jobs in the big city. However, the bustling suburb was beginning to be known as an "Edge City," defined as a town that bordered a major metropolitan city but had a unique identity, an economy that was independent, and held its own when it came to cultural events. It was beginning to become a destination rather than a bedroom community. There was even a defined "downtown" with busy shops and businesses, including a 120-room hotel and a four-star restaurant that had been written up in *Metro Philly* magazine.

There were ninety-four officers on the force, and Lt. Jason Coulter was the commander of detectives. Mostly, the city had problems with property crimes like burglary and car theft. Occasionally there was a murder, typically resulting from domestic violence or other crime of passion. Jason greeted his coworkers that were on the day shift this morning, including an imposing looking black man hunkered over his standard issue gunmetal desk. Charles "Cab" Calloway was a senior detective. Big by any standard, Cab always claimed he got his nickname from the association between his last name and the famous musician, but most of the squad believed he earned it the hard way, by eating his way to the size of a taxicab. He was 6'3", 260 pounds of black fury, as he himself always said. There was a running debate on whether his girth was muscle or fat, and Jason bet it was a little of both now. But he suspected that in his heyday as a linebacker for West Chester State University, Cab was a sight to behold. At thirty-five, he was a couple of years younger than Jason, but way ahead in terms of life maturity.

Cab had started his law enforcement career with the Philadelphia Police Department. After only six years, Cab was assigned to the narcotics squad, and spent four years undercover, ferreting out some of the most notorious drug dealers in the city. He received numerous commendations for outstanding work, and was involved in a shooting where he shot and killed a scumbag dealer who had wounded his partner. Shortly after, he began to get death threats from the dealer's gang-banger friends and he was transferred out of narcotics into the West Detective unit.

He married his wife Shawna that same year, and less than one year later, his son Maurice was born. It was then that his wife talked him into leaving the city force, claiming it was much too dangerous for a new father, and Cab wound up in Highland Park. He was only the second black officer in the department, but he had no problem fitting in. His experience with PPD and his sports background made him an instant favorite among his peers, and his ability and skill won him a spot in the detective unit after only two years on the street. In this relatively small department, Cab's experience as a decorated big city cop was a valuable commodity, and he was already considered a shining star. Although he was his boss, Jason considered Cab a mentor in many ways. Not only was Cab a crack policeman, he had one of the most stable home lives Jason had seen for a police officer, and he was truly in love with Shawna and his little boy. Jason looked forward to the nights when Cab would invite him to dinner with his family, and it made him feel good to be part of this kind of family living. It was something that was missing from his own life, something he soon hoped to change.

Chapter 3

"Well, Cab, what do we have today?"

"Not too much, usual stuff . . . a few burglaries, a couple of drug complaints, several retail thefts and a sexual assault in the mall parking lot. They're all assigned already, so there's no need for you to look them over. However there are some supplements in your bin waiting for your approval."

As their supervisor, Jason routinely reviewed the supplemental reports completed by his detectives. Today, there was the usual stack, nothing Jason needed to be concerned about. He reviewed them mechanically, scrawling his initials in the proper box and placing them in his "out" bin.

"Oh yeah, there's also a couple of prisoners Philly is holding for us. I sent Jenkins and a uniform to get them."

Being so close to the city of Philadelphia, Highland Park police officers frequently arrested perps wanted by Philly for major offenses, including rape and murder. They were often picked up by the locals for shoplifting or minor drug offenses, and NCIC checks would reveal they were felons. This worked the other way too. Jason had spent many a night in the Philly Roundhouse, a nickname for police headquarters, waiting to get a prisoner who had committed a robbery in Highland Park and hightailed it back to the big city to disappear. These trips served to remind him why he was glad he did not choose to join the PPD. The convoluted bureaucracy and wasted time would not have suited him at all.

He didn't like to stand still for too long, and in the Philadelphia Police Department and the city's overloaded municipal courts, not much was accomplished without waiting around for extended periods of time. Jason glanced at two red folders lying on the corner of his desk. Murders. They contained reports on the only murders in Highland Park over the last five years. One was a simple domestic related homicide that occurred over six months ago. Husband kills wife. The police were called by a neighbor who heard sounds of an argument. When they arrived, they found the wife's body. She had been

16

bludgeoned to death. Of course, the husband was the instant suspect, and the fast and furious investigation revealed that he was indeed her killer. This was not a difficult case, but Jason had still assigned it to one of Highland Park's more experienced investigators. Since they didn't get many murders in this town, he wanted it handled right. Even with it being assigned to a competent detective, Jason insisted on monitoring the investigation until they got either a guilty plea or a conviction in court. This was not exactly great supervisory practice. He knew he was driving the detective nuts with his constant questions about the status of the case, but he wanted to be sure everything possible was done to prepare for trial, especially since in the chain-of-command he was the one ultimately held responsible for the police prosecution.

The other case was fresh. The victim, Amber Mathieson, was drop dead gorgeous. When Jason first saw her the morning her body was found, he thought that she could have been a member of the Tuesday Club. Amber was discovered on May 5th by an early morning jogger at Mill Road Park, a small wooded nature area infrequently used during most weekdays, but heavily traveled during the summer months and on weekends. The coroner said she was dead less than a day when her body was found. The autopsy revealed she died of strangulation, and there was a lot of bruising and scratches on her face, arms and legs. Most of these were attributable to being dragged through the underbrush to the spot where her body was obviously dumped. There was some heavy bruising around her mouth and lips, and Jason was anxiously awaiting lab results that might provide some clues to the exact manner of death. It was one thing to know she was suffocated, quite another to know how it was done. There were no homes around the park, and a canvass of the area had provided no real evidence or witnesses. The investigation centered on her lifestyle and friends, but progress was slow. Cab was assigned to lead this investigation, but once again, Jason was taking an active role. Yes, the term anal-retentive did come to mind, but he didn't really think of it as a weakness.

Jason picked up the file as he sat at his desk, and started reviewing the details of Amber's murder. It had been four days since she was found, and he was still tired and sluggish from the initial exhaustive effort to discover clues about her killer. It was like a bad case of jet lag, his body clock just couldn't get back on tract after he put in thirty hours straight right after she was discovered and then resumed the investigation after a brief three hour nap. He knew this case would consume him until it was solved.

His thoughts drifted to the day of Amber's murder. He received the call from police dispatch at 6:30 AM on May 5th. Jason was in the process of getting up anyway, when the phone rang . . softly. The phone next to his bed chirped like a single cricket at dawn's light. He had shopped a long time until he found a phone with such a low ring. He got calls at night often enough that he came to abhor the loud shrill sound of a normal ring, and since he was a light sleeper, did not appreciate being awakened so abruptly. He went through three phones before he found one to his liking. Sure, the ring volume was supposed to be adjustable, but all of the previous models were still too loud for his taste. They may have sounded okay in the store, but in the middle of the night all three had been deafening. This new phone was perfect, providing just enough of a ring to shake him from whatever dream he was having, without abruptly jolting him awake and leaving him with a headache to boot. He answered the call and fumbled for a small pad and pencil he kept on his nightstand. A few minutes later he was on his way, dressed in a pair of jeans and an old college sweatshirt. He grabbed a jacket to throw in the car, in case the morning chill was too much. His hair was still tousled from sleep, although he had tried in vain to run a comb through it to make it presentable.

It took him fifteen minutes to reach Mill Road Park. Three squad cars were already on the scene, and Cab's blue unmarked Taurus was also in the small cinder parking area next to the woods. Jason grabbed his jacket from the car, and also retrieved a baseball cap with the police department's logo from the trunk. He didn't need any smartass remarks about his hair. Cab was near the woods line, talking to the shift sergeant. No matter where Cab was, or how many people were around, he was easy to spot. Not only was he huge, he loved to wear bright Hawaiian style shirts, even to crime scenes. He must figure as big as I am, why try hiding. This morning he wore a particularly shocking blue, green, and orange print, about as large as the screen at one of those Cinema 16 movie theatres. Cab was not wearing a jacket this morning, rarely did. He didn't feel the cold. Girth does have some advantages. He nodded toward Jason as he approached.

"This one's a shame, Jason, nice looking girl, mid-twenties."

"Any I.D?" Jason asked, carefully scanning the landscape as he moved gingerly toward the crime scene.

"Not yet, but we haven't gone through the body . . . waiting for county forensics and the coroner."

Highland Park was too small a department to support its own forensic unit, so the local police relied on the county detectives, who worked for the District Attorney, for these specialized services.

"Let's take a look."

Jason and Cab walked into the woods, about fifty feet from the left edge of the parking lot. The body was lying in a small clearing next to a large Willow tree. The dead woman was dressed to party, in a fiery red short dress and matching heels. She also wore light beige stockings, not pantyhose, and garters. She was not wearing panties, although one of her garters was still fastened, so this may not be meaningful to the crime. Same with the absence of a bra. The dress was designed to go without. More significant, the dress was not overly soiled, and the victim's hairstyle and makeup were still relatively intact. It was quite obvious the body had been deposited here, killed elsewhere and brought here to hide, for awhile anyway. Judging from appearances, it didn't look like a vicious struggle had occurred before death. Most of the injuries were localized. But Jason would draw no conclusions this early in an investigation.

"I know what you're thinking, Jason, and I agree."

"Yep," Jason replied, "this is just the dumping ground. No sign of a struggle around the body, and no real damage to the underbrush leading from the parking lot, so the victim wasn't struggling or being physically forced to this clearing. From the looks of it, I'd say the suspect carried her here from the parking lot. She was already dead or at least unconscious. Still, there could be some trace evidence here, too bad the area is all tramped up."

Jason was alluding to the jogger's tracks, and those of about four careless police officers who had stomped all over the area where the body was found. The chance for getting a footprint of the killer was slim. The chance of finding other identifying traits of the suspect, perhaps hairs from the head or fibers from the clothes, was also slim. Still, there was probably plenty of evidence on or in the body itself or on the victim's clothing, so the scene was not a total loss.

"Request County to get what they can," ordered Jason. "And have them take the cop's shoes for comparison, that'll teach them to tromp on potential evidence. Training classes just don't seem to get the message to them."

Cab winced. *That* order was not going to be popular. Cops don't like to be embarrassed, even when they know they've fucked up.

"I also want her hands bagged, in case she scraped her assailant with her nails, and I want a full sexual assault work-up, especially swabs. I want swabs of everything, including the webs of her toes . . . everything. Never know what sicko you may be dealing with. And make sure the coroner's crew doesn't let anything leak out of an orifice during transport. Pussy, ass, mouth, ears, eyes . . . and any other hole they find!"

Cab wondered how they were going to do that, shove a cork up her ass? Sometimes his boss could be obnoxious. Nevertheless, he wrote everything down and would pass it on to the coroner. He also noted the time. He was excellent at keeping a running log of events and actions taken during crime scenes, and just as important he didn't want to forget to have any of Jason's orders carried out. The only times Jason really got ugly were right after a failed relationship, which there were many, and when one of his detectives failed to do what he had ordered, which thankfully was rare. A lot of officers got pissed at Jason during the early stages of an investigation. He was demanding, and sometimes went overboard telling them to do the obvious, but the investigation was his responsibility, and he took his job seriously. Cab admired this trait. He knew this control-freak attitude was just Jason's own way of making sure everything got done right. He was essentially thinking out loud, running through the fundamentals. Jason himself knew he appeared controlling, even somewhat obnoxious, but he also knew by communicating in this fashion he was providing the opportunity for other cops to learn what he was planning, and to speak up should he forget anything . . . like there was ever a chance of that happening.

The County forensic team and the coroner arrived simultaneously. Cab hurried over to Detective Tom Stanford, the county's evidence technician, and a former Philly homicide detective. He wanted to diplomatically emphasize Lt. Coulter's requests, for he knew if Jason did it in his tactless crime scene manner, it would piss off the experienced technician. Stanford had already retired from the Philadelphia force during the time when Cab was working there, so he didn't know him all that well.

"How goes it, Tom?" asked Cab, approaching with an outstretched hand.

"Top of the morning to you mate," replied Tom, warmly shaking the big paw presented to him. "What do you got for me today?"

"Young woman, dead and dumped."

"Hmmph. Sure that's not dumped and dead? That's an epidemic lately. Woman pisses man off, man dumps woman, woman finds another man, first man kills woman. Dumped and dead."

Cab laughed. "Come on Sherlock, that's a theory. It's way too early for theories."

"Yeah, you're right. But I'd be right more than half the time with that one."

What he said had a ring of truth to it. Montgomery County had seen its share of domestic related homicides over the last few years, and Stanford had surely had his fill of them in Philadelphia. Certainly, if the dead woman had a husband or boyfriend that's where the investigation would initially begin.

"What can I do to help you, Tom? Let's get started before the media circus arrives."

"First thing you can do is to order one of those shoeless flatfoots to get me some coffee."

The dead and dumped woman's name was Amber Lynn Mathieson. She was only twenty-four at the time of her death. There was not much on the body, and no purse was found. Amber was identified by a medic alert bracelet she wore on her wrist. She had been diabetic, and police were able to trace a number on the bracelet and get some of her medical history. In her file at St. Joseph's

Hospital, police found her vital statistics, including her address, and the name of the person to call in case of emergency, one John Mathieson, age thirty-eight, of Atlanta, Georgia. Detectives back at headquarters were trying to contact him. She lived in Rockledge, a small town near the eastern edge of the county. She had no husband, and no current boyfriend, at least none that was common knowledge.

Nevertheless, with the way she was dressed when she was found dead, Jason suspected there would be a man in this mystery somewhere. Jason and Cab had spent the rest of the morning and most of the afternoon hoofing around Rockledge. They knocked on doors near Amber's apartment on Fourth Street, and checked with local stores to learn more about the victim. They entered dry cleaners, grocery stores, and liquor outlets and interviewed scores of people. The only person in the neighborhood around her place that knew her was Tran Vu, the owner of Tran's Quik Dry about two blocks from Amber's apartment. She frequently brought in clothes for laundering and dry cleaning Tran told them in broken English. "Nice girl, no problems, always pay."

Her landlord and an older woman who lived, respectively, in the apartments below and above Amber's were not much help either. Her landlord was a squirrelly old guy about 70 years old. She had leased the apartment only four months ago, and was always on time with the rent. She listed her brother John as a reference, and did not list a job or source of income. When questioned about this, the landlord said, "she had an honest face, and one thousand dollars cash."

There was something about this old guy that made the little hairs on Jason's neck stand up. There was probably nothing to it, but he looked like a pervert. Jason made a mental note to check for hidden peepholes or cameras in the apartment. A search of her apartment also revealed little of her life. It was sparse but tastefully furnished. Some of the pieces were nice. There was an Ethan Allen sofa and matching chair in the living room. Most pieces looked old and well used, like she acquired them at second hand shops or estate sales. There were a few knick-knacks scattered about the apartment. Jason saw candlesticks, wooden carvings of birds, silk flowers in vases. Typical possessions for a girl this age.

He noted some knick-knacks on a mantelpiece, some carved wooden articles that looked like souvenirs from a vacation or business trip. He carefully picked one up, a small wood framed clock. He turned it over and saw from some markings that it was made in Mexico. He smiled, pleased with himself. He knew it was making correct assumptions that made a detective worth his salt. Some guys had it, some never would. For him, it was almost an obsession. He made deductions and assumptions about everything; people, trends, activities, objects. Not much fun at parties maybe, but an important habit for his line of work. He set the clock down and resumed his search. There were some inexpensive prints hanging on the walls, mostly floral scenes to brighten the place up. There was nothing out of the ordinary.

There *was* a striking portrait in the bedroom, above the double bed. It was of a dark-haired woman in a long, flowing champagne colored dress, a tight ring of pearls around her neck. She was fingering the pearls, and looking toward the viewer with what Jason could only describe as a come-hither look. She was fetching, and the painting was well done. Jason wondered if it had any special significance to the victim, or whether she just liked the way it looked. Amber had nice clothes, and Cab counted at least two dozen party or cocktail dresses among the items hanging in her closet.

"Jesus," Cab exclaimed, "if Shawna got a look in here, I'd never hear the end of it. This woman has more dresses, purses, and shoes than the Chief has hemorrhoids."

"Think she's a working girl, Cab?"

"Could be, but there's other clothes here too, regular stuff. Besides, you know the type of clothes these young girls wear today. They all look like hookers."

"Spoken like a man who has only a son. Just wait till you have a daughter and we'll see what she gets away with!"

"Wanna bet?"

Cab searched through all the drawers and counters in the kitchen. He piled her mail and bills into paper bags for further review at headquarters. There were a few dishes in the drainer, and a couple of coffee mugs lying around, one in the bathroom, one on the counter near the microwave. Cab also collected these for processing. Jason had called for county to process the scene, but Tom Standish was not around and it would have to wait. Cab didn't want any items to disappear or get broken, so he collected what he thought may have value as evidence. She did have a computer, an early Pentium, three-year-old technology at least. It would have to be boxed and taken to the station, where experts from the Pennsylvania State Police would unlock any mysteries it might hold about Amber. Jason walked through the apartment again and again.

"Christ, Jason. Stop pacing," Cab told him. "Stop pacing, it's getting on my nerves."

"I'm not pacing, I'm studying. We're missing something here. This is where she lived, this is her most intimate place, her castle," Jason rattled. "But it seems kind of barren. I'm trying to get a sense of her from her home . . . but I'm not getting much at all."

"I don't know," replied Cab. "Check out these CD's." Cab was rifling through a large stack of compact discs on a cheap but tasteful entertainment center in the living room.

"Mostly top hit stuff, a few Sting CD's, some select female artists. No country, no rap. She's like fifty million other women her age, ain't that enough personality for you? Want to check out her underwear drawer? Silk or cotton, leather and lace? I bet she has panties and bras to go with every dress in the closet."

Jason considered that last comment. He never liked this part of the job, going through people's things. He felt invasive. He knew some cops leapt at the chance to take hours tossing a perp's room, or rummaging through the personal effects of a missing or deceased person. Some specialized in lingerie, others rooted for dirty photos hidden away in secret locations. Many such photos were discovered in envelopes taped to the back of a dresser drawer. Occasionally, a cop with a life outside the job would marvel at a collection of paintings, or recognize fine antiques, or appreciate an assortment of artifacts brought back from trips to places far away. Jason knew that information gathered from this invasion of privacy was often vital to a case, but always felt more like a burglar than a cop when he had to do it.

"There's not enough for me," Jason echoed. "There's not enough personality here to suit me. I can't picture her here . . . how she lived. Where was her favorite spot?"

He pointed to a chair. "Did she sit *here* when she was reading or listening to music? Okay Cab, you check the panties . . . I promise I won't tell Shawna."

"Shit! I'll tell her myself if I find some nice things in here. There's got to be panties to go with them dresses."

When he learned of her murder from HPPD detectives, Amber's brother had flown immediately to Philadelphia International Airport and took a shuttle to Highland Park. Jason and Cab sat with him in one of the department's interview rooms. He gave the detectives his sister's history, and he openly discussed what he knew about her life. "I'm sorry," he said after he gave a quick rundown on Amber's life in Marietta, Georgia, the town where she'd grown up. " I wish that I could help more, but I really didn't know her that well. She was nine when my parents adopted her, and I was twenty-three and already in college. I lived away from home."

"Is there anything else that you *can* you tell us about her?" Cab said. "Something more personal, something about the kind of person she was? Was there any indication early on that her lifestyle may have contributed to her death?"

"Well, even though she was just a kid, she *was* a handful. Before they adopted her, she had spent time in five foster care homes, and my parents picked her up from the county shelter, where she had been staying for the last five months. Apparently, she caused more disruption than a lot of families could handle."

"Was there anything specific that may have caused problems between her and her foster families?" Cab had to ask, even though he had little hope of getting a good answer.

"I don't really know, but she was a wild one, so I wouldn't be surprised if the other families simply couldn't cope. She had a smart mouth and wouldn't listen to anyone. I tried to become more involved in her life, but because of our age difference, she regarded me as a pseudo-parent, and I never could get close to her."

"Unfortunately, that's not an unusual situation for a child these days." Cab said. "We see a lot of kids from broken families passed from home to home. Must be a hellava life. What about her education?"

"She went to public school in Marietta for awhile. But she got in trouble there too, and then went to boarding school. She hated the regimen there, and ran away when she was sixteen. My parents agonized about that, but we could never find her."

"Did you help look for her?" Jason interjected. He was trying to gauge how much John had cared for his stepsister.

"I made some calls to the county about her, and went with my Daddy once to see the juvenile detectives a few months after she left. They had filed a report, and told us she was in the NCAP or something, but they didn't have a clue."

"NCIC," Jason said mechanically. "The National Crime Information Center. It's a computer system that provides information about missing and wanted persons to police nationwide."

"Yeah, that's it. But we never heard anything. Then out of the blue, Amber showed up one day."

"When was that? Recently?" The detectives' ears perked up, but the news was stale.

"Christmas. Two years ago. She came into the house liked she owned the place. I had moved back after college, and she picked right up, just like she'd seen me yesterday. She had changed a lot. Physically, she had grown from a scrawny girl to a voluptuous woman. A remarkable transformation. I don't know whether it was real, or plastic if you know what I mean . . . "It wasn't plas . . .""

"Hhrruumph," Jason cleared his throat loudly, cutting Cab off before he could confirm that there was no plastic surgery involved in forming Amber's voluptuous curves. Cab knew this from the autopsy. She must have been a late bloomer.

"Excuse me. Go on Mr. Mathieson," Jason prompted.

"More significant than the physical changes, her personality was much different. She was mellow, more confident, and almost worldly. Even her voice had changed. It had a sweet singsong quality. Her makeup was different too. More pronounced, but not overdone. Like it was done by a cosmetic counter girl, one who knew what she doing. There's no doubt, she had become more refined, and more like the Southern Belle mamma would have been proud to claim. Tragically, Mamma and Daddy died just three years after she ran away in an accident on Highway 20. They never got to see the young lady Amber had become."

"I'm sorry to hear that, John." Jason said. "It must have been devastating to lose both your parents at once."

"Thank you, Lieutenant. Ironically, they were heading toward Augusta at the time of the accident to check out a juvenile the police had in custody. The girl fit Amber's description, and she refused to give her name to authorities. It wasn't her though."

"Is there anything else you can tell us about the last time you saw Amber?"

"Well, I can tell you this; even though she changed so much, something was not right with Amber. She was hiding something from me I thought, avoiding my questions. To this day I don't know why. I remember asking her about the years she was gone . . . here did she live, what did she do, but she didn't tell me much. She stayed a few days and then left again. I never saw her again . . . until now." Mathieson hesitated, and Jason sensed he had told them all he knew . . . or all he wanted to tell.

"After that visit, did you have any contact with Amber?"

"Only once. She called a few months ago to tell me she had moved, lived somewhere near Philly." Mathieson smiled, remembering the conversation. "I didn't understand what she meant . . . Philly. She laughed and said 'Philadelphia, the city, you know . . . home of the Liberty Bell and the Declaration of Independence.' Everybody called it Philly she told me."

Up until his last statements, Amber's stepbrother had seemed detached. Cab noticed a bit of emotion creep into his voice as he answered their last question. Cab reasoned that he felt kind of helpless, and maybe regretted something he did or didn't do in regard to Amber's well being. The detectives both got the feeling that John Mathieson was generally a cold fish, but he was telling the truth. They wondered if his parents had been the same way, a little distant and unattached. Maybe that's why Amber didn't get along with them too well. She probably needed more attention. At any rate, they didn't learn much today that would help them find a murderer.

Just a few miles away, Amber's killer was very, very agitated. The images of his deed were flashing through his mind at warp speed. Bits and pieces of scenes; the silky look and feel of her red dress, her wide open mouth trying to shriek but making no sound, thick cords of blond hair twisted around his hands as he forced her head down toward his erect penis. She had offered little resistance. The combination of the alcohol she drank while dancing and the drugs he managed to slip into her last drink made her almost puppet-like. He felt the rush even now as he remembered. She fell for his ridiculous story hook, line and sinker. He got her to feel sorry for him, told her he regretted losing her, and although he was dealing with it, was in great pain. Maybe one more good memory to hold on to? She was so gullible for a woman of her experience. *Does the Lexus man know how foolish you are?*

He had pushed himself into her open mouth and came immediately. He held her against him, gratified even more as he heard her gagging and fighting for breath. He pulled her head back and replaced his member with a torn shirt, stuffing it into her mouth and over her nose. He held her face tightly against the cloth, feeling the contours of her nose and jaw against his one hand, while firmly holding the back of her head with the other. It was over in less than a minute. His breathing returned to normal, his racing mind slowed. He killed her . . . just like that. He glanced upward, waiting expectantly for some sort of emotion to sweep over him, but it didn't. No remorse. No disgust. No guilt.

Chapter 4

Janet was happy. She had finally gotten up the nerve to approach Jason, and it went well. Although she hated to use the story about her ex, it seemed like a good way to start a conversation with a cop. He seemed really genuine too, not like the other men she had met recently. She also admired his lean, hard body and his mature good looks. They had some nice discussions over coffee. With the ice broken, she was confident they would wind up dating. It was a long time coming. She and Robert had broken up months ago, and it was time to get back on the horse. Other than Kyle, she had not met any men who really caught her interest and she was tired of trying. Of course, as much as she admired Kyle, yes . . . even desired him, Christine was her friend, and she knew the couple was really good together. It was Christine who had introduced Janet to the Tuesday Club, and this opened a whole new world for her.

Besides, as open as Christine was with her marriage to Kyle, they both were really fun to be around, and she would never do anything to jeopardize that. She longed for a love like Kyle and Christine's. *Jason Coulter,* suave, handsome, brave cop . . . maybe a chance? Maybe her luck has changed. This is going to be really good, I can feel it, she thought. Janet finished dressing, and left for her shift at the hospital. Glancing at her Cartier watch, a gift from Christine, she realized that she had only a half-hour before she was expected to begin her shift in the emergency room. No time today for her usual post-workout snack of a cinnamon bagel and double mocha cappuccino. *God,* she bemoaned, *it would be a long time till lunch.*

Jason stuck his head outside his office, calling for Cab in the bullpen. The bullpen was the name Highland Park detectives had given the large room where they worked. There were eight desks and twelve detectives who shared space in this area. Some years ago, partitions had been set up to give the detectives some semblance of privacy, but in actuality, they only gave the appearance of privacy. There were no secrets among Highland Park detectives.

"Hey Cab, what's this message from Kyle Price? When did he call?"

"Shit, he called about ten times in ten minutes. What's up with you and that rich dude anyway? Is he still falling all over you for getting his little girl back?"

"Kind of . . . but he's okay. We hit it off. Besides, it nice to see how the other half lives."

"I hear ya! I thought that about white people when I was growing up in the ghetto. Now that I see how you all live, the myth is destroyed!"

Jason had met Kyle Price when Kyle's sixteen-year-old daughter Natalie was kidnapped three years ago. Jason was one of the detectives assigned to the case. It was probably the biggest case he was ever involved with, at least in terms of notoriety. In the first few days after Natalie was found to be missing, he must have received twenty calls a day from Kyle. It was incredible, even for a grieving father. The calls slowed down after she was found safe and sound, but Kyle still called several times per week to inquire about the case of the two men charged with her abduction.

"Bullshit, you grew up in Germantown, in a house bigger than my whole block. It was a step down for you moving to Highland Park. And speaking of myths, remember, I've seen you in the shower."

"Gutter mouth. That should be your nickname. You can turn any conversation into a sexual thing. No wonder you like Kyle Price."

"What did Price want anyway? Did he say?"

"Yeah, he heard something about an appeal for the two jackoffs that kidnapped his kid. He wanted to see if there was anything to it."

"They both got forty year sentences. They're not going anywhere soon. Even if they find a dipshit attorney willing to get involved in a losing battle, no judge would dare touch this case. The sentence will stand."

"Yeah, well call him back anyway. He's all revved up about it, and I'm tired of playing secretary."

Truth be told, Jason had come to like Kyle during the investigation. He even admired him in a way, although he wasn't sure if the man was a sincere community spirited benefactor, or just another talented con artist. There was no doubt he gave a small fortune to charity, and he and his wife were seen at just about every fund raiser and community do-gooder event in Highland Park. But then, that type of visibility was always good for business, and there were other local businessmen who did the same, and some of them Jason *knew* were more con than contrite.

Kyle Price was one of the most prominent businessmen in Montgomery County, and this case had been very high profile. He had made televised appeals for information about his daughter's kidnapping, and had offered a reward of fifty thousand dollars. In short order, there were hundreds of tips, mostly from opportunists and quacks, and none of them had proven fruitful. Nevertheless, it made life very busy for Jason and the other HPPD detectives working on this case. Jason had his own fleeting moment of fame during the initial stages of the investigation. Kyle Price had arranged for him to make appearances on several Philadelphia TV news and morning talk shows, where he was called upon to detail the facts of the case and answer questions posed by the hosts. Jason told everyone he really hated doing that kind of stuff, but secretly, he had been thrilled and it made him feel important. He thought Cab was the only one who saw through his denials, because Cab never joined in when the other detectives chided him about the media appearances. Cab only smiled slightly, and shook his head slowly whenever Jason insisted that he wished he never had to go on television again.

Price owned an import-export business, but his real passion was his daughter. Her, and his association with the Apex Gym. He was part owner, and sponsored several unique weightlifting and bodybuilding events each year that were attended by all the beautiful people who came to see and be seen. Kyle was married to Christine Ballentine Price, a gorgeous raven haired former model...of course...no surprise there. The surprise was that Christine was *not* the second wife, the "trophy" wife. She was the one and only, married to Kyle twenty-three years ago. From the investigation of Natalie's kidnapping, Jason knew that Kyle was forty-five and Christine two years younger, although both of them could easily pass for Jason's age. He saw them working out at the Apex once in awhile, sometimes together, sometimes apart. He had also seen them with Marjorie Jo Propenski in the nooks. This surprised him a bit, because most wives would not be comfortable sharing their husbands with someone so fetching, and so accessible, as Marjo the Pro. Of course, Jason did not know this from experience, but he had heard quite a few locker room rumors about Marjo's freewheeling sexual adventures. If even a fraction of it was true, she was quite a girl, and not the kind you bring home to mother.

It had been a very interesting case to work. Natalie, an avid gymnast, got picked up after practice every day by her father's chauffeured limousine. Even though she attended Wordsworth Academy, an exclusive school for girls, the sleek black stretch limo far outshined the Lexus's and BMW's that waited for the other teens. At first glance, the day she was abducted was no different than any other. A black limo pulled up, waited in the queue with the other cars, and witnesses saw Natalie emerge from the school about four in the afternoon. She headed toward the limo and jumped into the back seat. It was only later police learned that there was one big difference. It was not the limo sent by her father.

It seems a couple of ambitious young gangster wannabes decided to launch a plan that would earn them some big money the easy way. Oscar and Dominick, who delivered fish to one of the restaurants in the Apex for a company based in Kensington, found out about Kyle and his money during their twice-weekly deliveries. They also learned about Natalie, and over too many beers at the corner taproom one night decided that they too should be rich and famous. So they hung around Highland Park after the deliveries, did a little snooping around, and figured the quickest way to the cash was kidnapping the rich guy's precious little girl. It didn't take them long to learn about Natalie's after school routine, and they also found out that Kyle Price's driver usually took a mid-afternoon break at a local diner before he picked her up.

Being the imaginative characters they were, they concocted a surefire plan. So shortly before 3:30 PM on October 12th, which was almost three years ago now, they made their move. They rented a limo the morning of the twelfth from an uncle of Dominick's friend Larry who had a livery on Allegheny Avenue. Then they drove to Highland Park and staked out the diner, waiting for Natalie's chauffeur to take his break. Sure enough, he shows up shortly after 3:00 PM. The boys park their limo out of sight a short distance from the diner. Oscar, who could not quite match Dominick's superior eighty-five IQ and thus was not the brains behind the operation, was sent by Dominick to puncture one of the tires on the real limo. Oscar does this without a problem, as it is something he often did for fun anyway back in his old neighborhood. They figured that the chauffeur would come out, see the flattened tire, and either change it or call for service. Either way, it gives them time to make the pickup at Natalie's school.

Surprisingly, the pickup went smoothly. Natalie was accustomed to just hopping in the limo, and her teachers and coach, if they noticed at all, would not look twice at the long, shiny black limo that pulled up to get her this day. Nothing out of the ordinary for anyone to take note. Natalie was greeted by Dominick in the passenger compartment while Oscar drove away quickly. Dominick had a gun, and told her he would shoot her if she uttered a sound.

They took the girl to the small apartment they rented and led her quietly in through the back door. Oscar stayed with her while Dominick returned the limo and picked up his own battered Chevy. The police were able to get some good leads shortly after the kidnapping. Several people in Highland Park had spotted the suspect's rented limo near the diner. Witnesses at the school had verified that Natalie was picked up "as usual," and Price's chauffeur, devastated by the turn of events, had managed to fill in the rest of the story. Every available detective was called in to work the case. Jason had five of them calling every company in the book that rented limousines, hoping to get a good lead before the trail went cold. He treated the case like a whodunit homicide, using the theory that if you don't solve it in the first 24 hours after the killing, odds of success plummet.

He figured that the theory also applied to this type of case, except instead of solving a murder, his objective was to prevent one. He had each witness questioned twice, each time by a different detective, and had the rest of his squad checking into Natalie's activities for the past week, starting with the most recent hours and working backwards. When one of the detectives asked him how far back he should go. Jason bristled.

"Until you find a fucking clue we can act on." As he spoke, Jason looked at the other man with angry, piercing eyes, defying him to respond. To his credit, the detective realized this was not the time for smart-ass remarks or a cynical roll of the eyes directed at his peers. He remained silent until dismissed, and then quickly huddled with the others assigned to the same task. The detectives worked around the clock for the first day, and then fell into a schedule of twelve hours on, twelve hours off, which Jason planned to continue for at least two weeks. A task force was also formed, headed by the FBI out of the Philadelphia office.

Oscar and Dominick kept Natalie with them for four days before Philadelphia police stakeout officers took out the door and swept into the place like a horde of invading Huns. A phone call to the police hotline made by one of the wiseguy's nosey neighbors led to the break in the case. The call led them to the kidnappers. For once, a media blitz had paid off. The neighbor, watching TV, saw Jason and Kyle Price on "Good Morning Philadelphia." He knew these two numbskulls, he had told the FBI agent who answered the hotline number, and saw them with a black limo the day of the kidnapping. After that tip, it had only taken police a short time to find out who the numbskulls were, where they lived, and to get a no-knock warrant to search their house. The tough guys gave up without a struggle when confronted by the imposing SWAT trained officers. Natalie was found dirty and emotionally traumatized, but otherwise unharmed.

Jason dialed the number from memory. Mrs. Price answered. "Hello?"

Jason pictured Christine cradling the phone, running her fingers through her deep chestnut hair, smoothing it back from the earpiece.

"Hi Christine, this is Lt.Coulter… Jason. How are you today?"

"I'm fine Jason, how are things?"

"Not bad. How's Natalie?"

"Doing just fine. She's in Paris you know. Part of her schooling. She's spending a year in Europe travelling from country to country. She asks about you all the time. You're her hero."

"Well, if I'm the best she can do, she may be in trouble."

"Nonsense. You're my hero too. Anything new on the appeal?"

"No, not really. But don't worry about it. Those assholes aren't going anywhere. I got a call from Kyle a few minutes ago, is he in?"

"Yes, hang on. Hey! Before I get him, I wanted to tell you that I've been talking with Janet about you, and . . . "

"Really?" Jason interrupted.

"Yes, *really*. She's been waiting for a call from you. She thought you two had some nice conversation and expected you to ask her out. You aren't going to disappoint my best friend are you?"

Best friend, Jason thought. *You must have twenty best friends.*

"Ah, I wanted to . . . I thought about it a lot. I started to . . . "

"Geez, Jason, just call the girl will ya! I'm tired of dealing with this issue myself. She's dying to get to know you better, so please just give her a call."

All of a sudden Jason felt sixteen instead of thirty-six. This banter was making him feel foolish.

"I'll call her. Is Kyle there?" Jason wanted this subject to end.

"Sure, I'll get him. Nice talking with you, Jason . . . by the way, she also said you have a nice ass."

Geez indeed.

It turned out Kyle was not calling him about the case, but wanted to invite him on a trip to Atlantic City. Kyle often invited Jason to dinner, ball games, and parties. Despite his reservations about hobnobbing with the rich and famous, Jason enjoyed these little escapes. But things were pretty hectic right now, and Jason knew he didn't have the time. So at first, he declined. Kyle would have none of that.

"Well, I don't want to force you buddy, but I know you haven't had much time to relax lately. Tell you what, come with me this once and if you don't have one hellava good time, I'll never darken your door again. Come on, Christine will already be down there this weekend, we'll have a good time."

Jason relented. "Okay," he said quietly, "I'm in . . . when and where will I meet you?"

That Friday night a white stretch limo pulled up in front of Jason's house. Kyle only used white or silver colored limousines now, ever since Natalie's kidnapping. Weird, Jason thought, but everyone has his or her own way of dealing with stuff like that. Jason had bought the house about eight years ago. It was small, just a two bedroom, but it beat paying rent, and Jason liked the fact that he owned something like a house. He was building up equity already, and the mortgage helped lower his income tax. He picked up his small overnight bag and walked out the door, carefully checking to make sure the lock caught. Kyle had the door to the limo propped open, and a cold longneck in each hand.

"Come on Jason, he said, "let's get this weekend started."

It was about a one and one-half hour trip to the beach. Or, if you counted the time in longnecks, it was about a fourteen-neck trip! Kyle drank about nine of the frosty lagers, and Jason the rest. The time on the road passed quickly. Deter Schmidt, the manager of the Apex Gym and a friend of Kyle's for years, served as the driver. By the third beer, Jason started to feel good, and he and his host settled into long, sometimes spirited, always raunchy conversations about business, sports, politics, and of course, women.

They had dinner at Trump's Taj Mahal, at one of the steak houses there. Jason chose the petite filet. It was very good, and along with the steak, he enjoyed a fine glass of a deep-bodied Cabernet Sauvignon. Deter and Kyle had large portions of the filet and were eating with gusto. They probably did everything with the same zeal. They were all pretty mellow from the trip, and ate in relative silence. Afterwards, Kyle told Jason he had a special treat for him. They left the hotel and walked a few blocks back from the boardwalk. As they came upon an attractive but nondescript looking lounge Kyle turned to go up to the entrance. At first glance, it didn't seem like the kind of place Kyle would patronize. Jason knew he slummed it once in awhile, especially when he went to some of the more notorious exotic dance clubs in Philadelphia. Kyle did have an eye for pretty women, and was not above getting down and dirty, despite his wealth and lofty social status. But this place just looked like a neighborhood lounge, nothing special at all.

"Best kept secret in town," Kyle said. "Come on in, Christine is waiting here for us."

Jason soon learned his first impression was mistaken. Inside, the club was amazing. The lights were low, but it wasn't dark. Jason looked around and could see that this was a well-appointed, decidedly upscale establishment. Plush leather booths and polished tables with candlelight gave one an immediate warm and relaxed feeling. Expensive looking prints hung on the walls, bathed in soft accent lighting. The patrons were not the jeans and tee shirt set, but were dressed in what is commonly called "business casual." Some were more formally attired. Jason noticed a number of stunning women dressed in elegant eveningwear, seemingly overdressed even for a swanky bar. Probably refugees from some fancy corporate party in the casinos.

They were met by a very comely hostess who was wearing a very low cut gown. Deter bent to whisper something to her. She led them through the dark maze of tables and banquettes to a booth where Christine was already seated, gingerly fingering a long stemmed glass. Jason was looking around in wonder. He saw a few women wearing sexy, skimpy dresses, obviously paid escorts, a common sight in a gambling town like A.C. or Vegas. Mostly however, the clientele consisted of casually attired men and women, obviously enjoying the quiet elegance of this place, miles away from the din and bright lights of the casinos. It was an incongruous mix of people, and yet it all seemed comfortable and natural. They all fit, despite the opposite-pole variations. Damn, this was some club, not like one he had ever been to.

"What do you think of our little place?" Christine asked Jason.

"What?" Jason replied, still distracted. He looked around the club again, mesmerized by the opulence of the room and the beautiful people who were obviously used to such splendor.

"Like it?" Kyle repeated.

"What's not to like. This is incredible. I've never seen anything quite like this."

"Well, there are others, but not many." Kyle said. "I bought into this one a few years go, thought the high rollers might want to leave the casinos once in a while and try some different type of stimulation. I was right, and this place has been doing very, very, well."

"Your clientele seems pretty high class. How do you keep out the rift-raft?"

"It's a private club. One thousand dollars a year for full privileges. We do accept nightly memberships for a hundred dollars when another member sponsors them, but most of our business is regulars wanting to be amongst their own, something that is becoming increasing difficult in Atlantic City. Even at a thousand dollars for someplace they may visit only a few times a year, most of my customers think it's a bargain. Let me show you around a bit."

Jason felt a little awkward. It was he, Deter, and Kyle and Christine Price. At first he thought it strange that Kyle would bring his wife to such a place, with the painted face escorts moving freely about, but he soon found out that there was much more to this place. It was more like a country club, with a restaurant, lounge, game room, and a beautifully landscaped private courtyard complete with swimming pool, several whirling spas, numerous lounge chairs for sunning, and glass topped tables and chairs for outside dining and drinking. The place didn't look nearly this large from the outside. After a quick tour, they returned to their table.

When his eyes finally adjusted to the dim lights and he was through soaking in the rich atmosphere, Jason turned his gaze to Christine. She was dazzling. She had almost twenty years on most of the beautiful young escorts, but lost nothing in comparison. She almost always dressed in impeccably tailored suits, at least once Jason had spotted an Armani label on a jacket she laid down in the nooks, and tonight was no exception. Tonight, however, the suit was a bit naughty, at least by her normal standards. She wore a tan jacket and matching skirt, very sleek and silky. It was not exactly tight, but seemed to draw taunt in just the right places as she stood and took a few strides to meet him. The skirt fell almost to her knees, but with a left-front slit cut high. Her shapely thighs, a shade darker than her suit, flashed with each step. Under her jacket, she wore an off-white shear blouse with a plain three layer gold necklace setting off the outfit nicely. Well, *plain* is not quite the right word, but the necklace was just right, beautiful but understated . . . just perfect.

Deter and Kyle were discussing an upcoming weightlifting event at the Apex. It was sort of a celebrity bench press contest, a yearly event to raise money for the Muscular Dystrophy Foundation. It sounded like a funny idea, but the event raised over thirty thousand dollars last year, and was a resounding social success too. Local "buff" celebrities were paired up with real lifters to form teams. The team that lifted the most weight, as compared to their bodyweights, was rewarded with a huge trophy (for the usually rich and vain celebrity) and a trip to Las Vegas, (for the usually poor but trophy rich weightlifter). The attendees bet on the outcome and those who win are rewarded with a hodgepodge of donated goods and services. Restaurant certificates, massages, workout gear, and gift baskets stuffed with cosmetics and perfumes were among the prizes.

"Deter," Kyle asked, "how many are signed up?"

"Only about 15 lifters so far, but we have enough celebs to match, that is if Jason agrees to take part this year."

"Oh no, not me," said Jason, shaking his head to emphasize his reluctance. "I am not strutting my stuff, such as it is, for that group. This is my hometown. I have to live and work here. They would eat me alive!"

"Nonsense," Christine chimed in, "you would be marvelous, just what the event needs, a real man . . . a cop. Why, this is a great idea, you must do it. It will lend a different flair to the event!"

"No way, and that's it. Even thinking about it makes me need another drink." Jason raised his empty glass toward a passing waitress. Christine pretended to pout. She leaned over to pinch his cheek, a consummate female symbol of cutesy dominance, and her jacket gaped open at the bodice. She was not wearing a bra, and Jason could plainly see her right breast through the sheer blouse. She had large nipples, his favorite. He glanced away, but she had already noticed his eyes on her chest, and smiled devilishly at him.

"Come on big boy, show Miss Christine how you lift those heavy, heavy weights. You know you want to."

Jason wanted to show her something all right, but right now it was not his bench press he was thinking about, it was those jutting tits and deep red pouting lips. Christ, this woman is fucking beautiful. If he were Kyle he'd keep her locked up.

"Besides," Jason stammered, embarrassed that he got caught staring. "I can't put up the bucks to get in this thing anyway. The entry fee is outta my league."

"You are covered, my man," Kyle chimed in. "I can't let Christine down, if she wants you, she has you."

Now this was an accommodating man, Jason mused. The cocktail waitress arrived with a fresh Tanqueray martini for him. He knew Christine was watching him as the waitress bent over the low table to set down his drink. Her tits were also very nice, and the tight bustier she wore put them on a lacy shelf, the cups cut just above the nipple line. This time he met Christine's eyes and smiled, shrugging slightly as he shifted his eyes from her to the waitress and back again. Jason was aware that she was flirting, and he was starting to relax and enjoy it a bit. He picked up his drink, took two very large sips, and agreed to participate in the charity event. What the hell, he thought, it *was* for a good cause.

Chapter 5

Lt. Jason Coulter was different from a lot of supervisors and commanders. He still enjoyed the street. He would often jump in a car and accompany one of his detectives on a case. Sure, this was always the way the movie stars did it, and they could crack the toughest case in a couple of hours max. He was always amused at these shows. The movie and TV cops never had any paperwork to complete. What a joke. In reality it was rare to see a Lieutenant actually performing police work, unless he was ordering somebody around or chewing them out for fucking something up. Today, he decided to accompany Cab as he checked out a report that a crackhead was threatening to kill his father.

Cab had heard the call come in, and told the uniform cops to hang back until an unmarked car could cruise into the area and take a look. He figured he might avert a standoff if they could approach this nut by surprise. They arrived on location in minutes. Jason and Cab drove slowly along the parking lot of the apartments, using the access drive closest to the buildings. There were five buildings in the complex, each facing the others, with a large courtyard in the middle, and a circular driveway going completely around the outer edge of the courtyard. Each building had three sections, with twelve rental units in each. The suspect was supposed to be around building "D." At the front of each building there was a covered porch that led to the doors of four of the units, two along the back and one on each side.

No one was visible outside, but since the alcove was recessed from the front exterior walls of the apartment, the doorways couldn't be seen from the street. In fact, the detectives could not see into the alcove until they were almost alongside, raising their level of caution. Cab slowed and eased the nose of the car forward, both detectives peering intently toward the recessed opening, waiting for the doorways to enter their field of vision. A second later, he was there, just a few feet from the right side of their vehicle. The crackhead, who Cab knew to be Nathan Perry, was sitting on the cheap green outdoor carpet.

"He's there, son of a bitch," muttered Cab.

"Yep, and he's got something for his Daddy too," Jason said, spotting the shotgun Nathan was holding at port arms. Jason could see the kid's glazed eyes as they drove past. Nathan was slowly and gently rocking his upper body, and with his window open Jason could hear low moaning, almost like a mantra.

"He musta just copped. He's a space cadet, and I don't think our presence registered yet. Pull alongside of the building and drop me off," Cab ordered.

"Are you crazy? Let's call for backup, form a perimeter, get the SWAT guys out here."

"Nah, that'll take hours. Shawna's cooking something special tonight, and if I'm late, she'll kill me. I got an idea. We can take him now before he comes out of the fog he's in. If we wait for everyone, he'll likely sober up some and will be a real pain our ass. Listen up, here's what I need you to do . . . "

After quickly giving Jason some directions, Cab hopped out. He made his way along the side of Perry's apartment building, hugging the wall and stepping lightly . . . no easy feat for Cab. When he reached the corner, he was only about twenty feet from Nathan, although he could not see him tucked back into the alcove. Jason drove out to the street, and re-entered the complex just as Cab had ordered. He drove as close to the alcove as he could without being in Nathan's field of vision. He was approaching from the opposite side of where Cab was waiting, and Jason spotted his partner hunkered down next to some shrubs, ready to spring.

Jason stopped the car, drew his .40 caliber semi-automatic pistol, and took a position of cover, keeping the vehicle's engine block between him and the spaced out kid with the shotgun. He looked at Cab, who flashed him the thumbs up. He took a deep breath, and yelled toward the alcove as loud as he could,

"NATHAN, YOU WORTHLESS PIECE OF TRASH!"

He saw Nathan lurch forward into his view, the business end of the shotgun still pointed toward the sky, but starting to swing down. Nathan looked in Jason's direction . . . toward the sound he'd heard, muffled by his drug induced fog. With that, Jason got a glimpse of Cab powering forward, moving fast and low, quite fast for a man that carried as much weight as his partner did. He got a good jump, but Nathan heard him coming, alerted either by the big man's footfalls, or the panting sounds that escaped his partner's lips as he struggled to maintain full speed. But fortunately for Cab, Nathan was slow to react. He seemed to turn toward the black behemoth in slow motion, and by the time he realized what was happening he had no chance to avoid the rush. Cab had closed the gap and was coming at him like a blitzing linebacker with a bead on the quarterback. The crackhead crouched, and started to swing the shotgun toward the charging detective. Cab took one last stride and leaped, arms outstretched, literally launching himself at the confused man.

It was a beautiful thing, Jason thought as he observed the drama from his ringside seat, like a tiger leaping at its prey. Nathan collapsed in a heap as Cab hit him. Cab's bulk virtually enveloped the much smaller man, and for a second Nathan's body was virtually invisible under Cab's sprawling girth. Cab rose quickly however, and keeping one knee on Nathan's back, took out his cuffs and slapped them on Nathan's scrawny wrists. Not a peep came from Nathan Perry, a circumstance that would have made his old man jealous, having suffered though years of his son's backtalk and curses. Cab made enough noise for both of them, sucking wind like a vacuum cleaner with something stuck in its hose, making a shrill whistling sound that made Jason wince.

Nevertheless, Jason was duly impressed. "Damn, Cab, you could have killed the kid with a hit like that, either that or smothered him with that big ass of yours."

"Fuck you," The big man spit out, gasping for air. "Next time *I'll* scream, *you* pounce."

The big man was sweating, and wiped his brow with a handkerchief. He yanked Nathan to his feet while Jason used his portable radio to call for a patrol unit to transport the prisoner. Jason looked the boy over. He looked like he'd been run over by a steamroller. He was limp, and sweat caused his clothing to stick to his body like leaves on a wet pavement. His eyes were darting around wildly, hearing the voices of the detectives, but unable to pinpoint the source. He was still spaced out. This was gonna be some story at roll call tonight.

He was having another episode, another blackout. Some of the nightmares faded as he got older. Some of them only grew more intense. The one he confronted now was one of the worst, it was giving him a searing headache as he tried to will it away. It wouldn't go. He tried to picture something more recent, like the bar in the Apex gym . . . the woman who had wanted him to fuck her, but the demons were taking over. He lost control. He held his head in his hands as the visions rushed in like always, overpowering his senses. He remembered what happened . . . just like it was yesterday. This was one his recurring horrors, a memory from his boyhood. The day he was remembering now started out pleasant enough. He had forgotten to tell his mother that he only had a half-day of school today. Not that it mattered really, he took a bus to and from school, and when he got home, his mother was rarely there anyway.

So today was no different, except he still had had the lunch he grabbed on the way out the door this morning. He didn't have to open the rumpled brown bag to know what was inside. Peanut butter and jelly on white bread. Everyday

39

without fail his mother made him the same sandwich. She said it was good for him, and even though some of the other kids had thermoses filled with soup, and fancy sandwiches with ham, turkey, and cheese, he never doubted her. Sometimes, when she was feeling good, she would let him help make the sandwiches. They would stand at the counter near the sink and lay out the bread on a paper towel. Then he would get the jelly from the refrigerator while his mother got the peanut butter down from the cabinet. He liked the smooth kind, and that's what she always got, even though he knew she would have preferred the kind with the little bits of nuts in it. Once in awhile, she would lean down and kiss the top of his head when they were finished. Later, he would realize that this was one of the few rituals the two of them shared when he was a child, and it was one of his fondest memories. He remembered his mother clothed in her pink terrycloth robe, hair still disheveled from the night's sleep, She wore no makeup yet, and looked fresh scrubbed and wholesome. This is how he liked to picture her, but too often less flattering images were the ones that filled his mind.

The bus ride was over a half-hour, and when he passed through Crabtree Corners, a small village that featured the area's only supermarket and the town post office, he would snap out of his daydreams, and begin to look for his stop. He got off the bus a mile later, and strode down the block to his house. There was a strange car in the driveway, and he wondered whose it was, although he was not alarmed or surprised. His mother often had people he didn't know visiting, mostly men. They usually left shortly after he arrived, and most of them didn't even glance at him at all. He would often bound in the door, calling for his mother and running to the sound of her voice, but just as often he would quietly go in through the unlocked front door and head straight to his room. Whatever suited him at the time. He always went with his feelings. Today, he slipped in quietly, anxious to discover who was visiting. He tried the door, expecting it to open as usual, but today it was locked. He fumbled in his pocket for the single key he carried, attached to a small red plastic key fob with the logo of Jim's Texaco, the combination gas station and bait shop where he and Jack used to pick up worms and minnows before heading for the lake.

There was no one in the living room or kitchen when he entered, but he heard muffled sounds down the hall, where the two bedrooms were. He crept quietly down he hall, passed his open bedroom door, and listened at his mother's door. The door never quite closed since the wood had swollen and the door didn't quite fit snug into the frame anymore. Well, that's not quite true. It would close tightly if you slammed it hard enough, which he knew from the times his mother stormed into her room and really, really slammed the door shut. So hard the house rattled. He cocked his head and leaned forward as far as he could without touching the door. He could see into the room. His mother's dresser was in view, and above it was a large mirror where his mother would stand and brush her hair every night. From the angle he was looking the mirror reflected a good portion of the small bedroom.

What he saw in that mirror was a fairy tale gone awry. It scarred him forever. Even now, so many years later, he was tormented by an image so vivid he swore it was burned onto his brain. The mirror was old even then, and the fluid glass had settled some, causing the reflection to be somewhat distorted. In this case, the distortion only served to worsen the effect. He saw the reflection of his mother, naked except for some black lace stockings and what appeared to be some black leather straps crisscrossing her bare back. He could only see her from the rear, but knew it was she by her hair and by the deep red rose tattoo on her hip. Also in the mirror, he saw another figure. It was a man dressed in shiny leather. He thought it was a Halloween costume at first. It covered the man's chest and his legs down to the knees, and his head was covered by a hood of the same material, with small cutouts for the eyes and nose. There was a zipper along the hood where the man's lips should be, and the zipper was closed. The boy recoiled when he saw that the man's penis was sticking out a hole in the leather costume. The man was writhing, seemingly in pain, and in the mirror he saw his mother raise a whip, and he saw her strike the man again and again. He knew the man was crying out in pain, but because of the zipper his lips and mouth did not work right, and only muffled groans were heard.

He stood transfixed, unable to react. He was shocked and afraid. After a few moments, some sort of basic instinctual reaction kicked in, and horrified, he ran out of the house, down the street and into some nearby woods. He ran and ran until he collapsed on the ground, sobbing and gasping for breath. He stayed there for a long time, his body retching. Hours later, confused and not knowing what else to do, he found his way home. His mother was very angry because he was late, and smacked him several times on his buttocks and once across his face, cutting his lip. He did not cry out nor did he speak. He took the beating, went to his room and burrowed beneath the covers.

Chapter 6

The nooks and crannies were hopping this morning. There was an unusually large breakfast crowd, and the two waitresses on duty were having fits trying to keep up. The Tuesday Club was going strong. Half-eaten plates of fresh fruit and cottage cheese were strewn around haphazardly, and an etched crystal pitcher of Mimosas was sitting in the middle of the small round table like a centerpiece. The pitcher was almost empty. The women, sated from food and drink, were bitching about their husbands and boyfriends, a usual part of their once-a-week ritual. At the moment, Laura had the floor.

"Let me tell you something about Earl," Laura ranted. "He is the biggest, fattest, most disgusting husband in the world. I have no idea why I stay with him, let alone try to make him a good wife. Here's just one of many examples I could give you. The other day I came into the bedroom after glamoring up and putting on this little Victoria Secret number with sheer cups and a thong, which by the way, the saleswoman said was guaranteed to jump start any man, and there's Earl, propped up on his giant pillow watching TV. He's got a bowl of potato chips resting on his fat belly and two, not one, but two beers on the nightstand. He's wearing only a pair of oversize boxers and the way his legs are bent I can see right up his freakin' pants leg to the sight of his balls just flopped over his leg."

A chorus of groans and yucks accompanied the visual image flashing in each of the women's imagination. Michelle, the young teacher, made a face like a Cabbage Patch doll sucking a lemon.

"Wait, there's more. Before he sees me coming he lets out this big fart. Oh, God, how disgusting. I mean, he knew I was around, you'd think he'd watch for me and not get caught doing something so disgusting! Damn, I don't think it would have made any difference if he *did* see me coming. I called him a pig and walked back out. Not that my revulsion even registered with him, I swear I heard him crunch down on a chip as I was leaving."

42

The other women made appropriate noises indicating their disgust. This would be a hard story to beat today. Of course, everyone knew why Laura stayed with Earl. He was worth at least sixteen million dollars. Besides Christine's husband, Earl was the richest man in town, and had set her up in business. As a result, she owned and operated a sleek advertising agency that had done well from the onset. She was a talented, imaginative woman, and like the other members of the Tuesday Club, turned quite a few heads everywhere she went. Besides, she was exaggerating about Earl. He was a bit overweight, and watched too many sporting events on TV, but really was a pretty decent guy, even for a lawyer. Aside from the farting, that is.

"I guess that beats my husband David," laughed Michelle. She glanced over at Marjo, who was still literally doubled over with laughter. She was having trouble catching her breath, making a series of gasping, horsy snorts.

"David is kind of the opposite." She continued, "he is a neat and clean freak. Every time he showers, he needs a clean towel, and on the weekends he changes clothes every five minutes. Let's see, there's the running gear, the lawn mowing clothes, the 'let's play handyman' getup he wears to the Home Depot, and finally his casual wear. I practically live in front of the washing machine. At least he puts his dirty stuff in the hamper. Some days I'm tempted to fish it out, shake it off, fold it and put it back into his bureau drawers. He also holds inspection every Saturday morning. He goes from room to room checking for clutter. Anything not part of the furniture, or anything not *officially* part of his exacting décor, is held hostage for immediate disposition. Drives me crazy."

The women believed this story. Michelle was the youngest of the Tuesday Club members, and not as adept at trashing her husband. Being so young and inexperienced in the ways of the world, she lacked the ability to exaggerate and embellish life's moments that had become a trademark of Tuesday Club stories. Besides, having a neat freak for a husband may be annoying to her, but most women will take it anytime compared to some of the other winners out there.

Across the table, Christine was sitting quietly, sipping on her third Mimosa. She was amused by both stories. This was a regular feature of the Club's meetings in the nooks. Story telling. Sometimes they talked about work, sometimes about kids, and sometimes about men and sex. A throwback to the old coffee klatches, with a millenium twist. Even though the women gathered here today were very different, she liked and admired all of them. Michelle and her husband were very sweet. She had an aura of innocence about her that Christine hoped she would never lose, although she knew better. Michelle and her husband were good, church going people with strong family ties and a couple of really cute kids. The older of the two boys was only three. Laura, on the other hand, was worldly, sophisticated, and liked being in business. She held her own with the men she dealt with, and they respected her for it. She gave a lot of money to charity, always helping with fundraisers, special events, and even chipped in for political causes. She was a mover and shaker in Highland Park.

"Hey Michelle," chimed Marjo, "tell us more about playing handyman and the helpless housewife. Does Dave wear a tool belt and steel toed boots?"

"Yea, and nothing else?" added Laura.

"I had a boyfriend once, a cop, who always wanted me to play 'escaped convict and the warden's wife.' Now that was kinky."

Marjo was the exact opposite of innocent, and always had plenty of stories to tell, almost all of them about her sexual adventures.

"Really," purred Laura, "tell us more."

"Well, it involved a dark room, a wooden chair, handcuffs, a blindfold, leather chaps, and whipped cream. A lot of poking and prodding too!"

Laura chortled.

Michelle gasped.

"Why the chaps?" asked Christine, who was trying to picture this bizarre combination. "They don't fit the scenario."

"You're right, they didn't. Hell, he just liked the way those chaps framed my bare ass!" Once again, very unladylike laughter filled the nooks. When it subsided, it was Christine's turn.

"You all know Kyle is really a great husband. But this one day I was lying out back by our pool sunning, totally naked. I was trying to get a jumpstart on my tan because we were planing a trip to the Greek Isles in a couple of weeks. Now being naked in my own yard is usually not a problem, since it is very secluded and no one can get in except through the house, the locked gate, or the door leading to the yard from the garage.

"Don't you know Kyle had gone to the gym and forgot his house keys. So when he comes home, he parks in the garage, finds the connecting door to the house locked, and comes through the gate into the yard unannounced. Right behind him were two fitness instructors Kyle had invited back for a beer! They got more than they counted on! Boy, did those young men get an eyeful." She waved her finger in front of her in a scolding manner, "and Kyle didn't get any for a week! Thank God there's a heavy turnover of fitness instructors. Until they left, I turned beet red every time I saw them at the gym."

"Shit, Christine," said Marjo. "What's wrong with you, girl? I would have just stretched out and let them soak in the view! It's not often you get to pose for some real beefcake . . . especially in front of your husband! Make him sweat a bit."

"You all are just awful!" groaned Michelle, secretly delighted to be part of such decadent discussion. "You ought to be ashamed. But I guess that's why I love you so much!"

"Live and learn, girl . . . live and learn," advised Marjo the Pro. "Janet, what about you? What's your story today?"

The sleek looking nurse swished the remains of her drink around the bottom of her fluted glass, and downed it in a single gulp. She flung her head back, tossing her hair from her face and set her glass back on the table. She purred before speaking, just for effect.

"Damn," she said finally, genuinely disappointed she had nothing worthwhile to add. "I don't think I can compete with you today, ladies, but I'm working on one for next time. Stay tuned."

Janet looked at Christine and winked. Christine knew Janet was referring to Jason Coulter, whom she hoped to have an adventure with very soon. She was sure the sultry blonde's next story would be one worth waiting for.

He sat in front of the computer, his fingers flying furiously over the keyboard. Although he never learned to type, could work a keyboard as fast as many trained secretaries, a skill he attributed to his unique mental abilities. His mind just took over his body, just did what it had to do, subconsciously most of the time, acting on the same involuntary urge as did a beating heart. He didn't have to think, it just happened. As he had hoped, this trait also carried over to other things. It had been two weeks since he'd done Amber, and still no feeling of remorse had come over him. He took it as a sign, and believed that this lack of emotion meant he was justified in his actions. After all, if his conscience did not bother him, if he had absolutely no regrets about killing his ex-girlfriend in a manner that bought him great satisfaction, who was he to argue? He had put up with enough in his life, more than most men would have been able to stand without killing themselves or someone else. He had been miserable before he killed her, plagued by headaches and strong feelings of self-doubt and loathing. Something had to give.

Really, it had come down to two choices. Was he going to kill himself and end the torture? Or could he end this anguish by exacting revenge on those who brought him this unbearable pain? This was the question he pondered for months before reaching a difficult decision that now seemed so crystal clear he didn't know what took him so long. After he killed Amber, he felt peace. The pounding in his head slowed and even stopped for a while, and his thoughts became clearer. He was like a junkie who had found and taken the ultimate fix. And there was no turning back.

He knew he would kill again, and even though there was no one in his life anymore, there were plenty of women who given the chance would treat him like the others had done. Even his mother had fallen into this category. They had relied on him for as long as they needed someone in their lives, wanting him to be there, willing to give him control and placing their destiny in his hands. He responded by being there for them, regardless of the time of day or the trivial nature of their request. As long as he could do for them he was wanted. But little by little his attention became less endearing and more possessive, and that's when the trouble always began. He knew this happened, but to him it was the natural course of relationships. They were his, and he was theirs, what's wrong with that?

He concentrated on the task at hand. This program he'd just come up with needed a little more tweaking before it was ready to use. When completed, he would be to able scan thousands of computers using ISP's in search of additional unappreciative women. Women like Amber Mathieson. Best of all, they would have no clue that they were being "watched," or that they were being targeted. He would scan thousands of messages sent by unsuspecting women but only a select few would receive his personal attention. Those chosen few would be selected on the basis of carefully designed criteria that he created based on his own needs and desires. Essentially, he had created a sophisticated virus that would monitor millions of data packets being transmitted over the Internet. It was designed to search for key words and phrases that would screen potential targets. If there were enough of these phrases originating from a single unique identifiable source, the virus would hone in and trace the message back to the point of origin, which would inevitably be a personal computer being used by a beautiful young woman. There was no doubt about that. He had carefully constructed the intelligence gathering capabilities of his unique virus to recognize and record only messages coming from women. Well, the beautiful part was not always true, there were some ugly ones caught by the virus too. But even this he would find out sooner or later, and usually well before he actually laid eyes on his prey, saving him some effort. He had no interest in homely women. They were miserable enough already, and posed no threat.

The program then sent him a message verifying a hit, and he would then review the messages coming from his new potential victim. If it looked good, he sent them a seemingly innocuous email. When they opened it, the second phase of the virus would infect their computer, allowing him to mirror everything the women sent, received, or even typed into their machines. From the information he'd intercepted, he knew their tastes and habits. It was easy to construct a virus carrying an email message that had enough appeal for them that they opened it without hesitation. Sometimes, when he had gotten their information, he used the names of their friends as the senders. This would disarm even the most cautious user. It was an incredible feat, even for him. Just a few more hours and his search would begin. Just in time too. His headaches had come back, and grew in intensity each day. He needed some relief, and he needed it soon.

It was shortly after ten on Sunday morning when Jason received a call from the police station. It was Sgt. Adams, one of the patrol shift supervisors. Jason had been dawdling over his morning coffee and thinking about Janet Witherspoon. The last time he'd saw her at the gym, he'd gotten up the nerve to ask her out on a real date and she'd accepted. She had to work last night, so tonight was the night. Adams' booming voice interrupted his musings.

"Lieutenant, we just had a hit and run accident on Plum Street, the 200 block, near Vista Drive. It looks bad."

"Victim?"

"A seventy-five year old woman. Get this; she was crossing the street after church services had let out. She coded in the ambulance, she had serious head trauma."

"Do you have any info on the striking vehicle?" Jason asked.

"Yeah. It was a blue truck, maybe a Ford Ranger. There were two occupants. We have three officers on scene, protecting the evidence and canvassing neighbors. Officer Stowart is on his way in for the accident reconstruction."

Stowart was one of the department's trained accident investigators. Police work today is highly specialized. Most police agencies now had officers capable of combining complex measurements and mathematical formulas to determine a number of factors in vehicle collisions, such as speed before and after impact, direction, displacement of force based on vehicle weight and velocity, and other items important to an investigation. Jason knew however, that the most important evidence in this type of case would probably come from people, both witnesses and suspects, and from the striking vehicle itself, if they could find it quickly.

"Okay, Jack. What do you need from me?"

"Detective Dumont was on call, but his wife just gave birth yesterday and I thought you might come out for this."

"No problem. Be there in fifteen."

So much for real police work, Jason mused. TV cops never get called out on a Sunday to handle a fatal hit and run, especially Lieutenants. He was pleased to do it, however, especially to give Dumont some extra time with his new baby. It was his first, so Jason was sure he and his wife were preoccupied. Because he was single, and some would say had no life, he was often called to substitute for a family man caught in the throes of fatherhood or some domestic emergency. It was becoming more frequent with the new generation cops. Years ago when on-duty cops learned their wives went into labor, the Sergeant covered for them while they rushed to the hospital and waited for the delivery. Afterwards, the new father would return with a fistful of cheap cigars, turn in his remaining paperwork, and go home. Without exception, the officer would show up to work his next scheduled shift while his mother-in-law fawned over mother and baby. Today, officers' plan for the event like it was the Normandy Invasion. They take classes, have dry runs to the hospital, pack his and her suitcases, and have vacation time approved in advance so that they can take at least a week off to bond with the new baby. A week's vacation spent with a screaming baby, a postpartum wife, and your mother-in-law who *stills* comes to fawn even though you're there too. Go figure. It's a sure bet the mothers-in-law don't like this either.

Jason arrived at the scene 16 minutes after hanging up the phone. He approached the yellow barricade tape and ducked under it, walking toward a uniformed officer. Immediately, he saw the blood marking the spot the victim had fallen. She had almost made it. It seemed like she was just about to step back on the curb when she was struck. This was a bit strange, as most pedestrian accidents occur as the victim steps off the curb, from between parked cars, or around the bend of a sharp curve.

"Nice to see ya, Boss," said Officer Frank Michaels. "There's a couple of potential witnesses at 104, standing on the front porch." Michaels pointed toward two men standing on the stoop of a nearby house. "Otherwise, we got this handled."

"I can see that. How about going over there and moving those two *potential witnesses* apart a bit." Jason spoke with frostiness in his voice. He did not like the senior officer's attitude. Although it was a small thing, he should have known to put some distance between the witnesses. Every cop knows eyewitnesses' stories tend to mesh if they start talking to each other, and standing together at this type of scene is surely going to get their gums flapping. In addition, Jason did not like being called 'boss.' This was how ranking officers were referred to in some big eastern cities, but Jason thought it was unprofessional. Michaels shot Jason a look, but shuffled over to the witnesses.

Jason stood back and surveyed the area. He always liked to visit the crime scene as soon as possible after an event. He thought it was very important to get a feel for the scene, how it looked, how it smelled, the conditions of the lighting and shadows. He even wanted to see the people who were hanging around . . . all of this helped him begin his investigation. Some investigators would have just directed patrol to take the witnesses to the station for interviews and met them there, but Jason thought that type of procedure was a mistake. It was better to get

48

a first-hand look at the scene. It made it easier to picture what the witness was describing, and there was less chance of missing a critical point. This scene was simple but disturbing. The striking vehicle laid about 80 feet of skid a half-block up the road, but there was none approaching the spot where the woman had been struck.

There was also no debris from the striking vehicle, which is not that unusual in car versus pedestrian accidents. Jason confirmed that the accident investigator was taking measurements and walked over to the witnesses. Not surprisingly, neither of them actually saw the collision, but did hear the sounds of severe braking and then rapid acceleration. They heard tires spin as the truck "peeled out." When they heard the commotion, they rushed outside in time to see the striking vehicle leave the scene. One of them got a partial license number, and the other gave a sketchy description of the driver, a white male with a light beard, probably in his early twenties. Jason jotted down the information, asked them where he could contact them for further assistance, and thanked them for their help. He then went into the trunk of his unmarked Impala and brought out his Olympus digital camera. It took him about fifteen minutes to photograph the scene, and he discreetly took a couple of shots of his witnesses for good measure.

Finally, he used some glass vials, envelopes, and paper bags from his evidence kit to gather the few items of evidence he found, including a sample of the blood coagulating on the street. He looked at his watch.

"Hey Michaels, anybody at the hospital with the victim?"

"I guess just a couple horny nurses, Boss. We're a bit short."

According to cops like Michaels, police were always understaffed. Most of the time it was just an excuse to get out of some work.

"Never mind, I'll do it." Jason figured he might as well see this thing through. The victim was probably declared dead by now, but he could get some particulars for his report before the medical charts were sent to the hospital's records unit. It would save him some time getting the information now rather than having to get a subpoena later. Once the patient's chart went to the medical records unit, privacy laws forbade it from being disclosed to anyone without a release or some type of court order. He hopped back into his car and headed downtown toward Mercy General.

Chapter 7

Jason arrived at Pompano's Willow Grove Inn at precisely half past seven. He had to rush a bit after finishing up the hit and run investigation, but did not feel hurried as he entered the restaurant. However, he was a little anxious about tonight. He was always concerned about what his dates thought of him, which was in direct contrast to his cavalier attitude at work. On the job, he didn't care whom he pissed off or what his fellow cops thought of him. But tonight, he was more apprehensive than usual. Most of his coworkers and friends, except for Cab, would be surprised by his feelings. He had a reputation as a ladies man, and like every other red blooded American male, Jason did all that he could to maintain that image. In reality, he was not nearly as bold as he let on, but he was confident of his appeal to the opposite sex, and rarely worried about meeting new people.

But for some reason, he was a bit intimidated by his date tonight, perhaps because of her high brow appearance. Maybe it was only because he'd waited so long for this evening. There was a time when he didn't think he would ever have the balls to ask her out. Janet had suggested they meet at Pompano's, and he was pleased with her choice. The Grove, as everyone called the Highland Park landmark, was one of the most popular fine dining establishments in the county. It was an intimate setting, with tables adorned with white tablecloths and fresh flowers. The tables were set among large lavish plants and intricate arrangements of potted flowers that created a very private garden-like setting for each patron. The owner had taken care to arrange each table so that it was offset and secluded from the others, yet they were only a few feet apart. Strategically placed tiki torches, whose dancing fingers of flame added to the warm and seductive ambiance, augmented the low house lights. It was like seeing the world through a filter, or at least through rose colored glasses as the old saying went. Almost anybody could look good in here, Jason thought. The Maitre D met him immediately.

"I'm meeting someone," Jason said.

"Of course," the man replied with the slightest patronizing smile, like this was something he heard dozens of times each night, which was true of course. "Ms. Witherspoon is already at your table. Please follow me."

Jason obliged; not surprised that Janet had alerted him to watch for her date.

Janet looked absolutely ravishing. A lump caught in his throat as he approached the table. She was watching him, smiling, seeming to size him up a bit and realized he was nervous. Jason bent to give her a soft kiss on the cheek.

"Good evening. You look gorgeous, Janet." She really did.

"Thank you. You're very kind, but I think the lighting helps." She smiled again, with a mischievous glint in her deep blue eyes. Her eyes may have been the most beautiful of all her outstanding features. Jason would not doubt that those eyes, combined with the obvious feminine wiles of the intelligent woman behind them, captured many a heart . . . and broke more than one. The two started with the usual first date banter . . . the weather, the need for a vacation, the different trials and tribulations they were facing . . . just scratching the surface of a lot of topics. They were waiting for that comfortable feeling that comes after a couple realizes they truly like one another and begins to relax and enjoy their time together. If that moment never came, there would be a mutual awkwardness and two sad souls straining to devise plausible excuses for calling it an early evening.

"I'm really glad you suggested this," said Jason. "I'm probably a fool to admit this, but you intimidated me bit."

"Ha! *You're* a cop, and *you* were intimidated! How do you think *I* felt? Here I'm going out with a man who can find out all sorts of things about me before we even talk, how nerve-racking is that?"

Jason smiled. It was a common misconception that cops had access to all sorts of inside information about people that they could use whenever they liked. Actually, there were strict guidelines on the use of police records, including driver's licensing information, and tracking mechanisms that kept private lives private, even from curious cops. Besides, you could usually pull more off the Internet than you could gather from police sources. However since she'd brought it up, Jason couldn't help wondering if there was something about her she didn't want him to know. Does she have a record . . . a secret past? Maybe she was just referring to the problems between her and her ex-husband that she alluded to the first time they had spoken.

"Oh, we don't really do that kind of stuff, check up on women like that," he said smiling. "But we could, I guess. I hate computers anyway, never waste my time sitting in front of a cold, impersonal monitor when I could be doing something useful; working out, taking a long drive in the country, doing a little mountain climbing . . . that sort of thing. I'm more of the outdoorsy, adventurous type. Besides, I prefer to get my information the old fashioned way . . . interrogation! Now, my lovely suspect . . . let's begin."

Jason learned quite a bit about his date that night. He learned that Janet was raised in Swathmore, a suburb of Philadelphia considered part of the Main Line, a nickname for the posh western communities bordering the city. *Obviously, there's some family money here,* thought Jason. Not too many nurses drove cars as expensive as Janet's and hung with millionaires. She was Catholic, attended Villanova University where she majored in Biology, and graduated summa cum laude. He also learned that she was a regional finalist to become a Sunset Swimsuit model in 1988, and had a passion for Siamese cats. The modeling part caught his attention. Janet told him she entered a contest in a local college pub during her junior year, on a dare from some female classmates. Four of them entered, and much to her surprise, Janet won over nineteen other girls. She went as far as the East Coast finals, finishing third. The top two from each region went to Hawaii to compete for the title. She had to keep the whole thing from her parents, as she was living at home at the time and such a banal undertaking would have sent them through the roof. Actually though, she was quite proud of her showing, and ranked it right up there with her diploma and graduation from nursing school.

Jason asked her how she got into nursing, and she said it stemmed from her contact with a nurse she befriended while taking a friend to the emergency room one night after the girl had accidentally cut herself while slicing a bagel. She had been so impressed by the calm professionalism and caring attitude of the nurse she came back later to see her and they quickly became friends. After graduation, Janet got a lead on a job at Mercy Hospital in Highland Park and the rest was history; she'd been working there for the past eleven years. She glossed over her marriage, which was fine with Jason, and as he watched her speak, her eyes dancing as she smiled and frowned in accordance with events in her life, he was taken with her subtle sensuality and her unabashed revelations.

After a delicious dinner they languished over coffee for quite some time, not realizing the late hour until Jason saw the waitress looking over at them and checking her watch, obviously sending them a message. Not wanting to leave just yet, they had a couple of drinks at the piano bar, and he was pleased at how easily they talked, and at how comfortable he felt telling her about himself. That was something he rarely did. They also chatted about the Apex, and later traded war stories about work. Cops and nurses always seemed to be a good fit.

There is a natural attraction based perhaps on the high stress of the work, and the fact that both professions deal most often with people at their worst. Of course, both jobs were somewhat altruistic, attracting wide-eyed do-gooders who want to help people and change the world. But after just a few months of dealing with the drunk and disturbed while working midnight shifts, they begin to think most people are assholes. Then they realize that the only people with whom they can really relate are those who deal with similar challenges and who put up with the same assholes. There was definitely an attraction between *this* cop and nurse.

Jason walked Janet to her car. As she turned to say goodbye, she swept her hair behind her ear and looked directly at him, which Jason took as a sign she wanted to be kissed. He obliged, and a chaste closed-mouthed kiss turned quickly into a warm embrace. He felt Janet's arms encircle his waist and her hands moved along the sinewy muscles of his back. Their lips parted and he hungrily sought her tongue as their breathing quickened in response to their rising passion. He moved even closer, sliding his thigh between her legs and felt her grinding into him as she enthusiastically returned his kiss. He was getting hard. Suddenly she pulled away, moving her face to the side, breaking the heat.

"Yo sailor," she said in a low raspy voice. "We better slow down a bit, or we'll give the whole place a free show."

"Shall we take this somewhere else?" he replied softly, hopeful to continue what they had begun.

"Not tonight sweet cheeks, but I know we will . . . and soon."

Trooper John Woodson called Jason about ten o'clock the morning after his date with Janet. He was still thinking about her, and the shrill ring of the telephone interrupted his daydream. These phone interruptions were beginning to become a habit, one he didn't like at all.

"Detectives . . . Lieutenant Coulter."

"Lieutenant, Trooper Woodson here, from the forensic computer section." Woodson was the state police expert who had taken custody of the computer found in Amber's apartment.

"Yes, Trooper. What do you have for me?"

"We analyzed the computer in the Amber Mathieson case, and found an interesting quirk. We checked all of the programs and files. There were all the usual things typically found in a home computer. There was correspondence, a check register, photos, and a bunch of miscellaneous programs you'd expect to find. All were consistent with the computer being exclusively used by a female in her 20's, and there were enough identifying links in there to be reasonably sure the computer was Mathieson's."

"Okay," Jason said, "then what was there that caught your attention?"

"It's what *wasn't* there that jumped out at us. There are no records of email or Internet transactions. No current messages, no old files, no dumped files . . .

53

nothing. In fact, there was not even any ISP software in the system, including the one that comes installed when you buy the thing."

"Are you telling me that Amber never used the Internet?"

"No, I'm telling you that, in my opinion, all evidence of her use of the Internet has been deliberately and expertly destroyed. There's not a trace of anything."

" Are you certain? Why would anyone do this?"

"Oh, I'm certain," the trooper intoned. "Let me explain."

Jason could tell by the tone of his voice that Woodson was intrigued by his find. His duties usually included cracking passwords and codes to download child porn from a pedophile's computer, or examining boring accounting files in cases of embezzlement and fraud. He realized that this information may shed some light on a murder case, and was relishing his involvement. Despite the growing use of computers to commit crimes and the vast wealth of information available to the investigators who took the time to delve into their secrets, computer cops were still regarded as nerds. Working on a homicide case helped improve their image. Jason knew he would get maximum cooperation from the computer unit on this case.

"First," Woodson continued, "the absence of any Internet transactions is highly unusual, since virtually everyone who owns a computer these days hooks up to the web at some point. Second, it took a person with really detailed knowledge of computer operations to destroy any trace of messages and information downloaded from the net, and there is nothing in Ms. Mathieson's known background that indicates she had this type of knowledge. And finally, your inventory of bills and papers taken from her apartment shows some purchases made using e-sites. So there is evidence, easily verifiable by checking with the vendors, that she at least occasionally made purchases over the web."

"That *is* kinda weird," agreed Jason. "Even if Amber had the capacity for doing it, can you think of any practical reason she might have cause to destroy those files?"

"No, not really; unless something really sinister was going on. It seems more likely the killer did it, ether before or after he murdered her, or someone else did it after the fact . . . between the time of her death and the time police arrived on the scene."

This was new territory for Jason. He considered himself computer literate as a user, but knew little about how they worked, and even less about the inner workings of the Internet. He needed some help from Woodson.

"Is there anything else we can do to learn more about the victim's use of the Internet, try to find a link between this development and Amber's murder?"

"Right now the only thing I can think of is to find out what company she used for an ISP, and get a warrant to search their records. We can check the more popular providers, like AOL, but there are literally thousands of them out there. We'll hit all the local providers too. Many people use a discount service in their own towns to access the Internet. I'll do what I can if you'd like me to handle that."

"Okay, Thanks Woodson. Please do. When can I expect your written report?"

"I'll get it to you in two days, Lieutenant. It'll be my top priority. Let me know what else I can do to help," Woodson said hopefully.

"You bet I will. If this information means anything at all in relation to the victim's homicide, you and I will be spending lots of hours together. Thanks for your help."

Jason thought hard about the information Trooper Woodson had just given him. If the killer had wiped out the computer files, why had he done it? What could be in there that linked him to the crime. He thought of the different possibilities. The most obvious was that the killer could have had a relationship with her on the net, either forged in a chat room and maybe embellished by instant messaging, or by email. Option one meant that the killer would *probably* have started out as a stranger to Amber, while option two, using email to talk back and forth, meant that the suspect *might* be someone she already knew. At any rate, there was not a lot to go on, but at least it was something.

Chapter 8

It was a few weeks since Jason had promised to enter the charity weightlifting competition, and it was now time to put up or shut up. Jason couldn't believe how nervous he was about the event. He regretted giving in to Christine in a moment of weakness, or more accurately, a moment of horniness. The things you agree to when you think with the little head! He had been lifting weights on and off competitively for much of his life, but still got that "butterflies in the stomach" feeling. Tonight was no exception. Even though tonight's event was as much a fundraiser as a competition, it was an American Federation of Weightlifting sanctioned event. This meant that all the rules were going to apply, and any records set here by the lifters would count. There were about seventy lifters entered in the contest, including fifty-three non-celebrities. Many of these men, and a few women, were serious about their sport. Jason saw that the entrants included three state champions and a couple of national caliber competitors. They were scattered about the warm-up room. Many of them were huddled with trainers, lifting partners, and others who assisted them during the event. It always amazed him to see these guys donning specially constructed skintight bench pressing shirts. These were made of lycra, spandex type material that provided resistance while lowering the bar to the chest, and then provided a burst of concentrated power as the lifter thrust the bar upward. It took two guys to help a competitor in and out of these shirts, and Jason could not figure out why they were legal, since the shirts gave the lifter an edge over others.

There were also wraps for wrists and knees, lots of pungent sports cremes and smelling salts, and an assortment of other accoutrements. Some amounted to nothing more than good-luck charms or superstitions. Seeing all these men going through the pre-competition rituals always gave Jason the feeling that he didn't belong . . . that he was not a serious lifter.

It had been four or five years since he last competed, in the Pennsylvania Police Olympics in Lancaster. He had taken the silver medal. Since then, he had not really trained much, but stayed in good enough shape that he was able to get ready for this event and build up to some decent poundage. At least for a non-serious competitor. As he felt another twinge in his belly, he wished he had not allowed Christine to goad him into this, but immediately reminded himself it was for a good cause, and that he was entered as a "celebrity," and would not really be expected to perform like the others. Before entering the locker room to get changed and weigh-in, he looked over the platform and equipment he would be using in the competition. There was a wooden platform, about ten-foot square, at the front of the large aerobics room. On it was the standard eight foot long Olympic size bar, and a couple of racks holding hundreds of pounds of precisely weighted metal discs.

Jason was pleased to see that the Apex was using equipment manufactured by York Barbell, a Pennsylvania company that had a long tradition of sponsoring the USA Olympic and National teams. There were three chairs for the judges, one directly in front of the platform and one each on either side. These three judges would make sure the lifters made a "good" lift by following the proper form and successfully completing the movements required. For a sport characterized by brute strength, there was a lot of technique and finesse involved in getting a few hundred pounds from starting point to finishing point.

"YO JASON," a loud voice bellowed from across the room. It was Cab, standing in the entrance to the aerobics room. "Are you ready?"

"How about we forget this and get a beer," Jason countered.

"Don't even think about it. You're already listed in the program, and besides, you can't disappoint your fans. There are at least two of them, not counting me."

"Who's that?"

"The tantalizing twins, Christine and Janet. Are you sure you're not doing one or both of them?"

"Okay, okay. Actually, I could use some help warming up. Let me weigh in, and I'll be out in a few minutes. You can spot for me."

Jason balanced the scale at one hundred seventy eight pounds. This put him firmly in the light-heavyweight class, and he gave his opening lift as three hundred fifteen pounds. He had a routine he followed before every lift. First, he chalked his hands, mentally trying to clear his head and prepare for the lift. The chalk was the same type used by gymnasts, about the size of a bar of soap, and was designed to keep the hands dry and prevent the athlete's grip from slipping. Although he did not use chalk during training, it was part of his ritual during competition. He then walked directly in front of the bench and looked at the bar sitting on sturdy steel racks perpendicular to the flat bench. He examined the metal plates on each end of the bar, counting the number of plates and adding up the total poundage. Mistakes were sometimes made by the spotters who loaded the weights and stood by in case a lifter failed to complete the lift, and an unevenly balanced bar could spell disaster for a competitor. Not only would any difference in weight distribution screw up the lift, it could also result in injury to the athlete.

The plates were balanced, and the amount of weight was correct. He lay supine on the bench, and reached for the bar. He planted his feet firmly on the plywood platform, knowing that lifting a foot off of the platform would also result in failure. Form was just as important as strength in these competitions. He used some grooves cut into the bar to set his hand space. He used a slightly wider than shoulder length grip, which brought the large muscles of his chest into play as he pushed the weight upwards. Finally, just before "liftoff," that point when the lifter removes the weighted bar from the supporting racks that held it, he closed his eyes. As always, he envisioned his arms as pistons, and pictured them driving the weight up smoothly and forcefully. Then, he took a deep breath and lifted the weight off the racks.

As nervous as he was, the first lift went well, although one of the judges told him to watch his control as he lowered the bar to his chest. Apparently, he dropped it too fast for the one judge, and that could have cost him. Minutes later, he heard the announcer call his name for his second attempt. As he was approaching the bench, he spotted Christine and Janet in the audience. They waved at him, and Janet smiled and gave him the thumbs up.

Knowing they were watching gave him an extra surge of adrenaline, and he took the bar off the rack and slowly but steadily lowered it until it touched his chest. At the judge's signal, he thrust it upward with as much power as he could muster, and after a moment's hesitation, the bar went up smoothly. Three hundred and thirty pounds! Not too bad for his current state of fitness. He was tempted to try 350, but didn't want to miss it badly and be embarrassed, so decided to go with 340 for his last attempt. As he walked to the scoring table, he caught Janet leaning over to Christine and whispering in her ear. He was sure it was something about him. He checked on the other lifters in his class, and saw that two of them had not even started yet, which meant that they would almost assuredly be hoisting significantly more than he could do.

However, he also noted that he was ahead of four others in his class, and another was set to try 350 for his last attempt. Again Jason thought about trying the 350, realizing that he had weighed in lighter than this opponent and thus would beat him in the event they both lifted the same poundage. He decided to stick with his original plan, and five minutes later, was called for his last attempt. He was all business now, chalking up his hands and shrugging his shoulders to loosen them up. He strode to the bench, and got into position quickly, lying on the bench and placing his fingers around the bar, about eight inches from the inner collars. Just before he took the bar off the rack, he had a fleeting thought. The way he was positioned on the bench, Jason realized his crotch was the most prominent part of his body facing the audience, and all of a sudden felt a little exposed. Unlike many other lifters who wore spandex shorts or lifting suits, Jason wore a pair of cotton knee length shorts, and hoped they were not gapping open at this point! Maybe that was what Janet was whispering about.

Jason could often tell as soon as he took the bar off the racks whether he had a good chance of completing a successful lift. He was one of the few lifters who refused help to lift the loaded bar from the rack to a locked arms position over his chest, although such assistance was permissible in competition. He trained that way, and liked the feeling he had when the bar came smoothly off the racks and up into position to start the lift. As soon as he pushed the weight off the racks, he knew he had the strength to bench the 340 pounds. It felt steady in his arms, and not overly heavy. He wished he had called for the extra ten pounds, but quickly shook that thought off and concentrated on his form. He did not want to lose this attempt by lowering the bar too fast or pushing it back up without coming to a complete stop on his chest.

He lowered it slowly, pausing at his chest for just a second, just long enough for the head judge to signal "Press!" He pushed for all he was worth, imagining the pistons driving forward. The bar rose off his chest, and he felt his arms quiver a bit as the strain of hundreds of pounds put pressure on his wrists and elbows. But the bar kept moving up, passing the halfway point and even gaining speed as Jason forced himself to breathe, gaining a burst of strength with the forceful expulsion of air from his lungs. He locked the bar out, and held it steady until the judge yelled "Down." The spotters grabbed the bar, one on each end, and guided it back onto the racks. Jason sat up, turned to look at the scoreboard, and saw three white lights, signifying a good lift. He felt great.

It turned out the other competitor missed his attempt at 350 pounds, and Jason won third place. He stepped up to receive his award, and despite himself grinned broadly at Janet and Christine as Kyle handed him the two foot trophy, adorned with a gold plated figure of a weightlifter at the top. Cab approached, clapping him on the back so hard he lost his breath.

"You fucking wimp," Cab joked. "You were good for at least twenty pounds more. But, for an old guy like you, I guess it wasn't too bad."

"Thanks, pal," Jason retorted. "Looks pretty easy from your chair doesn't it? Next year let's see how much your ass can push up there!"

He chatted a bit with the women, accepting congratulations and a squeeze on the bicep from Christine, and then went to the locker room to shower and change. Twenty minutes later, he was scanning the nooks for his friends, and spotted them crowding into a corner booth. Cab was shaking hands and preparing to leave as he approached. Kyle had risen to bid farewell to Cab, and Janet and Christine were seated across from each other.

"Leaving so soon?" Jason asked. "Aren't you going to join in my almost victory celebration?"

"Well," said his partner, "first of all, you lost first place by forty pounds. And second, I have to catch an early flight to Atlanta tomorrow, and want to spend some time with Shawna and the kids tonight. See you all when I get back." He shook hands with Kyle and Jason, and walked quickly to the exit.

"I'm really jealous of that man," Jason remarked to no one in particular, thinking about Cab's loving wife and kids. "He really has his head on straight."

"Is he going to Atlanta to investigate the Amber Mathieson killing?" Kyle asked.

"Yes, he is. I hope he comes up with something. We don't have much to go on at this point."

He slid into the booth next to Janet. He could smell the dusky fragrance of her perfume as he drew near. Her usually alluring scent was slightly altered by the smells of the gym that were transferred onto her clothing during the day's events, a not-so-pleasant mix of liniment and perspiration. Nevertheless, Jason found her irresistible. He glanced at her, caught her eye, and held the look for just a few seconds, trying to communicate his intense interest in her. At least that was the look he was going for. He hoped he didn't look like a serial killer sizing up his next victim.

The group spent the next half-hour celebrating Jason's performance and discussing the weightlifting event. Kyle ordered champagne and they all drank heartily. Kyle told them that the preliminary tally of the proceeds exceeded thirty-five thousand dollars, more than last year, and he was pleased with both the amount of money raised for charity and the success of the actual event.

"And we owe it all to Lt. Coulter's participation," Christine offered, raising her glass in a toast. "I saw quite a few eligible ladies watching him as he lifted. No doubt he was a big draw this year."

"Here, here," Kyle enjoined, raising his glass and touching it to Christine's, Janet's, and finally Jason's. "To Jason, and to success."

Glasses clinked all around the table as Jason mockingly accepted the praise, bowing slightly, and winking at Janet.

As they were toasting, Marjo the Pro approached their table. She was wearing tight black spandex pants, and a silvery sequined top, cut low and tied at the waist. Her hips had a rhythmic sway as she walked, like a model parading down the runway, one foot crossing in front of the other. The motion gave the professional models an exaggerated shimmy as they walked, and it worked for Marjo too. Her hips and backside swayed so much it was almost obscene. The sequins on Marjo's blouse caught and reflected every ray of light in the dimly lit lounge, causing an aura-like effect about her body and face. It was vintage Marjo. She could steal attention from movie stars at the Oscar's if she ever got the chance.

"What am I missing," she cooed, spreading her arms wide and tilting her head from side to side, encouraging an answer from her friends. "Y'all are making a lot of noise over here."

"We are celebrating this fine evening," Kyle told her, rising from his seat and extending his hand for her to take. "Please join us."

Marjo took his extended hand, and Kyle bent to kiss her. He missed her cheek and his face burrowed into her neck as he planted one just below her ear. He was in there a little too long for a simple social greeting, and Jason wondered if there was something more going on here. Christine's expression didn't change, so whatever it was didn't register with her, or else she just didn't care.

With Marjo joining the group, the conversation got raucous, often punctuated with guffaws and snorts, the latter coming from Marjo, whose laughter was so intense it caused her to inhale sharply to get enough air back into her aching lungs. Jason imagined the effect that laugh would have at a stuffy social event attended by Highland Park's upper crust. He pictured Marjo seated at the dinner table, looking all prim and proper with her hair up and a demure gown that buttoned up to the neck. Another guest cracks a joke, and all of a sudden Marjo breaks into her loud, horsy guffaws, startling the others and making her and her now embarrassed date the source of unwanted attention. She's not the kind of girl you take home to mother, he thought. Kyle had ordered a second bottle of champagne when Marjo sat down with them, and was now gesturing for a waiter to request a third. Christine asked Marjo if she was seeing anyone now, which was a lot like asking a porn queen if she sucked a dick lately. Not that Marjo was a porn queen, or even a slut, but men were the staples of life for her, and she made no excuses for it.

"Actually, I am," She replied, as if *that* answer was really necessary. Christine should have asked *who* was she seeing now, but either way the group would soon know.

"I'm seeing Deter. He's been asking me out for months, and a couple of weeks ago, I agreed."

She was talking about Deter Schmidt, of course, the club's manager. It was no mystery that she preferred handsome, well-built Adonis-type men, and Deter fit the bill nicely. He was a cross between Sly Stallone and Jean Claude VanDamm, except his hair was blond and his eyes a clear, cold blue. When he looked directly at you, it was as if he was looking *through* you, and his eyes were expressionless. Jason thought that having such penetrating eyes would be a good asset for a police officer to possess. It was a bit unnerving to experience the glare from these orbs, and used correctly, it could make a suspect very uneasy.

"I always thought Deter would be wild and crazy," She continued. "And he is, but he's also sweet and very protective. He makes me feel good about myself. I really like him, much more than I thought I would in the beginning. I really just went out with him because he was so persistent. But now . . . well, he's just great."

"That scoundrel, as close as I am to him, I had no idea he had a thing for you," Kyle said. "I'm glad you two are getting along well. Next time we all get together, why don't you bring him along."

Despite his friendly tone, Jason thought he picked up a twinge of jealousy in Kyle's voice. There *is* something between the two of them. He'd bet on it.

"I can't wait," she answered, seeming to be excited about joining Kyle's circle of friends. "Let's do it soon."

Several hours later, after coming home from the gym and fixing himself a final drink before turning in for the night, Jason found himself examining his relationship with Kyle Price. When he was a rookie, all spit-shined and sharp-creased, he would never have allowed himself to accept the offerings of such a man. He had entered police work just as the decline in petty corruption and graft was taking hold in the bastions of law enforcement. He had heard stories from veteran cops about how they visited all the local businesses at Christmas, and came away with more bottles of booze and thick envelopes stuffed with cash then one could imagine. Of course, in some towns, such gratuities were not limited to the holidays, but occurred routinely for special considerations and favors. During his first few years on the force, he witnessed some of the older cops accepting bottles and gifts of food and merchandise.

Trying to wean the men away from such conduct, the Chief decided to implement a policy regarding gifts. He would accept contributions from individuals and businesses on behalf on the entire department, and the gifts would then be used to put on a holiday party and a summer picnic for the officers and their families. The Chief was broad shouldered enough to turn away any contributors who tried to use their contribution to get a little extra service from the police department, so there was no quid pro quo. After some initial grumbling from the older cops, the idea worked well. It may not have been the best policy in the strictest moral sense, but for the era, it was a pretty gutsy move. The Chief's decision represented a major change for the Highland Park Police Department, and Jason admired him for taking the initiative. Nevertheless, cops still manage to get in trouble. There are a variety of ways a cop can screw up, some subtle, some not. However, the three major weaknesses that lead to the downfall of police officers are greed, anger, and lust.

Jason had long struggled with the legal ethical dilemmas connected with the complexities of law enforcement and the criminal justice system. Young men and women who became cops, no matter what their background had been, confronted parts of this world that few people ever got to see. Cops not only saw and heard too much, but they were forced by their duties to become inexorably involved. They routinely made difficult decisions, and used their judgement and discretion to determine the fate of others. Sometimes, their decision involved issuing a traffic summons, or taking a person into custody and transporting them downtown for booking.

Sometimes, they played referee, trying to determine the facts from the various stories they were barraged with from combatants in hundreds of disputes they were called to settle. The stories ranged from convincing half-truths to wildly fictitious renderings that the creators of the X-Files would deem too strange for prime time. Cops could take away a man's freedom, or his life, in a heartbeat. There are few individuals in this world who possess the raw power of a police officer. However, few citizens are pleased with the actions they take. Cops almost always deal in the negative. They put people in jail, they make them leave their homes after fighting with the wife or kids, or they insist on asking the most personal or inane questions and demand answers.

Even on a good day, Jason thought, cops wind up interrupting somebody's daily life and getting blamed for any inconvenience, such as directing traffic around the scene of a motor vehicle accident. Its no wonder police officers are a high-risk group for divorce, alcoholism, and suicide. It's worse in the urban areas, but being a cop in Highland Park is no box of chocolates either. Spend twenty years in *my* world, and see how normal *you* are!

There was one incident that occurred years ago when he was a young street sergeant that had a significant impact on his sense of justice and his professional ethics. Prior to this incident, he had become quite a scholar in regard to the laws regarding arrest, search, and seizure. In fact, he enjoyed the intricacies of the legal parameters of policing so much he'd become an instructor for the Montgomery County Police Academy, a position he had held for eight years. Consequently, he was very conservative, and officers who sought his guidance before making an arrest or conducting a search were often dismayed by the seemingly impossible standards to which he held them as he grilled them about probable cause and other legal requirements. His scrutiny of criminal complaints and search warrant applications had caused many cops under his supervision to scramble for additional information and gather more facts before Jason would allow them to go forward.

However, a heinous rape inside a building at the Sweetbrier Office Complex had changed all that. It was about seven one night when a janitor passing by the women's bathroom on a fifth floor hallway of building number 1501 heard scuffling coming from within. He opened the door and found seventeen year old Jessica Fountain inside, hands and feet bound with duct tape, and a dirty cloth stuffed inside her mouth, secured by another piece of the tape. She had been bleeding from her nose and lips, but the blood flow had stopped and the blood had coagulated on her face. Jessica was nude, her clothes strewn about the room. The responding police officers had carefully removed the tape to protect any fingerprints and found her hysterical and incoherent, crying uncontrollably. After calming her down a little, they managed to get a brief description of her assailant, and she indicated to them that she had been assaulted hours ago. She also confirmed that she'd been raped.

Jason arrived on the scene shortly thereafter, and was briefed by the patrol officers. By this time the girl had once again lapsed into hysteria, and the medics had arrived to treat her. She described her attacker as a black man, medium height, wearing a blue baseball cap with the insignia of the New York Yankees. Officers at the scene found the remains of a couple of Marlboro cigarettes in one of the stalls. Upon asking the victim about the cigarettes, she said that she thought the man was smoking when she walked into the restroom and saw him standing there. She could not recall any other clothing, marks, or distinguishing features about her attacker, but Jason was glad they had gotten as much as they did given her condition at the time.

About forty minutes after police were called to the scene, one of the officers checking the neighborhood had stopped a man waiting for a bus on a nearby street corner. He was black, and wore a blue baseball cap with the initials NY stitched in front. He was smoking a Winston cigarette, and had papers identifying him as a resident of New York City. He told police he was visiting a friend, and gave an address in a neighboring town. The officer radioed to Jason that the man was not hostile, but was not cooperative either, and had refused the officer's request to voluntarily come back to the scene or go into the police station for an interview, saying he didn't want to miss his bus.

When he learned this, Jason wanted to have the victim immediately transported to the scene of the stop and see if she recognized the man as her assailant. Drawing on his knowledge of the latest case law regarding eyewitness or victim identifications, he knew he didn't have enough probable cause to put the man inside a police car and bring him back to the office complex for the girl to view. Being black and wearing a hat with initials on it was not enough, in

Highland Park a half dozen people in the span of a few blocks would fit that description. His only option to find out if police had stopped the right man, he reasoned at the time, was for the victim to go to the location where the officer was detaining the suspect and make an identification. One look at the shivering, whimpering young girl convinced him that would not happen, and although he made the request, he didn't push it. She was probably too traumatized and distraught to make a good ID anyway, even if she'd agree to try. Jason knew he was on thin legal ground, but his instincts told him to push the envelope, do something to give police a chance to prove or disprove the man's involvement before letting him go. But before he could think of a solution, the man's bus approached, and Jason was forced to make a decision. Jason gave the order to record the suspect's information and description, and let him go. He remembered feeling sick to his stomach as soon as he'd spoken the words.

Sure enough, police soon learned that the man was a convicted rapist from New York City, having served a term in Rikers. He had a rap sheet three pages long, and the offenses included drug violations and petty thefts as well as the rape. Highland Park and New York City detectives spent days canvassing the neighborhoods surrounding the last known address of the convict, but failed to locate him or uncover any leads. Jason beat himself up over this for weeks, second guessing his decisions and wondering if he was even competent enough to lead future investigations. He was never able to completely forgive himself for letting the rapist go. He vowed that he would never again allow himself to be so swayed by the letter of the law. Given a similar set of circumstances, he would do what was necessary to take a predator off the streets. For the rest of his career, he would use this incident as his guide in making decisions and taking actions. In his investigations of serious crimes of violence, things would be done in the best interest of the victim and the community. He would see to it.

Shortly after he made this promise to himself, he resigned his position as a police instructor.

Chapter 9

Despite the long drive, he was not tired when he arrived in Albuquerque. He had decided to take a flight to Dallas, and drive to New Mexico from there. He thought it best never to take a direct route to a city where one of his chosen lived, desiring to muddy the trail as much as he could. Besides, the quiet drive gave him a chance to think about the events to come. He got some of his best ideas while on these long drives. Add that to the excitement he got from anticipating carrying out the act, similar to the type of excitement one got from planning a vacation, and the whole experience was rather pleasing. It also made each killing more vivid, and more memorable. It prolonged the pleasure of the event, and he liked being able to relive each one in a logical sequential form. He was nothing if not logical. He had a few things to do on this trip.

He had learned much about Melina from his virtual intrusions into her world, but it was now necessary to map out specific plans, and that would take some familiarity with her real world, not just her virtual one. He wanted to follow the routes she took to work, to the shopping center, to the gym . . . every place that was part of her routine. He also wanted to check out her neighbors and coworkers, just to make sure there were no substantial risks. He needed to know if she had a neighbor who was a Navy Seal trying to get into her pants, or an old lady who sat by the window for hours spying on her neighbors for entertainment. He didn't need some nosy old woman or an overly protective macho man watching out for her and her things.

This trip was not overtly risky. He was not going to do anything illegal, so even if he were spotted following her or snooping around the neighborhood, nothing would come of it. Hell, even if he were pulled over by a cop, there was little to fear. However, it would mean that Melina would become off limits. The worst thing about getting compromised at this point was that he would have to spend countless hours finding another woman who captured his fancy. This was not likely to occur, since he was so careful, but if it did by some chance he would have the discipline to abandon his pursuit for safety's sake. He knew this about himself. He was a patient man, and would not compromise himself for the fleeting feeling of euphoria he got from one of these adventures. He liked the sound of that . . . adventure. It made it seem like he was on a bold mission to fulfill a driving, lifelong quest. Of course, that didn't mean he would not consider an abandoned victim at some future time, if she were really worth coming back for.

He never forgot any of the fascinating women he mirrored or pursued. Sometimes, being off limits was like an aphrodisiac, causing him to want a victim even more, driving him crazy with desire. There were a couple of women in his life that he wanted to take so badly he could taste them, but they were too close, it wouldn't have been a wise choice. He was always able to keep himself under control in these instances, at least until he found another victim to satiate his desires, or until the coast was clear and he could pursue his original prey. Either way, this would make the next killing very special. He felt the first twitches of what would soon be a throbbing headache.

He thought about what he was going to do to his next victim, pictured her writhing in his arms, her mouth open wide as if to scream. But in his thoughts she was too terrified to make a sound, and he looked down the chasm of her throat, and pictured filling the dark, moist void with his manhood. These thoughts dulled the pain, and allowed him to continue planning for the actual event. Ah! Sweet passion does soothe the beast raging within.

He planned to spend two days in Albuquerque, which should be enough to accomplish what he needed. He checked into a Holiday Inn downtown using a credit card that he'd obtained "legitimately" using manufactured identification. He had a half-dozen of these at any one time, and using his computer design skills, had created driver's licenses from six states to match each card. He paid all of the bills on time, so the cards were good, and he established a line of credit for each name, just in case he needed money fast. Of course, all of the addresses were fake, but since the bills were forwarded to a series of commercial mailbox locations, he was almost untraceable. Tired from the drive, he slept soundly. The alarm went off at six the next morning, and he was dressed and headed toward Melina's house by seven o'clock.

It was about a 30-minute drive to the foothills where Melina and her husband had purchased their modest three-bedroom home. Just as he thought, Melina Oberman lived in a trendy neighborhood in the foothills of the Sandia Mountains. From mirroring her internet transactions for the past several months, he knew that she was a stylish young women of twenty-eight, recently separated from her husband, and just coming out of that fog that envelops those who

67

experience such an emotional trauma. Get ready girl, you are about to disappear into a fog for good. He laughed, amused at his cleverness. He had also learned that Melina had two very good women friends, Terry Scholl of Albuquerque and Carolyn Helmsley of New York City. She and Terry were friends from work, while she and Carolyn had been roommates in College at Pepperdine University. She spent endless hours with them on the computer, swapping recipes and stories, and sharing their trials and tribulations. Dot-com friends. Melina liked to order DVDs, shoes, and lingerie over the net, the latter from an Australian company called Wonder Down Under. She also had a fondness for Swiss Chocolate, which she ordered direct from Lucerne. She had found a quaint shop there right after college during a trip with her fiancée, now her soon-to-be ex-husband.

Melina lost her virginity at age seventeen in the basement recreation room of her parents home, always wanted to travel to Istanbul because it sounded exotic, and had a not-so-secret fantasy to share her bed with two men, including her husband. It was amazing what people would chat about on the Internet, and he loved taking full advantage of the information he garnered from these lovely women. Of course, he had to intercept hour upon hour of boring nonsense before he would find an interesting or stimulating woman, one worthy of his time and his unique passion. In monitoring over a thousand people who were using email, spouting off in chat rooms, doing their shopping, and browsing for information, he had found only a couple dozen who captured his sustained interest. From these, he found only a few who excited him enough to drive him to seek them out.

Melina was one of the chosen. He had intercepted her picture, sent to a man that she was chatting with a few weeks ago. She was a lovely woman of Mexican descent, her long black hair cascading almost to her shoulders. It was pulled back on one side, revealing a delicate ear with a diamond stud. She had brown, almond shaped eyes, and her skin was a light mocha. She was five foot six, one hundred and fifteen pounds, but he had not seen how it was distributed. All of the pictures he had seen were headshots. She was an account executive for a local firm, sold scheduling and time-management software. He liked this about her. It spoke of some precision, a trait he greatly admired. There was other stuff too. Since she paid many of her bills over the net, he had as much financial and statistical information about her as did her mortgage company, her bank, and her utility providers . . . and so much more. He knew her habits, her preferences, and even her dreams. Whatever she chose to reveal to anyone via her ISP . . . her internet service provider . . . she revealed to him. He alone had all the pieces of the fabulous puzzle that was Melina V. S. Oberman. V for Valerie. S. for Sanchez, her maiden name.

He thought about what was to come. Now it was time for the revelations to cease, and for the revelry to commence. Reality would become absurdity, quiet would become cacophony. Sensation would overcome the hapless woman he had silently pursued and would soon possess. He could feel the first stirrings in his groin. To choose and control. To fuck and to kill. This was now his fate.

Cab caught a Tuesday morning flight to Atlanta. He had arranged to meet Amber Mathieson's brother again for a follow-up interview, and to spend some time in the area where she lived before she came to Pennsylvania. He arrived at Harts Field at 10:10 AM, only fifteen minutes behind schedule. That was considered an on-time arrival for USAir, and given the reputation of the airlines these days, Cab was not disappointed. He took the shuttle to Hertz, picked up a Cavalier, and headed for Buckhead, the fashionable part of Atlanta that John Mathieson called home. Traffic was horrendous, and it took him over an hour to make the short trip through Center City to John's modest but fashionable brick townhouse. John was pleasant when he answered the door.

"Come in Detective. Make yourself comfortable. Can I interest you in some lemonade, or sweet tea perhaps?"

"Sweet tea would be great," Cab replied. "I remember my grandma making that for us when I was a kid. She was from South Carolina . . . Aiken, and we would visit her every summer. Just can't get it up North you know."

"Ahhh, Aiken, that's jus ov'r yonder," John mimicked, lapsing into an exaggerated drawl. "Did you know that South Carolina was the last bastion of the Stars and Bars? I must say, I was elated when they finally removed the Confederate flag from the Statehouse. It was inappropriate, to say the least."

Cab knew he was referring to the flap a couple of years ago, when the NAACP and numerous other groups, both black and white, had boycotted the State of South Carolina over its refusal to lower the Confederate flag from the peak of the Statehouse in the capital city. State leaders finally relented and lowered the revered symbol of the War of Northern Aggression, relocating it to a Confederate memorial nearby. Cab wondered if John was playing the race card, and personally didn't care too much one way or the other about that flag. Born and bred in Philadelphia, it didn't affect him much at all.

He took the sweet tea John handed him. It tasted really good, just like he remembered. He always marveled that plain old tea could taste so fine, and that its distinct southern flavor was never duplicated north of Virginia. John seemed a nice enough person, but Cab couldn't help thinking that there was something brewing beneath the surface.

"John, tell me again about Amber's life here." Cab took a big sip of tea and replaced the glass in the coaster John had handed him. He was trying not to slurp, but it was hard. The tea was good, and he was thirsty. "It's been awhile since we talked, and I want to see if you remember anything else that may help me with this case."

Of course, Cab remembered every bit of the statement John gave to him and Jason a month ago. He had a copy folded in the pocket of his suit coat. But he wanted to test John; see if there were any inconsistencies that emerged between then and now, a common but effective police interview technique.

An hour and a half later, Cab left the house. His next stop was Marietta, Amber's girlhood home. He had one new piece of information from the second interview with John. Amber's brother had given Cab the name and address of a childhood friend of hers that still lived in Marietta. Her name was Nancy Lynn Longstreet. Although she no longer lived at home, where he'd first gone after leaving John's house in Atlanta, the girl's mother gave him her new address. She was glad to help, she told Cab after he had identified himself and told her the reason for his inquiry. She told him Amber and her daughter were inseparable almost the whole time they were growing up, especially in their teens. Amber spent many a night in her house, she related, and was a nice girl. It was a shame she ever left Marietta and went North, she should have stayed here, among kin and friends.

Nancy Lynn now lived in an apartment complex on Johnson Way, just off Highway 127, the main east-west route through town. It was a modest neighborhood, but the buildings were well kept and the grounds nicely landscaped. If the theory of opposites attracting applies to best friends as well as lovers, this was surely such a case. Nancy was a plain looking girl with short dark hair and thick tortoise frame glasses. In today's world of endless choices, her pick of this heavy, uncomplimentary eyewear spoke volumes about her personality.

As he talked with her, Cab realized his initial judgement was accurate. Nancy was a bookworm. She was a grad student at Georgia Tech, majoring in chemical engineering. Her apartment was cluttered with numerous books and what appeared to be science projects strewn about both the living and dining area. She wore a pair of plain Levi jeans and a rumpled sea foam green knit pullover. Although she was not an emotional person, Cab could see she was distraught over Amber's death. She was not reluctant to tell him about her. The two had been very good friends, at least up until Amber left for Pennsylvania. Cab learned a bit more about Amber from her roommate, the kind of things girls tell each other. He was most interested in her love life, since with the possible exception of drug related deaths, husbands and lovers accounted for most of the murders of young women.

He was not surprised that Amber had many boyfriends. Nancy Lynn remembered them in great detail, and Cab couldn't help but wonder if she lived vicariously through her more comely friend's conquests. He jotted down information on four men that Nancy knew, and unconsciously sighed as he realized his trip here may have to be extended to track them all down. He was finishing up the interview, closing his notebook and thanking Nancy for her cooperation, when she interrupted him.

"There is one more thing, Detective," she said. "I'm a little embarrassed to bring this up, but I think you should know. I don't want to be accused of hiding anything from the police."

Cab settled back into the chair, waiting for her to continue.

"Amber worked in a club a couple days per week. A strip club . . . a nice one, but nonetheless a strip club." There was a slight note of disapproval to her tone, or maybe it was envy. " She made great money, and seemed not to mind the work."

"Did she ever talk about the club?" Cab asked, keenly interested about this development. "Did she ever mention having trouble with anyone, or discuss her work there with you?"

"Well, she did feel uncomfortable in the beginning. She talked about how she felt weird being stared at, exposing herself like that. But after a couple months it became routine, like any other job. At least that's what she said. She said she would occasionally run into some guys from school, which is the only time she felt funny. But other than that I don't recall her mentioning any real problems. Quite a few girls from school work those clubs for awhile, usually when they get behind on car payments or credit cards. It's a chance to make some good cash quickly."

It had been over a year since Amber would have worked at the CatNipsU, the strip joint her roommate told him about, but Cab needed to check it out. Amber's life was getting more complex. There were more variables popping up than even her brother had known about her. His stay in Atlanta would definitely be extended. He needed to break the news to Shawna, but figured he'd stop by the strip club first, before fighting the traffic to get back to his hotel. Cab entered the bar. It was a typical southern strip bar, dark and cavernous. There were at least forty tables, each capable of seating eight customers. Even though it was only afternoon, it was already busy. Heavy smoke hung in the air, despite large overhead fans, giving the stale air a bluish hue as it swirled above the crowd. Three long bars framed the room, one on each side, and one along the back. Rows of wooden stools provided seating for even more customers. A stage was located up front, all done up with velvet drapes and gold tinsel. At least two dancers were on top of each bar, working customers for tips.

Cab coughed, silently cursing the toxic mist and headed for a sign marked "no smoking." Sitting at a table by himself, he did not get much relief from the smoke. Before he even got settled in his chair, a thin, raven-haired dancer sauntered over and asked if he wanted a table dance. A table dance, he remembered from his long-past college forays, entitled the customer to get an up close look at a dancer's usually hidden attributes as she undulated naked on top of his table, each dance lasting the duration of a song the DJ was spinning. Years ago, it was ten bucks. Cab wondered how much inflation had driven up the cost of staring at a woman's pussy as she straddled your drink.

"Not right now, sweets." He told her. "I just got here. I need a drink."

"Okay big stuff," she cooed. "When you're ready, call me. I'm Vicky." And as quickly as she had approached, she disappeared into the maze of tables and smoke.

Twenty minutes later, sipping on a Jack and Ginger, Cab motioned to another passing dancer, and asked for Vicky. He didn't know why he sought her, since he could start with any of them, but he figured maybe she would appreciate the loyalty and be more inclined to answer his questions. She appeared in a flash.

"I knew you'd be askin' bout me big stuff," she said, bending to whisper in his ear. He could smell the dusky scent of her perfume. The girls must apply a spritz every few dances, to mask the odor of smoke and perspiration. It only partially worked.

"Are you ready for a little personal attention?"

"Depends," he said. "You know what you're doing? How long you been working here?"

"Here? Over two years now. It's helping me pay for college. Don't worry, I know what you want, honey . . . just relax and enjoy the show."

He slid a fifty-dollar bill toward her transparent silver spiked heels. She danced for three straight songs, and Cab's neck was getting stiff from looking up. He wondered if he should try to hide this line item on his department expense account voucher or tell the truth. Cab hoped the Chief would understand why he spent fifty bucks in expense money for table dances in a strip bar. After the third song ended, he helped her off the table, and held her flimsy top as she rehooked her front clasp bra. The dancers got undressed and dressed each time they performed for a new customer. They must do this fifty times on a busy night. Cab asked Vicki to sit for awhile, quickly adding he would like to buy her a drink

"Of course, big stuff," she replied, as she motioned to a waitress. "Champagne please, honey."

Damn, Cab thought, *the Chief is not going to be happy with this.* But over the next two hours, Cab managed to become very friendly with Vicki. Of course, the other fifty dollars he dropped helped, but he thought he did okay anyway. She was starting to loosen up and trust him a bit, and didn't seem to mind answering questions about Amber.

Cab told Vicki he knew her through her roommate, and after relating a couple of stories told to him by Nancy Lynn, she was very forthcoming with information. Amber's stage name was Ambrosia, and Vicki said she was very popular with the customers, which made her not so popular with some of the other girls. Amber was really pretty, and had this quality about her that attracted men even from a distance. They used to walk clear across the room, passing plenty of other dancers, just to tuck a dollar into her stockings. Cab asked what she thought that quality might have been, and laughed when Vicky replied, "innocence." He laughed not because it was absurd that an exotic dancer would exude innocence, but because he knew that many men who came to strip clubs were under the illusion that *one* of the dancers was special. They would seek out the one that appeared a bit unsure, a trifle bashful, never suspecting that she was just playing a role. Cab decided to push a little further.

"Vicky, Amber's roommate told me about some of the guys that became hung up on her. Do you remember any of them?"

Actually, Nancy Lynn had remembered no such thing, but Cab was taking a shot in the dark. Reticent witnesses were much more likely to talk if they believed the person looking for information already knew at least part of the story. "Did any of her customers get out of line with her?"

"Nothing out of the ordinary," she replied. "Just the usual creeps and weirdoes you expect in this job."

Cab figured as much. Even if there were some strange character in Amber's past, in two years their antics were likely to fade from memory. A girl like Vicky saw so many horny men in the course of a few months that it would take a real wacko to set off any alarms. His ears perked up as he thought he heard the dancer say something else. He cupped his ear and leaned closer, straining to hear her above the din of the music and the crowd. Once again, he was preparing to end an interview. Once again, his witness had a sudden revelation. The proverbial light bulb lit up, although in Vicky's case, it cast only a dim glow. Too much alcohol and cocaine, he thought. Party girls burn out quickly. Vicky leaned toward him too, giving any bystanders the mistaken impression that the two were engaged in intimate conversation.

"You know, on second thought, there was this one guy . . . "

Chapter 10

Cab called Jason at home that evening. He filled him in about his interviews in Atlanta, including his visit to the strip club.

"Jason, this dancer, Vicky, was giving me the creeps as she talked about this guy. She described him as *vacant . . . .*like he was talking and everything, but he wasn't really there. She said his eyes had no sign of expression. Even when she danced for him, his face never changed. Vicky avoided him, but she told me that he and Amber were often together at the club, and that he dropped hundreds of dollars on her every time he showed up."

"Sounds like an odd duck," Jason admitted. "But like she said, the girls are bound to encounter some strange characters in their line of work."

"I realize that, but this one apparently was different than the usual. Vicky said he became obsessed with Amber. Ignored the rest of the girls completely, and even became angry one time when he came in when Amber was supposed to be working one night and she wasn't there. Vicky said the guy was pretty good looking, and was a smooth talker too, but something about him turned her off. She said most of the other girls felt the same way."

"Still not much to go on."

"Yea, but listen to this . . . Amber left the club suddenly, no notice or anything. After she left, this guy never came into the club again."

"And how long ago was this?"

"Fifteen months this week. Eight months before her death."

"Still a long time before her murder to get too worried about it. Can the dancer describe the guy well enough for a composite drawing?"

"I think so, she's willing to try anyway. Do you want me to see if the Atlanta police will provide an artist for us?"

"Yeah. Why don't you do that? If the lead were stronger, I'd fly one of our own county guys down to do it. But considering the time that elapsed between this contact and Amber's murder, it's a slim chance they're connected. I got

74

some bad news from the lab today. There were no semen samples in the swabs we submitted from Amber."

"Jesus, I felt sure we'd get something."

"So did I, however they did detect some small shreds of latex in the samples from her mouth."

"So our suspect wore a condom? How considerate of him."

"Looks that way. I don't think he was thinking about *her* though. I think he's smart enough to know about DNA and used the rubber to avoid identification, which could mean he has a record, maybe even spent some time inside. Check and see if the Atlanta P.D. has had anything like this in the past year or so, will ya?"

"Okay, Boss. I'll get it done. How's things at home?"

"Your home?" Jason teased. "Well, Shawna misses you a little. At least that's what she told me when I left her this morning after bringing her breakfast in bed."

"Fuck you. You're a terrible liar. Everyone knows you can't cook. Besides, if you were with Shawna last night, you'd still be gasping for breath."

With Cab in Atlanta, Jason called on Amber's employer, Cisco Industries. They had gotten the company's name from some check stubs the detectives found in her apartment, and Jason had called to make an appointment with their human resource director. He arrived at the company around ten o'clock in the morning, and walked into the spacious lobby of the modern steel and glass building located in the newer of Highland Park's two business campuses. The receptionist, a prim but well dressed woman in her mid-forties was busy answering phones behind an expansive console that looked like a control center for NASA. She smiled at him curtly and held up a finger as she conversed with a caller.

"Cisco Industries, good morning. How may I direct your call? Please hold, thank you." She pushed another button and repeated the same greeting.

This happened four times before she looked at Jason again, giving him an exact replica of her earlier smile. Jason thought of asking her just how many times per day she repeated this routine, but figured he'd better not; he didn't want to remind her how droll her job seemed, just in case. Some people were touchy that way. He once said something similar to a turnpike toll collector, and the enraged man almost came out of the little booth to get him, launching a tirade of obscenities and threats toward a very surprised Jason. Some people have no sense of humor.

"Good morning, sir. I'm sorry to keep you waiting. Can I help you?"

Her voice had changed. It was softer, more personal than her phone demeanor. Jason was glad he'd kept his mouth shut.

"My name is Jason Coulter. I'm here to see Mr. Stoner."

The phone interrupted her again. Twice. She reverted back to her phone persona to handle the callers, and then turned her attention back to Jason without missing a beat.

"Yes, of course," she replied, checking her computer calendar to verify his appointment. "I'll let his office know you've arrived. Please sit down."

Within minutes, a woman who had been called to escort him led him up to the fourth floor. She took him into an office where a balding man greeted him in his fifties, dressed in a pair of chino slacks and an oatmeal mock turtleneck sweater. He came around his desk to shake hands, and had a look on his face that matched his casual attire. Jason liked him immediately. Stoner had the natural warmth and charisma that Jason thought was necessary to be an effective people person, and certainly this was a required attribute for a human resource manager.

"Lieutenant Coulter? Ken Stoner. I'm the assistant director of H.R. for the company. Glad to meet you. Please sit down. Can I have some coffee brought in?"

"No, thank you. I'm fine. I appreciate you taking the time to meet with me personally."

"No problem. We were sad to hear about Ms. Mathieson. She was a good employee during the short time she was here. More importantly, I hear she was a good person, well liked by her fellow employees."

"Did you know her personally?"

"No, she was hired by our director, Mr. Wagner. He's in Europe on vacation this month, so I'm filling in. I've met her a couple of times, but never really had the opportunity to sit and chat with her. We have over four hundred full-time employees, and at least a hundred more part-timers. Many of them come and go, especially those in repetitive, manual jobs. We try to offer incentives to stick around, and pay a competitive wage, but it's tough. I'd like to get to know them all, but it's impossible. Would you like to review her personnel file? Normally we do not make those available without the written consent of the employee, but in this case . . . well, it's different."

"Yes it is different, murder is nasty business. Thank you for being so cooperative. And besides looking at her personnel file, I would appreciate it if you could arrange for me to talk to any employees with whom she was friendly."

Amber Mathieson's personnel files revealed little of note. She had been hired only three and one-half months ago, as an entry-level graphic artist in the company's advertising department. Her job mostly consisted of creating drawings and graphics to supplement pictures of company products, which included a variety of air-handling devices used for filtration and exhaust systems. Not very glamorous work, but Jason saw that she was paid $17.50 per hour, not too bad for an entry-level position.

Her fellow employees also added nothing significant to the investigation. Although she was very cordial, they said, she didn't socialize with anyone after work and none of them knew if she was dating someone from the company, or had even been approached by anyone to ask her out. Jason dutifully reviewed his notes before he left the company, being careful to make sure he had all the names of the people he had talked to for his report. He made a note to call the director of human resources upon his return from Europe. He was nothing if not thorough. He stopped back briefly to see Ken Stoner and handed him two of his business cards, one for him, and one for Mr. Wagner. Jason again thanked the amiable man for his cooperation and left, disappointed that no further leads were discovered.

Chapter 11

The neighborhood was all kids and dogs at this hour, and he was just a bit concerned about all the noisy kids and mothers moving about getting their little urchins off to school. Mothers were always on-guard these days, with all the hype about child molesters and all. It really made life difficult for a working man like him! He had glued a small goatee to his chin, and wore a pair of sunglasses and a nondescript baseball cap to mask his face. He drove down her street and stopped a few doors away from her home to check it out for a few seconds. He was really impressed by how well she was able to maintain it. He took note of a rock and cactus garden in the front yard and the well manicured green grass lawn. It wasn't easy to keep a lawn in these rocky hills, and it showed Melina took her lawn care seriously. He drove past her house, turned around about a quarter mile away, and finally found a good spot a block away, out of the school bus route, but with a good view of the lower half of her driveway. Like a cop on surveillance, he settled in to wait.

Half an hour later, he saw her red Jeep Cherokee backing out of the driveway. He started his car and began to follow her. Since he knew where she worked, and had already mapped out the probable route she would take, he made sure he stayed far enough behind to be inconspicuous. Traffic was light, and he had no problem keeping up with her. She deviated a bit from the route he'd picked, but because of so many new developments in this city, the streets had changed. He praised himself for being so thorough. These walk-throughs eliminated any surprises on game day. He watched her park and get out of her car, gathering up her purse and a morning newspaper from the front seat.

Her employer, LaMar Business Systems, was a small firm with about thirty workers. Melina was one of only four account representatives, a fancy title for saleswoman. He watched her walk to the front entrance, cocking his head from side to side in time with the sway of her buttocks. *She moves her ass real nice.* Her dark wavy hair also bounced with every step. Wearing an expensive, fashionable taupe linen suit and tan pumps, she made a nice appearance. He liked women who dressed nice, even beyond their means. However, he knew she was a successful businesswoman too. Maybe he should make an appointment.

After she'd entered her office, he left, got some breakfast at a local diner, and then drove back to her house. Now after nine o'clock, there was nobody on the street. He parked his rental right in front of the home, and went to the front door, pretending to ring the bell, and then knock. He then walked around the home, scanning the neighbors' houses for movement. Seeing none, he grew bolder, stepping up to the windows and peering inside. The windows were fastened with a standard lock, and would provide no serious obstacle. There was no evidence of a security system. He tried to get further insight into Melina's personality by looking at her furniture and decorations, but his view was obscured by window treatments.

He had been out of his car about ninety seconds. He took another careful look at the surrounding properties, saw no signs of anything unusual or potentially alarming, like a big doghouse or dog chain, and left. He would return shortly before five o'clock to watch her leave work, and to see how she spent her evenings. Meanwhile, he would switch rental cars, tell the clerk he needed a bigger car. Just in case this car had been seen near her house by a nosy neighbor, he would get a fresh one before he returned. One can never be too careful.

The clock in his new Concord LSI read 4:45 when he drove into a side street near her office. He did not need to get too close, nor did he need to follow her direct path home. He was content just to watch her leave, and parallel her route to her house. She still looked fresh as she emerged from her office shortly after five. She flung her head back as she stepped from the building's vestibule and ran her hand through her long tresses in what seemed like a liberating gesture. She walked briskly to her car. She drove straight home, and this time he did not stop and continue his surveillance, but simply cruised by to insure that she was inside. He then left the area in search of some Mexican food. Fitting choice for the occasion, he thought.

About two hours after he'd watched her go into her home, he drove back to her neighborhood and parked a block away. He waited to see if she would go out this evening, or if she had any visitors, especially any male friends he may not have known about. It was dusk, the block was quiet, and he felt safe. He let his mind wander, and was soon thinking about some of the women who had recently caught his attention. There was that really haughty woman in San Francisco who had quite exquisite taste in fashion and spent hundreds of hours searching sites like Halston and Versace for new finds. He liked the upscale tone of her email conversations and could envision the twisted look of horror on her delicate face as he held his face inches from her and smiled, all the while driving his engorged dick into her with a vengeance. It would be the best fuck she ever had for sure. The sluts were fun to fuck too, but his greatest thrill came from the classy ones, the ones who were used to being spoiled. Most of them were very proper, and liked to be in control. Rough, shove-it-in fucking caused them to quickly go into shock. Beside sheer terror, these women displayed such a look of complete degradation that he could not help but delight in their reaction.

He was still daydreaming when he saw Melina's car backing down her driveway. She turned left, headed away from his position. He started his car and followed, being careful not to get too close. Fortunately, night had fallen and there were few streetlights in the subdivision. She turned onto the main street, headed for the freeway, and drove west toward the city. He kept his distance, but had no trouble keeping her in sight. He saw her turn signal flash, and followed her off the Ramsey Street exit. Three minutes later, they were both pulling into the South Park Mall, and he grinned as he realized they were going shopping. He would get his chance for a close encounter. He stuffed a green floppy canvas hat into the pocket of his reversible windbreaker and tucked a pair of amber lens glasses into his breast pocket. He could change his appearance quickly if she so much as glanced at him before he was ready.

Luck was with him today. It was an easy assignment to tail someone in a mall. He enjoyed watching her browse. Of course, knowing her interests and taste in clothing and such, he could predict where she would stop, and made a game of it. He was not surprised when she entered Nordstrom and headed for designer dresses. As she paused to sort through a rack of Liz Claiborne's new line, he stepped behind a display counter where he had a good vantage. He took a few moments to appraise her appearance. She was a very pretty woman. She had changed out of her work clothes and was dressed casually in a pair of blue jeans and an oversize pink pullover sweater. He was disappointed that her clothes were not more form fitting so he could really see what he was getting, but nevertheless could tell that she was at least acceptable.

He decided to approach her, and his heartbeat quickened. Several steps later, he was at the same display, standing next to her. He took a slow deep breath, inhaling her scent. He was several inches taller than she was. He liked the way her fine black hair blended into the nape of her neck, and pictured himself standing behind her, his lips on her neck, smelling her sweet perfume and feeling the silky texture of her on his nose and cheek.

"Excuse me," he said quietly, not wanting to startle her. "Are you very familiar with Liz?"

She turned toward him, her face only a couple of feet away. Her skin was smooth and somewhat lighter than it seemed in the picture, but her features were so delicate she reminded him of a porcelain doll. He smiled just a bit, hoping to appear a bit unsure and embarrassed to be bothering her.

"I'm sorry," she replied, noticing him for the first time. "Were you talking to me?"

"Yes, I am trying to pick out a birthday present for my wife. I know she favors Liz Claiborne, but I remember her saying something about her sizes being different than other designers. I just can't remember what it was she said. Can you help me?"

He knew that Liz sizes tended to run large, that if a woman usually took a size eight, a Liz size six would fit nicely. He saw the corners of her lips crinkle, and her eyes met his. His disarming approach had worked. In a few seconds, he went from imposing stranger to loving husband. He appeared to her to be very thoughtful, and not hard to look at either. She was only too happy to share her knowledge.

"You did good to remember that much." She told him, smiling now. "Liz runs big. What size does your wife usually take?"

He knew what he was about to say was trite, and that it was an oft quoted line used by men in lingerie shops, but he couldn't resist. Trite as it was, it usually worked.

"She's about your size, and just as pretty too." He reached for her, and with the slightest touch, let his fingers rest on her upper arm as he spoke. He removed them quickly, before she could become alarmed. He was testing her, to see how she would react to his intrusion. She did not flinch, making him bolder. He began rifling through the rack, looking for a prop to continue his charade. He found a four-button vest, and held it up for her to see.

"This is something she might like," he said. "Would you mind slipping this on so I can get a better look?"

She smiled and took it from him, slipping the vest over her shoulders. He waited until she looked up at him expectantly and then quickly reached toward the back of her neck. "Your hair is caught," He said, as he ran a hand through her fine hair and briefly caressed the nape of her neck with his trailing fingers, pretending to pull her hair from the collar of the vest. *So soft.* He stepped back, seeming to admire the vest, but secretly enjoying his racing pulse and the stirring of his growing excitement. She was really going to please him when the time came. He looked at her for a little too long, and she diverted her eyes.

"No." He finally spoke, almost barking out the word. "It is not quite right for my wife. But I truly thank you for being so nice, and hope I didn't inconvenience you too much."

"Not at all," Melina replied, feeling just a bit unnerved by the sudden tone of his voice. She was still wearing the vest as he walked off, quickly disappearing from sight. That was an odd exchange, she thought, as she placed it back on the rack. She felt a slight chill that made the hairs along the back of her neck stand up, and ran her fingers through her hair, much like the stranger had done moments before. She suddenly had the feeling something was amiss, but had no idea why.

Jason pulled into the driveway of the Calloway's brick Cape Cod. The one with the forest green shutters, Cab had told him the first time he gave directions to his house. Shawna roared when Jason had related this to her.

"Forest green, forest green," She repeated. "That man can't tell the difference between *red* and green, let alone know what forest green looks like."

It was true. Cab was essentially color blind, barely discerning enough of the basic colors to qualify as a police officer. When you talked shades of color he was lost. Yet he almost always used nuance to describe things. It was "robin egg blue," or "a subtle teal," much to Jason's delight. Besides food, it gave him another way to chide his partner, especially during those long stakeouts.

"Hey Cab," Jason would say in a mocking tone, "isn't that salmon car the one we want? Or is it that chartreuse one over there?"

"Fuck you and your pasty white ass," Cab would always shoot back.

Tonight, Shawna had made a roast duck, one of his favorites. It was a dish he did not often get to enjoy, especially with the pungent spices and slow roasted way Shawna made it. It was one of the most mouth watering, savory meals he'd ever had, and he made sure she knew it.

The evening spent with Cab and Shawna caused Jason to reflect on his own life. He wasn't getting any younger, as the saying goes, and he missed having a family like Cab. Cab seemed so grounded. Often, Jason found himself envying his best friend. He knew that many admired his rise through the ranks, and he enjoyed his professional reputation as a crack detective and tough but fair supervisor, but convinced himself he would trade it all for a family like Cab's. There were too many nights he came home to his empty townhouse, wishing he had a wife and a couple of kids who were glad to see him after he spent all day in the trenches. Actually, a day in Highland Park wasn't exactly the trenches, but he did get worn down by the daily grind of police work, even in a small city. Jason had never been married, although he lived with a woman once for four years. They were very much in love, but something kept him from making a total commitment to the relationship. Physically and emotionally they were extremely compatible.

More importantly, they both realized they were soulmates. Karen was not the most beautiful woman he had ever been with, but she was the most sensuous. Her eyes spoke for her when he gazed upon them, and he could read her perfectly by their expression. Jason had never experienced a greater attachment to another human being than he had felt with Karen. He still compared every woman he dated to her, and none of them had even come close to evoking the same strong feelings. However, there had been significant differences in their values, and this ultimately caused the relationship to fail. He wondered whether he would ever meet his Shawna, or maybe he was aiming too high. Maybe his memory of Karen was becoming distorted. Mostly, he only remembered the good times. He had to think hard to recall the time he came home unexpectedly and caught her smoking marijuana to "calm her nerves," and the frequent violent outbursts of temper. Many a plate and glass were shattered against the walls of the small apartment they had shared during some knock down, drag out arguments.

Still, every couple had some troubles. No one was perfect. Karen's good qualities far exceeded her bad. Maybe he was holding out for too much. After all, he was no prize either.

Chapter 12

Detective Paul Patterson poked his head into Jason's office. He waited a few seconds until Jason was finished on the phone.

"Lieutenant," he said. "Got a minute for me? I think I have something going on at the Apex."

"Come in, Paulie, sit down. Whatta you got?" Everybody called him Paulie, after Rocky's friend in the movies. He looked just like him, but without the tough guy image.

"Ben Dickson, you know Ben, don't you? He's that powerlifter from Rockledge who set a national record in the deadlift a few years ago. Lifted something like nine hundred pounds."

"Yeah, I remember, vaguely. He's only about five feet five inches tall, but built like a tractor."

"That's him alright. He was just hauled in by a couple of the patrol officers. He was in a fight down at the Wayfarer Pub. Seems like he got into a dispute with another customer about smoking. You know Ben hates people who smoke while he's trying to eat, and wound up clobbering the guy when the guy mouthed off to him. Witnesses say that Ben started out okay. He just asked the guy to put out the cigarette, but when the guy gave him some lip, Ben hauled off and ripped the poor slob a new asshole. They said Ben went from zero to sixty in three seconds flat."

Jason wondered what kind of moron would spout off to a guy who looked like Ben Dickson. Even in street clothes, Ben looked like a miniature mountain. He had arms the size of tree trunks, and his trapezoid muscles were tied directly to his head; he had no visible neck.

"That's interesting," Jason replied. "But what does it have to do with me?"

"Right, here's the thing. Ben started sobbing in front of the cops, blubbering that he's real sorry about clobbering the guy, and blames the steroids he's been taking. The patrol guys call me in for the interview, and badda-bing, I get his whole life story. And guess what?"

"Tell me," Jason said patiently, looking at the detective's animated expression and realizing just how much he *did* look like Paulie from Rocky.

"He also goes for your hit and run. You know, the one where the old lady was killed. He said he got into an argument with some kids playing in the street who refused to move as he drove near. He stops, gets out of his truck and gets in a screaming match with them, but says they were too young for him to clobber, so he jumps back into the truck and floors it, careening down the street and hitting the old lady. He says he didn't even see her. He was seeing red."

"Yea, and Anna Cuzzi saw blue," Jason said, referring to the old woman and the color of the truck that hit her. Jason always referred to dead victims by their names, unlike many cops. He thought it was a sign of respect to them and their families. Jason requested to talk with the suspect, whom he knew casually from the gym. Paulie led him back to the interview room, a small, stark room with a table and four chairs. Ben Dickson was sitting quietly, his head in his hands. He looked up when the two men entered. Jason saw his eyes had a look of desperation. The gravity of his actions was beginning to sink in. There wasn't much more they needed to solidify the hit and run case against Ben. The steroids, however, really interested him.

"I'm sorry Ben," Jason said. "I know this is not like you, but I've got to tell you, this is serious business."

"I know man. I can't believe this whole thing. I just been going off lately. It's the juice . . . the anabolics."

"How did you get them," Jason asked. "Maybe you've been getting some bad stuff . . . .making you act this way."

"Shit, all of this is bad stuff. Should have stopped long ago. Been doing this for ten years now, ever since I went into competition back in my teens. I get the shit from all over, man. Friends, doctors, even the Internet. This stuff's called green monster."

Jason had heard about buying drugs on the web, mostly getting them from Mexico. Up to now, he'd never had much cause to investigate this type of claim. They talked to Ben for another half-hour, mostly about his use of steroids. He refused to be more specific about his source, and he had none on him when he was arrested. He also steadfastly refused to give up the passenger in his vehicle, although it really didn't matter. Jason was more curious then anything. It would be tough to charge the passenger with committing any crime. Jason thought about Anna. Sad thing. Two lives wasted, although it's ironic that Ben can salvage his if he tries.

At about the same time Melina was trying on the Liz Claiborne vest in Albuquerque, Janet was slipping a body hugging cotton-spandex slip dress over her head and working it down over her sumptuous curves. The little black number was one of her favorites. It was sexy and showed off her figure well, but the look was not overdone. She looked at herself in a full-length mirror, was satisfied with her image, and started downstairs to wait for Jason's arrival. He was picking her up in fifteen minutes. She hesitated before she took the first step down, went back into the bedroom, and straightened up a bit, making sure the room was presentable. She expected to be back here with Jason in a couple of hours.

He was five minutes early, and she met him at the door immediately. He was dressed casually in a knit polo shirt open at the throat, and a pair of highly pressed Khakis. A navy blazer added a nice touch, and Janet thought he looked more laid back than usual. He took her to a new restaurant that just opened in Valley Glen, and held the door for her as they entered. Jason led her to the lounge, and they took a seat at a small table adorned with a short linen tablecloth and a crystal vase with freshly cut flowers. She was pleased that he put so much thought and effort into this date. Jason ordered his usual, a Tanqueray martini, and Janet asked for a glass of Chablis. He asked her about work, and she told him about her day, which was a typical Friday for the hospital . . . lots of patients and not enough staff.

Knowing her interest in health and fitness, Jason told her about Ben Dickson and the hit and run accident. She also knew who Ben was, had seen him at the Apex a few times. He was not a member, but because of his status as a world class weightlifter, Kyle liked to have him work out there, and he had an open invitation.

"I'm really not surprised about Ben," Janet said. "I see a lot of guys built like him and I think quite a few are on steroids. If not steroids, they're into some kind of new supplement to pack on the muscle."

"Yeah, I know. But I knew Ben since high school and he seemed pretty squared away."

"You know what's interesting, last week we had another guy from the Apex in the ER. He was pretty strung out too. Cut himself while working on his house. He was cutting plasterboard when the knife slipped and sliced his other hand open. It wasn't a bad cut, but needed a few stitches. He gave the nurses and doctor a real hard time about waiting his turn. He was really agitated and paced back and forth, sometimes muttering to himself, sometimes yelling at the nurses.

He was glaring at the other patients in the waiting room, and we called security to stand by. He seemed like a time bomb waiting to blow."

"Did anybody ask him about drugs during his treatment?" Jason asked.

"Sure, it's routine. He denied taking anything, but when his girlfriend came to pick him up, I overheard him tell her something about the *roids*. I wouldn't have thought much of it, but we've had a few similar problems lately, and the doctor's are talking about some toxicology screens revealing the presence of steroids."

"I'll look into it a bit more tomorrow. Can you give me the guy's name?" Jason waited, wondering if she would give him this information. Unless it was part of an official investigation, hospital personnel are instructed not to release such information to the police.

"Sure. I'll get it for you . . . just don't tell anyone who told you."

"My lips are sealed," he replied, smiling at the ease in which she confided in him. "At least on this matter."

"I hope that's true, about keeping a secret I mean," Janet purred. "Christine and Kyle have a special night planned for us soon, but they're counting on me to let them know if you can be trusted to remain silent about it."

"Really? Sounds interesting. Unless we're going to engage in illegal behavior, you have my word."

"Illegal . . . no. Licentious, scandalous, even reprehensible . . . yes."

"Sounds even better," Jason said. "Count me in."

As she predicted, Jason accepted her invitation to come inside her house. Although they had only been seeing each other for a short time, she was ready to take the relationship to a more physical level. He was really an engaging, attractive man, and she found herself growing more and more excited as the evening progressed. She went into the living room, and turned the lights down low. He stood patiently while she lit a couple of candles, and watched the slim blades of flame cast shadows against the white walls of the room, like dancers undulating in the moonlight. She offered him a drink, and he took a seat in the living room while she mixed a couple of cocktails. He was standing when she returned, looking at a painting that she had picked up during a visit to New York. It was an abstract work, a swirl of color and texture that was open to interpretation, but one that spoke to her strongly. It took on a mystical aura in the ever-changing candlelight. She put the drinks on a table and slipped up behind him, putting her hand gently on his back. She was almost as tall as he, and put her face close to his neck as she spoke. He could feel her soft breath against his skin.

"Do you like it?" she asked.

He reached behind and found her hand. He held it gently, and leaned back ever so slightly into her as she stood her ground behind him. A primal, but subtle and sensuous ritual had begun. Already they both sensed what would soon follow, but neither would take any shortcuts.

"Yes, I do like it, but I'm not sure why. It grabbed my attention because of the mix of color, but the longer I look at it, the more I see. What is it?"

"It's my spirit," she said. "That's what it represents to me anyway. Don't ask me why, but I see myself in there. See here? In the center of the painting there's a woman's face, but a face without boundaries, a face with only a hint of form. That represents the woman's core, her center. The swirls of color emanating from the core depict the plethora of her hopes and dreams, her thoughts and her emotions. Where the color is singular and deep she is sure of herself, confident in who she is and what she wants. But where the colors begin to swirl together and one fades into another like leaves on a tree in autumn, there is a realm of doubt, feelings of uncertainty and maybe even confusion. Do you see it?"

She had stepped in front of him as she talked, pointing out some of the features of the painting, showing him as well as telling him how it spoke to her. He felt her brush against him as she moved, and looked at her in profile. She was a beautiful woman, and in this soft light looked more delicate and desirable than he would ever have imagined. He took a few moments before he answered her.

"Only because your description is so vivid. Looking at it from your perspective, it's beautiful, almost haunting. I have to admit though, I never would have made the same connection without your guidance."

"I probably shouldn't have told you what it means to me. I probably should have first asked you what you see when you look at it. Can you still tell me?"

He was so close to her now. He gently kissed the side of her cheek, and then lightly brushed her neck with his lips. She sighed faintly, and turned toward him. They were standing face to face, the swirling colors of the painting now serving as a vivid symbol of their growing passion. Jason slipped his arms around her waist. She lifted her head and met his gaze.

"I'd rather show you," he said quietly, and bent to meet her waiting lips. She kissed him back, gently at first, and then with more fervor, hard and wet. Their breathing became quick and shallow and their hearts raced. Janet's arms encircled Jason and she pulled herself into him. Jason hands began exploring her lithe body as their ardor increased. Her thigh slid between his legs, she could feel him harden as she moved against him. He reached to stroke her leg, pulling her dress up as he did. He worked the dress up to her waist and beyond, and she raised her arms as he lifted it clear of her head.

She used her hands to toss back her hair, and smoothed the errant strands into place. He took that moment to look at her standing there, wearing only a pair of white lace panties. Although he had seen her many times at the gym, he was still taken with her body. He kissed her on the mouth again, tasting her sweet lips and tongue. Soon, he moved down her body, planting light kisses on her neck and shoulders. He brushed his lips against her flesh as he slid his face down to her breasts, and she shuddered slightly as her nipples grew hard even before his warm mouth enveloped them and his tongue explored each of them in turn.

He took his sweet time, his lips tracing a path of warm wetness against her soft skin. His hands caressed her back as they moved lower, coming to rest on her smooth round ass as he reached that part of her body which was aching for his touch. He entered her with his tongue, not tentatively, but with the certainty of one who knows the purpose of his actions. She felt a rush of moisture as he changed tempo, now lightly circling her clitoris as she ran her fingers through his hair, pressing him into her to insure he didn't stop until she was ready. There was no need, as he hungrily continued to lick and suck her.

She felt her legs weaken, and awkwardly lowered herself to the floor, bringing him down with her. They were apart for only a few seconds, and then re-coupled with even more purpose. Jason alternated between light butterfly kisses and pointed probing of his very talented tongue. *The boy has stamina*, she thought. Unable to hold back any longer, Jason entered her. Janet felt the first signs of an impending orgasm, and moved her hips in rhythm to Jason's now ardent and deep thrusts.

"Oh, Janet," he called out softly, as they came close to orgasm.

She moaned as feelings of ecstasy swept over her, and became lost in a swirl of senses as she closed her eyes and let herself go.

If the first time is supposed to be quick and awkward, then the next time they made love it would probably drive her crazy with pleasure. When he had finally entered her, he was slow and gentle, better than she imagined, much more sensitive than she would have ever expected from a cop, especially a hard-boiled one like Jason. But he let his rough exterior peel away like so many layers of clothing, and their passion grew with each passing moment until neither of them could take any more. In the end they came together, much like the colors in her painting, not sure where one ended and another began. Jesus, she thought as she lay beside him in bed, still panting from what seemed an eternity of sensual exertion. She was tingling all over. She'd had her share of lovers, but it never felt like this before. *Don't let him go. Don't let him go.*

She called him the next morning with the name of the man treated for cuts. The hospital's records showed he was Tim Weidner, age twenty-five, from

Stenson Street near the Philadelphia border. Jason ran him through local records, and also checked with Philly P.D. He was clean. Nonetheless, Jason was growing suspicious. Was this just a coincidence? All he had was two men, both of whom frequent the Apex, attracting attention because of their behavior. He asked Janet if she would nose around the files and get the names of other patients who had tested positive for steroids. She balked at first, but agreed when he told her he just wanted to see if they had a connection to the Apex. He hoped there was no such link, but the detective in him needed to find out for sure.

She wasted no time, and only an hour later had the names of three men who were treated recently at the hospital and had tested positive for steroids. Jason recognized one of the three as belonging to the club. A few phone calls later, he discovered a second man was also an Apex member. He still wasn't sure he had anything. Steroid use among lifters was fairly common, and just because they worked out at the same club didn't mean there was a conspiracy. He thought about asking Kyle about it, to check and see if he had ever seen or heard about steroid use at his club. Kyle and he were fast becoming friends, and Jason felt he would be straight with him, but decided to do some snooping first. He thought about using a narcotics officer he trusted who worked for the county District Attorney's drug task force, and decided to give him a call and see if he was available to assist. No time like now, he reasoned, and reached for the phone.

Chapter 13

She was right on time. She pulled into the driveway at 5:11 PM, and he waited as she walked to her front door. As soon as she unlocked the door and entered her home he sprung into action. He walked swiftly to the side of the house, and opened the window he had jimmied earlier. He had thought about entering her house earlier and waiting for her in her bedroom, but believed that presented an extra risk he was not willing to take. He thought it best to wait outside to make sure his victim arrived alone. The window sash lifted noiselessly, and he could hear her moving about upstairs, in her bedroom. He carefully pulled himself up and through the window opening, paused inside, and listened. The shower was running. There was a steady cadence of waterfall; she had not yet stepped in to bathe.

He went to the stairs and carefully but swiftly mounted them, the plush carpeting cushioning his footfalls. He saw her walking from the bedroom to the hall bath, naked. She was even prettier up close, and her body was lithe and smooth. She had beautiful small breasts, which bounced just a bit as she walked. She saw him a second later and a look of surprise and then terror fell over her face. She froze momentarily, a common reaction of many victims taken by surprise. It always amused him how defenseless people became when they were suddenly confronted by a situation they didn't expect. He probably could have stood there smiling at her for minutes before she could even move her feet enough to flee. He wanted to prolong her terror, and already was growing excited by her reactions. He enjoyed that fright-frozen expression on her pretty face and could smell the fear already emanating from her sweat glands. Nevertheless, he gave her no time to set up a defense. He leapt from the top step and was on her in a second, punching her hard in the head, knocking her down and drawing blood from her nose. He looked back into the bedroom, and then at the bathroom, shower running, steam beginning to fill up the small room, and grabbed her by the hair. He dragged her into the bathroom. She was conscious, but not resisting. She was making small, whimpering sounds, like a beaten dog.

He threw her roughly into the shower stall, and she collapsed onto the floor, blood from her face mixing with the running water to create a swirling pink stream. The blood excited him even more. He stood outside the stall, stripping off his clothes. He was already hard and knew his excitement would cause him to climax soon. He put his arms around her waist and picked her up, grinding his penis into her backside as he straightened her up and then bent her over from the waist. He slid one of his hands up to her breast and grabbed it tightly, squeezing the nipple hard, causing her to scream in pain. He entered her forcibly from behind, and came immediately.

Still holding her tightly, he reached for the towel bar and removed a dark green bath towel. Again grabbing Melina by the hair, he began to stuff the towel into her mouth, prying her jaw apart with his hands and pushing it deeper and deeper down her throat. He felt her body tighten, and could sense the wave of panic come over her as she realized he was going to kill her. He was still inside her, and liked the sensation caused by her panic. She bucked hard, and tried to swing her legs up and push off the wall, but he wrapped one of his own strong legs around her and kept her from getting any leverage. He held her very, very tightly until the bucking slowed to a shudder, and then stopped completely. She became heavy in his arms. The bleeding had stopped, and the water ran in clear rivulets down their bodies. Melina was lifeless when he simply let go and dropped her hard to the shower floor. He rinsed himself off after using some of Melina's perfumed soap, *the better to remember her by*, and stepped out of the shower. He retrieved his pants, reached into the pocket and removed a diskette. He walked naked into her bedroom, leaving a trail of water between the rooms. He found her computer, turned it on, and inserted the disc into the floppy drive. A few commands later, the virus he introduced into her system eradicated part of her hard drive, leaving no trace of his correspondence.

Returning to the bathroom, he took a second to stare at Melina's crumpled body, still flush and pink from the hot water cascading over her. He dressed quickly, decided to leave the shower on, and left the house through the front door.

Kyle Price owned property in Cajuani, Mexico. Cajuani was a small town located on the pacific coast, about 70 miles south of Acapulco. Primarily a fishing village, it was also the location of Price's largest warehouse, and the manufacturing plant that produces several attractive, quality built keepsake items. Among the biggest sellers was a small teakwood music box, complete with a trio of brightly dressed, twirling Mexican dancers inside. There was also a unique clock, built with the same teakwood, having some indigenous semi-precious stones in place of the numerals marking the time. Both items, though not expensive, were well made and very attractive. They're the types of items often seen on home shopping networks.

The plant employed fifty-eight Mexican workers, who make the wooden boxes designed to hold the works of the music boxes and clocks. The mechanical parts were made in Germany and shipped to the plant for installation. Eduardo Perez Santiago, a native of Mexico, was Kyle's plant manager. Eduardo had been a Mexican policeman for almost twelve years. He became tired of the work, but had grown used to the graft and corruption that supplemented his paltry police income, so Kyle thought it prudent to hire someone to keep an eye on him. The former policeman was, however, a gifted negotiator, and seemed to have some power over the locals. Disputes were quickly settled, and there were no real labor problems in the fourteen years Kyle had owned this plant and warehouse. Maybe it was because Eduardo used to be a cop...it didn't really matter, as long as he kept the production line running smoothly.

The plant was prosperous. It was the mainstay of Kyle Price's import business, and was responsible for most of his fortune. He had managed to successfully promote a few items, including a few of the clocks and music boxes that proved very popular in the States. But his business really took off when he took advantage of burgeoning Internet sales. His was one of the first companies to offer retail sales on the web, and his operation was up and running the first Christmas season that people really used the web to buy gifts. That year, Price's sales topped five million dollars. The profit for just the three-month holiday season topped 2.3 million. Since then, business was steady. Without needing to rely on costly retail outlets and high maintenance sales staff, the profit margin remained high, and production costs in Mexico were very reasonable. Kyle realized that many companies that had experienced great initial sales had waned quickly once more and more companies started to take advantage of computer sales. But Kyle had been careful not to sink all of his profits back into the business. He kept his overhead low and did not seek to expand more than absolutely necessary. As a result, even if things went bust, which was a real possibility for any dotcom-based company, Kyle was set for life.

There was also an American, George Dellatorre, who was the man he hired to keep an eye on Eduardo, as well as oversee the overall operation of the plant. Dellatorre was an interesting character. He was born in Texas, the son of Mexican immigrants, and spent about half of his life working for his father's uncle, who owned and operated a small resort in Acapulco. It was there that he became very familiar with those who had money, and soon learned the art of sucking-up. Dellatorre still preferred the seamier side of life, but could clean up in an instant when he had to. It was a necessary skill in the resort business, and Dellatorre could change his persona as quickly as a chameleon changed color, appearing to be whatever suited his guests. He had also developed a keen business sense, and together with Eduardo kept the plant running smooth. The pair of swarthy men reminded Price of swashbucklers, and he enjoyed their rough manner and salty language. In turn, Dellatorre was impressed by his boss's smooth style, and his ability to make others feel at ease, no matter what their station in life.

He had first met the Price's at the resort, where Kyle and Christine occasionally vacationed. Kyle treated a housekeeper just as well as he treated the aristocrats that stayed in the resort, and this left a lasting impression on the resort manager, who was used to the shoddy treatment most of the wealthy guests bestowed on the hired help. Although Dellatorre himself viewed the employees with disdain, he saw that Kyle got better service by pretending he liked them. This was a tactic to remember. When Price had asked him if he were interested in becoming his plant manager, he jumped at the chance. After all, if he heard it once he heard it a hundred times from the rich fat cats who lay like beached whales poolside, sipping their imported scotch and regaling each other with their latest conquests . . . both financial and sexual. *Opportunity doesn't knock twice.*

About twice a year, Kyle took a trip to visit the plant in Cajuani. Although Christine preferred to stay home, Kyle always made a fuss about her coming with him, every time convincing her that he really preferred that she accompany him, that it would be a boring and unbearable experience without her. She never ceased to be flattered by his attention, and did look forward to the romantic evenings he planned while they were in the land of sun and surf. She enjoyed the beach, and the times they spent sailing in the azure waters of the Pacific Ocean. This trip would be even better, since Kyle had invited her friend Janet and her new boyfriend Jason Coulter to join them tomorrow. The Price's left on Thursday in their private jet, arriving at the small airport near the city around two in the afternoon. Dellatorre had sent a driver for them.

Christine felt the burst of dry, hot air as she deplaned. The heat felt good on her face, and there was a nice breeze that made for a comfortable afternoon. They arrived at their house a half-hour later. The villa was a large bungalow, kept exclusively for their use, and that of a few business associates and friends that Kyle sometimes allowed to use it for vacation. It was only a few blocks from the ocean, but the property had its own large pool that had been built and landscaped to resemble a tropical pond. The house had a second story veranda overlooking the pond, and it was Christine's favorite spot to relax and unwind. The veranda looked toward the west, and provided some of the best views of a

Mexican sunset one could ever imagine. It was postcard perfect, second only to being on the water watching as the sun dipped below the horizon in a dazzling array of red, orange and yellow.

After freshening up, the couple drove downtown to one of their favorite cantinas, a small hole-in-the-wall with some of the best home-cooked Mexican dishes you ever tasted. They were to meet Dellatorre for drinks and dinner, and Kyle would receive a briefing on plant operations. They were greeted warmly by the proprietors when they arrived, and Christine saw Dellatorre and another employee, Ted Sykes, seated at a corner table adorned with fresh flowers. As plant manager, she had met George plenty of times, but had never seen Ted before today. He was some sort of computer genius, one of the first to realize the commercial value of the internet. He had been hired recently to help Kyle take advantage of this ever-changing technology. She knew her husband admired his abilities, and rewarded him well. She figured that this chance to dine with them was another perk for Ted. Both men stood as the couple approached them.

Christine didn't like Dellatorre, and her first impression of Ted wasn't so hot either. Both of them seemed cold-blooded and just plain creepy. She caught Ted staring at her several times, and when she met his eyes, he made no attempt to divert his gaze. She was used to men looking at her, she usually didn't even object when it was obvious that they were sizing her up, often checking out her breasts, or trying to peer up her skirt. She took it in stride, a hazard of being an attractive woman in a man's world. While some things were changing, some remained annoyingly constant.

The world was slowly becoming more accepting of women's talent, ambition, and their drive to become movers and shakers when they had the right stuff. But some things, like the leering look of a man on the prowl, and they all were, remained the same. She had accepted that, and even learned to use it to her advantage. The looks did not usually rattle her at all. But Ted's gaze did bother her. It sent shivers down her spine. Even though he was sexy in a rough kind of way, with a hard, sinewy body and a rugged but handsome face, she did not welcome his attention. Dellatorre, on the other hand, was just plain ugly. He was a big man, powerful looking but turning soft. His ample belly protruded from his unbuttoned silk shirt. She could tell he was covered with hair, and hoped she would never have to see him without his shirt. The less time she and Kyle had to spend in the company of these men the better.

She liked coming to Cajuani, but vowed to skip this meeting in the future. Kyle thought it was good for her to accompany him and learn more about the plant and the men who ran it. While she was pleased he wanted to include her in the business, she would rather stay at the villa. There, she could soak up the sun on the veranda or take a short hike and sit on the white sand beach at water's edge, enjoying the warm surf lapping at her toes as she reclined in a low slung canvas lounger. She watched with interest as Kyle interacted with these men. She wondered just what her husband saw in them. Dellatorre seemed much too rough and tumble for him. He had a grating New York accent that seemed contrived. Although she knew he was well paid, he dressed poorly. He had no sense of fashion, wearing mismatched clothes that looked like they were pulled from the hamper. He always had a few days growth on his face, and his hair was unkempt.

In addition, he was always downing the locals, which Kyle usually despised, and complained about everything from the bugs to the food. Christine knew that this slovenly man had once run one of the most accomplished resort hotels in the country, and figured his mode of dress was by design, maybe a conscious decision to change his once opulent lifestyle. He was more like a beach bum now. Ted seemed more refined, but there was something unsettling about him too. Despite his disarming southern accent, he seemed to be always probing, always trying to step into other people's space. He seemed to want a level of intimacy that Christine reserved for her good friends, something Ted would never be considered.

"Well, sweetheart, what do think of George's idea?" Her husband's voice interrupted her thoughts.

"What? I'm sorry, what did you say?"

"George asked if we'd like to go for a twilight cruise tonight. He'll grill some lobsters and we can watch the sun set."

Christine hoped no one noticed the sour look that suddenly appeared on her face.

"I like the idea," she lied, "but I'm feeling a bit queasy, and afraid I'll get sea sick. You go if you like, it can be men's night. You're always saying that you need a night out with the boys. I'll just watch the sunset from our veranda."

Kyle considered it a moment before replying.

"Naa, wouldn't be the same without you. George, how about we take a rain check?"

"Of course. But I'll hold you to that," Dellatorre replied, looking at Christine and smirking. It was like he knew she was begging off because of him and Ted. Was she that obvious? Well, who cares. The thought of taking a sunset cruise with these two is too revolting to consider, even if she normally would love such an experience. Christine believed nothing was more sensual than being out on the water, anchored well offshore, sipping champagne and enjoying the spectacular flameburst that is sunset on the Mexican Riviera.

None of them took a sunset cruise. After Christine had been driven home, the men began to talk about the other business that took place at Kyle's plant. The steroids now accounted for sixty five percent of the entire profit margin. Internet sales were booming, with a distribution network surreptitiously operated through a complex maze of computer routers in twenty states and thirty-nine cities. Sales in the United Sates were now in the millions of dollars, and this did not include legal sales made in Mexico and Europe, where regulations about steroid use and distribution were less stringent. Kyle was very pleased by the report.

Although he considered himself a good man, he knew what he was doing could bring potential harm to the habitual users of his products. Nevertheless, he rationalized his involvement in the illicit trade by maintaining the U.S. government and the American Medical Association had erred in the decision to ban the unrestricted sale of mild steroids that boosted athletic performance. He was filling a demand that would be met one way or another, so why not do it right; manufacture a quality product, and make a few bucks out of it. Besides, he was also providing a means for a few hundred local villagers to feed and clothe their families. He paid more than any local tradesman could muster and even more than the resort jobs in Acapulco, which were hard for the average Mexican to get anyway. Besides, he let them buy some of the trinkets the plant manufactured, and resell them to tourists for a nice profit. All in all, he rationalized that what he was doing did far more good than harm, especially for the athletes who relied on his products and the locals who relied on his business for survival.

Eduardo Santiago prowled a catwalk above the warehouse floor. He kept a close watch on the twenty or so workers who toiled beneath. Five of them were sitting in front of computers, taking orders off the web site and relaying the purchaser's personal and credit card information to five other workers seated at old metal desks behind them. These people also had computers and phones. They would take the information, complete an electronic form for a credit check to the various card companies and send off for a quick verification. Upon getting a positive response, the order and a shipping label would be sent a third distinct area of the operation, where packers would pull the product from shelves and prepare it for mailing.

Watching the packers was his main concern. Although all of the workers wore special smocks with no pockets or lining to secrete the tablets, Eduardo was very aware that an innovative worker could stash a hundred pills into a bra or other undergarment. Some had even been caught stuffing the steroids into bodily orifices. The temptation was great, especially when you consider the

97

workers had next to nothing. They lived in shacks, had meager rations and sparse personal possessions, and little hope of changing their status in life. Eduardo guessed that it was the "next" to nothing that kept most of them in line. They had enough to sustain themselves and their families, and to get caught meant losing everything.

However, some did try, and some succeeded. It was necessary to make an example of those that got caught, and that was part of Eduardo's duties. At first, he did this himself, but found it revolting. Since simple arrest would do nothing to dissuade the workers, Dellatorre insisted that those caught stealing be severely beaten. This most often involved breaking bones by repeatedly hitting a subject's head and arms with a baseball bat, or striking them across the face with a nightstick, shattering their nose and orbital bones. The beatings often were conducted within earshot of the rest of the workers, and they could hear the crack of splintering bone and the haunting screams and moans of the accused. Sometimes, the disfigured workers were paraded across the plant floor days after the incident, so others could see their swollen, broken faces. It was a great deterrent.

Beating the offenders like that sickened Eduardo, and he was always on the lookout for someone willing to do this for him. He had tried several local banditos, but they tended to brag about their deeds. Eduardo was still forced to do some of the dirty work himself, less he be branded a coward. He had to find someone who could keep their mouth shut, for if it were discovered that he had no stomach for violence, his reputation and his effectiveness would be ruined, and he would surely be fired by Mr. Dellatorre. He did not have to look far to find someone. A wretched new employee named Ted Sykes, whom he was introduced to recently, was more than happy to take on the assignment. Ted was one of the computer whiz kids the company had found to keep their web site running. He was some sort of wizard, Kyle Price had told him and Delattorre, and in a matter of weeks, had expanded and modernized the whole Internet sales operation.

No one knew much about him, and he only came to Mexico a few times, preferring to do most of his work by modem. But in the future, Eduardo hoped to see more of him at the plant. Sykes would be an asset in more ways than one, he thought. He could relieve Eduardo of the burden of dealing with these thieves. Sykes wasn't a bad looking guy, with longish blonde hair he kept in a ponytail and slender, pointed features. He reminded Eduardo of a fox. His eyes were cold and empty looking. He could be smiling or scowling, but his eyes never changed. There was no expression in them, no clue as to what he was feeling.

He had also heard Ted mocking the "simpleton peasants" and calling them slimy lizards. He believed that those caught stealing should have their fingers crimped with the wire cutting pliers used by the shippers to package the steroids for shipment. An occasional amputated finger, left on a table in the product prep area would send the right message. Such a graphic example would have the desired effect, he overheard Ted say one day.

He invited Ted out for dinner one night, and then took him to his favorite nightclub where they had a few drinks. Eduardo led the conversation to business, particularly the thieving peasants, and Ted was more than willing to listen to his proposition. He would pay Ted fifty bucks to take care of a worker who stole any of the wooden novelties they make, and a hundred bucks to severely beat those caught stealing steroids. Ted thought he was a cheap bastard, suspecting he didn't have the balls to do his own dirty work, but took the job nonetheless. Hell, he would have done it for free, just for the thrill. It kept him warmed up for his real passion.

Two weeks later, during one of Ted's visits, Eduardo and a couple of his goons took hold of a worker suspected of stealing and dragged him from the plant, kicking and screaming. Eduardo was grinning at the other workers as he led the grim entourage out the door, where the unfortunate worker was thrown roughly into the back of an old pickup truck. Two of the goons jumped in after him and Eduardo sped away. Ted was waiting for them just a short distance away, in what Eduardo called his torture chamber. It was nothing more than an old shack that had been used to store farm equipment before the plant was built. Inside, he had rigged a number of devices that he used to strike fear into the hearts of his victims, including a makeshift guillotine and a chair with straps to fasten the wrists and ankles.

The guillotine was for show, although he had once held a worker's hand under it to scare him and accidentally hit the release lever. The blade fell and sliced the poor man's hand off clean. Eduardo was shocked by the accident, and surprised that his homemade appliance functioned so well. News of this cruel act spread quickly, and Eduardo's reputation was safe for awhile. The chair with the straps and a set of old fashioned stocks, actually a part of Mexican history, completed his implements of torture. Mostly, the devices just held his victims in place while he beat them. He wore an old, bloodstained pair of leather gloves while he beat them, and occasionally he used some things he'd gotten from his cousin, who was still a local police officer. These included a blackjack, and a riding whip.

Finally, there was the cattle prod, an amusing little weapon that provoked quite a reaction, especially when used on the genitals. When he had shown his collection to Ted Sykes, the young man's eyes showed genuine interest. These items would be more than just props to him.

Ted heard the pickup rattling down the dirt road leading to the shack and walked out to greet it. The worker was now franticly trying to escape and the two goons struggled to keep him down. *Calm down, moron,* he thought. *You'll live, if you don't die from a heart attack.* Ted directed the goons to put the wild-eyed, sweating worker in the stocks. Eduardo had told him that this guy was actually a pretty good worker, he had more intelligence than most and seemed to take some pride in what he did. Nonetheless, he was caught stealing, and discipline must be maintained.

The worker was secured to the stocks, and Ted ordered that all of his clothing be removed. He reached for the cattle prod, and placed it against he man's clavicle and pressed the on button without hesitation. The man's eyes went as big as saucers, and he screamed as the current pulsed through his whole body. Ted stepped back, and backhanded the man in the mouth with his gloved hand. The rough glove split open his lips and blood began to flow. Ted approached the man again, holding the cattle prod near the worker's eyes, speaking to him softly about how the juice would make his eye explode, about how he would look in the mirror every day and see the burned out socket. The man was sobbing, and babbling incoherently about being sorry. *Would that be enough to stop him from stealing again?* He then lowered the prod slowly, skimming the man's neck, chest, and stomach before letting the prod come to rest on his penis.

"Well, my friend," Ted said as he waved the prod around the man's genitals. "Do you want it on your dick, or your balls?"

Eduardo thought the crazy son of a bitch would do it, and felt nauseous. He wanted to leave but saw the goons were leaning forward eagerly, and knew it would be taken as a sign of weakness if he did not stay. The goons would spread that word around the plant in no time flat, and he would lose control of the workers. He breathed in deeply let it out slow, trying to slow his pulse rate and keep control of himself. If Ted fries the poor workers balls, he thought, I'm going to lose it right here.

But Ted didn't. He knew the man was absolutely terrified, and that he all he had to do was mark him up a little for show, and then he would be done with him. A straight razor suddenly appeared in Ted's right hand and he made two quick passes across the man's face, slicing twin four-inch gashes in his left cheek. Blood flowed profusely, and Eduardo gagged, trying to cover the sound by coughing. The goons looked at him, waiting to see if he reacted further.

Ted followed with a quick poke of the cattle prod to the stomach, hitting the button to release the current, causing the stricken worker to scream in pain. He then struck him hard in the eye with the back of his gloved fist, enough to give him a black and swollen eye for a couple of days. Finally, Ted punched him full in the face, hearing the crunch of bone and cartilage as the man's nose broke, and blood flew from his nostrils. The goons' attention was riveted on the action, and they didn't notice Eduardo slip away and head for the side of the shack, where he promptly vomited.

Chapter 14

This was going to be a nice break from the recent pressures Jason had been facing at work. Besides, a trip to Mexico with Janet would likely move their relationship to the next level, something that he wanted for the first time in many years. He was growing tired of the one night stands and girlfriends who lasted just a few months. Despite what many men thought about the love'em and leave'm theory, dating really wasn't much fun. There were a lot of wasted hours involved, and Jason did not have the time to spare. He guessed that he was ready to settle down. The envy he felt whenever he visited Cab and Shawna was a good barometer for his feelings.

He glanced over at Janet, seated next to him on the airplane. She was reading a copy of "People" and was absentmindedly massaging her temple with well-manicured fingers. As usual she looked exquisite. Wearing a light blue, knee length skirt with an eggshell muslin blouse adorned with blue and mauve southwestern designs, she was the epitome of casual chic. He felt like a ragamuffin next to her, even though he went to great pains to match her fashion sense. He also felt something deep inside that couldn't be ignored. He knew he was already falling in love with her. Although he enjoyed the comfortable warm and fuzzies such a feeling brought, there was a part of him that was frightened by the implications of it all. Significant change would soon follow, and Jason was not fond of anything that interrupted his routine, especially in his personal life.

Janet looked up from her reading and smiled. She reached for his hand and squeezed it gently. It was almost as if she sensed his misgivings, and was giving him some assurance in her quiet, subtle way. The flight attendant passed by, and Janet stopped her and ordered two glasses of white wine. The couple toasted the beginning of a wonderful excursion. The flight to Acapulco was just under three hours, and after a couple more glasses of wine, both of them were feeling mellow. They were caressing each other's arms and shoulders, and bantering about a variety of topics ranging from the trivial to the philosophical. It was a delightful experience. The flight went quickly, and a burst of hot, acrid air greeted them as they deplaned. Almost immediately, Janet felt beads of perspiration form under her blouse and looked forward to getting to Cajuani and getting out of her clothes.

After clearing immigration in Mexico, they were led to a limo Kyle had sent for them. The trip to Kyle and Christine's villa took only about an hour. Weaving around the serpentine back roads leading from the airport to their beachfront destination, the two of them became distracted by the lush foliage and dappled sunlight streaming through the tall trees. Jason had opened the skylight in the limo, and the air was much cooler under the canopy of leafy trees. They marveled at the many varieties of tropical plants and flowers growing wild by the side of the road, and the limo became filled with the sweet, fragrant scents of some of Mexico's most prolific flora. Janet quickly forgot about the stifling unpleasantness of the airport, and relaxed into Jason's arms as the trip progressed.

Christine was waiting for them when they arrived. She was dressed for the warm weather in a floral print bikini with matching cover-up, and a pair of open toed leather sandals. She greeted each of them affectionately as they stepped from the car, and Jason was enveloped by the spicy scent of her perfume as she hugged him close. He helped with the luggage as the two women, holding hands, walked to the villa. The front entrance to their home away from home was up a small rocky incline, and there was a rough-hewn wooden staircase leading to the front door. The house was spacious but simple. They obviously wanted it to be that way, kind of a no frills oasis. It was designed to be rugged outside, blending in with the surrounding countryside. The floors inside were native tile, and the furniture was locally crafted from indigenous fruitwoods. A leather sofa and matching loveseat were the only luxurious exceptions to the décor. Nonetheless, the place was marvelous, and reminded Jason of a Caribbean bungalow.

Christine showed them to their bedroom, which featured a single king sized bed and a large chest and closet. It may be simple, but the home didn't lack amenities. Jason and Christine walked out to the veranda at the back of the house while Janet unpacked, and eager to shed her sticky clothing, jumped in the shower.

"I'm so glad you and Janet could make it. It's been awhile since anyone has been here with us. Since Kyle is so busy, I'm here alone most of the time, and it gets pretty boring."

"We appreciated the invitation. It's so good to get away for a bit, and this place is great. Janet and I were looking forward to this ever since you asked us." Jason walked over to the edge of the veranda and gazed at the beautiful landscaping surrounding the pool. He could see the Pacific Ocean to the west.

"The view here is spectacular. I could spend many hours just sitting in one of these lounge chairs sipping a drink and soaking in the atmosphere."

"It is nice," said Christine. "Just wait until sunset. The colors are so intense just before the sun drops below the horizon. I hope Kyle gets back beforehand so we can all watch it together. He left for the plant right after breakfast and promised me he'd be back by five."

They continued chatting for another fifteen minutes or so, and Janet emerged from the house. She had changed into her bathing suit, and her hair was still wet from her shower, tied back from her face. Jason liked her fresh scrubbed look. He also liked her tiny bikini. It was metallic silver, and seemed to take on different hues as she walked across the deck. It had quite an appealing effect, like a moving hologram. The parts not covered by the suit had an appealing effect too, and he smiled approvingly.

"My turn for the shower," he said. "Would you like me to make you some drinks when I'm finished? I'm a pretty fair bartender."

"How about a batch of Pina Colada's?" answered Christine. "They go down real smooth in this hot sun. All of the makings are in the kitchen, including some fresh pineapple I cut this morning."

Jason showered quickly, and pulled on a pair of shorts. He padded barefoot to the kitchen and assembled the ingredients for the drinks. He got the pineapple from the fridge, and slipped a piece into his mouth. It was sweet and delicious. There was a well stocked bar, and he made a large pitcher of the tropical drink, and sipped a little for taste. It was good. He poured the mixture into three tall glasses and found a tray to put them on. He carried them to the veranda, and saw that Janet and Christine were lying on lounge chairs facing the west, where the exposure to the sun was best this time of day.

As he approached he noticed that there were two bikini tops flung over the chairs, one floral, one metallic silver. Walking closer, he could see the women lying on their backs on the partially reclined lounges. He didn't need Sherlock Holmes to deduce this one. They were topless of course, and their bodies were glistening from the mix of lotion and perspiration, compliments of the blazing Mexican sun. He hesitated for a split second, thought maybe he should go back and give them some warning that he was coming, but then remembered that they were expecting him with the drinks so they must have known he would walk out on them this way. He continued on, stepping over to Janet first and handing her a drink. Smiling, she lowered her sunglasses to show him her twinkling, mischievous blue eyes. She reached for the glass, giving him an exaggerated "Thank you, sir."

He then went over to Christine's chair, where she was lying in a semi-reclining position, her seat back halfway between straight up and fully reclined.

He couldn't help but notice the fine beads of perspiration between her nicely formed breasts and clinging to the areola of her large nipples. He traced the line of perspiration down her stomach to her navel, where the thin stream made a right turn and meandered to the top of her bikini briefs. Her dark glasses prevented him from seeing her eyes and her facial expression did not change as she accepted the drink, but her long fingers caressed his hand before they encircled the glass. The women had positioned a third lounge chair between them, and he took the last drink, set down the tray, and settled into the chair.

After only an hour in the mid-day rays, Jason looked at his reddening skin with concern. He was not prone to sunburn, but the Mexican sun was stronger than he was used to, and he knew it was time to get inside. He glanced from side to side, once again enjoying the superb bodies of the women who flanked him. They were both well tanned, and tolerated the sun better than he.

"Ladies, I've had enough sun for today. Can I get you anything before I change?"

"No need," said Christine, sitting up to look at him. "I've had enough too, time to shower and get ready for dinner. We're going to one of my favorite places tonight. They have great seafood, and the lobster bisque is to die for. I'm getting hungry thinking about it. Kyle better be back soon."

She stood up and stretched, a half-moon of white skin appearing below each of her uplifted breasts. She grabbed her bikini top from the top of the chair, and turned to walk into the house. Jason admired the rhythmic sway of her ass as she strode across the deck, looking like a haute couture model parading down a Paris runway.

Janet called after her. "Let me know when you're finished in the shower. I'll stay out here till then. I still need a little more sun on my back."

Kyle returned a little before seven, and Christine gently admonished him for being late. He apologized to his guests.

"Being the boss is not always fun and games," he said. "There are times I think I should just sell all my businesses and retire to a life of decadent luxury."

"You wouldn't last a week," Christine replied. "And neither would I. It would drive me crazy trying to compensate for your boredom. You're like a shark, you have to be swimming all the time, taking it all in, checking it all out. If you ever stop, I'll know there's something seriously wrong. Hey! Let's get moving, We have reservations for seven-thirty. I'll fix you a drink while you get ready to go. You are already several behind us."

Dinner was nice, although Kyle seemed distracted. Christine and Janet carried the conversation, and Jason was content just to look and listen to the two beautiful women. They were totally engrossed in conversation, the dancing candlelight providing a soft, fluid glow that served to accent the uniquely beautiful features of their faces. He briefly imagined them as lovers, picturing the lithe bodies he had seen earlier entwined in a passionate, glistening embrace. Well, this was another fantasy of red-blooded American males wasn't it? He glanced over at Kyle, and saw the other man was looking at him. He felt sheepish, wondering if he'd been caught staring at the two women. He'd better chat up his host a bit.

"Everything okay at the plant, Kyle?"

"Not bad, really, but there's always problems. Today we caught a guy stealing. It makes me angry. I try so hard to treat these people well. We pay them a decent wage, give them more breaks then we have to according to Mexican law, and try to make them feel part of a team, but there are still too many that want to take advantage of it. It just burns me sometimes, and today was one of those days."

"It seems that you deal with some of the same kind of people I do. Thugs and thieves. You know, I've never been to the plant. Why don't you take me sometime. I'd like to see the operation." Jason envisioned a dark, dirty warehouse, hot as hell and filled with the sweaty stench of too many bodies and not enough air.

"Sure, but it's not very glamorous. Just your typical production oriented industry."

"Machine or manpower driven?" *Not glamorous, that's an understatement!*

"We use machines for some things, but we mostly rely on local craftsman to design and build the products, and we employ a lot of women to do the assembly, cleaning and packing. As you know, the labor market is good and cheap here, that's one of the reasons I'm in Mexico. Of course, being near the warm Pacific is a bonus for a fisherman like me too. If you're really interested, I'll take you to the plant next time you come to visit."

"Sounds good. Now let's hear about those fishing trips!"

Later that night, after returning from dinner and enjoying more cocktails on the veranda, Jason and Janet said goodnight to their hosts and retired to their bedroom. The room was equipped with a CD player and Jason found some soft rhythm and blues just right for this evening. He turned the music on low and turned the lights way down. Janet lit some candles, and the room was quickly filled with the subtle fragrance of lilac. A light breeze coming through the open windows caused the flames to dance, reminding them of their first encounter. Janet loved candles, and rarely spent an evening without one kind or another sending a warm, sensuous glow throughout her own home. The mood set, their eyes met and locked. They watched each other undress, and moved into a comfortable embrace.

Jason could still smell the fresh scent of sea mist and tropical flowers in her hair, and he thought this was as close to paradise as he would ever get. They made love slowly, savoring each moment and imprinting it into their minds so they could remember it forever. They held each other like it was the first and the last time combined, with the excitement and freshness of a new relationship tempered with a past of broken promises and fleeting loves lost. When they finished, they lay in each other's arms, breathless and completely spent. It was several minutes before either spoke.

"Jesus, Sweetheart," Jason said in a low, raspy voice. Even his mouth and lips were sluggish, exhausted from kissing and licking and sucking each and every part of her lithe, moist body. "I didn't think it could get better than our first time together, but you were just incredible. I've got nothing left."

She smiled broadly, and sunk even deeper into his inviting warmth. She couldn't get close enough to him, no matter how hard she pressed against his flesh. She would have climbed inside him if she could, and remembered screaming with delight a few minutes ago when he penetrated her and thrust deeply in a slow, arrhythmic pace, causing her almost unbearable anticipation as she waited for the next tantalizing stroke. It was too hard to resist, and at one point she had reached behind him and pulled him deep into her, holding him so he couldn't withdraw.

When they came together she had wrapped both her arms and legs around his hard, lean body, and held him as tight as she could, feeling wave after wave of shuddering orgasm envelop her being. Her ability to see and hear faded as her other senses peaked, soaking in the touch, sound, and smell of their lovemaking. She was also drained, and her throat was dry.

"Sweetheart," she echoed when she could finally speak again, loving that he called her that and letting him know she felt the same. "Would you get us something to drink? My throat is parched."

"Great idea. Don't move, I'll be right back."

Jason pulled on a pair of shorts and padded out toward the kitchen. As he entered the dark living room, he heard muffled sounds. They were coming from the veranda. He walked toward the sounds, and recognized them as the same kind of moans and sighs that were coming from his room just a few minutes earlier. As he looked outside, his assumptions were confirmed. Kyle and Christine were making love. She was straddling him across one of the lounge chairs, her torso rising and falling as she rode him. He had a side view of the action, and could see them in profile, watching the muscles of her legs ripple as she moved her body up and down, fucking her husband for all she was worth. The couple was backlit by the moonlit sky, and Jason could not divert his eyes from this unexpected sensation.

As he watched, Kyle buried his face in Christine's hair, kissing and nuzzling the nape of her neck. She turned her face to the side to give him more access, and her eyes fell upon Jason, standing transfixed at the edge of the veranda, just inside the open sliding glass doors. She smiled at him, and then leaned back from Kyle, stretching her upper torso as far back as she could while still mounting him. Her breasts were pulled taunt, and Jason could see the dark tufts of hair down where the couple was joined together. He turned away, embarrassed but stimulated, and made his way into the kitchen where he quietly poured two glasses of orange juice.

Despite his recent activity, he felt a familiar stirring, and hoped Janet was ready for round two. As he turned around, gingerly balancing the drinks, he saw Janet standing in the same spot he'd just left, looking out at the veranda. She saw his look of surprise and extended her hand for him to join her. She took one of the glasses from his hand, turned her head to watch the couple once more, and then led Jason back into their room. No one slept much that night.

Jason walked up three floors to the offices of the county drug task force. Its headquarters were located on the top floor of a nondescript brick building in Norristown, the county seat of Montgomery County. There were no signs indicating the presence of the task force, and no one would get any ideas of the office's true nature by watching the bedraggled, sometimes unkempt occupants climb the stairs. These would be the detectives of the Montgomery County District Attorney's Drug Task Force. They were a force of about 20 detectives and narcotics officers from around the county. Eight of them were county detectives, in the employ of the D.A. The other dozen were officers from different municipalities around the county, on loan from their own police departments to work on the county's drug problems. Their duties entailed surveillance, backup details, and undercover work. They also partnered with the Pennsylvania State Police, the Pennsylvania Attorney General's Office, the U.S. Drug Enforcement Agency, and the FBI, depending upon the needs of the investigation and the target. Jason had done a one-year stint with this group several years ago before he was promoted, and had some appreciation for the gritty work they did. It wasn't something he had wanted to do for long. The targets were too slimy, and he felt dirty being immersed in their world for any length of time. It took a special breed to be a narcotics investigator.

He was breathing hard by the time he got to the small third floor landing. He had gotten back from Mexico late the night before, and needed sleep badly. He felt funny coming here, especially after leaving Kyle and Christine's villa only twelve hours ago. Now he was about to have an investigation launched with Kyle and one of his businesses as the main targets. Probably, if something was going on at the gym, Kyle had no knowledge of it. After all, steroid use was commonplace wherever serious athletes trained. Nevertheless, it was possible that he was involved, and Jason would do well to keep this in mind. But at this point, there was no need to break up their friendship. He would just have to keep the investigation secret, and hope his friend would understand when it was all over. Who knows, Kyle might appreciate what he did, especially if the investigation proved he was running a clean place.

Jason pushed open a glass door into a six-foot square vestibule, and faced what appeared to be an ordinary, well-worn wooden door. It was in fact a solid steel door and frame with a wood façade, designed to protect the police officers inside should embattled drug lords ever discover the office's true purpose and plan an assault. Besides the fortified door, Jason was aware that he had been watched by closed circuit cameras from the time of initial entry into the building. He also knew that sensitive eavesdropping devices picked up the sound of his voice, or any other noise he made. He paused at the door.

"Lt. Coulter, here to see Bill Ramos," he said into thin air. He heard a metallic click and pulled on the handle of the door. It swung open noiselessly, and he entered the Task Force headquarters. The inside was almost as dull as the outside, only cleaner. It had the look of a time worn military outpost, with hand-me-down scarred wooden desks and dark paneling on the walls. There were a few official photos that passed as decoration, and the rugs were fairly new, a commercial variety, beige of course. The rugs were the only improvement made since he had worked here six years ago. The offices were neat, however, and the Spartan look contributed to the military feel of the place. This atmosphere was no accident either. For the past twelve years, the Task Force had been commanded by Lieutenant Anthony D. Broscolli, an ex-marine colonel who spent twenty years with the Drug Enforcement Agency and had joined the D.A.'s office when he retired. He put up with the disheveled look of his investigators, which he could justify as being necessary for the work they did, but he insisted on a clean, orderly, no-frills office.

Jason was greeted by the secretary, a young woman whom he didn't recognize, and then he saw Detective Ramos coming down the hallway.

"Jason, its great to see you again, buddy. How long has it been?"

"Its been four years since I worked here, but I'll tell you, coming up those stairs and through that door, it feels like just a few months. And it doesn't feel too good either," Jason laughed and shook his head as he spoke.

Bill Ramos knew Jason didn't enjoy narcotics work, which was a natural fit for Ramos. He was Jason's alter ego. Jason was always very well groomed, dressed fastidiously, and kept his small home so clean it looked like a model in a new development, complete with furniture that never got used. Ramos, on the other hand, always sported a three day growth of beard, wore jeans and one of four sweatshirts he owned, and lived in a trailer in one of the most rural sections of the county. Ramos loved narcotics work, and got his biggest thrills from going undercover during prolonged investigations. He was part of an exchange program the county had with other cities and counties, where a "fresh" face was needed for these types of investigations. He estimated that he spent about seven months every year assisting other police agencies. As they walked into his office Jason saw the bulletin board Ramos had put up when he started with the District Attorney's office ten years ago. On it he had placed the shoulder patch from every police department he had worked with, and there were almost fifty pinned to it so far.

He poured himself a cup of coffee, and lifted the pot toward Jason. Jason waved him off and took a seat on the beat up sofa, which he suspected Bill often used for a bed. He sunk low in the tired cushions.

"I know you didn't come here for the coffee, or just to see your old friend," Ramos said. "So what can I do for you?"

"I'm not quite sure, Bill. We've got a bit of a situation in Highland Park, and I'm kind of caught up in it personally. Not anything illegal or unethical, just a little too close, if you know what I mean."

He knew he was not explaining himself well, but felt better when he saw Bill nodding his head. He told him all about the reports of steroid use at the Apex, and his suspicions that the club might be supplying its patrons with the product. He also told him about Kyle, and how he had befriended him during his daughter's kidnapping investigation. Of course, he left out the more sordid details of their relationship. Ramos remained quiet until he had finished speaking.

"Really, Jason, that's not much to go on. A hit and run suspect who admits using steroids, a gym patron who tested positive in a hospital lab test, and locker room conversation where one jock tells another how to go about getting some Nandrolone. Doesn't really make an epidemic, nor does it necessarily establish a link to Kyle Price if that's what worries you."

"I know, but I *sense* something is there. Besides, if I don't check it out and something turns up later, it won't look good for me, being friends with him and all. Can you help me?"

"Sure, I'll do it next week. I'll get one of those trial memberships to the club, and nose around a bit myself. If there is a connection to the club, or to Price, I should be able to get a whiff pretty quickly."

"Thanks, I really appreciate it."

"It will cost you, you know! Remember what I want?"

Jason did. Ramos wanted an officer from Highland Park assigned to the task force. The department hadn't sent anyone for a couple years. It was about time they coughed up some help.

"What's Calloway doing these days?" Ramos was trying to get Jason to commit. He knew about Cab's splendid record as a narcotics officer, and would bust a nut to get him. Jason on the other hand, was scared that Cab might start to like the work again, and he would lose his partner and best friend to the County.

"We'll talk, Bill. We'll talk," he replied with a sly smile. *Not in a million years*, Jason thought to himself, as he shook the detective's hand and left the office.

Chapter 15

Detective Ramos was amazed at the scope of the Apex Health and Fitness
Center. He wandered around the building, taking in the various high tech
machinery and the glitz and glitter of the décor . . . and the people. For him,
walking the dog nightly and an occasional stroll down the country lanes near his
home passed as an aerobic workout, and he kept his muscles taunt by a daily
regimen of push-ups and crunches. This place was too much. Men and women in
designer garb strapping themselves into various black and chrome apparatus.
There were pulleys, and springs, and levers and cams. Each machine worked a
different body part, and it seemed to Ramos that there were enough pieces to
pull, push, stretch, and compress every muscle in the human body, and then
some. He was relieved to see a row of treadmills and rowing machines lined up
on the outside perimeter of one cavernous room. They were not like the vintage
machines he had used in his twenties, but at least he knew what they were
supposed to do, and figured he could stick to a basic routine during his
investigation and not draw any attention to himself.

He strode over to one of the treadmills, surveying the blinking electronic
lights of its controls. He hopped on, and read the directions three times before
successfully starting the motion. Fortunately, he was naturally athletic, and had
no problem keeping up with the program he had set. He jogged in pace to the
revolving deck of the machine, and after settling into a smooth steady rhythm,
began to systematically scan the room. It was late afternoon, and the gym was
pretty sparsely populated. But looking out the massive picture windows into the
parking lot, he could see cars pulling onto the lot, and patrons emerging with
gym bags in hand. It wouldn't be long until they were lined up waiting for some
of the popular exercise machines, and there would be a steady flow of women
heading toward the next aerobics class. Ramos searched for burly men who
might be likely steroid users. There were a few possibilities on this main floor,
including a very large man working the pec deck with an intensity only seen in

serious lifters. Although he was big, his muscles lacked that "cut up" look sought by bodybuilders, and his shoulder and trapezoids were more like those developed by weightlifters who pushed and pulled heavy poundage for just a few repetitions. This contrasted with the style of the bodybuilders, who usually lifted less weight, but performed many repetitions to build definition into their physique as well as increasing their strength.

Mostly however, this part of the gym appealed to the more moderate crowd, whose goal was to tone their body and look buff. This was the room that Jason told him would smell a bit like sex. He also said this was the best location to people watch. And he was right. This was not bad duty at all, Ramos thought, as he watched a steady stream of young women stride past the rows of exercise equipment and enter one of the aerobics studios. He had not seen such a spectacle since he was on that nude beach in Jamaica. Many of the women were very attractive, and very fit. They were not wearing the old gray sweat suits he was used to seeing at the police academy gym. Instead, he saw a variety of skintight lycra, spandex bodysuits, some of them cut high and low to display the wearers most prominent features. With all these distractions, he almost forgot the strain and breathlessness he was feeling as he tried to keep up with the tortuous treadmill. It wasn't hard for his imagination to kick in as he unconsciously licked his lips. In fact, he almost forgot his purpose for being here, but a loud grunt from the guy using the peace deck brought him back to reality. The plates dropped an inch, ending with a huge clang as the man pushed himself off the small bench and rose to his feet. Ramos whistled silently. He's at least six foot five, and must weigh about two hundred and sixty pounds. He's as big as Cab, and looks just as strong too.

Ramos watched as the big man collected his towel and walked toward the free-weight room. This was the part of the Apex where the serious lifters hung out. It was like a jock fraternity. A lot of men felt like outsiders if they entered this room. All eyes turned to newcomers, sizing up each one and determining if they really belonged. Men in here lifted by the ton. They used the Olympic style bars and forged iron plates that were hung on heavy welded racks and also strewn about the lifting platforms and benches around the large open room. From outside this part of the gym, members could often hear the grunts, groans, and muffled shouts of men pushing themselves to the limit. This place was anything but pretty, and Ramos would be lying if didn't admit that it didn't smell so good either. Nonetheless, the detective jumped off the treadmill and followed the big guy. The room was big, like its inhabitants. Mirrors lined three of the walls, reflecting people and equipment and making the room appear even larger than it was. The big man was wandering around the room, shaking hands and being clapped on the back by the dozen or so men working out here. They were calling his name, Ivan. Ramos grabbed a couple of twenty-five pound dumbbells and began pressing them overhead. He faced the mirrors and could watch Ivan's reflection as he settled down at one of the bench pressing stations and started to work in with a couple of other brawny men. Obviously, Ivan was a regular here, and from the way the others treated him, a well-respected weightlifter. He watched Ivan as he lay down on the bench and reached for the bar overhead. Two of his buddies stood on either side of the bench, ready to help if he needed it. Ramos tried to count the amount of weight on the bar. Three of the biggest plates were on each side, and one more moderately sized plate also. A quick check of a nearby rack holding a stack of assorted size plates gave him his answer. The large plates weighed forty-five pounds apiece, and the smaller plates were twenty-five pounders. Ramos knew that the seven-foot bar itself weighed forty-five pounds, so Ivan was attempting to bench press three hundred and sixty five pounds. And press it he did, about twelve times. The weight went up and down like a broom handle, and Ramos soon learned that this was just a warm-up for Ivan. This man could be his link to a steroid connection at the club, and Ramos tried to blend in while he waited for Ivan to finish his routine.

He followed Ivan to the locker room, being careful to keep his distance. Ivan walked toward one of the many rows of lockers, placed his towel and oversized gym bag down on a bench, and twirled the dial of the combination lock on the one he was using. Ramos dropped his own bag on a bench at the edge of the same section of lockers, quickly peeled off his sweats, and headed straight for the showers. He was lathering up in one of the stalls when Ivan entered. The big man, in all his naked glory, was a sight to behold. While not a classic bodybuilder, he had the "V" shape envied by most men. His huge shoulders were one of his outstanding features. They were wide and thick, with his beefy trapezoid muscles connected almost directly to his head. His shoulders were capped at each end by a massive deltoid, a rotund mound of muscle and bone as big as a softball. The effect was nothing short of Herculean, and although he felt somewhat chagrined to be looking at a naked man this way, Ramos was duly impressed by the dimensions and proportions of Ivan's body. He figured him to be about thirty-five, but the effect of gravity had not yet taken hold. Ivan's stomach was not flat, but was trim and hard, and the muscles of his abdomen could be seen tensing as the big man moved and twisted. Ramos finished showering, and went back to the lockers to dress, moving slowly so he could still be there when Ivan emerged from the shower. He greeted the still dripping man as he passed Ramos' locker and engaged him in small talk as they dressed, being careful not to overdue it during this first contact. He just wanted the big man to start to recognize him, and start to feel comfortable around him. Ramos asked him about his lifting routine, and for some suggestions on improving his own strength, and Ivan was pleased to respond, even jotting down some details of an exercise sequence he would recommend Ramos follow to get the results he wanted.

Little did he know it, but Ivan was about to become Ramos' confidential informant. He was using the big fellow to gain entrance into the world of weightlifting and bodybuilding at the Apex. This would lead to the discovery of any underground steroid operation centered at the club, or would reveal that there was nothing of the sort happening. Either way, he would get the information he needed, and help out his friend Lt. Jason Coulter. It didn't take much time for his answer to arrive. Ramos started by learning more about Ivan, whose last name was Petrolovich, and who lived in Highland Park, close to the Apex. He was not a world class weightlifter, which Ramos had originally thought after seeing him perform, but had been a champion at the regional and state level. Ramos could only imagine the strength of those who rose to be national or world champions. They must be amazing. About three weeks into his investigation, he was at the gym, spotting Ivan on a bench press of four-hundred seventy five pounds, when another spotter asked Ivan about a drug called Dianabol, a popular performance enhancing steroid. The spotter was a gangly kid, big but lacking the proportions of most of the stronger lifters. He could not have been more than eighteen years old. Ivan replied, his voice low and heavy like a growl.

"Listen to me kid, don't fool around with that junk at your age. It might give your lifts a little boost, but the price is too much. Makes you mean and ugly too, like me. It also makes your balls shrivel and your dick soft. You want that?"

The kid looked terrified. All of a sudden he wanted to be anywhere but here. He looked around, searching for a quick way out if needed. The huge man was still looking at him, expecting a reply. The kid gulped, his Adams apple bulging noticeably. He hoped the words came out as he struggled to speak.

"Ah, no sir, not the soft dick part anyway. But I do want to be stronger."

"Well then, watch this," Ivan said, and reached for the bar. He took three deep breaths, lifted the bar unassisted off the rack, and lowered it slowly to his massive chest. When it just touched his chest he exploded upward, pushing the weight for all he was worth. The bar rose, hesitated a bit a foot away from completion, then rose again as Ivan's face turned red and his arms began to quiver. He locked his arms, and Ramos and the kid assisted him in racking it. He sat up, exhaling deeply.

"That was a drug free lift," He told the kid, looking directly at him with just a hint of a scowl. "It's also as far as I'll probably get, I've pretty much reached my potential. If I wanted to go further, I might have to consider using something. But I got this far without it."

"So why don't . . . " The kid started to talk, but Ivan cut him off.

"So why don't you wait until you reach *your* potential before even considering taking something that may alter your personality and shrivel your dick? When and *if* you get to that point, then make the decision. But you've got a long way to go before you have to make that call."

The kid walked away, nodding his head slightly, but without commitment.

"That was some speech," Ramos said, his admiration for Ivan rising. He was surprised by the big man's expression of concern for the kid.

"Shit, just trying to do him a favor. Look at the kid. He doesn't have it anyway, he won't get to the stage where steroids will help much. Why risk screwing up your life if you're not going anywhere near the top?"

"Still, it was good of you to say what you did."

"I ain't no saint, and I lied about the steroids. I did take them, a long time ago when I still had hopes of making the Olympic team." He got up and started taking plates off the bar. Ramos helped him.

"How do you get them anyway," Ramos said, realizing he had an opportunity developing here. "Is there a place around here?"

"Sure, you can get them easy, practically anywhere. That kid could-and may buy some stuff despite what I told him. But buying them on the street adds to the risk. You never really know what you're getting. Most of the stuff is marked, but just like other drugs, steroids are not hard to counterfeit."

"What could a serious lifter do to make sure he was getting the right stuff?"

"Know your supplier, of course. Find someone you trust, someone with connections, and tap into their source. Still risky, but a lot less so."

"Is that what you did when you took it?" Ramos wanted to push this as far as he could. He knew this might be his best opportunity for awhile to learn what he needed, and he had already invested several weeks into this investigation. He couldn't spend much more time on this one, there were cases piling up on his desk in Norristown. For some reason, Ivan seemed to like him, and did not seem reticent talking to him about this subject. Actually he liked Ivan too, he was a pretty intelligent guy, and spoke his mind. He looked like a big, dumb ox, but like many stereotypes, he was anything but what your first impression indicated.

"Yep, and I never had a problem either. I bought it off the net, using a place recommended right here. Best I could find out, it was a Mexican company that sold it, since most steroids are legal there."

At the risk of being shut down completely, Ramos decided to go for the gold. "Who recommended it?"

Ivan laughed, and then focused his steely gaze on the investigator. "Why, are you thinking about trying some? Didn't you listen to what I just said? Hey, you're further away from needing them than that kid."

Ramos laughed also, breaking the tension. "Naa, just curious I guess. Forget I asked."

"I will tell you this much; the person was someone I trusted, and very close to this club, if you know what I mean."

Ramos was thinking about this when Ivan spoke again.

"And he doesn't do it for the money either."

Bingo. The source was right here at the Apex. He was halfway home. If he could find the supplier, Jason would owe him big time. Maybe he could finally get Cab as an undercover for a few years.

After Ramos obtained the lead from Ivan, it only took a few days to piece together the rest of the story. He called on the other club members who had tested positive for steroids at the hospital, and their information was enough to convince Ramos that somehow the Apex was connected to the use of steroids by club members. He was careful when he contacted the men whose names Janet had given Detective Jason Coulter, not wanting to implicate her or the hospital. He simply told the men they were named by sources as being steroid users, and the police were seeking their cooperation in this matter. It was inferred that if they cooperated, and kept their mouths shut about the ongoing investigation, they would have immunity from prosecution. It was all bullshit, of course, as police had no case against them. There was no evidence they could rely on, and using the information obtained from hospital records would not be admissible in court, and bordered on an ethics violation. But it worked. The men were willing to cooperate, fearing that exposure could complicate their lives, even without the threat of criminal charges. Both men gave Ramos the name of an internet site from which they purchased the drugs. Both of them told Ramos they got the name of the site from an Apex employee. One of them claimed the employee, whom he refused to identify, jotted down the name of the site on a piece of paper during a workout. From there, it was only a matter of time before the parts of the puzzle started to fit together. If the two club members kept their mouths shut like they were told, the detectives would have enough time to locate the site, find out where it was based, determine the storage and shipping points for the drugs, and put together a raid. It was a big "if" though, because people liked to talk. As soon as one of those two men mentioned that the police were questioning them about steroid use, it would be a short time until those involved were informed, and a cover-up would quickly commence. And in a small town like Highland Park, news of such an investigation would spread like wildfire.

Ramos, Jason, and Trooper John Woodson sat around a small conference table at Highland Park Police Headquarters. They were joined by Special Agent

Philip Kelly from the Philadelphia office of the U.S. Drug Enforcement Agency. Woodson was doing most of the talking.

"We logged on to the website where the steroids were reputed to have been obtained. Sure enough, it was a virtual online pharmacy for performance enhancing drugs. Steroids like Dianabol, Nandralone, and everything in between. The prices were good, according to our drug guys. They offer most of the items for less than the legitimate outlets here in the states."

"What do we do next," Jason asked. "How do we pinpoint where the stuff is coming from?"

"We place an order," Woodson continued, glancing at Agent Kelly. "Actually, we'll place several orders, using different credit cards the state police use for fraud investigations. Some of the orders we put through just like we were regular customers. Nothing special is done, and the orders should be handled without a problem on their end. The goods will be shipped to a cover location we designate. Once received, we try to trace the package back to the source through the shipper. For any of these businesses to be lucrative, they have to use commercial shippers, like Federal Express or UPS. Some even use the U.S. Postal Service."

"What if they use a dummy address? You know, like a vacant house where the bad guys stick some lackey to hand the package over to UPS. We trace it back, and come up empty . . . no one home."

"That's possible, Lt. Coulter, but even that scenario is time consuming and burdensome if the illicit company is dealing in volume. More probable is that there are *several* locations involved in this process, to make it difficult to trace back to the source of the product."

Jason noted Woodson's use of his formal title. The trooper also used the term "product," which was often used by narcotics agents when referring to drugs. No doubt, he was trying to impress the DEA agent with his knowledge. He was relishing his fifteen minutes of fame as a detective.

Woodson continued, once again glancing at Agent Kelly expectantly, looking for signs of agreement. Taking the cue, Kelly nodded his head approvingly.

"First, there will be a site to accept the customer's order. This may or may not include a series of pass-through routers that kick in before the order is actually picked up by the order-taker. Electronically speaking, of course. In the real world that would be like a series of couriers following circuitous routes before delivering the goods to the final destination. It's designed to throw off a tail."

Jason cocked his right eyebrow. He wondered if anyone else was having trouble following Woodson's analogy, not to mention the meaning of the word "circuitous."

"Then, the order will be passed on to a second site, which accepts payment, verifying the credit card information and putting the charge through. This site is usually a place that harbors a legitimate business as well as being a front for the drug sales. The most frequent type of business used for this is a mail order house, one where a number of products are inventoried, cataloged, and offered for sale. Today, many of these have websites, which dovetail nicely with the drug sale operation. The same technology and the same general techniques are used for both operations, so it's unlikely that anyone will suspect anything strange is going on. Finally, the order will be forwarded to the source, a warehouse if you will, and the drugs will be shipped."

"With that in mind, what's our next step?" Jason asked. The trooper started to speak, but Agent Kelly beat him to the punch, leaving Woodson with his mouth open and a finger lifted for emphasis.

"I've had some experience with this part," Kelly said. "Our next step is to place a few orders, attach a Trojan horse of our own to a couple of them, and see who gets the message. From there, we'll try and determine the source. Usually, the dealers will accept the order with the Trojan horse, and it sends back a message to us with information on the ISP and specific message identifier. From there, we contact the ISP and find out where *all* the computers involved are physically located. Piece of cake! However, if the operation is sophisticated enough, they'll have a expert on board to constantly update their virus detection software to scan for Trojan horses."

Woodson once again began to chime in, and this time it was Jason who cut him off.

"If the virus is detected, does that ruin the chance to find out the location of the drug warehouse?"

"It does complicate matters," Kelly said. "But that's why we also place a couple of orders the regular way, with no attachments. Hopefully, the operation does enough business that our regular orders blend in with tens or even hundreds of others, and they get processed and filled as usual. If the dealers get too spooked by their discovery of the Trojan horse though, we're screwed. They'll probably pack up and be moved within hours, long before we can pinpoint them and move in for the arrest."

"Maybe we should try to trace them using a regular order first," Ramos volunteered. "Once we get the product delivered to us, we can secure a search warrant and obtain the ISP customer identification, and move in from there."

"We could try that. But chances are that these dealers have things set up to stymie such an investigation. The info we get from the ISP company will likely lead to a dead end. Hitting a place and coming up with zilch will do nothing but alert the bad guys we're hot on the trail, and they'll scatter like cockroaches. With the Trojan horse in place, the virus we introduce will silently backtrack through their whole system, no matter how many relays or routers they have set to cover their tracks, and give us a record of everywhere it's been. From all that data, we'll be able to figure out which location is the source...the warehouse. I say let's go that route."

Jason considered Special Agent Kelly's plan. He looked at Woodson, who had become quiet and withdrawn since he was no longer leading the discussion. "John, what do you recommend?"

Woodson looked up slowly, his eyes brightening. He looked at each of the other men in turn, like a master making sure his proteges are ready to accept his sage advice. "I say let's go for it. I think my boys and I can sneak the virus past'em, and give you a chance to catch'em sleeping."

"Okay," said Jason, "that's it. I'll clear it through the chief, and then we'll get to work. Ramos, can I see you alone for a second?"

As the others left the room, Jason addressed Ramos in a low tone.

"Do you think Kyle Price is involved in this? It blows my mind that someone with his credentials would even have knowledge of this, let alone maybe be involved himself."

"Anything is possible, Jason. You know that. But I really would be surprised if Price knew anything about this. Why put his business reputation in jeopardy by selling steroids, or by allowing someone else to do it using his gym? Look at that place, it's a gold mine. I saw more socialites and business moguls working out there than I see at the annual Chamber of Commerce dinner. It's a good show, why chance ruining it?"

"Thanks, bud. I appreciate your opinion."

"You're welcome. But remember, just cause I say it doesn't make it so."

"Well, there's just one small problem with your idea." Chief Forestall said to Jason, who had come into the Chief's office to tell him about the plans he and the other police officers had made to interdict the steroid sales operation.

The Chief was not pleased about the idea of putting a virus into cyberspace. Joe Forestall was a 32-year veteran of the Highland Park Police Department, having risen through the ranks to become Chief almost 12 years ago. Like most chiefs, he had a well-worn appearance. His eyes had the look of someone who had seen too much too often, and although they showed signs of experience and wisdom, they no longer twinkled with excitement, or beamed with anticipation.

His years of law enforcement had greatly tempered the enthusiastic, optimistic attitude he had as a young recruit. He was only fifty-four years old, thought Jason, but many officers referred to him as "the old man," and Jason himself thought the Chief should be winding down, preparing for retirement. The Chief, however, had never talked about such a move. He continued to address his Lieutenant.

"Introducing this so-called Trojan horse raises Constitutional issues," he said. "It may even be a violation of the Pennsylvania Crimes Code. There have been a number of amendments recently dealing with such matters as they relate to computer fraud and destruction of data. We will need to get an opinion from the city attorney before we can proceed. We also need to get an opinion from the District Attorney about any requirement we may have to secure a search warrant before proceeding with this action. Remember, Pennsylvania law is a lot more restrictive than federal statutes."

"Yeah, maybe. But if we don't move soon, we could have another victim on our hands. What's worse?"

"It's not a question of what's worse. It's what's right. And even if you don't agree, it's the law. We have no choice but to comply. Besides, what if we move on this, get the guy, and lose it in court on a fourth amendment violation? The killer walks and we have to start over . . . with egg on our face."

The Chief was right, of course. In his zeal to investigate this case, Jason had completely forgotten to consider some very basic tenants of criminal procedure. He was surprised none of the other investigators had brought up the issue either. Maybe the old man was not yet ready to be put out to pasture.

Sure enough, a check with the District Attorney backed up the Chief's opinion. They could not introduce the invasive virus based on their current case. They needed just a bit more, maybe a statement from a purchaser who was willing to step forward and be named in the warrant. This individual would also have to be prepared to testify in court if necessary and that was going to be a problem in this case. Those persons who had purchased steroids were not the type to get involved publicly, and since the police had gotten their names through Janet's employment at the hospital, it would be foolish to even try. Janet's involvement in the somewhat unusual, if not borderline manner in which the police acquired the information would surely come out in court under the scrutiny of the defense attorney. This would more than likely get Janet fired, and severely impugn the image of the Highland Park Police Department. Nevertheless, Jason had no regrets regarding his decision to get the names of these men from hospital records. The stakes here were high, and unlike the Jason of years gone by, he firmly believed that in cases like these, the end justifies the means.

121

Chapter 16

"Cab, what's it like to be married?"

"Huh?"

"Married, I'm asking you what it's like."

Cab stopped poking the keyboard of his laptop and lowered his glasses to the tip of his nose. He peered at Jason with a quizzical look for what seemed like an eternity, but was only seconds.

"Does this have anything to do with a certain woman and a recent trip to Mexico?"

"Maybe. Just answer the question, will ya smart ass?"

"Since you asked me so politely, sure. It's kinda like this job." He leaned back in his chair and put both his hands behind his head, fingers clasped together. "What I mean is, it's mostly routine, at least after the first couple years. But there's always something ready to blow, just beneath the surface . . . if you're not careful."

"Interesting . . . I guess," Jason said, unconvinced.

He was hoping for more. Men don't usually talk about things like this, unless they were kidding, or unless they were couching such talk in euphemisms or stories of wild antics and fantasies. Anything that disguises the fact that they are reaching out to another man for some insight relating to matters of the heart. Serious stuff. The stuff of life fathers don't talk about to their sons or buddies over coffee or a few beers.

"You know how the first couple years you're fascinated by the job. It's new, exciting, and mysterious. All your senses are heightened, you try to take in everything; some of it makes sense, some it washes over you without really sinking in. All of it has an impact on what you become as you advance through your career, whether you realize it or not. If you're lucky, nothing will come your way that is too difficult to handle, or forces you to make a decision you're not yet ready to handle."

"You mean like coming face to face with a gunman holding a hostage on your first day?" Jason quipped out of habit.

"Sort of. Because something like that forces you to make a decision that could affect the rest of your career, or even your life. Same thing in marriage. An early crisis can create a chasm that will never be bridged."

"Or," said Jason, warming up, "it could result in an experience so intense and so shared that it cements the relationship, like shooting the hostage taker right between the eyes, and boinking the swooning babe hostage in the back of your patrol car!"

"Exactly, my perpetually horny friend." Cab smiled. He knew his friend was serious here, and that his humor was to make it appear as if he wasn't. Standard macho bullshit. Cab was happy that Jason may have found someone who he really cared about. He was also proud that his boss, and his friend, wanted to hear his advice.

"Your examples are way off, but you get the idea. If you make it the first couple of years, you start feeling comfortable. You know each other well, you learn about habits, you learn which triggers to pull and which to leave alone. Sometimes you work well *with* each other, other times it's best to work *around* each other. You compliment each other, begin to rely on each other's strengths, shore up each other's weaknesses. Most of the time this goes on subconsciously. You're too busy making a living and raising a family to dwell on it, it just happens."

"Sounds too good, you're not telling me the bad stuff."

"Oh, there's plenty of bad stuff. Like noticing a hundred things about your wife that bug the shit out of you, things you never noticed before, or never mattered before the big commitment, but seem very important now."

"That's it! Here we go," Jason interjected gleefully.

"Like stopping the world for awhile and really thinking about your life. Did you make the right decisions, is she really the love of your life? Is there something more for you out there someplace? That's dangerous stuff, cause you may not like the answers you give yourself. And if you don't, you got problems. You only got two choices then, and both of them are bad."

"And they are . . . "

"They involve a major change either way. You leave, start over, which I think would be frightening for most of us, to say the least. Or you stay, reconcile yourself to the fact that you will live life unfulfilled at best, maybe miserable. Not pleasant."

"You and Shawna . . . you two seem to have this marriage thing down pat. True?" Jason was surprised at himself for asking such a personal question, and was even more surprised at Cab's instantaneous response.

"True," The big man said quietly but firmly, in a way that meant business. He leaned forward, and Jason did the same. Unconsciously, Jason looked from side to side, like he was about to get some important information from an informant, and wanted to make sure no one was eavesdropping. Cab continued.

"In the deep of the night when we're sleeping, when the loudest sound is the rhythmic breathing of two souls who share one space, I'll awaken and look at her. Her sweet, sweet face pressed against her pillow, strands of tousled hair against her cheek. I look at the shape of her mouth, framed by full, sensuous lips. I look at the shape of her eyebrows, the slight arch that makes her have a slightly quizzical expression that intrigued me from the very first time I laid eyes on her. It gives her a cynical look, and thinking back on it, maybe the cop in me appreciated that. I look at her smooth cocoa skin, the way her nose brings singular beauty to the face that is uniquely Shawna. And as I watch her sleep, the comforting rise and fall of her chest as she breathes, I think about how much a part of me she has become, and if I'm lucky, will always be. It wasn't always that way, my friend. We had tough times like most other couples, but I think we always knew we would make it work. And we did. I love Shawna like you wouldn't believe and I'd soon as cut off my right arm then lose her for an instant. And that's no bullshit."

Wow! That was pretty amazing. Jason had never heard his partner talk this way. Jason thought about his only true relationship. He remembered the time they went to Ocean City and stayed in a beachfront motel. He had been so enamored with her that his whole world seemed to revolve around being with her. One night he found himself watching her as she slept. He stared at her for what seemed like hours, until suddenly she opened her eyes and smiled sweetly at him. She wasn't startled at all to find another person staring at her in the dead of night, like she'd known she was being watched the whole time. He wondered now whether that was the feeling Cab was talking about now, or was it just lust. He wasn't sure at the time, and he still wasn't. He looked over at Cab, who was still leaning back in his chair with a smug look on his face, like he'd just given Jason some pearl of wisdom. *Can't let him get away with that!*

"You know, that was really nice. Thanks for sharing. I do have one question though, being the ace detective I am."

"Okay, Ace, what's the question. You want to know if you can have the same thing?"

"With Shawna? Man, you're sick. No, I was wondering how you could see all this in the deep of the night, wasn't it dark in there?"

"Shithead! I pour my life out to you and you think about some stupid question like that. Nightlight! We keep a little nightlight on in case we have to pee. Which, by the way, is happening more often lately, something to do with age no doubt."

"Now I understand, it's not love that wakes you up and prompts you to wax philosophical in the middle of the night, its your bladder calling. I knew there was a more logical reason for your alleged insight."

"Fuck you and your pasty white ass."

He was not like other killers. He didn't take trophies . . . items to remember his victims and to relive the excitement of the kill. He didn't have a favorite method of murder, other than evoking sheer terror from his victims as they realized his intent and then slipped away into death's grasp. If he did have a signature, he guessed it would be stealing their privacy, which he did well in advance of the actual killing. This is what set him apart, his ability to learn so much about his intended prey without any of the in-the-flesh risks usually associated with stalking a victim. He would know everything there is to know before he met them. It was easy for him. The random scanning of data packets flying all over the country through thousands of internet providers was like shooting fish in a barrel. His "eavesdropping" program searched billions of bytes of information looking for certain combinations of words and phrases that indicated a possible subject. When one was identified, the unique source was identified and captured, and the virus was injected into the victim's computer. The virus was quite intrusive and did not necessitate the victim opening up an email attachment or any such overt act. It attached itself to an incoming data packet and rode into their system unnoticed. Once in the operating system, the virus mutated into the mirroring software that would now relay every incoming and outgoing message to his computer. Simple when you know how.

He had misspent his youth locked in his room with his computers. Countless hours were spent exploring the possibilities of the virtual world. He learned quickly, obviously having an innate talent for this technology. For a full year, he had held down a job in a bookstore, and stole just about every book about computers in the inventory. He also had a variety of jobs with Radio Shack, a couple of independent computer outlet stores, and an electronic repair shop. He used these jobs to refine his skills and learned even more about the principles and practicalities that would solidify his abilities as an ace hacker....a master at this game.

Even so, it took countless hours to scan, read and develop the leads necessary to find the kind of women who piqued his curiosity. He spent four to six hours a day trying to find women worth pursuing, and he could spend months in fruitless searches. Although the frustration was great at times, the thrill of finding the one woman in a thousand who excited him was a necessary part of his existence. It started when he was thirteen, after a teacher in middle school took an interest in him and began to teach him about computers. He took to it immediately, and the teacher arranged for him to get a used computer that was donated to the school so any needy children could learn computer skills. Although the computer itself was little more than yesterday's technology, he explored every facet of the new world it opened up for him. He soon became more proficient than his instructor and was able to take his computer apart and make it more powerful. Once he started working for Radio Shack, parts became easy to get and he began to build his own machines. They were just as fast and capable as the major brands, and he was getting a reputation as a wizard at age sixteen.

But he had a darkside, and he saw his unique skills as a way to get things denied to him in the past. He quickly learned how gullible people were, especially those that floundered around on the net making purchases, bidding on items offered by online auctions, and sending money to complete strangers whose true names and addresses were unknown and undiscoverable by the average person.

His second chance for salvation came during his second year at college. He had survived a disastrous freshman year, both academically and socially. That first year, he'd taken all the required subjects he could, hoping to get them out of the way before his enthusiasm for school wore off. However, they proved to be too much for him. He simply couldn't generate any interest in these courses, and he almost flunked math and economics. He barely escaped with two "D" grades, which he knew were gifts from professors who felt sorry for him. Worse yet, he just didn't fit in, and had a hard time making friends, even with the other so-called computer nerds. He wasn't openly ridiculed or anything, so it wasn't as bad as high school, but he wasn't included either.

He stuck it out though, knowing he'd been through worse in his life, and looking forward to the computer classes he would begin in his sophomore year. Sure enough, things got much better. He loved the three computer-based courses he was taking, and he had met Carol. She was a pretty blond with a slim yet curvaceous body. She had a laugh that came easy, and eyes that seemed to exclude all else when she focused on him. He fell for her immediately, and she seemed interested in him too. He met her in a class on web design, where she sat at the next terminal. Carol was amazed at his prowess, and marveled at the intricate designs and complicated links that stymied most of their classmates, but came so easily to him. She called him her little genius and he responded by batting his eyes rapidly at her and smiling broadly. It was the most human he'd ever been. For the first time since his mother's friend Jack had spent time with him, he was in a relationship that felt good. More significantly, he thought, it was a positive relationship with a female. He hoped it would wipe out the memories of the many years of abuse he suffered at the hands of his mother. He had even showed Carol a crude version of what would become the intricate virus capable of intercepting personal data flying around cyberspace, and tracing it back to the originating P.C. He remembered her looking at him in awe as he explained how it worked, telling her it would then mirror everything a person did on their computer. She began to call him "Mirror Man." He liked that, it was kind of like a pet name, something real lovers gave each other as a sign of their affection.

For over a year, the relationship flourished. They got together several times a week, and he was feeling pretty good about her, and about himself. It had been a long time since he felt this way about anyone, and this was the first serious relationship he'd ever had with a woman, except for his mother. Things were right on course he thought, until the day along Burnside Hall when he was walking on campus and turned the corner toward the student union. He saw her standing not ten feet way, talking to Brad Stewart, a student he recognized but didn't personally know. Brad was a starting linebacker on the football team, and he felt his stomach suddenly turned upside down. He quickly turned around and walked away, hoping Carol would not see him. He went back behind Burnside, then went into the building and walked to a rear window, a position where he could watch the two of them without being seen. He watched them for fifteen minutes, which he knew because he carefully timed them, and continued watching as they said goodbye and parted, walking in opposite directions. There was no touching, nor did he see a flirtatious look or a big smile.

Although it seemed an innocent encounter, it was the beginning of the end between him and Carol. Later that same day, he caught up to her in her dorm room, and casually he began to ask her a few questions about her day, trying to see if she'd tell him about meeting with Brad. If she talked about it openly, then it didn't mean much, just a passing encounter between students. But when she didn't mention it, he became suspicious. It never occurred to him that she might not mention it because it meant nothing, that the brief encounter was already forgotten. His questions began to intensify, and soon Carol was the subject of a full-fledged interrogation. From that point on, she saw him in a different light, and began to withdraw from him. This behavior only made him think the worst, and he stepped up his efforts to track her every move. Following her was risky and proved harder than he thought. However, there was a way to keep tabs on her that was risk-free, and undetectable. Using every bit of knowledge he had gleaned, he went to work. Mirror Man was born.

Chapter 17

Jason drove through light traffic on his way to appear at the preliminary hearing for Ben Dickson. As the detective of record, he was expected to act as the prosecutor for the case and present the evidence necessary to have the matter bound over for common pleas court. Since Dickson had admitted to driving the vehicle that had struck and killed Anna Cuzzi on her way home from church, there shouldn't be any problem. Pennsylvania law requires that prosecutors present a *prima facia* case at the preliminary hearing held in a district court. Prima facia is a Latin phrase that roughly translated means "at first glance." Theoretically, only two items have to be proven for the case to move forward at this step in the judicial process. First, the State must prove that the crimes specified in the criminal complaint have been committed. Second, the State must present enough evidence to demonstrate that the accused *probably* committed the crimes for which he is being charged. The burden of proof in the district court is not nearly as severe as in the County Court of Common Pleas, where it must be proven beyond a reasonable doubt that the defendant is guilty. Sometimes cases were dismissed at the District Justice level, but it was pretty rare in Montgomery County, because most cops only brought good cases to court. When they were dismissed, it was usually because the District Justice, of which there are twenty-five in the county, went beyond the scope of his or her duties. Some of the local District Justices tended to regard themselves as full-fledged judges rather than as preliminary arraignment and screening officials.

Their main purpose is to insure the defendant's initial procedural rights were followed, including the right to bail, and the right to be informed of the charges against them. At the preliminary hearing, many of them act like Supreme Court jurists, listening to lawyers argue fine points of law and make accusations about evidence collection and statements that should be ruled on by the higher court. Too often they go way beyond their responsibility to insure the prosecutors present a *prima facia* case. What makes this practice even more trying for the local police is that the arresting officers often stand in for the District Attorney and serve as the prosecutors in all but the most serious cases, mostly felonies like rape and murder. Police officers present the evidence needed to bind over the defendant, including the questioning and cross-examination of victims and witnesses. They have to deal with the objections made by defense attorneys and raise their own objections when warranted. Virtually all defendants at these proceedings are represented by attorneys. If they are indigent, unable to pay for their own lawyer, the county is required to appoint one to represent them from a list of qualified local lawyers who agree to do this for a moderate fee paid ultimately by the county's taxpayers.

Often, these attorneys will take advantage of the police officers by barraging the Court with case citations, and trend setting precedents. Another favorite tactic was to constantly raise objections to testimony. All of these, in Jason's opinion, are attempts to fluster the police and impress the District Justice with their superior legal prowess and diligent case preparation. Since District Justices are not required to possess a law degree, and are former teachers, businessmen, and tradesmen who qualified for the job by winning an election and passing a three-month course, the ploys often worked. This leads to frustration for the police and others on the side of the law, and serves to add to the woes of an already overburdened justice system.

The Highland Park police decided years ago to deal with these tactics by assigning an experienced detective to handle all felony and many serious misdemeanor cases at the preliminary hearing stage. The detectives usually appeared in court much more often than patrol officers, and were involved in investigating and testifying in more complex and serious cases, thus increasing their knowledge of court procedures. After a little while, Highland Park detectives became very proficient at prosecuting, exceeding the ability of many new assistant district attorneys and even outshining some of the local defense attorneys. Since instituting this practice, Highland Park rarely lost a case in front of a District Justice, and several other departments followed suit. Jason had started this initiative and was proud of the record he and the other detectives had amassed since it started.

As a Lieutenant, he no longer regularly presented cases in court, but was looking forward to today's hearing. He had spent several hours getting the facts and testimony he wanted to present in order and even jotted down a checklist of evidence and information he wanted the District Justice to hear. The judge presiding today was Walter Quincy. Walter used to be a schoolteacher, and after presiding over the fourth grade for fifteen years, he decided to do something a little less challenging. He was raised on Perry Mason reruns, and spent much of his spare time as a committeeman for the Republican Party in Montgomery

County. It was this combination of experience and skill that he thought qualified him to sit on the bench, and the people of his district apparently agreed, for he won the election in a landslide. Of course, his democratic opponent, a local plumber, did not have the same "outstanding breadth of experience" as Walter's campaign ads related, so the populace voted for the less incompetent candidate. The voters had elected him into office four years ago for a six-year term, and Walter had learned just enough in those four years to make himself an obnoxious boor to all who appeared before him. The Court had a full docket today, and the small waiting room was packed, resembling a doctor's office during flu season. Jason recognized a couple of Highland Park P.D.'s regular customers waiting for their court appearance. He nodded to Judy, one of the clerks who kept things running in a relatively timely manner. She was standing behind a counter that separated the waiting area from the court office. Judy was a long time county employee who had worked for three District Justices. She chided Jason for being "late as usual," and told him the rest of the police officers, the defendant, and the defense attorneys were already in the courtroom.

He walked down a narrow corridor that led to the courtroom. Inside, he saw that besides the regular players, the victim's son and daughter were seated in the rear. There were also a couple of what Jason assumed were grandchildren present and a woman seated on the other side of the room who Jason did not recognize. Although he had told them they did not have to come for this initial hearing, he was glad to see them. The presence of grieving family members tended to insure that everyone played by the rules. Sometimes friendship between officers of the court or reputations of attorneys could affect the rulings of the District Justice. Even if nothing out of the ordinary was afoot, courtroom demeanor was more proper when interested relatives and friends of heinous crime victims were seated in the courtroom. Since all court hearings were open to the public, it was unusual but not unheard of that disinterested citizen decided to wander in and observe the criminal justice system at work. Most often, such observers were middle or high school students fulfilling the requirements for a civics class, and given his background, District Justice Quincy encouraged their attendance. He always saved his best performances for them, especially when one of his former colleagues was present to monitor their students. However, despite his best efforts, Walter Quincy's courtroom rarely resembled an episode of Perry Mason. Jason liked it when the proceedings were formal and proper. It seemed to him that was the way American justice should be conducted. He hated when the sanctity of any courtroom was degraded to a good ole' boy's backroom study.

Before heading for the prosecutors assigned table, Jason stopped briefly to acknowledge Mrs. Cuzzi's relatives and went over to the defense table to shake hands with the attorney representing Dickson. His name was Matthew Pitts. Pitts was almost sixty, and had spent almost his entire career with the Montgomery County District Attorney's Office as a prosecutor. He went there fresh out of law school at the University of Delaware, and had risen through the ranks to become the Chief of the Trials Division before retiring at age fifty-five. Since then, he opened a small private firm that practiced general law, and had offices in Highland Park and Norristown. He employed four other lawyers. Once in awhile Pitts showed up defending a client in a criminal case, and he was still a force with whom to be reckoned.

He returned Jason's handshake vigorously, and they exchanged a few memories about their former roles as assistant district attorney and street cop. Officer Stowart and Detective Paul Patterson, who had respectively investigated the accident and interviewed Ben Dickson, were already seated at the prosecutor's table. Jason joined them, placing his briefcase on the table and taking the third and last available seat. He passed copies of his checklist to them, and whispered to Stowart that as the accident investigator, he would be called to testify first.

Shortly after, the District Justice entered the courtroom from a side door leading to his chambers, and took his seat behind the raised bench. The *bench*, court terminology for the large desk the judge sat behind as he presided over his courtroom, was a source of amusement for Jason. He had been in many courtrooms throughout the county, and even some out-of-state. He noted that there were vast differences in the type of bench judges selected, as well as a significant difference in how far they were raised above the floor of the courtroom. Some were simple and utilitarian, set only about a foot above the other seats in court, just enough so everyone could plainly see the judge. Others were very ornate, made of rich cherry and grossly oversized. Jason had seen benches as high as five feet above ground level, almost giving participants and onlookers neck strain as they craned their heads upward to see the high and mighty jurist. He firmly believed that there was a direct correlation between the height of the bench and the ego of the presiding judge. Quincy's bench was about three feet off the floor, which may not seem too ostentatious, but then he was only a District Justice, not a county judge.

Before the proceeding commenced, Jason noticed Ben looking over his shoulder at Anna Cuzzi's family. He was fidgety, wringing his hands together nervously. At one point, Pitts reached over and placed one of his hands over Ben's to get him to stop. Ben did cease for a few seconds but before long was once again casting furtive glances toward the back of the room and tapping his foot compulsively. Jason knew the family's presence was making Ben very uncomfortable, and figured that for the first time since the accident he was coming to grips with what he'd done. He was realizing that his actions not only caused the death of an innocent elderly woman, but had a profound impact on the lives of others who he had not faced until today. He also knew that Pitts would be silently cursing, because this type of behavior would be noticed by everyone, especially the judge, and would probably hurt any chance Ben had for a dismissal or lessening of charges. Sure enough, just before District Justice Quincy entered the courtroom, Pitts leaned close to his client and they spoke in hushed tones for a few seconds. Jason saw Ben shake his head up and down, seeming to agree with what his attorney was saying, and he lowered his head as the Judge entered and sat behind the bench. As soon as he was settled and had called this "matter before the court" to order, Pitts rose from the defense table and addressed the Judge.

"Your honor, my client has reconsidered his plea at this time, and would like a few minutes to conference with Lt. Coulter concerning our options before we proceed."

"Lt. Coulter, do have any objections to this?" the Judge asked.

"No your honor, I'll be pleased to meet with them."

Jason sensed a victory, not only in the case at hand, but perhaps also in his investigation of the steroid operation centered at the Apex. He was only too happy to oblige.

"All right, we will take a one hour recess. I have another hearing in one-half hour, and we'll reconvene after that one is through. Be ready to proceed by ten-thirty."

Jason told Officer Stowart to go get a cup of coffee or something, and asked Detective Patterson to accompany him to the small conference room available for these types of meetings. Of course, Stowart was more than glad to take the opportunity to grab breakfast on company time, and Jason didn't want to see his rolling eyes and exasperated grunts while they listened to what Pitts and his client had in mind. Patterson on the other hand, was most knowledgeable about the case, and was savvy enough to interject only when his information would help Jason get what he wanted from the defense. Pitts and Ben followed the detectives into the conference room and shut the door. When they were all seated, opposing sides facing each other across the table, Pitts began talking.

"Gentlemen, I'm going to put all my cards on the table here. No holding back. I think you'll agree this is a tragic situation, and my client is genuinely remorseful of his actions. As you know, it was completely out of character for him, he has had no other significant run-ins with the law, and will have to carry the burden of what happened that day for the rest of his life. While we certainly want to acknowledge the victim here, you must also consider the complete devastation Ben feels for causing the death of the old woman."

"Anna," Jason interjected with a sign of exasperation. "The woman's name was Anna Cuzzi."

"Yes, of course. But as I was saying, Ben is very upset by what he did. He'll have to live with this the rest of his life. And remember, Anna Cuzzi was into her eighties, she'd lived a long, full life. Besides . . . "

"What the fuck Matthew, give me a break!" Jason had enough. "First of all, there is a whole family sitting out there in the waiting room that will also have to live with Ben's action. They will never get to be with their mother and grandmother again no matter what her age. By this man's enraged, thoughtless act, he took her from them, suddenly and permanently. We've both been around the block a few times, so let's knock off the bullshit and get right to your proposal."

Jason thought it was pretty amazing the way an attorney could turn a straightforward proposal into a diatribe for the sainthood of his client. In this case Pitt's speech was being wasted not only on his client, since Ben Dickson wasn't the flowery type, but on the detectives also. Jason wished these guys would really just get to the point like they always claimed they would. After years of listening to lawyers in interviews, during court proceedings, and in the countless exchanges he had with them during his time as a police detective, his attention span had grown short. He no longer had the patience to sort through all the bullshit and pull out the important stuff.

"Okay, Jason, but there's no need to be vulgar. I'm just doing my job here too. I have to point out the factors that may influence my client's case. You know that."

Pitts leaned forward in his chair, and placed both his hands on the table, one on top of the other. Jason remembered this quirk from years ago. Pitts did this when he was finally ready to make his proposal. He wanted everyone to think he was about to impart some sage advice, and when he leaned in toward his listeners, he found that they inevitably leaned in also. Pitts finished the effect by talking in a very low voice, almost a whisper. This heightened the effect he was trying to create, and essentially forced everyone in earshot to huddle closer to catch all his words. Jason liked the technique, and often copied it for his own use. He smiled now as he leaned over the table to hear what Pitts had to say. The former assistant District Attorney continued.

"My client believes that he has some information you may need to successfully conclude an investigation you're working on. He is willing to talk to you about this in exchange for your support regarding a plea in the case at hand. Interested?"

"Go ahead, Matthew, we're interested." Jason leaned back in his chair, and placed both his hands behind his head, fingers intertwined. He wanted to portray a look of causal openness.

"We are willing to waive this preliminary hearing, and Mr. Dickson will plead guilty to manslaughter and leaving the scene of an accident. The charges of homicide by vehicle, reckless driving, and all drug related charges will be dropped. You will make a recommendation that Ben get probation, and undergo counseling, something along the lines of an anger management course. Do you still have the authority to make this deal yourself, or do you need to call the Chief or District Attorney?"

Jason leaned forward and dropped his hands on the table, mimicking Pitts' posture. They were face-to-face, like two confidantes exchanging secrets.

"I can do the deal." Jason said, turning to glance at the detective seated next to him. "As long as Detective Patterson and I agree."

Patterson took his cue.

"*If* the information is good, and *if* we make an arrest for distributing the goods we're talking about based on Johnson's information, and *if* he testifies in court as needed, I'll agree, except . . . " Detective Patterson continued, "the drug charges stand."

Before the lawyer could react, Jason chimed in.

"Let me add this, Matthew. If we really get something notable out of this, like a good seizure of steroids or if we uncover a sizable organization, we'll recommend the D.A. dismiss the drug charges, similar to what we do for informants whose information pays off big time. Of course, as you know, if your client doesn't come through on his part of the deal, all charges will be reinstated. Is that acceptable?"

Attorney Pitts huddled with his client a few minutes before responding. The deal was forged, and Jason and Pitts went back into the Judge's chambers to work it out with Quincy. Jason signed off on the proper documents, and so did Pitts. The case was waived to the County Court of Common Pleas. The detectives would take Ben Johnson to police headquarters for a statement. Along with the witnesses he had gotten from Janet, Ben's information would probably lead them further toward establishing the connection between the distribution of steroids and the Apex. Of course, this also meant an increased possibility that his friend Kyle Price would be involved, or at least that his establishment was being used for drug trafficking. No matter how you couch it, trafficking was serious business, and even if he had no knowledge of what happening at the health club, Kyle's reputation would be impugned by any scandal at the Apex. Nevertheless, it was Jason's duty to carry out the investigation no matter where it led.

Columbia, Missouri is a city of nearly 80,000 people. It is home to the University of Missouri, a college famous for it's school of journalism. Not coincidentally, the city is crawling with media types. There were the real media, always hot on the latest political fracas, or pursuing an endless string of feature stories with the goal of winning a Pulitzer. Then there was the college media, a bedraggle collection of students hoping to find a story that will give them their first break in the business, and insure that their mommies and daddies did not pay their tuition in vain. Often, the professionals and the amateurs covered the same story, and sparks flew as they practically ran each other over to get the scoop. There was quite a bit of competition in a relatively small market. Considering that Columbia was more like a big Mayberry than a small St. Louis, a fender bender involving the Mayor's wife was liable to wind up on page one.

Nevertheless, Mirror Man liked this town. It was technology friendly, and with all the pretty coeds and trendy coffee shops where they hung out all hours of the night, he felt rather comfortable. Hell, this is a place he could call home in a few years. He was sitting at a table for two in the Tiger Cup, a coffeehouse just off campus. It was a typical college joint, with small glass top tables decorated with thick candles resting on cheap, but heavy glass candleholders. Images of tigers, the mascot of the University's sports teams, were everywhere. The place wouldn't win any awards for cleanliness, but it managed to keep one step ahead of the city's health inspectors.

He surveyed the usual assortment of fresh faced post pubescent women and their seemingly immature, younger male counterparts. College girls always looked older and worldlier than the men. It was Wednesday, and on Wednesdays, one could expect to see Sonja Peterson at the Tiger Cup. It was her after school hangout, and according to the information he had intercepted, she would more than likely be there tonight. He looked around, but did not see anyone resembling her. Of course, like the others, he was able to get some pictures of her from the internet and was confident he would recognize her the moment he saw her. She was a buxom young woman, and looked a bit like Marjo the Pro, only younger and a little less well endowed.

She was only twenty-one years old, which would make her his youngest victim to date. He was surprised that she managed to catch his attention, being so young and all, because he usually went for women who had accomplished more in life, had interesting experiences that intrigued him, or at least had some seasoning. However, Sonja seemed mature for her age. He had learned that she had skipped her last year of high school in her hometown of Olathe, Kansas, and received a music scholarship to the University of Missouri. She played the flute, and at the age of fifteen, had made regular appearances with the local symphony in Johnson County, and had even appeared as a special guest flutist with the St. Louis symphony.

He was sipping his coffee when he noticed a table of three coeds giving him the eye. It as a pretty slow night and he guessed they were looking for a little male companionship, probably just for some flirtatious dick teasing. Two of them held no interest for him, but the third, a slim brunette whose finely chiseled features were framed by wisps of silky hair splayed over her forehead, was definitely a possibility. She had an innocent, farm girl look keeping with her Midwest birthplace, although she was raised in a subdivision of three hundred thousand-dollar houses and had never so much as set foot in a cornfield. He directed his smile at her, and the other two girls looked at their friend and started whispering advice, or maybe warnings. He thought he saw her blush, and wondered how their girlish bravado would change if they knew who he was, and what he would do to them if they were one of the chosen. But of course, he never, *never* killed without first carefully selecting his prey.

Maybe he should play with these three a bit, let them pick him up, drive out of town to a highway motel, and show them a night that would be burned into their brains forever. He never fucked three girls at once, and imagined lining them up, arms overhead and secured to the bed frame, the inner legs of the girls on the end tied to the legs of the girl in the middle. *Three little pussies all in a row.* He would gag them, but would hear their muffled screams and see them writhing in terror as he approached each one and stuck his hard dick into their dry, impossibly tight young pussies. He would look at the other girls while he was fucking the first one, giving them a toothy grin that would literally frighten them out of their wits.

He wouldn't kill them, just fuck'em. This way he wouldn't violate his ritual. Maybe tune them up some, so they would be forced to tell others of their shame. All three of them were still flirting with him across the room, and he decided to go for it, give them what they deserved for playing with fire. They ought to have more sense. He picked up his coffee cup and started to his feet when he heard the little bell on the door jingle softly. Another customer coming in. He settled back into his chair and turned toward the door. It was her . . . Sonja. She was alone, and walked into the shop with the ease of familiarity.

Her face was unmistakable, although in person she did not look as much like Marjo. She was also heavier than he thought she'd be, judging from her pictures. Still, she was pretty, and had big tits. He looked at her lips after she had taken a seat. They were full and moist, and he imagined them pursed around her flute, with her well-manicured fingers working the keys of the instrument with confidence. Yes, she would do fine. He drained the last drops of now lukewarm coffee from his cup, and rose to leave. He didn't give the three coeds a second glance as he walked out the door.

Chapter 18

Ben had good information. Turned out it was even worth the song and dance he had to go through with the burly weightlifter's crotchety attorney. Jason left his car at the District Justice office, and rode back with Detective Patterson and Ben Dickson. He would send a patrol unit to pick it up later. They had some trouble convincing his lawyer to let him ride with them, but made it part of the deal, and Ben himself had no problem with it. In fact, before returning to the police station, he told the officers to stop by his house. He had something for them that might prove useful. They accompanied him into his small, disheveled apartment, not trusting him to be alone and a little suspicious of his motives. He was a high-strung man, even without the after effects of steroid use, and Jason felt he was a suicide risk. After all, killing the old woman kind of branded him, and the accident had received enough publicity to make Ben a household name in Highland Park. He was now infamous, and even though his fifteen minutes would pass, and people would forget his name and face a lot quicker then he could imagine, some people just couldn't bear the furtive looks, obvious stares and the snide comments Ben would experience for a few months. Even if he were emotionally stronger than he appeared, the cops didn't want to take chances. Imagine how it would look if their prime witness killed himself while the police were taking him in for questioning. When Ben made a sudden move toward the bathroom, Jason stepped in front of him. Ben stopped and put his arms up, like he was surrendering.

"Yo, man, I'm just going to take a piss. Whatta you wanna watch?"

"Fuck you, Ben. Just hold on a second. I gotta make sure there's no evidence in there. It's routine."

Actually, Jason wanted to make sure there wasn't anything within easy reach in case Ben did want to harm himself. A quick check revealed no items of concern. No straight razor or scissors, no thin sharp blades, only those cheap disposable safety razors. There were some pills, including a bottle of steroids, all

138

of which Jason put in his pocket, just in case. He would put them back, minus the steroids, after Ben was through using the facilities. Once they left his apartment, the rest of the trip was uneventful, with Ben sullenly seated next to Patterson in the back of the detective's car while Jason drove.

The detective's efforts proved fruitful. Not only did Ben give the detectives the web address for the site where he purchased the steroids, he supplied them with some of the bottles, packing material, and shipping labels from his last order. However, he made no mention of Kyle Price, even when questioned directly about the gym owner's involvement. Jason was mollified. If Ben learned about the web site through the Apex, but never heard anything about Kyle Price being involved, then his friend was probably in the clear. Although he would surely be embarrassed by this type of activity going on right under his nose, Jason was sure he would cooperate with the police and clean house when the investigation was over. It would be a public relations nightmare for the guy, but he was personable enough and had great media connections that would enable him to escape serious harm and public persecution. He could call in a few favors. Jason thought that he might be able to help out with this, which would smooth out any ruffled feathers caused by Jason's duty-bound involvement in this whole mess.

The next morning, Mirror Man was up early. He had a lot of work to do. Sonja lived off campus with two other women. He would never select a victim who lived in a dorm. Still, since there were other people involved, there was an added element of danger, a greater chance of discovery. He would have to be especially careful, and needed to research the habits of not only his intended victim, but her roommates as well. Fortunately, most of the women he selected in the past had lived alone, but Sonja captured his interest in a big way, and he wasn't going to let some minor complications stand in the way of his good time. He had identified the two other girls, although he decided not to mirror their computers. It was a safety issue. It would be too cumbersome to try and find all their computers after the killings and wipe out their memories. He was also aware that college students frequently owned laptops, which they used for their studies and also to log onto the Internet. He didn't want to take the chance that he would not be able to access one of the computers immediately after the killing. That could prove to be devastating. If discovered, and if the cops were smart enough, which they probably weren't, it could fuck up the whole deal. He wanted to end this when he was ready, not anyone else. So it paid to be conservative, just like in business. He would find out about Sonja's roommates the old fashioned way, he would spy on them. It would take time, and present some calculated risks along the way, but he had a feeling his efforts would prove to be rewarding.

It took him almost two weeks of following the girls before he had a handle on their routines. Fortunately, their class schedules were different, and he had discovered several days of the week and time periods where Sonja was likely to be at home alone while the other girls were still at class. One of them even had an evening class, business law, on Wednesdays, and the other roommate had an aerobics class Monday and Wednesdays at the University's wellness center. He took this as a good omen because he preferred to work at night, there was less chance of being seen in the dark. This was particularly important around a college campus, where people were out and about at all times of the day and night. Even though he blended in easily with college age kids, he did not want to risk being seen and remembered by passing students or staffers.

The next step in his quest was to survey the area where the girls lived. He did this to learn about the neighborhood, the comings and goings of people who might be concerned about a stranger in their midst. This might include the landlord, other students, delivery persons, and the mailman. He was concerned about anyone who had a routine that he should know about before striking. Once he knew all he could about this, he would be ready to pick his time, and the killing would go smoothly, like the others before it. Fortunately, there were not many people he had to work around. During the two weeks he spent in Columbia, he was able to get all the information he needed to assuage his reservations about being inadvertently discovered in this busy college town.

He learned that the landlord lived out-of-town, and the mailman came like clockwork between 1:00 and 2:00 PM daily. The only variable seemed to be a cleaning lady who serviced one of the apartments in the same building as the girls. There were four apartments in all, and all of the other three tenants worked full time during the day. They all left by eight-thirty in the morning and never returned before five o'clock. One of the apartments was occupied by a discernibly yuppie-like couple, both of whom had professional careers in separate downtown office buildings.

The cleaning lady worked for the yuppies. She was a middle aged white woman, not half-bad looking for her age. Her appearances over the last couple of weeks concerned him a bit at first. She came four times during the two weeks he was watching the area. Two of the days were Mondays, one was a Thursday, and one was a Friday. He figured the lady was scheduled to clean on Mondays and Thursdays each week. He bet that something came up on that second Thursday, and she was delayed until Friday. Somehow, this schedule made sense to him. The yuppies wanted their apartment cleaned Monday, just after the weekend, and Thursday, just before. It seemed to him a schedule the youngish couple would set for their lifestyle. Nevertheless, based on the cleaning woman's appearances, he eliminated all three of these weekdays. Of course the weekend was also out, so that left Tuesday and Wednesday. With both of Sonja's roommates gone on Wednesday evenings, this was his first choice. He had also checked out the security at the apartments; there were no extraordinary measures, no video cameras, no exterior premise alarms, and no one had any dogs that he could detect. The girls' apartment was located on the first floor and they also shared part of the basement, which had been converted into a small laundry room.

Toward the end of his two-week surveillance, dressed in the brown shirt and pants of a UPS driver, he had entered the apartment house through a common vestibule door. He had been prepared to jimmy the lock if necessary but found that the door had not fully closed and the lock had not caught. The door to the girls' apartment was secured, but it was one of the standard interior locks that even a kid could slip, and he had no difficulty with it at all. Once inside, he took his time getting to know the layout, and found several places where he could hide. He rummaged through some drawers, focusing on a large hutch that seemed to be the gathering place for mail, magazines, and the other remnants of the students' daily life. Lying in a basket on the hutch were numerous keys, some on key rings and some singles. He examined them, discarding the obvious car keys before finding a couple of keys on a cheap plastic fob that looked like door keys. They were either keys to a parent's home, a boyfriend's apartment, or spare keys for this place. He tried both in the front door, and one of them turned the lock. He bet the other key on the same ring fit the vestibule door, and he pocketed them.

This was falling into place nicely. He thought it best to enter during the day, when no one was around, and remain hidden for several hours. He relished the thought of the girls coming home from class, and going about their business not knowing that death was so close. Waiting silently in the dark, he would hear the sounds of the young women as they chirped and babbled to each other about their day. He would smell the mix of their perfume as they came within inches of his hiding spot. He remembered when he had done this before once, and it had been euphoric. He recalled the rush it had given him during the event and for weeks afterwards. For such a feeling, he was willing to take the extra risk.

Besides, he had cased this place enough to be sure that he would be okay. Even if he would be inadvertently found by one of the girls, he would be able to escape and flee the area before an investigation could be started. Police always focused on the neighborhood first, believing that most perpetrators don't travel far to commit their crimes. Usually, they were right, and that was what gave him such an advantage. He never did anything like this around his home; don't shit where you eat. There were always exceptions, of course, but it was a good rule to live by . . . or die by, depending whether you were the predator or the victim.

Sonja liked to think of herself as athletic. He had learned this from mirroring her computer transactions, and although she limited her workouts during the week to a brisk evening walk and some free weight exercises at home, he knew she went for a six mile run every Saturday morning at eight. He knew she ran six miles because he had traced the route, twice. This Saturday, she would have a partner, as least for a short while. He arrived at the Tanemend trail at a quarter to eight Saturday morning, all decked out in a nylon shirt and an oversize pair of running shorts he had purchased the night before. He wanted to look the part, so when she appraised him she would label him as a jock, and not be apprehensive about his presence as they both ran on the trail, a former railroad line that had been converted to a jogging and biking path.

Sure enough, like clockwork, Sonja arrived at eight sharp. She pulled her well-used Honda Civic into the small gravel parking area beside the trail. She was wearing a green and tan warm up suit, with the zipper of the jacket pulled down to her waist. He could see a flesh colored sports bra underneath. He greeted her with a quick smile while he stretched his calves and thighs, trying hard to look at ease. She smiled back at him, and they exchanged brief greetings. He continued to stretch and warm up, biding his time before starting to run. Sonja went over to a fence, put her leg up on one of the rails, and began her own pre-run routine. After a couple of minutes, he started down the trail, hoping he had timed things right, and Sonja would follow shortly. The trail was beautiful. The city had done a great job of reclaiming the neglected railroad bed and turning it into a wonderful tribute to nature. The trail itself was about eight feet wide, with a soft surface made of a recycled mix of pea gravel and pulverized rubber tires. Along each side was a level berm planted with wildflowers. At regular intervals there were landscaped gardens and small neatly trimmed shrubs, courtesy of the many garden clubs and civic organization that had sponsored the trail. Finally, a border of tall, mature trees served as nature's frame, lending an aura of majesty to the runner's world. The scenery allowed many a runner to forget about their aching lungs and legs and focus on the beauty and splendor that was Earth at its best. Even Mirror Man was enjoying this fine day, breathing deep the crisp, sweet morning air.

He had gone only half a mile when he heard her footsteps approach from the rear. He allowed himself a quick backward glance to make sure it was Sonja and not another runner who had passed her by. Seeing it was she, he continued to run for a few hundred yards more, and then suddenly feigned a fall onto the trail. He cushioned his fall with outstretched arms, and came to rest with his legs splayed across the trail. Sonja pulled up to help him.

"My God, are you all right?" She asked him, her voice heavy from exertion.

"I'm okay," he replied, reaching out to rub his right ankle. "But I think I've sprained an ankle. Can you give me a hand?"

She reached for his arm, and he grabbed her wrist, wet with perspiration. She pulled, and he stood up, pretending to favor an injured leg. He stumbled a little, and she bent and placed his arm around her shoulders to support his weight. He was very close to her now, and could smell her, an intoxicating scent of perfume and perspiration. Not a stale smell at all, but rather the clean, pleasing scent of a freshly showered body at work. It was arousing to him and he leaned in toward her head to smell her hair.

"Could you give me a hand over to the rocks?" he asked, indicating some large boulders just off the trail that he could use to sit on.

"Of course, just hang on."

She started to move with him off the trail, and he let his arm slide down her back and encircle her waist. Quickly, he burrowed his hand under the back of her warm up jacket, his fingers and hands now on her moist, silky flesh. He held her tightly, feeling the firmness of her waist as she moved toward the rocks. She bent once again to lower him gently to the rock, and he let his hand roam down off her side along her hip, and daringly squeezed her ass before he sat down. She looked at him hard for a second, but wrote it off as an inadvertent act rather than a cheap feel. But when she stepped back and looked at him again, he had a strange twisted smile on his face. It made her feel uncomfortable at once, and she shivered with a sudden top to bottom chill before speaking once again.

"Will you be okay now? Do you want me to call someone for you? Shall I call 911?"

"No, no . . . thank you," he said, still holding that strange smile. "I'll be fine in a minute. Please finish your run. Thank you for all you've done for me."

He watched as she ran away, moving his head from side to side in time with the rhythmic movement of her hips. He breathed deep the crisp morning air. What a wonderful day, he thought.

Chapter 19

The unique experience Janet promised him began at the home of her close friends, Kyle and Christine Price. Jason had wrestled with the idea of becoming further involved with Kyle. He tried a couple of times to tell Janet he was not coming, but just couldn't do it. Besides, since his interview with Ben Dickson turned up no mention of Kyle being part of any steroid deals, he felt a little more comfortable about his flamboyant friend. He decided to go. After all, there was another couple also going out with them, and most of his attention would be on Janet anyway. He was looking forward to another fun evening spent in her company, and with Kyle arranging things, it was likely to be luxurious as well. He needed a night out. He and Cab were not able to develop many leads on the Mathieson murder, and the pressure from his chief and the media for a break in the case was mounting. This seemed a perfect way to forget about work for awhile.

It was indeed a special evening. He picked Janet up at five o'clock and drove to the Price's exquisite home in Highland Park's posh Emerald Point development. How the exclusive subdivision got its name is a mystery, since it was not located near the confluence of any bodies of water or roadways. Nevertheless, it was the most distinctive address in this part of the county. The whole development consisted of only six custom built houses, each at least five thousand square feet, and each vastly different than the others. When they arrived, Jason turned into the home's long, circular driveway, and noticed a limo parked just outside the portico covering the front entrance. He pulled behind it, and quickly exited and walked around to open Janet's door. Before they could ring the bell, Kyle opened the front door and greeted them warmly. Jason had been to the house before, but never ceased to be awed by the splendor of its foyer and public rooms. A large crystal chandelier served as the center point as guests stepped toward the house. It was plainly visible from the outside through a large two story tall window located just above the ornate front doors. Inside, you could see that it hung from the 25-foot tall ceiling and was framed by the window and a large brass and glass spiral staircase leading to the second floor.

Off to the left was a formal sitting room, where Jason had first broken the news of Natalie's kidnapping. It was not a large room, but very well appointed, with a floral theme done in various shades of red, mauve and green. There was not a single item out of place. On the right was the dining room, a magnificent room with a huge cherry china closet, which was one of the most dominant pieces of furniture Jason ever saw outside of a museum. There was also a table for twelve, in matching cherry of course. All of the pieces were trimmed in brass, which blended nicely with the foyer. Between the dining room and the staircase was a hallway leading to the kitchen, family room, and study. Kyle led them to the family room, which featured a built-in media center with three televisions, one with a six-foot screen. The others flanked it on each side, and had more modest thirty six-inch screens. They were all on, tuned to ESPN type channels. Kyle took his sports and movie viewing seriously.

Christine was inside, and so were Marjo the Pro and Deter Schmidt. They were sipping drinks and smiled at the newly arriving pair. Christine nodded knowingly at Janet and lifted her drink in a salute.

"I figure we'd better take the limo tonight," Kyle said. "If we're going to do some serious partying, we don't want to worry about Jason's boys messing with us! More importantly, we don't want anyone left out of the fun. There will be no designated driver in this group."

Jason wondered what was in store for him tonight, but already knew that Kyle and company liked to party. He figured it would do him good to relax and enjoy himself. It had been a long time since he had gotten anywhere close to being drunk, and tonight was as good a night as any. It was obvious the couples were feeling good tonight. The women seemed especially ready to let their hair down. Marjo, always looking hot, was wearing a fiery red minidress cut low, and it appeared more of her tanned breasts were outside the dress than inside. Never shy, Kyle slipped behind the wet bar and let everyone know he noticed.

"Marjo, let me be the first to buy you a drink. With that dress I'm not gonna get through the crowd around you later."

Marjo whipped her long back with a flip of her head. "Glad you approve," she purred.

All of the women would be guaranteed attention tonight. Christine's stylish raven hair was set off by a teal two-piece knit blouse and skirt that accentuated her generous curves. She wore white stockings that complimented her outfit nicely. Jason glanced at Janet, who certainly held her own in this group. She was wearing another slinky black dress, shorter than he'd ever seen her wear before. There was just a hint of soft cleavage visible below her silver necklace. Black must be her signature color, he thought, and she looked great. The dress showed off her slim figure nicely. The looks on the faces of the other men indicated their agreement. Janet couldn't wear a bra with this dress, and the outlines of her nipples were clearly visible. If she knew this, it did not seem to bother her, and she was smiling as she sipped her white wine and looked back at her date, seeming to realize that he and the other men were eyeing her up. Kyle interrupted his thoughts.

"Jason, can you come into the study with me? I want to show you my latest toy."

He accompanied Kyle into the well-furnished room, full of the man's personal taste. It was definitely a masculine room, with rich dark wood furniture and a floor to ceiling bookcase that lined the entire east wall. Besides the books, some of the shelves held quite a collection of sports memorabilia and photographs of Kyle posing with various famous people. Jason saw two ex-Presidents and some movie stars included in this menagerie. Kyle pointed to a sleek display sitting on his massive desk. It looked like a miniature dispatch console, with a multi-button phone, and a fifteen-inch flat monitor. It even had a type of microphone built into the display, which Jason figured was some kind of hands free calling feature.

"Like it?" Kyle asked.

"Sure, but what exactly is it? Some kind of high-tech phone system?"

"Don't let anybody tell you you're not sharp, my friend. That's what it is. It's based on a digital wireless system, only it's equipped with GPS. You know about GPS don't you?"

"Global Positioning System. It uses satellites to track and pinpoint locations. We use it with our police radios. Hell, we even have it installed in our police cruisers. All of the patrol units are displayed on a monitor like you have, and the police dispatcher can see which of those are closest to an emergency. They dispatch the closest one and cut down on the response time. Good way to save a life or stop a crime. It also keeps the cops safer. If they get in trouble and can't radio their location, GPS tells us exactly where they are, and we send the Calvary. Pretty neat stuff. From my office computer, I can see the location of each one of our squad cars. They could drive clear down to Virginia for a coffee break and I could see them passing through Baltimore."

"I'm not surprised the police have caught on to this. Well, this is the same thing. I have my own personal wireless network here with GPS. I've got a half-dozen cellular phones hooked up to it now, and at the push of a button, the monitor shows me where each of them is. Coolest thing I've seen in awhile."

"Its great," Jason said, trying to muster up some enthusiasm. "What do you use it for?"

Kyle laughed. "Okay, I'll admit it. It's really just a toy right now. I call Christine every once in awhile just to tell her where she is. Sooner or later I'll find a good business use for it. Right now, though, I'm just trying to keep up with the changes in technology. If you don't use these things, you'll find yourself falling behind the leaders, and you know me, I can't have that! Do you want one?"

"Thanks for the offer, but I'm not sure I want you to know where I am all the time! Besides, you know me. Technology passed me by a long time ago, ever since they created self-programming VCR's. I spent months learning how to program mine, and then these new models came out, rendering my newfound skill useless. Naa, I'll stay in the dark ages."

"Okay, suit yourself. But if you need one or two for something, just let me know. We better get back to the others, before they wonder what devious undertaking we're up to."

The men walked back and joined the others, with Kyle letting out a loud whistle to get their attention.

"Down your drinks and let's get going. The limo driver gets paid by the hour!" The three couples went outside and slipped into the sleek black stretch limousine. Kyle had the limo stocked with the makings of everyone's favorite drink and prepared another round for all. The lights were subdued, and smooth jazz was playing softly. Along with the plush seats and shiny silver and black accented mini-bar, the car was transformed into an intimate setting rivaling an upscale lounge. Just right for Kyle's taste. As his eyes grew accustomed to the dark interior, Jason took the opportunity to look around. Christine was seated next to him on the one side, and as she settled into the couch-like seat, her skirt slid above the tops of her lace trimmed thigh high stockings, and Jason was immediately appreciative of the mode of travel tonight. Janet was on his other side, and was leaning forward to hear something Kyle was saying. As she bent over, her breasts became much more visible, and Jason knew Kyle would make this a long conversation! Good for him, he thought. It was a great view. Across the limo, Marjo was in a reclining position with her legs pulled onto the seat. She was wearing nude lace trimmed stockings with garters, and her red panties were visible at the top of her well formed, tanned legs. Jason thought that life didn't get better than this, and exhaled slowly as the drinks started to take effect. He soon accepted another from his host.

"Extra dry," he said as he took a sip. "Just the way I like them."

All of them had more than a few drinks by the time they arrived for dinner at McAfee's, a four star restaurant in Philadelphia. The driver didn't even raise an eyebrow as the three gorgeous women alighted from the car, slightly tipsy and not too careful about showing too much flesh. Dinner was slow and elegant, and conversation ranged from families to vacations, to the latest gossip around the Apex. As is typical of couples who feel close and comfortable with each other, the talk turned to relationships and sex. Kyle in particular complained about how their busy lives allowed little time and energy for enjoying married life, especially sex.

With Marjo taking the lead, much to Deter's embarrassment, the couples swapped stories about keeping the spice in a relationship. The stories included everything from skinny-dipping on an island vacation to watching dancers in an exotic strip club, something Kyle and Christine seemed to enjoy. It was obvious to Jason that these people had a penchant for the erotic, and he was a bit surprised that Janet was so comfortable discussing these topics. However, fueled by the alcohol and the sexy, cavalier attitude of his friends, Jason found himself at ease, and hoping for this exciting night to continue. He would not be disappointed.

After dinner the couples returned to the waiting limo for a trip to a waterfront night club. As Jason waited to get in, he watched Christine slide down the bench type seat, making room for the next person. As she moved, her legs separated, and he caught a glimpse of her upper thighs, and then a thatch of dark hair between them. She was not wearing panties. Feeling slightly guilty but unable to take his eyes off her, he watched her slide all the way to the end of the seat, hoping to catch a second glance. He didn't have to wait long, because by the time she reached the end her skirt had ridden so high that her bush was in constant view of anyone seated across from her. He sheepishly made eye contact with Janet to see if she'd caught him watching. He saw that she had noticed, but rather than flashing him a scolding look, she was smiling seductively, obviously letting him know that she too was enjoying the show. Suddenly her fingers moved up his thigh, and came to rest against his hardening dick.

The nightclub was noisy and very crowded, but they managed to find a table. The earlier conversations continued, with Kyle and Deter discussing some Apex business, and Janet and Christine sharing some information about a charity event that they were planning. Marjo had left the table, but returned shortly with a waitress bringing shots for everyone.

"Enough shop talk, she said, "let's have some fun!"

After downing several shots, Kyle asked Janet to dance, and she readily agreed. Not to be left out, Jason grabbed Christine and led her to the dance floor. Deter and Marjo followed. It wasn't long before the effects of those shots became evident. All of the couples were getting looser and started dancing closer. Kyle was running his hands up and down Janet's thighs as they slid up against each other, and at one point he cupped her ass and pulled her in close, rubbing himself against her. Normally, this type of behavior would have pissed

Jason off big time, but tonight it didn't faze him at all. In fact, he found it exciting, maybe because he didn't feel threatened by Kyle, or maybe because secretly he had wanted to do the same to Christine for a long time.

Deter and Marjo were also dancing close, and it seemed like her breasts would fall right out of her dress as she shimmied to the music. A slow tune came next, and Jason pulled Christine close, feeling the heat from her body and breathing in the tantalizing scent of her perfume. Knowing she was not wearing panties excited him. He had always had the hots for her, especially since that night in Mexico, but never dreamed he'd be in a position to do anything about it. Feeling the liquid courage, he let his hand slide down from her waist and squeezed her thigh and ass, pulling her into his hardness. She moaned softly, and he felt her sweet breath against his ear.

Kyle had his head buried in Janet's long blond hair, and was inhaling her fragrance and kissing her neck and ear. They danced over close to Jason and Christine. Janet smiled sweetly at Jason and winked. She then moved one of her arms from around Kyle's shoulders, slid her hand slowly down his chest to his waist, and then went lower, rubbing her hand against his dick for a moment. She reversed the path slowly, sliding her hand back up his chest and around his shoulders where it had rested seconds earlier. She again looked at Jason and smiled. Christine saw this action, and mimicked Janet, wrapping her well-manicured fingers around Jason's hard dick and squeezing gently. This was unbelievable. Jason had never experienced anything like this before. He had a fleeting thought that he was compromising his professionalism, not to mention breaking just about every moral rule he'd been taught, but in his current state of intoxication, found himself swept away.

After the set was through, the couples made their way back to their table. Kyle commented that he thought Marjo was overdressed tonight, and asked for her red thong panties! She issued a dare for him to get them. As the others watched, he reached over to her, his arms shielded by the tablecloth. She raised up ever so slightly from her chair as Kyle slipped off her panties and lowered them to below her knees. She kicked them off, and gave them to Kyle. They were passed around, and Jason could feel the moisture in them as he handed them back to Marjo. It was after 2:00 AM, they left the club and headed for home, feeling very sexy and very high. The next hour or so was kind of fuzzy for Jason, and he had trouble focusing his eyes. He was thankful that they were in the limo and that there were others who would take care of him if he passed out.

He remembered kissing Janet's lips and neck and ears, loving the taste of her and her familiar perfume. He slipped his hand into the top of her dress and cupped her breast, squeezing softly. Her breath quickened as he lowered his head and began circling her nipple with his tongue. Glancing around the dimly lit car, he saw that the other couples were engaged in similar activities. Deter had lowered Marjo's dress, exposing her large creamy breasts, and was sucking and licking them feverishly. Across from him, Christine's head was buried in Kyle's lap. She put her arms up as he lifted her blouse over her head and threw it aside. Her erect nipples strained the thin fabric of her see-through bra as she continued her up and down motion on Kyle. Janet leaned over toward her, and unhooked her bra and slipped the straps from her shoulders. Jason saw Janet's fingers lightly brush against Christine's large pink nipples as she reached around to remove her bra.

Jason noticed Kyle looking to his left, and following his gaze, saw that Deter had dropped to his knees facing Marjo. He pushed up her dress, and zealously went to work. Jason was soon distracted by Janet tugging at his zipper, and became lost in his own pleasure. The booz, the sex, and the fatigue of the long night all blended together, creating a surreal scene that Jason would relive many times over in his dreams.

Any remaining inhibitions vanished as the couples succumbed to the lure of unbridled sensuality. There was much moaning and cries of ecstasy as they all reached orgasm. The driver, discreet as he was, must have overheard the unmistakable sounds of sex. However, his face remained stoic as he opened the limo's doors when the couples arrived at their respective destinations. When they pulled up in front of Jason's house, Janet got out with him. He was already looking forward to round two as he led her into his house and up to the bedroom.

The next morning, Jason awoke with a headache. It was a long time since he had drank so much, and he was paying the price now.

"God," he mumbled aloud in voice that would have been inaudible, even if he wasn't alone in bed. "Did last night really happen?"

He couldn't piece it all together, but remembered enough to know that he had crossed the line. No question that he had compromised himself as a police professional, and maybe as a normal human being. *Damn! How could he have been so stupid?* Images of Janet popped into his head. Asked and answered. He wondered what she thought this morning, and immediately realized he would soon find out. As his senses awakened, he could smell her perfume lingering on the sheets, and he also caught the aroma of fresh brewed coffee.

She was in the kitchen, and now Jason was wide-awake, and apprehensive. He quickly rose and headed for the bathroom, hoping to get some nerve up before he had to greet her. Twenty minutes later, freshly shaved and wearing boxers and an oversized white muscle shirt that emphasized his broad shoulders and well defined triceps, Jason padded into the kitchen. Janet was seated at the table, the sun from the nearby bay window making her blond locks appear even lighter. She was scanning the morning paper. Jason noticed she was wearing a pair of his boxers, and a tee shirt with a logo and the words "Broad Street Run 2001" printed on the front.

"Hey baby," she cooed in a suggestive but slightly apprehensive tone. "Sleep okay?"

"How could I not?" he replied. "My body was totally spent. How about you?"

"Same. Except I was a little concerned about your reaction today. Caused me to toss and turn this morning."

"I know. But don't worry, I'm okay with it. Different experience. I feel a little strange. But look . . . we can now say, orgy? Been there done that! How many people do you know that can make that claim?"

"Well, six for sure!" Janet smiled. The ice was broken. Things would be all right between them. Jason noticed a cell phone lying next to some packaging material. It looked like Janet had been examining it.

"Hey Sweets, what's with the cell phone?"

"Oh, this is one of those Kyle was talking about last night. Christine offered me one and I thought I'd try it."

"You realize of course, that if you carry it with you, they'll always know where you are! Sure you want that?"

"It doesn't bother me. But I don't think either of them are going to be home watching the comings and goings of all their friends and associates. It's kinda cool really. I bet *you* would like to keep track of me, wouldn't you?"

"Yeah, maybe. But I don't have the time either, and you know how I hate to mess with this new age technology. It ruins my mountain man image."

"Didn't you tell me once that this 'mountain man' could cook? I'm getting awfully hungry. How about feeding a girl, willya?"

"You're on. Breakfast is on in fifteen."

"Great, I'll put some clothes on, and be right down."

'I like you just the way you are," he replied, as he bent to kiss her and slipped his hand inside the oversize boxers she was wearing and let his fingers brush against her. "Just the way you are."

As they ate the breakfast of eggs and home fries he prepared for them, Jason glanced furtively at her. She really didn't seemed to be bothered at all by the experience last night. She was light and bubbly, even more so than usual. It was like she accepted it without hesitation. Maybe it was not even a new experience for her. He wanted to ask, but couldn't get up the nerve. It could be he didn't really want to know the answer. For his part, the whole thing bothered him . . . more than a little. If only he didn't drink so much, maybe things would never have gone so far. It certainly complicated matters, not only with Janet, but for his

151

professional responsibilities as well. He hoped that Kyle was indeed innocent, because if he weren't, it would be a tough road ahead for both of them as Jason pursued his duties.

Chapter 20

Mirror Man checked out of his hotel on Tuesday morning, and registered at a Holiday Inn across town later the same day. He used a fresh credit card, one that he obtained just a week ago. He had made a couple of minor purchases to make sure it cleared. He did not want to take the chance of the card being questioned while he was in town on a mission. He called the airline to confirm his flight to Dallas the next morning, and settled in for a nap. He slept until 2:00 PM, showered quickly, and prepared his bag, a blue knapsack. The bag held the usual assortment of lock picks, screwdrivers, a short sturdy pry bar, two very sharp stainless steel knives, and of course, his on-the-fly disguises. He selected one of them to wear to Sonja's apartment, a non-descript brown wig and a pair of heavy frame clear glasses. There was rarely a need for anything elaborate. If questioned about seeing him, witnesses would only remember the basic details; medium height, brown hair, glasses, wearing blue jeans and a gray sweatshirt. That would fit at least two dozen students in a six block radius of campus.

He drove to a small shopping center a few blocks from the apartment, parked in a busy section of the lot near the Kroger's supermarket, and walked briskly to Sonja's place. It was 3:30, at least an hour and a half before anyone was expected home. He sat on the stoop of another building a few doors down on the opposite side of the street, watching and waiting. There was little activity on the street, and before long he felt fairly comfortable in the neighborhood. Hell, he had spent so much time here he almost felt as if he belonged. At 4:05 he rose and went directly to Sonja's, entering the door to the vestibule with his key. Once inside the apartment, he proceeded to the bathroom, and opened the door to a linen closet. After removing a couple of the lower shelves, it was just big enough for him to get in and sit on the floor. He removed his clothes, and carefully folded them and laid them on the floor beneath him. This would do nicely. He would browse around the apartment for awhile, soaking in the smells and rubbing himself on the frilly, feminine effects of all the young, pretty occupants. Then, about a half-hour before Sonja was expected home, he would wait in the closet.

He hoped she would take a shower. He knew if she came in and opened the linen closet door for a towel, she would surely spot him and he'd have to pounce. But there were several towels hung on racks in the bath, and he was betting that one of those would be hers and she wouldn't need one from the linen closet. Playing the odds made the experience more exciting, although he always made sure the odds were in his favor, and he always had a plan if things went awry. That's what separated him from a common murderer. Sonja was a fit, strong woman, and today he had selected a straight razor from his collection in case she put up too much of a fight. He retrieved it from his pants, unfolded it, and placed it under a corner of the small pink rug in front of the sink. He would be able to grab it quickly if needed.

What else? Ah, yes. He remembered that he needed to wipe the razor down first. He lifted the rug, picked up the razor, and carefully wiped the blade and the handle with a washcloth and replaced it under the rug. *Shame on you, that could have been a costly mistake.* If he didn't use the razor and forgot about it after the killing, police surely would have discovered it. He was not worried about DNA evidence, since they had to catch him before doing any comparisons, but he knew his fingerprints were taken once during an arrest for shoplifting when he was a kid, and feared they might still be on file somewhere. With the expanding AFIS network that he'd read about in IT journals, he knew such prints could be the first step to his downfall. He then took the eraser disk from the pocket of his trousers and dropped the pants back on the floor. He walked around the girls' apartment, stopping in each of the two bedrooms to rummage through their drawers, being careful to use the washcloth to open them.

He touched their clothes, feeling the silky texture of their underpants and reaching underneath for any hidden items, like photos or diaries that women often keep away from prying eyes. He was careful to replace each item exactly in the same position he'd found it, especially the underwear. He'd heard that they could get fingerprints from cloth now, but figured if an item didn't look disturbed, the police wouldn't risk destroying it just for the sake of thoroughness. He knew the cops didn't have the time or resources to print every item at every crime scene, even murders. It was a risk worth taking for the wonderfully stimulating feeling he got from touching and fondling the girls' personal items.

He examined their keepsakes, bits of dried flowers from high school corsages pressed in books and small lockets and charms from years past. Some of these items were for little girls, probably given to them by their fathers many years ago. He got an apple from the refrigerator, and sat on Sonja's bed as he ate, flipping through some photo albums he had found in her nightstand. She came from a good-looking family. He found a picture of her as a child, about four or five, being lifted off the ground and swung in the air between her parents, each holding one of her arms. They all had ear-to-ear smiles on their faces. Her mother's hair had fallen across her face and she was just starting to sweep it back with her fingers. Long, elegant fingers. From the pictures he surmised Sonja was an only child, as there were no other children present in the album. He never did pick up any evidence of siblings while he was watching her emails. He glanced at his watch. He still had time. She wouldn't be home for another thirty minutes. He went over to her computer, turned it on, and put the eraser disk on the desk. Plenty of time to erase the hard drive, he thought. He went into the kitchen and fed the apple core to the garbage disposal and went back to the fridge to get something cold to drink.

Suddenly, he heard the outside door open, followed by footsteps. He froze for a second, but then heard the sound of jangling keys and knew Sonja was home early. *It's ShowTime!* He ran as quickly and silently as he could to the bathroom, and took his position in the closet. Darkness enveloped his naked body as he shut the closet door, and he regulated his breathing so that he made almost no sound. He felt his hardness grow and knew he was ready. He retreated inside himself, and let his mind take him where it may, from the photos he had just seen to the jaded memories of his own family . . . his mother and her many lovers . . . especially . . . Jack . . . and the rubber man. In a matter of seconds, he retraced his steps back to the first encounter with Sonja at the coffee shop, remembered the firmness of her ass as he squeezed it on the trail, and then used his imagination to rehearse the action soon to come. This was the sweetest time.

Sonja unlocked the door and entered the apartment. He felt his hardness grow and knew he was ready. He heard her go into the bedroom, turn on the radio, and sing to the tune. He heard the refrigerator door open and close and a popping sound as she opened the top of a soda can. Her footsteps came closer, and he was grateful for the radio that masked the sound of his escalating breathing, as he anticipated the sheer pleasure and pain the next few minutes would bring for him and his prey. He started to sweat from the closeness and heat in the closet, and he detected the acrid smell of his body. He hoped that she would smell him also, and realize that something was wrong, just before he attacked. He hoped that when she looked at him that first second that he would see a spark of recognition in her eyes. That her face would scream *You, You, from the trail . . . I know who you are . . .* right before his hands encircle her throat and he squeezes the life out of her.

A shuffling sound drew his attention away from his revelry. He listened carefully. She was in the bathroom now, bent over the tub. He heard the faucets turn, and a steady splash of water followed. He saw her perfectly in his mind, her weighty breasts hung low, swinging slightly as she turned the handles to run the water. The curve of her hip and ass would be facing him as she bent over, inviting him to enter her. He reached up, turned the door handle slowly, and sprang from his crouched position to where he knew she would be. She was just where he pictured, naked . . . leaning over the tub adjusting the water flow. She didn't see him, but heard a noise behind her and turned her head toward him.

Like a leaping lion he was on his prey, hitting her hard and causing her to fall forward across the tub. She struck her head on the far wall, drawing blood. He grabbed her hair, and spun her head back violently so that she faced him, but her eyes were still closed from the shock of her collision. He forced his erection between the crack of her ass and moved it until he found an opening. Her pussy or her asshole, he didn't know and he didn't care. He felt a slight give and rammed it in hard. He had one hand around her waist, holding her up. *Just like Melina, but this one felt like dead weight. She's already gone*, he thought with disgust.

He slid his arm from around her waist and grabbed her hips with both hands. His penis slipped out and he cursed, removing a hand from Sonja's body to shove it back in. As he looked down between her legs, he saw movement out of the corner of his eye. He looked at her face and saw that her eyes were open wide, but before he could react she swung upward at him, and her elbow caught him just above the jaw. She hit him with enough force to cause his teeth to rip the soft tissue of his gums, filling his mouth with warm, salty blood. She was on him quickly, spinning around to face him, scratching at his eyes and bringing her knee up to strike him in the groin. She connected and he writhed in pain, falling to the floor, waves of panic coming over him for the first time since Carol had dumped him years ago. He was blacking out, seeing flashes of light and getting dizzy and nauseous. *No . . . must not lose control . . . must not black out . . . must win.*

He knew he had only seconds before he was finished. He shook his head, trying to think, trying to react. *Yes! He could reach it.* He slid his hand along the floor, feeling for the pink rug. She was pummeling him, beating her fists against him, and he bowed his head to protect his face. He had underestimated her strength and her resolve, and even as she beat him he admired her. That was a good sign. He was not out yet; he was going to be okay. He continued to sweep his hand under the rug, looking for the razor, and in a few more seconds was rewarded with the touch of cold steel against his fingers. His fingers found the handle and grabbed it tightly.

He looked up at her, could see the fury in her face and the blind rage with which she struck at him repeatedly. But, the blows had already softened, she was spent. He was the victor. She saw his face, and as he hoped, knew instantly who he was. She prepared to put all of her strength into another onslaught but was too late. In a swift, practiced move he swung the razor toward her face, slicing a deep, four-inch cut along her cheek. Sonja recoiled in pain, and he saw blood start to pour from her cheek, dripping on the pink rug. There was blood on the slick, smooth surface of the razor too, reminding him of that movie "The Shining." *Who's your daddy now, bitch.* He slashed again, and the razor opened up her left breast, spilling more blood. She was crying, a low whimper.

The fight in her was completely gone. She was a whipped dog. He put the razor down and grabbed her by the hair again. The pain was fading from his groin, but he knew that he would not get erect in time to fuck her again. He grabbed her by the throat and began to strangle her, watching the panic in her eyes grow even more extreme as she realizes he was going to kill her. He squeezed the life out of her, enjoying the gurgling sounds in her throat as she struggled to breathe and the flutter in her eyelids as she started to black out. He ground his face against hers, and rubbed his wide-open eyes against hers in some bizarre ritual only he could understand. Almost gone. He felt himself stirring in spite of the blow he took to his groin and thought about releasing his grip so he can re-enter her before she died. He reached down to stroke himself. But before he could continue he heard a voice. A melodic tone, inconsistent with the violent, tumultuous scene that was unfolding in the small bathroom.

"Sonja? Sonja? Are you home?"

FUCK! Someone was here. In the apartment. He didn't hear anyone come in but they must have entered during the struggle. The voice was female, young . . . probably one of the roommates. *GODDAMN BITCH. Got to get out.* He loosened his grip on Sonja, determined that she was unconscious, and set her head gently on the bathroom floor, not out of compassion, but simply to prevent any noise. Moving slowly and deliberately, he picked up his clothes and knapsack from the bottom of the closet and rolled them up under his arm. He looked around and spotted the bloody razor, picked it up, and stuffed it in the pocket of his pants. He heard the roommate's footsteps coming closer. Sonja moved her head and moaned softly. *She's coming to. Got to get out now.* He partially closed the bathroom door, hiding behind it as the roommate approached. Thinking about the struggle with Sonja and not wishing a repeat performance, he felt for the pocket with the razor, and slid his hand inside, grabbing the handle, just in case.

He waited for her to reach the door, and she screamed as she suddenly saw Sonja splayed on the floor, her face and chest covered with blood. At the same moment, he slammed the door against her, sending her sprawling to the floor, and ran out of the bathroom. He kicked at her head as he passed, trying to prevent her from catching even a glimpse of him as he made his getaway. He remembered the eraser disk, quickly retrieved it from the bedroom, and dressed as fast as he could before leaving the house. He walked swiftly down the block, almost running, and had to mentally force himself to slow down. Two blocks later he started to breathe normally, regaining his composure. *He should not have fled. He should have stayed and killed them both. What was wrong with him? He had panicked like a frightened child. Was it the unexpected resistance from Sonja? Was it because his act did not go according to plan? This was most disturbing, and most dangerous.*

He needed to think. The screams may have been heard by neighbors, the police may already be on the way. He needed to check himself for cuts or marks, make sure his clothing was in order, and try to blend in as he neared the shopping center to get his car. He found his car where he had left it, locked the knapsack in the trunk, started it up, and drove away from the neighborhood. There were faint sounds of sirens in the distance.

Columbia police officers that responded to a 911 call from her frantic roommate arrived to find Sonja semi-conscious on the bathroom floor. She was weak, but alive. The room was covered in blood, and it was apparent from blood spatters and smears on the wall, bathtub, and sink that a struggle had taken place. She was nude, and the officer saw a thin trail of blood streaming from her privates, indicative of forced penetration. Sonja was in no condition to utter even a single word, let alone give them a description to broadcast to responding units, so the officers concentrated on her roommate. They turned Sonja over to the paramedics, who had arrived shortly after the initial officer. One officer was detailed to take some quick Polaroid photographs of the bathroom and Sonja, and to record any changes that occurred to the crime scene as a result of the paramedics working on her.

The first officer on the scene was an alert second year patrolman who aspired to be a detective. Consequently he understood police procedure and investigative techniques and he knew the importance of documenting the scene and getting information about the suspect to other responding police units so they could search for the assailant. So even before speaking to the roommate, he broadcast to all responding units that they should be "on the lookout for a person, unknown sex, probably with bloodstained clothing, possibly armed with a sharp weapon, and with the appearance of recently being in a struggle."

A short pointed interview with her roommate allowed him to add, "the suspect is probably male, relatively young and fit." Although this may seem obvious to most, the young patrolman knew these sketchy details served a couple of purposes. First, the other responding patrol units knew almost nothing about the incident, so he was informing them about the nature of the attack. He included the information about the weapon to increase their awareness of officer safety issues should they stop a suspect. Second, he provided them with some legal grounds to stop a suspect. General as it was, the description was necessary to justify the brief detention and questioning of any persons stopped by police.

Sonja's roommate was seated on the bed, holding an ice bag to her forehead. She told the officer she had come home early from school, and upon entering the apartment, heard noises coming from the bathroom. When she walked into the doorway of the room, the suspect pushed the partially opened door into her face, and she fell back into the hallway. Before she could recover, she was kicked in the head and saw stars. She said she knew from her brief glimpse of the suspect that it was a male, and that he wasn't wearing any clothes. She surmised by his quickness and the fact that he was able to subdue Sonja that he was relatively young. She did not recall him speaking or making any other sounds that would be useful in identifying him. Twenty minutes after he had arrived, the officer heard several of his coworkers call out with pedestrian and vehicle stops of persons who might be the suspect. Although he had given out a description, he suspected that they were stopping everyone and everything that moved and was not old, female, or obese.

Cops knew that offenders were capable of changing their clothing and appearance pretty rapidly, especially if the crime was planned, so they considered any description that was broadcast as an advisory rather than a guideline. He also knew that in heinous crimes like this, the Boone County judges who would wind up ruling on any legal motions to suppress accepted such liberties. They might be lenient on drug and petty theft cases, but when you cut up and sexually assault a young college student in her own home, you were going to jail. Detectives had arrived on the scene by this point, and the young officer took pride as he detailed his initial findings and the actions he took to control the scene. The Detective Lieutenant in charge nodded as he spoke, and clapped him on the upper arm as he concluded his briefing, signifying a job well done. He returned to his patrol unit, determined to join the search before he got down to the mundane and cumbersome business of writing his report.

The next day found Mirror Man sitting in his apartment, alone as usual. The euphoria and excitement of the day before had subsided, much too quickly this time. His head was already starting to pound. He was thinking about his life and the miserable, uncontrollable chain of events that made up his sorry existence. Hard to even call it a life, really. The very word *life* conjured up images of vitality, of involvement, of hopes and dreams for a better future. He had none of these. He didn't remember when he first felt the rages of shame, and hate, and anger that so frequently enveloped him now. Or maybe he did. He was only nine years old when he caught his mother in a strange sexual act with a man he couldn't identify. And that was not his first indication that his life was different from all the other kids.

Even at age nine, he had seen countless men come and go from his home. Although he would not call his mother a whore, she did depend on men for her existence. She moved from lover to lover, and most of the men stayed many a night at whichever house, apartment, trailer, or motel room his mother and he called home for the moment. She changed lovers even more frequently then they changed homes, but only barely. All of the places he'd ever lived were hovels.

His mother hardly ever worked, and he remembered her lounging around the house watching TV, usually wearing just a slip or babydoll pajamas. She had lived with some of the men, always in her place, always on her terms. He surmised that the men supported her, but she always managed to have her own place, which came in handy when she inevitably gave the man the boot. Consequently, they moved frequently, and Ted was forever changing schools and friends. After awhile, he gave up on both, preferring to be alone in his room, or take frequent forays to nearby towns and interesting places, whatever provided him with some temporary relief from his dismal home.

Most of the men just ignored him, but some were abusive. His dreams were frequently about these men, but his mind played tricks on him. In his dreams the men acted differently. He dreamed about playing catch with them and being taken to movies and car shows and county fairs...all the things the other kids did with their fathers. As far as he knew he had no real father. He didn't remember meeting him and his mother never once mentioned him. Once, and only once, did a man show any real interest in him. A friend of one of his mother's boyfriends would come over and baby-sit for him while his mom and her boyfriend went out. His name was Jack and he was nice. They played board games and he often brought some videos to watch. He had overheard his mom talk about Jack maybe being a faggot but her boyfriend said no, that he was a churchgoing sort who just liked kids, that the kid would be all right with him. Ted wished Jack was his mom's boyfriend, and he asked Jack whether he could be, but Jack just smiled and tousled his hair.

Jack had taken him fishing once at a lake. They had gotten a small boat with an outboard motor, two fishing rods, and some worms and minnows for bait. Jack had a tackle box and a fillet knife in a leather sheaf that he wore on his belt. As a boy he loved that knife. He got Jack to show him how sharp it was and watched in fascination as he used it to cut up the crappies they had caught. The knife was the shiniest thing he had ever seen, and he liked the way the flesh opened and parted cleanly as Jack expertly sliced along the bony spine of the fish. He was not taken aback by the blood, or by the fishy smell that lingered over them the rest of the afternoon. To this day, the fishing trip was the singular memory he had of childhood happiness. He remembered every detail of this long and wondrous outing.

It started with the breakfast of ham and eggs Jack had bought him in a diner near the lake. He remembered how nice the waitress had been, and how good the food looked and smelled when she set the plates in front of them. He needed no prompting, and dug into the meal ravenously. Afterwards, they headed for the lake. If he closed his eyes he could still feel the way the sun beat down on his bare shoulders and back as he hunched in the boat holding his rod and continually casting and reeling as Jack had shown him.

That first time he'd felt his line snap taunt and the pole start to wriggle in his hands he thought there was no finer sensation in the world. Jack leapt to his feet to assist him, rocking the boat and causing him to let go one hand from the rod and grab the side, fearing he might be thrown overboard. But he recovered quickly and got a firm grip on the rod. Jack was telling him to pull up on the rod and reel 'em in and he grasped the knob and reeled for all he was worth. Jack bent over the side holding a long pole with a net attached. As his catch neared the surface Jack dipped the net under the water and pulled the wildly twisting, writhing fish into the boat. The fish's tail threw water on their faces and heads as Jack lifted him overhead and spilled him onto the bottom of the boat. Jack was smiling as he caught the still squirming fish and lifted it by the tail for Ted to inspect.

"Great job, young man. You're quite a fisherman. I'm proud of you."

I'm proud of you. This was to be the only time he heard these words in his young life. As he rode back home that evening with Jack, tired but happy, he felt real. For once, he actually did what he had imagined a thousand times in his dreams. He looked up at Jack, and Jack smiled down at him. He felt Jack's hand squeeze his knee, and slide up to his thigh, where it remained for the rest of the trip home. He was eight years old.

He'd been buddies with Uncle Jack for nearly three months when his mother dumped her latest boyfriend. After that, Jack stopped coming around. His mother never did give him a good explanation. She said something about Jack not having a way to come see him now, since her boyfriend was the one with a car. It hurt him deeply, though, and he once again became sullen and withdrawn. He felt as if this had been his only chance to be a normal kid, to have someone who cared about him and would show him all the wonderful things there were to do in this little part of the world. Instead, he sunk lower than ever. It probably would have been better for all if he never had that short time with Jack; if he'd never had that fishing trip. He'd finally found out what it was like to have a man take an interest in him only to have his hopes dashed by his mother's fickleness.

Chapter 21

Located on the lower level of the FBI Academy in Quantico, Virginia, the Behavioral Science Unit was the home of VICAP. The mission of VICAP was to identify serial crimes, especially violent rapes and homicides, by collecting data from police agencies nationwide. VICAP distributes a special form for police departments to complete and send back to the FBI, detailing pertinent facts of the crime that may be related to crimes in other jurisdictions. These reports are entered in a computer database that can be queried by any agency needing information about serial crimes or the known patterns of criminals. VICAP serves police agencies worldwide, and the information contained in its electronic files have helped to solve many crimes. There were ninety-five questions on the case entry form, plus plenty of room to expound on the answers as necessary. The questions include the following pertinent information.

- Name and description of the victim or victims
- Name and/or description of the offender(s)
- The modus operandi of offender
- The condition of the victim when found. This is a very important question, as many serial killers and rapists have a particular way they plan and execute their crime, which often entails a particular, sometimes ritualistic manner of death and can include "posing" the body to complete their fantasy.
- The cause of death or manner of trauma
- The details about any sexual activity
- Information about weapons used or displayed during the incident
- Vehicles used or involved in the crime, or simply possessed by the offender

Of course, there was also plenty of room for additional narrative that contained information, especially that of an unusual nature that may help identify a serial type offense. Analyst Devin Gray was pouring over a stack of newly arrived forms, mentally evaluating their importance before entering them into the system. All of the analysts performed this chore, mostly to see if any of the incidents were so ghastly or bizarre that they needed immediate attention by one of the special agents assigned to the unit. In addition, since their work often gave them an insight into the types of incidents that may be legitimate serial crimes, it had proven useful for them to actually read the material before typing it blindly into the database.

She picked up a report sent to them just yesterday by the Columbia, Missouri police department. Something in it reminded her of a murder in Albuquerque a couple of months before. In both attacks, the killer had been nude. Both had been very violent sexual crimes, and both were committed in the victim's bathroom. Although she recalled that the victim in Albuquerque was murdered and the one in Columbia was not, the police believed murder had been the intent of the assailant in both incidents. The victims were young women, described as very pretty. There were no links to anyone the women knew, which indicated they were both "stranger assaults," the kind that strike fear into the heart of a community. The distance between cities was fairly large, but Devin knew that this did not preclude involvement by the same perpetrator. Stranger assaults were the most prevalent reports that came into VICAP. Local police had difficulty developing leads in these cases. Often there were no good witnesses, and if none of the victim's friends, family, acquaintances, or enemies were suspected, there was zilch to go on.

She looked again at the stack of reports she needed to enter today, and concluded that she should not take the time to run a query right now, maybe she could get to it tomorrow. But before she put the report back in the pile she read the description of the brutal attack on Sonja Peterson. She learned Sonja was a few years younger than she and liked to jog, which was an activity Devin had recently began taking up herself. This struck a nerve, and she decided to run the query despite the pile of waiting forms. After all, she reasoned, she was an analyst, not a clerk, and this *was* the main purpose for her job.

She began the task of building the data and parameters for which she wanted the system to search. There were fields for suspect description, weapons used, and methods of operation, commonly referred to by police as *modus operandi*, or M.O. for short. Despite the volume of her other work, Devin took her time delving into the report from the Columbia police. She found many items that could help uncover a link between this and other assaults. It took her about an hour to prepare the query, including a call to the Columbia detective who was handling the case. She wanted a bit more information, and was lucky to get him on the line after calling the department's headquarters. Satisfied with the information she collected, she hit the 'enter' key, and waited for the results of the search. Minutes later, the printer near her desk came to life, spitting out sheets of green bar paper for her to examine.

She tore off about two yards worth of sheets that contained the summary information for more than two dozen cases, open and closed, which matched at least some of the criteria she set. She spread the sheets out on her oversized desk and scanned the material quickly. Immediately she eliminated eight cases that didn't fit, and a more detailed analysis ruled out six more. That left thirteen cases to examine. She took the sheets she needed and discarded the rest, feeding them into a shredder. She then noted that seven of the remaining cases were closed, which meant that they had been solved, usually by the arrest of a suspect. Six of those were murders that predated Sonja's attack but were less than a year old, so it was unlikely that these offenders had escaped the criminal justice system so soon and were back in operation. However, it *was* possible, and they would have to be checked out. Devin set them aside for some interns to follow up later.

That left seven cases. She would have to pull the original VICAP report on them, and contact the originating police agency to gain access to their complete files. This could be done promptly by the FBI field office closest to the city where the crimes occurred. Before pulling the reports, she noted a commonality in three of the six open cases. The *victim's computer was found to have been tampered with. All files were erased beyond recovery. Interesting*, she thought, *very interesting*. She picked up the phone to call the special agent in charge of her unit. This was too good to wait.

Three days later, analyst Devin Gray received all the packets she'd requested. She took them into a small conference room located among the offices of the Behavioral Science Unit, and spread them out on the well-worn oak table. Her instincts flared as she laid the paperwork out in neat rows, and arranged them in a standard fashion for comparison. She first reviewed the initial police officers' reports, then the investigators' reports, witness statements, and finally the lab reports. There was a suspect listed in two cases and she collected as much information as she could about them. She took a few minutes to run their names and identifying information through the VICAP database, but nothing of interest was found. However, her excitement grew as she continued to find some strong commonalties among the three cases that had originally drew her attention. It took six hours to review all the cases, and she began to list all the significant details on a large, pre-prepared grid she had designed for just this purpose.

There was a seventy five percent match in the critical elements of the crimes committed in Albuquerque, New Mexico, Columbia, Missouri, and Highland Park, Pennsylvania. Anything above sixty percent was automatically assigned to a special agent to further investigate the link between crimes. Despite the fatigue she felt from scrutinizing report after report from all the different police agencies, Devin was elated that she took the time and effort to look at all the information. The special agents would have to make the official call, but she had already made her decision. *She was looking at a serial killer, and a good one to boot.*

It was 9:30 when Joe Forestall came into Jason's office. The Chief's disposition looked as sunny as this fine September morning. He also looked excited, which was a rare emotion for the Chief these days, and he immediately took a seat opposite Jason's desk.

"What's up, Chief?" Jason inquired, putting down the pen with which he had been writing a memo and sitting back in his chair. He wanted his boss to know he had his full attention. Jason hated those people who continued to work on whatever was in front of them, even after acknowledging a visitor. That sent a clear message...you can talk to me, but I'm too busy with something more important to listen. Jason was careful not to do this when people came to see him.

"I just got off the phone with Quantico. They're sending an agent from Philadelphia to work with us on the Mathieson murder. Seems like a VICAP analyst found at least two other cases that showed strong similarities."

"No shit. I've never heard of a VICAP hit around here before. Do you think it's legit? Where did the other homicides occur?"

"According to the agent I talked with, it was a strong match between all the cases. It centered on the computers being tampered with, as well as the manner of death and the sexual overtones. They think it's possible these are serial killings. Actually, one of them is an attempted murder. The victim put up a fight and before the killer could finish her off, someone interrupted them and he fled. That one was in Columbia, Missouri, a university town about ninety miles west of St. Louis."

"Where was the other one?"

"Albuquerque, New Mexico. That was a homicide. They are checking into a couple of others too. They don't fit as tightly as the three we're looking at now, but there could be some links buried there. The FBI analysts are pulling all the case files on them now."

"Damn, Chief. This is unbelievable. What do we do now?"

"The FBI agent will be here first thing tomorrow. He'll want to go over the file with you and Cab, and then discuss the other cases. After that, detectives from the three sites, maybe more by that time, will get together and work on the cases as a task force."

The meeting with the Philadelphia FBI field agent was short. He was convinced that the murders were linked, and arranged a meeting at Quantico for the next day. Jason and Cab left for Virginia at 5:30 in the morning. It would be about a three and a half-hour drive, more if they encountered any traffic problems on the Beltway around D.C. The VICAP meeting was scheduled for ten, and Cab hoped his boss would stop for breakfast along the way. The last time the two of them had traveled any distance, to pick up a rape suspect in West Virginia, Jason drove for hours without stopping, despite Cab's constant nagging. The damn guy was like a camel, could go for an eternity without having to eat, drink, or pee. *Kind of goes along with his robot-like personality*, Cab thought. No wonder the guy can be so short, direct, and abrasive at times, he's not human...at least not *totally*. Come to think of it, he even walked with a measured, stiff gait, like he was all-purpose and no wander, always had a destination and was programmed to take the shortest route to get there. Cab made up his mind that they were stopping just past Baltimore for something to eat, even if it was only an Egg McMuffin or three.

He began to think up a ruse that would force Jason to stop should he resist. If he had to, he'd work up one of his killer farts. One time, he had caused Jason to stop in the middle of a busy intersection after releasing one of his potent bombs on the way back from dinner. He remembered the look on Jason's face as he turned toward him after the stench had first invaded his nostrils. His lips were unnaturally curled inward and his eyes were starting to tear. He was starting to gag when he suddenly slammed on the brakes, threw open his door, and leapt out into the busy street, cars honking and brakes squealing as other motorist swerved to avoid him. Geez, you'd think it was nerve gas for Christ sake.

On second thought, Cab figured he'd better not do that again. It would be hard to explain to the Chief why his partner got flattened in the middle of Route 95 during early morning rush hour. Worse yet, Jason would tell Shawna on him. And that would cost the big man plenty. She hated any time her man was so uncouth, wanted him to have *style*. And, like she had told him a hundred times about several different habits he had; "men with *style* don't do that." Cab wondered where all those men were, cause he surely never met one.

They lucked out. Traffic around Baltimore was manageable, and they were cruising toward the outskirts of D.C. with time to spare. Even more remarkable, Jason had suggested they pull in at a truck stop for some breakfast. Miracles never cease. It was twenty-to-ten when they pulled into the FBI Academy. Jason had a knack for always showing up right on time. Cab figured it must be part of his robotics package, a built-in fucking time-space calculator. They were waved through the gate and walked inside the main building. Jason walked up to the check-in counter, flashed his badge, and told the guard they were here for the VICAP meeting. Having attended the FBI National Academy where he spent eleven weeks using every part of this spacious campus, he shook off the man's offer to call for an escort. He led Cab down the long hallway toward the elevators, which they took to the basement offices of the Behavioral Science Unit.

There were well over a dozen people gathered around the large battle-scarred conference table in the sparse quarters that served as a briefing room for the unit. There were no paintings or decorations; just bland, beige walls, three of them covered with well used cork boards to paste up pictures, drawings, and documents from cases under discussion. A few of the participants were milling around, drinking from Styrofoam coffee cups and making introductions. A FBI agent called the meeting to order.

"Good morning all. I'm Supervisory Special Agent Thomas Parsons. Welcome to Quantico and welcome to the Behavior Science Unit. I hope our meeting today will be fruitful, and I hope that you all get an opportunity to learn more about your cases and possible links to some of the others. Let's begin with some introductions."

They went around the room, with the representatives from each agency identifying themselves, and giving a short synopsis of the cases they were bringing to the table. Besides the departments Jason was expecting today, there were detectives from Sparks, Nevada and Olympia, Washington. There were also FBI field agents from each of the regions covering these cities, and an FBI criminal profiler. Standing next to Agent Parsons was a red headed beauty introduced as Devin Gray, a crime analyst for the Bureau. He said she was the individual who discovered the links in the murders and assaults, and it was her alertness that brought them together today. Jason looked at her as her boss introduced her. She was really pretty, but seemed too young to be the catalyst for such an important case. But, she was probably in her mid-twenties, and in today's world of high tech gadgetry and space age information, she was in her prime. After all, this fast-moving, head-spinning world does belong to the young. She seemed a bit nervous, and Jason wondered if this was her first meeting of this type. However, once she spoke, her nervousness seemed to fall away and was replaced by a logical, factual cadence that bolstered her professional standing with the detectives in the room.

"It's my pleasure to be here today," she began, gazing round the table. "Let's talk about what we know."

She went on to describe her initial discovery of the links between each case, starting with the obvious computer involvement. Jason immediately regretted not inviting Trooper Woodson to come along today. He would have added to this discussion, and it would have been better for him to get information firsthand, rather than relying on Jason and Cab to brief him later.

"So that we can start to get a firm timeline, let's put the cases in chronological order. Please take notes so we can save any questions until after the presentation of all of the cases. First, we have a murder in Highland Park, Pennsylvania. This one occurred in early May of this year. The victim was a single, twenty-four-year-old white female, found strangled to death in a small park. However, it does not appear she was killed in the park, but was moved there after death. The scene was pretty clean, and the only evidence recovered was basically on the body. She was dressed in a short party dress, sans bra and panties, and had been sexually assaulted. There was bruising on her thighs and buttocks, and trauma to her vagina from forced penetration. Forensic examination found cloth fibers deep in her throat, indicating that some sort of gag had been shoved deep into her throat. Despite the sexual nature of this crime, DNA is *not* available from this case.

"Trace evidence, a small amount of latex rubber, *was* recovered from the victim's throat. This indicates the perpetrator used a condom. There also was a piece of what appeared to be hair under one of the victim's fingernails. Laboratory analysis confirmed it was indeed hair, but the type of treated hair found in a toupee or wig. So there was no DNA and the sample is little or no help in determining if we have a serial killer. There were no local suspects developed, and although the victim had worked as an exotic dancer in the past, there were no obvious indications that this work had anything to do with her selection as a victim. Nor was there any evidence of any current or past disputes or conflicts with someone who may have wanted her dead.

"Police in Highland Park did learn about a past contact in Atlanta, her home state, that could have some connection, but as of yet, nothing has panned out. At first glance, this case appears to be an acquaintance murder. You know, girl is picked up at local bar nightclub, gets drunk or high, and is assaulted and murdered by unknown suspect. Despite a pretty exhaustive local search, police were never able to find a bar or club where the victim was seen the night of her murder, so that's still a mystery.

"However, police searching the victim's apartment did find that her computer hard drive had been wiped out. It was not an accidental act or machine malfunction either. It was deliberately erased by someone who knew what they were doing. There was nothing in the victim's background to lead us to believe she had the knowledge to do this, so our theory is an outsider, possibly the killer, was responsible."

Not bad. Jason was impressed with Devin's research and the ease with which she recalled the details of Amber's murder. She seemed more mature to him now, and he liked her delivery. He bet that she was very thorough and methodical, much like him. He wondered if she was as obstinate too. She looked at him as she finished her discussion of the Highland Park incident, almost looking for his approval. He smiled and nodded slightly, and she moved on.

"The second case is from Sparks, Nevada. It occurred in early June, almost a month to the day after the first. In this case, the victim was a single, twenty-seven year old prostitute, a high-end call girl. She was found in a room of the NewWorld Hotel, which is one of Spark's nicest hotels. The victim was found naked, and her clothes were piled neatly on a chair next to the bed. She too was raped and assaulted, and was strangled. Although, in this case there was no cloth shoved down the throat, there were ligature marks on the neck that the coroner concluded were caused by a leather belt or similar object. The initial theory here was that some nutcase had picked up the victim through her call service, taking her to his hotel room for sex. After she disrobed, he let his real intentions be known and there was a struggle.

"He overpowered her, raped her, and strangled her to death. The reason this case is being considered by us is that there was a laptop found in the room, still turned on, connected to the internet, and it appears that someone used the computer to talk in a sexual oriented chat room. It's possible the perpetrator did this after the murder, so it's significant. There was also fresh semen found in this case, on the sheets and in the victim's throat. We are running the samples using PCR-STR analysis and will be able to compare the result with any other case yielding DNA evidence. As you know, this will identify the perpetrator with a one in quadrillion chance of error. It's virtually failsafe. In addition . . . "

"Excuse me for interrupting," Jason said, not really sorry at all. "But why did you say *fresh* semen?"

"Well, not to be disgusting or anything," Devin answered, "but the Sparks crime scene unit found six different semen stains in the room, on the mattress, on the rug near the bed, and on two of the cushioned chairs. I needed to differentiate between evidence and sloppy housekeeping. Need I say more?"

"Please don't," groaned Jason, as others in the room shook their heads knowingly. Anyone in the crime business knew how many hidden stains and bodily excretions existed in a hotel room, any hotel room. Maid service was ill equipped to deal with the fluids amorous guests often left behind. Fortunately, today's forensic technology could determine an old semen stain from a fresh one, so detectives did not have to waste time and expense checking them all out. For a large city or resort town, this was a godsend.

"As I was saying, the DNA result we found in the Sparks case will be entered into the FBI's National DNA Code Indexing System, which is a rapidly growing database of evidence and suspects, similar to AFIS. The information will be available for this and future investigations." She saw Jason look fidgety again, like he had something else on his mind. She held up a finger in his direction, and quickly continued.

"There are hundreds of surveillance photos available in Sparks. The room was on the sixth floor, so there is video from the elevators, stairways, and a little from the hallways, although it's possible to avoid the fixed cameras in the hallways if you're careful. Nevertheless, the Sparks police have these available for the task force to review anytime if you have anything to compare them with.

"The third case is from Albuquerque, New Mexico. It occurred in July of this year, when the single, twenty-eight year old victim was attacked in her own home. She was brutally beaten, with the perpetrator physically assaulting her and literally dragging her into the shower in the master bedroom. It was there police found her body, naked and bleeding. They were called the next day after she failed to show up at work, and the coroner determined she had been dead at least sixteen hours before she was discovered. This would place her death around five-thirty to seven o'clock PM. The water in the shower had been running the whole time, and no semen or bodily fluids, except for traces of the victim's blood, were found at the scene.

"There were wet footmarks outlined in the rug, and we're assuming the assailant was nude or partially nude during the attack. It appears he stepped out of the shower after killing the victim, and dripped all over her bedroom. There *was* forced entry, from a window at the north side of the house, but neighbors saw nothing. No prints, of course, and no other evidence, but they did take a lot of fibers and hair samples, some of which are *not* the victims. These are still in analysis. The hair samples had no roots, so they were not pulled out and without the root it's very difficult to get DNA...but we're trying. There was a computer here too, and the hard drive had also been wiped out, just like the Highland Park case. We view that fact as very strange, and it forges a strong link between these two cases."

Devin took a few moments to review her notes, and took a drink of water from a glass she had poured herself before continuing. She had lost all traces of nervousness, and was totally focused on her analysis. Jason found this very appealing.

"The fourth case is from Olympia, Washington. This case involves a twenty-one year old student from Evergreen College, who was found in her dorm room by her roommate. She had been bludgeoned to death, and there was quite a lot of blood in the room, all hers. There was a sexual assault here also, penetration of the anus by a blunt object, which was not recovered. The coroner's report indicated it tore the anus in a non-symmetrical manner, meaning the wound was not round, but rather rough-edged and uneven. No speculation on what the object might be, but the victim was alive during this assault, and would have suffered excruciating pain. This is the only case so far that has a suspect. It seems the victim had met a young man at a college dance. He was from nearby Granite Falls Community College, and apparently became quite taken with our victim.

"The feeling was not mutual, but he continued to pursue her, alarming her to the point that she told several of her friends about it, and then eventually filed a report with the Olympia Police Department. They interviewed him, labeled him a strange duck who was socially inept, and told him to cease and desist. All pretty much standard fare for a stalking incident. This was in April when they interviewed him, and our victim was murdered just a couple of weeks ago. There is no other evidence linking him to the murder, and detectives have said he refuses to be interviewed anymore. He's lawyered up.

"His background is not really significant as far as we are concerned, and there's no indication he has the ability to travel and the intellect to have been behind these other jobs, but he's still under consideration. Police are trying the hard way to reconstruct his activities on the days surrounding each of the murders, but it's painstaking and time consuming without his cooperation. Personally, I think he's a loony-toon who might be responsible for the one Olympia murder, but he's not our guy."

Jason saw Devin's boss lift his eyebrow disapprovingly at this remark. He did not like his analyst to be so forward.

"Finally," Devin continued, "we have the case of Sonja Peterson from Columbia, Missouri. This was an attempted murder, and the victim is very much alive, and very helpful to police. This assault occurred just a week ago, on Wednesday. It too was a brutal attack that occurred in the 21-year-old student's off-campus apartment. Police determined the perpetrator gained entrance to the apartment through the front door, probably by slipping the rather cheesy lock. There are also some keys missing from the place, which the guy must have took with him, or maybe gotten beforehand from somewhere. One thought is that he cased the place, slipped the lock to get a look-see inside, and found another set of keys that he took for future entry. Or, he could be an acquaintance, and been inside the place legitimately and hoisted the keys.

"At any rate, the perp was waiting inside the victim's bathroom and attacked her as she came in to run the water for a shower. Police found that he had hidden himself in the bathroom closet. When he lunged at her from behind, he first tried to strangle her, but she surprised him by fighting back. Apparently she came close to winning, but he managed to grab a straight razor that he must have carried with him and sliced her up pretty bad. This took the fight out of her, but he was not able to complete the sexual assault or the murder. Fortunately,

Sonja's roommate came home during the assault, and the perp bowled her over as he ran out the door.

"We have DNA from this job, from a sample of the perpetrator's own blood. Samples are in the lab now, and we'll have a comparison between the Columbia case and the Sparks case in a matter of a week or so."

"Is there a computer involved here as well?" Jason interrupted, once again breaking the rule about holding questions until the end.

"Yes. In fact, her roommate, even after she was kicked in the head, saw their attacker go back into the bedroom and pick up something next to Sonja's computer. She couldn't say what it was, but it was small, and fit in his hand."

"Was the computer on? Was it checked out yet?"

"Yes, Lieutenant, it was on, and it's been impounded by the Columbia P.D. for analysis. Our forensic people are going to look at it soon."

Jason thought of Trooper Woodson, and wanted to get him involved with this.

"Agent Parsons, if possible, I would like a computer expert from the Pennsylvania State Police to be in on any examination. He's already involved in our case."

If Parsons was annoyed by the request or it's timing, he didn't show it. Ms. Gray, however was looking somewhat perturbed by his constant interruptions. He was disturbing the flow of her thoughts, and she had to take another few moments to review her notes. This was no way to impress her boss.

"I guess we're ready for questions now," she said, with a touch of haughtiness in her voice. "At least Lt. Coulter seems to have some pressing needs."

"Well," said Jason, unperturbed by her mild rebuke. "Since you asked, what are the similarities between victims? You told us their ages, how about other characteristics, such as physical description, occupation, interests, philosophy of life. Also, were Ms. Peterson and her roommate able to give a description of their attacker? Is there a composite sketch being completed?"

"Unfortunately, there is no composite sketch. Neither Ms. Peterson nor her roommate could give us much. We do know the suspect is a Caucasian male, mid-twenties at least, about five-foot-eight to five-foot-ten inches tall, and does not seem to have any unusual features or marks on his body. He has blond hair, both top and bottom."

It was Jason's turn to cock an eyebrow. He was tempted to ask how come the girls remembered the color of the suspect's pubic hair, but could not recall any details of his face. In fact he started to speak, but the look on Devin's face silenced him. She was in no mood for such antics.

"There is one thing however. Although the girls could not give facial characteristics, both said he looked like a fox."

This time, he spoke without thinking.

"You mean the guy was a hottie?"

"No, Lieutenant, that's not what I meant. I mean fox, as in furry little cousin of the canine. Long, angular face."

"So what? Haven't you ever heard of fox face, pig face?"

Cab grunted loudly, hoping Jason would pick up his displeasure. We're guests here man. Never met any of these folks before, and first impressions count. Don't make all these FBI agents and other city detectives think we're a couple of assholes from Pennsylvania.

"Excuse me?" Devin looked at both Jason and Cab. She was starting to think they were a couple of assholes, but maybe they were just real good. True to her scientific training, she withheld judgement until more facts were known.

Supervisory Special Agent Parsons was thinking the same thing. Were these guys clowns, or did they know what they were doing? He shifted his feet and smiled lamely, giving them the benefit.

"You know," Jason continued, glancing at the others for signs of recognition. One of the cops from Missouri was shaking his head in agreement. "There's a theory that most human faces fall into one of two categories, fox face or pig face. If you look at people, you'll see traces of one or the other in their face."

Detectives looked at each other self consciously, trying not to be obvious, but thinking the same thing. Please don't let me be a pig face.

"Myself, I don't think all faces can be classified as such." Sighs of relief from some in the room. "But most can. Anyway, that's the theory. Please go on Ms. Grey."

Devin was incredulous, and her expression showed her disbelief and displeasure. The combination of emotions resulted in a sour look, like she had just taken a bite of a rancid peach. It took her a few seconds to realize that Jason had called upon her to continue, and she noticed that all heads had turned from the brash detective back to her. She hesitated an instant more, her face still twisted, and then regained her composure and forced a weak smile. She continued the briefing. Asshole, she concluded. Fucking asshole.

The rest of the meeting was uneventful. Fortunately for him and the reputation of the Highland Park Police Department, Jason was very convincing when he was called upon to provide the group with a more detailed account of the Amber Mathieson murder. The detectives were impressed with his knowledge of the case and the way he had picked up the salient points of Devin Grey's overview and worked them into his presentation. Even Devin herself was forced to reevaluate her earlier impression. She admired the ease with which Jason spoke to this group, and could see that unlike her, he was genuinely enjoying the spotlight. *So that's why he played the class clown*, she thought. He was trying to steal the limelight. Here was a man used to being noticed, used to being in charge. He didn't really like it when he was just "one of the boys." He *was* a bit arrogant, but he pulled it off in such a coy way that she found it attractive.

Despite her better judgement, she began romanticizing about the two of them. If he stayed around awhile, maybe she'd get some history on him, see if he was interested. She hated to admit it, but Jason was the sort of man she'd been drawn to since high school, when she dated the quarterback for two years. Although shy herself, she loved being attached to a man who garnered attention at every gathering. It got her introduced to the in-crowd, and made her feel part of an inner circle that otherwise would exclude the shy, introspective bookworm. Her relationships to these men had opened many doors for her in the past. In fact, she got her present job on the recommendation of a D.C. lawyer she was dating up until last year.

Her boss calling everyone to order again interrupted her thoughts. He went over some of the standard procedures for joint investigations, making sure everyone knew the FBI would be in charge. She watched the group for the knowing nods and quick disparaging glances exchanged by the city cops. Even in the information age, where the FBI was king, local cops resented being told the Feds were in charge of anything. However, there was no denying they had the best network for exchanging information, and even now Agent Parsons was distributing secure cell phones which operated off a special FBI network and was telling the detectives how to access investigative software using the internet. This software would connect all the involved cities and keep tract of clues, leads, and actions of each investigative team. FBI analysts would review it each day and make sure all the participants were abreast of any developments. In addition, a Bureau criminal profiler would also be assigned for the duration of the investigation. He would be headquartered in Quantico, but would visit each city and each crime scene to help him get a feel for what had transpired in each location.

That same evening, Cab and Jason drove straight through back to Highland Park. Cab was sleeping most of the time, and so didn't complain while Jason pushed the car mile after mile. They didn't stop until they reached Pennsylvania, and even then they just peed and grabbed some coffee. Jason was in his glory.

Chapter 22

The morning after he returned from Quantico, Jason found a whole slew of law enforcement types waiting for him outside his office. He shook hands with Agent Kelly from the DEA and a slightly built mustachioed man from the Office of the Postal Inspector whose name he didn't catch. Bill Ramos and Trooper Woodson were also there, so Jason assumed something broke in the case involving the steroids. It was after nine, and he felt a little guilty coming into the office so late, but he had been really beat from the drive, and had nothing scheduled for this morning. The men informed Jason they had reviewed the statements he had taken from Ben Dickson, and they wanted to move forward with the investigation. They had plotted a strategy for tracing the orders they would place for steroids over the Internet back to the supplier.

Jason tried without success to put the Mathieson murder investigation out of his mind as he listened to the plan. He found himself drifting off several times as Agent Kelly was talking to him. He had to ask Kelly to repeat several key parts, and noticed the agent's perturbed look as he discussed parts of the plan for the third time. Finally, Jason understood. He hated to make the briefing difficult and knew it made him look bad in front of the others, but it could have dire consequences if he screwed up the operation because he hadn't been paying attention and kept quiet about it. It was a mistake his own detectives sometimes made, and it wasn't going to happen to him.

They did it the old fashioned way. The detectives placed an order for steroids over the Internet, and put a reverse trace into effect with exactly twenty-four air-ground package delivery companies, including the U.S. Postal Service, UPS, and FedEx. It was not a sure thing, but chances were that one of them would be the carrier chosen by the steroid supplier. If it worked according to plan, any package with the final destination of 1238 Carpenter Street in Philadelphia, the dummy address used by the DEA for such operations, would be traced from its origin. After a little detective work, they would be able to identify the exact location from which the product was shipped, and obtain a search warrant for the premises within hours of receiving the information. All of the details were already typed into a warrant, and a team of detectives and swat teams from the DEA and the FBI were on standby. As soon as word came about a delivery, they would spring into action.

The company delivered as promised. The drugs were on their way within twenty-four hours after the order was received. They used a second address to mask the location of the warehouse, but they did such a high volume that determining the source location was not difficult for the federal agents. Once they had a suspect location, undercover agents from the DEA and FBI watched the drop point, and physically followed a passel of delivery persons back to the warehouse. Agent Kelly took the call from the agents who had discovered the source of the shipments, and quickly wrote the address down on a scrap of paper, which he handed to Jason while he was still on the phone. Jason immediately recognized the address. Cajuani, Mexico. A plant owned by his friend Kyle Price. Although it was no surprise, Jason had held out hope that Kyle was not involved in the drug connection at the Apex. His hopes were dashed with this news, and he knew that his friendship with Kyle had suffered a fatal blow. While the other agents and detectives exchanged high-fives over their success, Jason fought a wave of nausea. The next few days would bring him many challenges, both professionally and personally. It was the personal part that made him sick.

Less than fifteen hours later, they had the plant surrounded. Following a predawn briefing with the Federales, agents from the Drug Enforcement Agency, including their crack SWAT unit, had moved into place. Jason had conferred with the regional DEA agent-in-charge about the raid. They had decided not to request help from the Mexican Authorities until the last possible moment, fearing news of the raid would be leaked by corrupt policia. It was not unusual in Mexico for the local policia to be on the payroll of American business and industry, looking out for their interest in this foreign land. There was no evidence that it was happening in this situation, but no one wanted to take the risk. Things were getting better under the new Mexican President, and it was more prudent to contact the federal police, whose reputation was better, and as a courtesy inform them of the raid and request their approval and assistance.

In actuality, the raid was already fully planned, and there were enough DEA personnel present to conduct the operation without local help. The Mexican authorities would be miffed, knowing the arrangements were made without their blessing, but they would agree to the plan. Under their new President, the country was sincerely trying to improve cooperation with the U.S. government to stem the flow of illegal drugs into the United States. Any signs of reluctance by Mexican law enforcement or the provincial Governor would be frowned upon by the new administration. Besides, the target was an American company, and the fact that Americans were using Mexico as a base for drug running would play well in the news.

Jason was also there to participate in the raid, and had brought Trooper Woodson and one of his associates to delve into the computer network inside the plant. He and the other Pennsylvania police officers were inside a nondescript panel truck parked in a seldom-used dirt lot off the main road leading into the village of Cajuani. The truck was actually the command post for the raid, and was specially outfitted with workspaces and communications gear necessary to run such an operation. There were three DEA agents inside, including the agent-in-charge. The radios were humming with activity as SWAT supervisors gave various orders to their raid teams on the scene. It was approaching 6:00 AM, the time chosen for the raid to commence.

At two minutes past six, a single command started the action. The SWAT team commander, a leather skinned, veteran DEA agent Jason had met briefly only a couple hours ago, issued it. The message was simple. "All units, GO." The radios fell silent. This was the most stressful part of any tactical mission. Almost anything could happen during the seconds that the teams first entered a building. Despite any intelligence police develop prior to an operation, they are never sure what resistance they would meet, especially when confronting drug dealers, who are known for being heavily armed and for setting booby traps to injure police officers. The most dreaded sound during this time would be gunfire. Everyone on the perimeter remained quiet, listening for any sounds of resistance coming from the plant.

Although it took only eight minutes before the first transmission came from a SWAT leader signifying that the building was secure, it seemed like hours. There was a discernable sigh of relief in the command post, and Jason, the troopers, and a DEA agent jumped from the truck into a waiting car and sped to the plant. They approached the main entrance of the factory. There was nothing remarkable about it. It blended in with other buildings that he'd seen along the route, and except for the newer chain link fence topped by strands of razor wire, it could have been any other Mexican factory. Of course, most of the ones in Cajuani were garment factories, staffed by native women who were paid piecemeal for the garments they produced. He knew from discussing this operation with the DEA that many of the workers were younger than fourteen, some as young as ten, toiling in these hot, poorly ventilated sweatshops for more than twelve hours a day when not in school. As he approached, he nodded to the SWAT officers guarding the building. It was then he noticed the surveillance cameras mounted on the low roof of the entrance foyer. He looked for other signs of enhanced security, and found the front doors were made of steel, and the walls were thick, reinforced concrete. Although he knew Mexico had a high burglary rate, and banditos sometimes rampaged and plundered all over the province, this level of security was unusual. Jason was pretty sure he would find this particular factory was making more than trinkets and crafts.

The contingent of police detectives and special agents from the Federales and the DEA motioned him from a large room down the hall from the foyer.

"Senore," said a portly brown shirted Federale, a big round cigar bobbing precariously from his lips as he spoke. "We have found what you seek, come see what your American friend was doing in our town."

Jason was tempted to order him to put the partially smoked but unlit cigar back into his grimy pocket. In Highland Park, an officer who carried something into a crime scene like that would be subject to the full force of his wrath, but he was just a guest here, and held his tongue. He ignored the slovenly officer as he passed by and walked slowly and carefully into a large, dimly lit room, scanning the area ahead, especially the floor, before his footsteps fell quietly onto the harsh cement floor. He didn't even flash one of his patented icy looks as he made his way past, the man simply wasn't worth acknowledging. Besides, such a look would probably be lost on this dullard, who was on the one hand proud to be accompanying the fabled Drug Enforcement Agency on such a mission, but on the other looked for every opportunity to show his disparagement toward the Americans.

The room was about the size of a high school gym, only not nearly so high. There were the usual array of tables, benches, and chairs one would expect to find in such a place. But it was different too. Along the far wall, to the west, there was a comprehensive laboratory. Jason didn't know all that much about clandestine drug labs, though he'd seen a few during his time with the drug task force, but he knew enough to realize the scope of this one. This was no kitchen lab. It was sophisticated, and from the look of the rows of apparatus and racks of beakers, cylinders, and tubes he saw, probably capable of producing enough pills to keep an entire town supplied. He would later find out that he underestimated the plant's capacity. Actually, the lab made over 50,000 pills per day, enough to fill daily orders and have some left over for stock.

The DEA agents were systematically checking the equipment, making sure there were no imminent hazards that could endanger the agents and police. It was a well-known fact that the interruption of certain phases of the "cooking" process could lead to explosions if not handled correctly. The DEA had special lab teams that were trained to perform these delicate operations, and Jason was glad they were part of this raid team. Other investigators were busy taking photographs, and still others were searching for documents, order forms, accounts receivable, and any other evidence that would solidify their case. Trooper Woodson was scurrying about with the other eggheads, chirping about the banks of computers they found in another room, hoping they would be able to crack passwords and discover the online heart of the illicit steroid operation. Suddenly alone in the middle of the room, watching all the well-coordinated activity around him, Jason felt empty. He realized his suspicions, his fears, were correct. Kyle, his friend and sometime confidante, was a crook.

They were in the plant for over eight hours. During that time, agents from the DEA and Mexican Federal Police inventoried the contents of the laboratory, the stockroom, and even the thousands of legitimate craft products produced by the local artisans. Actually, samples of each of the different items prepared for export were pulled from the shelves and several of them were dismantled and examined closely. Jason stepped over to one of the tables where agents were working. He spotted a familiar item, a small wooden clock. It took him a minute to remember where he'd seen it before, turning the clock over and over in his hands.

Then it came to him. One of these clocks was in Amber Mathieson's apartment. He removed the cover to the battery compartment, and sure enough, the same hidden compartment was present. He caught the attention of one of the DEA agents, and pointed out the compartment. This was a surreptitious way to get a small quantity of drugs through customs into the United States or other destinations. Jason and the agent were able to pack four prepackaged glassine packs of steroids into the clock. With two dozen pills in each pack, they discovered that each clock could hold ninety-six pills. More importantly, hiding the drugs in these items meant that mass shipments could be sent to seemingly legitimate outlets throughout the country, and from there could be distributed without suspicion. This was another way to get drugs into the hands of dealers in the United States, drugs that would then be resold to the end users, probably thousands of weightlifters, bodybuilders and athletes throughout the country.

When the dust settled in Mexico, indictments were prepared for Kyle Price, George Dellatorre, and Eduardo Perez Santiago. The latter two men were picked up in Mexico, and were being detained in the local jail. Chances were they would face the wrath of their new President and a revamped justice system. Jason thought it possible that they could get long sentences and harsh prison treatment as poster boys for Mexico's new war on drugs. It was a strong case. Both of them were in control of the plant, and numerous documents linked them to the sale of steroids. In addition, several plant employees had come forward after the arrest with tales of terror and assault some workers had suffered at the hands of the two men, especially Eduardo, who by all descriptions was a sadistic son of a bitch. There was another man involved, an American, who seemed to take the role of an enforcer. Authorities did not have much information on him yet, but the locals had some recent tales that made Santiago's antics seem tame by comparison.

These acts of brutality against their own people had riled the village, and the local media was quick to feature the story of an American owned drug factory that used torture to keep workers enslaved. There was a chance the two men would never see the light of day outside a prison, and a greater chance they would be killed by friends or family of those they tortured. Kyle Price was in the U.S. at the time of the raid, and warrants would be issued for his arrest in the States. The Mexican authorities would push for him to be extradited to Mexico to stand trial for his crimes, but chances were the United States would prosecute him for the drug sales over the Internet first. Price's lawyers would be able to indefinitely stall any attempts to return him to Mexico, and the U.S. Attorney had already indicated he would forge ahead with a federal trial.

Upon his return to Highland Park, Jason met with Cab and briefed him on the raid and its aftermath. Cab had stayed in town to work on the murder case. Jason was anxious to take another look at the wooden clock they'd seen in Amber Mathieson's apartment and tell Cab about the obvious connection to Kyle Price. He was getting an uneasy feeling about Price. Was he leading a double life? Was he capable of murder? He laid out the details of the drug raid for his burly partner.

"Sweet Jesus, that's a hard one to believe."

"You know it, I was really shocked. I still don't know how to react."

"Kyle Price, pillar of the community, role model to hundreds of wannabe's like myself, uncrowned King of Highland Park . . . running an illegal drugstore. Hard to believe."

"Yeah, when I first got wind of it, I was really skeptical. But there was enough independent information, from different sources, that there had to be something to it. Once I figured there was foul play, I felt I had to act. Even though Kyle was a friend, and becoming a good friend at that, I had to find out what was going on. All the while I was hoping I was wrong, that there was just some sort of weird coincidence."

"So you went to the County Drug Task Force . . . "

"I figured that they would be the best agency to investigate the allegations. I would be considered personally involved, so we couldn't do it. There was not enough evidence to call in the DEA or FBI, at least initially, and the Attorney General's Office is still swamped with Ecstasy investigations at Rave clubs."

"And Ramos went for it? He's usually reluctant to use his resources for anything other than street dealings that cause violence and mayhem."

"I think he did it for me. Bill and I go way back, and I think he figured that if it bugged me that much, he'd do me a favor. He handled it himself, as a matter of fact, and did some good work. Even an old dog can still sniff around a bit."

Jason didn't mention Ramos' desire to have Cab work for the drug task force. That wasn't an issue he wanted to raise now, probably he would never want to raise it, but knew it was only a matter of time before Cab got the bug to return to drug work in some form. Selfishly, he thought that when that time came, he could join forces with Shawna to keep Cab home in Highland Park.

"How deep does Kyle's involvement go?"

"All the way, it appears. His plant makes the stuff, his network markets it, distributes it, and he collects one hell of a profit. We're talking about an organized drug organization here, Cab. If the case can be proven, and I think it will, he'll go away for twenty years."

"Won't there be a chance that he'll get less based on the fact that it's his first offense of any kind, plus his considerable reputation and generous contributions to the community?"

"Maybe . . . I don't know. With the County's zero tolerance policy and other stiff sentences handed down lately, I wouldn't count on it. Kyle's made a real positive impact here, though. The Judge, whoever that might be, will take that into account. The wild card is whether the case gets prosecuted locally, here in the county, or federally. If the FBI or DEA takes over the case . . . he's done."

"Do you have any say in that . . . whether the Feds step in?"

"Only through the Chief. I'm sure his input will be considered. But you know he never really liked Kyle, thinks of him as a rich grandstander, which he is of course. But he's also a genuine person, who despite his faults, tries to do good things. He certainly made a mistake in getting involved in this steroid operation, principles or no principles, and he's going to pay dearly unless his attorney can come up with a miracle."

"How do you think this whole thing will affect your friendship?"

"It's probably over. It will be a strain for sure. After all, I started the investigation, used some of his other friends, including Janet, who he may or may not learn, to carry it forward, and called for outside help. I was even in on the raid at his plant. There has to be some degree of resentment, even subconsciously, that will build up hard feelings. I don't know if it will be enough to sever our relationship, or if we can somehow get through this. It may depend on the final verdict and sentencing. Regardless, it will change the nature of our relationship. If he gets convicted, I can't associate with him directly anymore, you know, the whole 'known felon thing.' Christine will be my only link, and that's only if she doesn't hate my guts when this whole thing's over. It's an ugly scene."

"Well, one thing's for certain, you did what had to be done. Don't beat yourself up over this Jason, you did the right thing, no matter how it turns out."

"Thanks, buddy. I appreciate that. But there's more." And Jason began telling Cab about the wooden clock. "We may have a serial killer right here in Highland Park. We've got a lot more work to do."

Cab whistled softly and shook his head as Jason talked. Finding the clock meant that they had some suspects in the murder of Amber Mathieson. Given what they had learned about Kyle's two associates at the Cujuani plant, Dellatorre and Perez-Santiago, they now had two prime suspects. Men who were capable of such beatings were also capable of multiple murders. However, neither fit the physical description of the killer, but Cab knew that did not rule them out. It's easy enough to disguise one's appearance, and most eyewitnesses don't really remember much anyway. He glanced at his watch as he thought about their next move. He knew Jason would want to get to Kyle Price as soon as he could, before the wire services broke the story here in town, and before Price could meet with his attorneys and build up a defense. He thought he'd better call Shawna; he was going to be here for a long time.

Mirror Man sat in the hard wooden chair in his nondescript bedroom in his little apartment, mesmerized by the computer. This is unbelievable. This fucking chick is just too good to be true. She was one of the few he found not through the elaborate net he created to target the hapless women, but through personal contact. She was just too good to pass up. He would bide his time with her, wait until the moment was right, but he knew that eventually he had to have her. She was kinky and a bit perverse, and very beautiful. A fair-haired stunner, the rational part of him knew that she was off limits to him, it would be too messy, too complicated. It would be like advertising, sending out a signal, I'm here, come get me. It probably wouldn't be good in the long run, but he often thought about the kind of rush he would get from seeing her spread naked before him, terrified and helpless.

He used this fantasy many times to get himself off, imagining the sweat beading around her nipples, the tears streaming down her face . . . leaving a salty taste on her cheeks and lips. He loved the smell and taste of fear, and remembered the kisses and licks he gave to the women he'd already done. Salty tears and pungent sweat were aphrodisiacs for him, got him hard and ready . . . close to explosion. The fact that she was so near, the fact that she was connected . . . well, it made him think long and hard. Rational . . . no. But he was thinking less and less about caution these days, and more and more he was overcome by the strong need to taste the fear. Yes, the word addiction frequently popped into his brain now. He was familiar with addictions. His mother was addicted . . . to alcohol, to men, to depravity. Shit, no one will ever wonder what happened to him, it's so fucking obvious. They'll say "textbook." A classic case of Motherous Psychosorous. A fucking Freudian nightmare. Murdering bastard. It all fit, and he made no excuses. *I want to,* he thought. *I just fucking want to, and no one can stop me till I'm done.*

Only a short distance away and a few minutes later, Janet settled into the chair facing her electric blue-cased computer. There seemed to be no end to the shape and colors of computers these days. You could purchase one to fit into almost any space in your home, and in many designer styles and colors to match your personality. She was in a great mood tonight, even though she was due at work in an hour, and was feeling a little tired. Mechanically, she went through the log-on procedure and called up her e-mail. She had four new messages. One was from Christine, one was from her mother, still living in Swarthmore, and one was from a nurse she worked with regularly. The fourth was a message from someone that she didn't know. It was from someone with the screen name *Jayman,* and the message was titled *"About last night."* Of course! It was from Jason.

He had never sent her a message before, in fact he always told her he didn't have time for "playing around on the Internet," but she thought he was exaggerating for effect. He liked to portray himself as technologically challenged, but Janet was convinced he did that just to build up his image as a Marlboro man. Jason wanted to be anything but a computer nerd, and frequently made comments about those who spent much of their existence in front of a monitor. She chuckled to herself as she pictured him in his bedroom, slipping a laptop from under the bed, and logging on to a world he pretended to know nothing about, but which probably enthralled him to no end. He probably even locked the bedroom door when he surfed the net, like he was doing something dirty. It was a humorous mental picture. It was a ridiculous premise, Jason not being familiar with the Internet. How could he *not* use it, being a detective and all. Being familiar with the worldwide web would save him hundreds of hours in investigative time, and there were probably things online about a person that would never be revealed through traditional gumshoe methods.

She clicked on the message *Jayman,* and watched as a sudden starburst of color exploded across her screen. It was a beautiful spectrum of yellows and reds that were as brilliant as the evening sun over Mexico, followed quickly by an explosion of ice blue and silvery shards of light that made her squint as she sat transfixed, staring at the screen. Then, as the colors faded, the screen turned to black, and her name suddenly appeared in deep red, emerging through the blackness to form a stunning effect, something you'd see at the beginning of

Hollywood horror flick. She was startled at first, but then smiled. This was just like Jason, feigning ignorance at first and then using his hidden talent to beguile her later. Two can play at this game. I won't give him the satisfaction of asking him about this spectacular display, she thought. Let's see how long it takes him to become puzzled by my silence and start interrogating me about the messages I've received. In the end, he'll be too vain not to admit he's the creator, and then I'll tell him I knew all along. Take some wind out of his already inflated sails.

Meanwhile, as swift and silent as a deadly plague, the virus was already inserted into the targeted host computer. Another unknowing victim was chosen.

Chapter 23

Before talking to Kyle, Jason wanted to develop a strategy. He knew his one time friend would have an attorney present, and that he would only get this one opportunity to talk to Kyle. His attorney would never consent to a second interview. In fact, the only reason he would let Jason talk to his client at all would be to see how much they could learn about the police investigation and the possible charges that Kyle may be facing. They would not give up much to learn these things, since they had other methods at their disposal. But Jason was well trained in the art of interrogation, and he knew how to read body language and facial expression to detect a wide range of human reactions, from deception, to anger, to fear. A suspect under stress tacitly revealed all of these, and Jason was adept at picking up on the signs and signals betraying the range of human emotion.

There was no doubt Kyle already had a heads-up from his sources in Mexico. Mexican police do not extend the same courtesies as police in the U.S. do, so it was unlikely Dellatorre or Eduardo could have called him, but Jason knew Kyle would have friends in Mexico that would have called him about the raid long before Jason even boarded a plane home. He also knew that Price's attorneys would have already dispatched investigators to Cajuani. They would comb the village, the police station, and the jail for information about the raid and the evidence uncovered.

Despite the new President's firm stance on police corruption, money still was a factor prompting cooperation from Mexican police. They were paid a dismal salary. Jason also knew that Kyle's people would offer huge sums for good information, and realized that the lawyers would know just about everything concerning the raid and the evidence police found within 24 hours. Time was of the essence for him. He was thinking intently about his line of questioning when the phone rang, rudely interrupting him. He almost didn't answer it, but knew from experience that a missed call could mean a missed opportunity. As much as that sounded like a salesman's credo, he never could just sit there and let voicemail pick up like most of the other detectives did when they were busy on a case. Just an old habit.

Ten minutes later, he was thankful for old habits. He hung up the phone, his thoughts and emotions working overtime. Jason knew that the information he'd just received was crucial to his case. Standing alone, it didn't mean much. But combined with other circumstances, it was huge. In fact, he may just have gotten the clue that would solve a homicide, maybe several of them.

Kyle Price arrived at the police station an hour after Jason called him. Two other men accompanied him. One of them, Stanley Biggerstaff, was a local attorney who handled much of Kyle's day to day business and personal affairs. The other one, wearing a tailored suit that Jason figured would cost a detective a month's salary, was a new face in town. Jason extended his hand to Kyle, and his friend took it briefly, a perfunctory greeting at best. Jason then greeted Biggerstaff, whom he also knew professionally, although the lawyer's practice was mostly confined to business law. It was hard for Jason not to know most of the doctors, lawyers, and Indian chiefs in a small town like Highland Park. Sooner or later, someone *he* knew introduced him to someone *they* knew, and so forth and so on until he had met everybody who was anybody in this version of Peyton Place. Biggerstaff pointed at the other man, and introduced him.

"Lieutenant, I would like to introduce R. Chancellor Robertson, of the firm Jacob, Pullam, and Robertson. As you may know, Mr. Robertson is one of the premier attorneys in Philadelphia, and a close personal friend of my wife Katie and me."

"Good day Mr. Robertson," Jason replied curtly, reaching for the lawyer's outstretched hand. He shook hands like a limp dick, which Jason would expect from any man who chose to be called Chancellor instead of whatever the R stood for. Rumpelstiltskin would be a better moniker.

"I'm not one to mince words, Lieutenant," the man said as soon as he let go of Jason's hand. "I only agreed to have Mr. Price appear here because he wants to cooperate with you in every way possible. He has nothing to hide, but I will warn you, I am not about to have him subjected to a lengthy interrogation. Even by you, a friend, according to my client."

Robertson pronounced the word *friend* like it was a bitter potion he spit out just before swallowing. Jason had two thoughts enter his head simultaneously. *What rock did they find you under? Do you spit or swallow?*

He almost lost it and said something that would have ended the interview before it began. Maybe he was already getting too old for this business. It was getting harder and harder to maintain a calm facade when dealing with such unequivocal assholes. Instead he cocked the brow of his left eye and said, "I understand completely, this will only take a minute . . . or two."

Jason led them to a small, plain interview room. There was a small table and only three chairs. Biggerstaff was odd man out, and remained standing until another chair could be found. Thus, the pecking order was already established, and Jason saw that Robertson would be his nemesis in this investigation. Jason had taken some time to mentally prepare himself for this interview. Even though he was now in serious trouble, Jason considered Kyle Price to be a friend. He had arrested and prosecuted friends before, but never one so close, and never one who knew so much personal information about him. *Damn,* Jason thought, *I even fondled this man's wife.* He wondered if Kyle had told his attorney anything about their relationship, especially the trip to Mexico and that wild night out they had in Philadelphia.

Nothing he could do about it now. He wished that he'd thought with his *big* head that night instead of yielding to his primal urges. He had resigned himself to carry on just like it was any other interview. He would give a short speech about their friendship to get it out in the open, how he could not let it get in the way of doing his job, and that he hoped Kyle would understand. He sincerely meant it, and hoped Kyle would accept what he had to do without hating him. He knew that Kyle's attorney wouldn't care at all about their friendship unless he could take advantage of it to help his client. Thinking about that, Jason figured if Kyle did tell Robertson or Biggerstaff about some of the things they'd done together, he'd find out soon after the interview began. They would certainly use it to their advantage. On the other hand, Jason had saved Price's daughter. That would count for something with Kyle. Actually, it would count for a lot.

Jason decided to take the direct approach. He no longer saw the need to start slow. Kyle's abrasive attorney has seen to that. Jason decided to give him the worst case scenario; put so much fear and immediate anxiety in him that it will be beyond his attorney's ability to keep him from reacting. Of course, since every man is different, Jason had no way of knowing what would happen after he lowered the boom. As soon as they were settled, the spit or swallow man spoke again.

"I'll also tell you this right up front, just so there is no misunderstanding. My client will not answer any inquiry until I give him the signal. When I say the interview is over, it's over. No further questions, no further discussion. The door opens, and we walk out. Agreed?"

Jason ignored him and fired off his first question.

"Kyle, how long have you owned the plant in Cajuani?"

Price looked at Robertson before replying. The attorney nodded slightly.

"About seven years."

"Do you have any partners? Is there anyone else who owns a piece of the action there?"

Robertson interjected. "Whoa, Lieutenant, I really must object. Mr. Price is not here for any of his business practices. Let's stick to the subject, shall we?"

"Counselor, this is directly on the subject. Mr. Price is being accused of running a virtual illegal drug store from his place of business. I need to know if he is the sole owner, or if there are others who have an interest. That's pretty much on target, don't you think?"

"Nevertheless, his business practices themselves are confidential. Mr. Price is a successful international businessman, and you can't expect him to freely impart his years of experience and accumulated business acumen to you or anyone else. He is in a highly competitive field. You know the volatility of web-based enterprises."

"Certainly. However, this illegal enterprise does not just involve Price's plant in Cajun. We're talking conspiracy here. We're talking racketeering. This is indeed an international business, Mr. Robertson. The international drug business."

Jason rose swiftly from his seat as he spoke, moving toward Kyle seated across he table. Jason grabbed the end of the table with his hands for support and leaned far over, looming over Kyle like a dark rain cloud ready to burst. Kyle looked up, and quickly averted his eyes while slouching noticeably in his chair. The tension in the small room was thick, palpable.

As quickly as he'd stood, Jason returned to his seat. The tension still hung in the air.

"Okay, I'll drop that question for now. I can get that information easily enough anyway through the company's articles of incorporation."

Biggerstaff was shooting glances at Robertson and his client, trying but not succeeding to be nonplussed. He was second-guessing the decision to do this interview, and Jason sensed that he or Robertson would soon move to shut it down. It really didn't matter. He was going to pop the one question he was holding back anyway, even if it was after the formal interrogation was over.

Even Robertson, a veteran of court battles and certainly no stranger to pressure, looked troubled. Jason was pleased. His goal was to get Kyle and his attorneys rattled. Surprisingly, it was being accomplished with ease. He surmised that Biggerstaff had not gotten to spend enough time conferring with his client before this interview, and was unsure of the depth of Kyle's involvement in this and other shady business practices. And since Robertson was only feeding off the information supplied by Biggerstaff, he was in the same boat. Besides, after the phone call he'd received a short time before this interview, the sale of steroids was no longer his main concern. There was a huge new angle to his questioning, one that neither Kyle or his attorneys would anticipate.

He was now pursuing Kyle Price as a heinous criminal, a monster. He was surprised by his own thoughts about the man seated across from him, but at the same time was excited by the prospect of solving an important case. Jason had become a hunter with his prey in sight. Until a few days ago, this man had been one of his buddies, maybe not a close friend in the sense that Cab was, but at least a social friend. But the information he now held changed all that, even more than Kyle's obvious drug involvement. All bets were off. A few more direct hits and he would be ready. Without reluctance, Jason continued to set his friend up for the big question.

"Let's move on to something more meaningful. Kyle, were you selling steroids on the Internet?"

Robertson barked. "My client will not answer that, Lieutenant."

Biggerstaff nodded his head, adding emphasis to Robertson's short burst of forcefulness. He crossed his arms, and sat up straighter in his chair.

"Okay, let me rephrase. We know that your plant was making steroids, and we know that your plant was shipping steroids to all parts of the world. Did you have any knowledge of that?"

"Once again, my client will not answer."

"Mr. Robertson, is there any question pertinent to this case that your client *will* be allowed to answer?"

"Well, Lieutenant, perhaps if you tell us about what you found, what evidence you think you have that makes Mr. Price a suspect, we could give you a statement."

It was Biggerstaff this time. He didn't have the savvy of his Philadelphia associate, but he was no idiot. He realized he wasn't prepared for this question and answer format session and wanted to turn this into a fact-finding expedition for the defense. After he learns more about the police case, he'll allow Price to give a carefully constructed, and useless-written statement about his legitimate business practices. Normally, Jason would settle for that. He knew the attorneys would soon have, if they didn't already, all of the important aspects of the police case against his client. So he could give them some details in return for a written statement. As useless as it might seem, anything in writing could eventually come back to haunt a suspect, especially in a case as complex as computer crime and worldwide drug distribution. There would be too many loose lips out there somewhere for the operation to stay secret. The trick is to find them, and provide whatever grease was necessary to get their jaws flapping.

Jason was confident he could find these people just like he'd found the Apex club members who had already made crucial admissions. So right now, he was in no mood to acquiesce. He wouldn't be giving up much if the attorneys shut him down, and Jason decided to take the offensive. He looked directly at both men before replying.

"No counselors, I see no reason to waste my time or yours on that sort of senseless exercise. If you will not allow your client to answer even some basic questions concerning the charges against him, we'll just move forward toward the preliminary hearing. I thank you for coming in, and wish you a good day."

Robertson was aghast. Never had he had a detective end an interview so abruptly, especially when everyone was being civil. It was true he and Biggerstaff had been less than fully cooperative, but that was expected in a criminal inquiry. They were really just feeling each other out at this point, and Jason was not really pressing them. He had not tried to dance around the main issues in hopes of getting a tidbit of useful information, or even hoping for a slip of the tongue by either he or his client. After all, sometimes clients were known to utter a few incriminating words before their lawyers could shut them up. This was quite unusual. When he recovered from his surprise, he rose to leave, lightly grabbing Kyle by the elbow to make sure he promptly followed. He did not want the detective to take a parting shot against his client that might provoke an emotional response, something the police were fond of doing. Biggerstaff followed dutifully, glancing back at Jason as he went for the door first, preparing to hold it open for his two companions.

Robertson paused, checking Jason's eyes for some sign of trickery. Jason met his gaze, and the two battle-proven warriors locked eyes. Robertson found it unsettling, like looking into a deep dark well. There was no indication of what the blackness concealed.

"If that's the way you want it, we will be going. We'll see you in court, as they say." He started to extend his other hand toward Jason. The detective turned away from the proffered hand, pretending not to notice, making a pretense out of shuffling some papers. Cab had quietly appeared in the doorway, having come from the adjacent observation room when he saw the interview was concluding. "Detective Calloway will show you out."

Just before the men turned to leave the room, Jason spoke again, addressing Robertson but looking directly at Kyle Price, who unwittingly met his gaze.

"Oh, there is one more thing Counselor." Jason paused for effect, and satisfied that he had the full attention of all involved, continued.

"I need to know about the relationship between your client and Amber Mathieson, who was murdered here a few months ago. I hear they were more than just friends."

Biggerstaff blanched visibly and immediately looked toward Robertson and Kyle, whose jaw dropped noticeably.

Without shifting his eyes, Jason continued.
"If you have the time, now would be good."

After the initial shock, Robertson recovered enough to make a fuss about Jason's tactics and demand some private time with his client. This was granted of course, and Jason took this time to review what had happened in the last hour. The telephone call that he'd received before the now all-important interview of Kyle Price had been from Samuel Wagner, the human resources director at Cisco Industries, where Amber Mathieson worked at the time of her death. He was the man Jason tried to see months ago, but had been on vacation at the time and he was sent to the assistant director. The information Wagner had imparted was simple. Amber was referred to the company by none other than Kyle Price, friend and business associate. Kyle had personally called Wagner about her, and she had been hired immediately, and at an advanced salary to boot. Jason questioned the quick hiring and the relatively high salary, and the steely executive answered without hesitation.

"This is business, detective. We work differently than government. When a man of Mr. Price's means wants a favor, we tend to accommodate him. It makes it an easy decision if the favor benefits both parties, and Ms. Mathieson turned out to have real talent in her field. I would have taken care of Kyle anyway, but we did interview and test her skills before putting her on, and she was good. This was a no brainer."

"Did Mr. Price tell you anything more about her? Anything on a personal level?" Jason knew what the answer to this question would be, but he had to ask. Wagner did not prove him wrong.

"No, he didn't."

Short and sweet. One thing about powerful, experienced male executives; they don't mince words. Wagner was not going to volunteer anything that might prove embarrassing to Kyle or put him in a compromising position. In a way, Jason admired that trait. He wished he could instill it in his own police detectives, who too often got diarrhea of the mouth when discussing cases with other cops or police groupies.

Wagner sensed the pause on the other side of the line, and took advantage to close the conversation.

"Will there be anything else, detective?"

"No sir. I appreciate the call. But we may have to talk to you again. I would appreciate it if you didn't mention this discussion to anyone. Have a good evening."

As soon as he had hung up, Jason had completely reworked his strategy for the interview. Thinking about it now, he was happy with the result. He had gotten the men into the police station to discuss Kyle's arrest on the drug charges. This was legitimate, although he figured that Robertson and Biggerstaff were now infuriated and questioning his motive. When the phone call came from Wagner, it completely altered his agenda. He was no longer investigating an illegal steroid operation, he was probing a murder case. Nevertheless, the preliminary questions about the Cajuani raid had thrown the men off-balance, and set Kyle up for the kill.

He figured that even though they were royally pissed off at this point, the two experienced attorneys would be too curious and too apprehensive to walk away from further discussion. After conferring with their client, they would be back. The real question was how cooperative they would be at this point. If they came back to the interview room and began to answer most of the questions he would ask, it would indicate to Jason that Price was probably not involved in the killing, at least not directly. If this were the case then he would explore the nature of the relationship between Price and Amber. This may lead to discovering other clues . . . other links to investigate. Perhaps Kyle would even know who the killer might be. This happens all the time.

On the other hand, if his attorneys refused to allow Kyle to answer most of the questions proffered, it would be a sure indication Kyle has something to hide, and that something *could* be murder. He waited anxiously in his office. Cab would call him when the two men returned to the interview room. Jason had removed his tie and unbuttoned the top button of his dress shirt in preparation for the next phase of the interrogation. He wanted to be comfortable and appear relaxed and less formal. Actually, he was tight as a drum, and was trying to breathe rhythmically to bring his anxiety under control. Although he was always calm and cool at crime scenes, Jason had a penchant for becoming nervous and excited whenever he sensed a break in a major case was coming. He had that feeling now. Cab stuck his head in his office. They were back.

The two attorneys and Kyle had returned to their seats in the small room, and Jason saw Kyle pull his collar away from his neck. Yes, the temperature in the room had noticeably risen, or at least it felt that way to the lawyer and his client. They were right to feel this way. The room came with an individually controlled thermostat located in an adjoining room, and Cab had literally turned the heat up on the investigation. If Jason gave him the signal, based on cooperation, he would cool the room off quickly, facilitating a comfortable conversation. Jason saw that Kyle's attorney was struggling to keep himself under control. Biggerstaff was furious. He felt as if both men had taken him in. His client had failed to tell him about knowing the victim of a homicide, and the cop had played him and Kyle like a flute.

He figured the drug case interview was just a ruse. The detective really wanted to get them in this room to learn about his client's relationship with a murdered woman. Was Kyle so stupid that he didn't think it was relevant to tell his lawyer about his? Or did Kyle Price have knowledge of the killing? Worse yet, was his client involved? These questions and more had went through his mind as Biggerstaff struggled to make a decision whether to stay in the police station or take Kyle and flee to the safety of his own plush office in the law firm's downtown building. It was actually Robertson who convinced them to stay.

After talking to Kyle in private, he encouraged Biggerstaff to allow the interview to continue, mostly because their client had insisted on it, asserting that he had no knowledge of the murder. Biggerstaff had cautioned him about divulging too much information, not satisfied that his client was being truthful. Once burned, twice shy. Too many times this experienced lawyer had clients who swore to him they had nothing to do with the crime with which they were charged, only to have them admit later they lied to him, their own attorney. These admissions always gave him a queasy feeling in the pit of his stomach. Most of the time, they only admitted this to him after the police had revealed some irrefutable evidence of their guilt, and Biggerstaff wound up pleading the client for a much lessor deal than he could have secured had his client been truthful with him from the beginning. Biggerstaff had the same sick feeling now. But Robertson seemed self-assured, so he reluctantly gave in to the wishes of the more experienced trial attorney and their client, who would not relent. Biggerstaff hesitantly accompanied them back into the lion's den.

Robertson again took the lead. He was used to being in control, and his assertiveness left no doubt which attorney was calling the shots.

"Once again, Lieutenant. My client will only answer those questions I deem appropriate, and we'll walk if we feel you're getting offpoint or heavy handed. Agreed?"

"Agreed, Counselor." Jason picked up the exasperation in the attorney's voice, and would have given anything to be a fly on the wall during the latest discussion between attorney and client. He picked up exactly where he'd left off, word for word.

"I need to know about the relationship between your client and Amber Mathieson, who was murdered here a few months ago."

Chapter 24

The interview had gone well. Only three minutes into Kyle's response to the first question, Jason had signaled Cab, in the next room peering at them through a one way mirror, to lower the heat. Jason had the gut feeling that Kyle was being honest, although he never totally believed a suspect's story until the real perpetrator had been apprehended and convicted. Indeed, Kyle had opened up. He readily admitted knowing Amber Mathieson, and knowing her well. He was a bit sheepish about telling the whole story in Jason's presence, but had resigned himself that it must be done.

He met Amber in Atlanta, while she was dancing in the CatsNipU. He was there for a business trip, and stopped into the club because he'd heard it was a nice, classy place and featured good looking women dancing totally nude. He made no apologies for this, and Jason already knew of his penchant for exotic dancing and great looking women. He was taken with Amber immediately, not just for her good looks, but because once he'd had the chance to talk with her awhile, he found her to be an interesting, well-spoken woman. She seemed attracted to him also, and by the end of his first night at the club, they agreed to meet the next evening for dinner. Well, the rest was pretty predictable, but Jason couldn't help but think of Christine and if she knew about this liaison. He wondered how many of them there had been, and whether Christine had even participated in some or all of these sexual trysts.

Kyle reluctantly admitted to a torrid love affair with Amber, which went on for months and culminated in his getting her a job in Highland Park. Kyle visited her sporadically over a year's time, while she finished college. Sometimes he was on business, but sometimes he flew to Atlanta just to be with her. Jason watched him carefully during the interview. He was no expert, but it was obvious that Kyle had abnormal sexual desires. Of course, he knew this by the antics he had witnessed in the limo, but now his tendencies were even more apparent.

Jason figured Kyle was a sex addict. Even in the way Kyle spoke about this affair, Jason knew it was about sex and excitement, not about love.

Kyle readily admitted recommending Amber for the job at Cisco Industries, and after further questioning, admitted giving her rent money for the Rockledge apartment she lived in, and to continuing their affair in Pennsylvania. He denied any involvement or knowledge in the woman's murder, and claimed he had no idea who might have wanted her dead. This begged the question Jason loathed to ask, but duty dictated he did. After all, the primary suspect in a murder was usually someone that was involved with the victim in some way. A family member, a lover, a jealous husband or wife. In this case both Kyle and his wife fit the bill. If Kyle *didn't* do it, Christine was the next best possibility. Because of the sexual assault on Amber, and the evidence they had uncovered thus far, it was almost certain Amber was killed by a man, but Jason could not rule out murder for hire. Christine certainly had the means to hire someone to kill a rival, and this motive had to be explored. Jason had come to really like Kyle's wife, and hated to think of her as a suspect in a grisly murder. Nonetheless, he pursued this possibility.

"Kyle, did Christine know about Amber?"

"Yes, she did. But not in the way you think. We are . . . were all friends, and had been to dinner several times. We took her to Atlantic City of couple of times."

"To your club?" Jason was wondering whether she too had been part of a wild ride.

"Yes, at least once we went there. But nothing out of the ordinary occurred." Jason could read his eyes. Kyle was telling him there had been no sexual adventure with Christine. No one else would understand this message, and Jason felt uneasy with the hidden signal. He again cursed himself for succumbing to that night of drunken debauchery with his friend turned murder suspect.

"And you're telling me that your wife had no idea you were carrying on an extended sexual relationship with Amber?"

"As far as I know, Christine did not know. If she had, I think she would have confronted me with it. She is not the type to stay silent over something like that."

"Was this the first time you did something like this without Christine's knowledge?" Jason wanted to say "without Christine's participation," but knew that would surely open up Pandora's Box. He just hoped Robertson, Biggerstaff, and Cab, who was still watching from the next room, didn't pick up on the hidden meaning. Kyle, however, heard him clear as a bell. He lowered his eyes for a few seconds, more in contemplation than in shame, before he spoke.

"No," he said very quietly, causing Robertson to lean toward him to hear his reply. "I've done this before. I really do love my wife, but I have . . . damn, it sounds so trite, but I have . . . needs, appetites, that cause me to be with other women from time to time. I'm not proud of it, but I've come to accept it about myself. I've tried to stop, but quite frankly, there are too many temptations, even if I *had* the will . . . well, I just don't."

"Did Christine ever find out about any of these women? Did she ever confront you about any suspicions?"

"Yes, once. It was years ago when we were married only a short time. She almost left me then, but I convinced her to stay. After . . . I included her in some . . . "

"Let me get back to Amber Mathieson." Jason cut him off. He surmised what Kyle was going to say and didn't want to go there, not with witnesses. He knew. There was no need for others to know. Not yet, anyway. He could picture Cab's eyebrow raised behind the two-way mirror. His partner would be puzzled by Jason's abrupt interruption. You never interrupted a suspect when they were in the midst of giving up what could be valuable information. Hopefully, he could shrug off any questions about it Cab might raise later.

"Kyle, where were you on the night of May fifth, the night Amber was killed?"

Robertson finally spoke up.

"That's it, Lieutenant. I know my client has nothing to hide, he's been forthright in his answers, even to the point of revealing some embarrassing aspects of his personal life. But now you're asking him for specifics about a date in the past, and I don't think it's prudent for him to answer right now. Not that he had anything to do with the killing, but simply to protect his rights, and to make sure he doesn't inadvertently make a mistake in telling you about his whereabouts that night. Hell, I can't remember what I was doing a week ago, let alone remember my activities on a nondescript evening months in the past. What makes you think that you can just . . . "

"Unless on such an evening you committed murder." Jason said very matter-of-factly.

Robertson was clearly agitated now, and half rose from his chair as he spoke. "C'mon, Lieutenant, I told you no cat and mouse stuff. What are you getting at?"

"Okay, I hear you." Jason was still looking directly at Kyle, and waved a dismissing hand toward Robertson. "Let me ask you this Kyle. Are you willing to give us a blood sample? Just standard stuff in a homicide case. We'd like a sample of Kyle's blood for DNA. I'm sure you know Counselor, that it's a great way to prove he's innocent. Thirty percent of all defendants are proved innocent by DNA comparisons." *Of course, Robertson would do some quick math on this, and realize that left seventy percent guilty as charged.*

"That's it. We're outta here," Robertson said in a huff.

"I'm not saying we won't cooperate, but I don't like the way you're treating us right now, and we're leaving. Good day, gentlemen."

The now red-faced attorney rose and turned to leave, once again followed by his comrade and their client. The three of them filed out of the small room, waddling like ducks in a row.

A few minutes later Jason was slumped in one of the hard backed interview room chairs, oblivious of the way the sharp edge of the chair top was digging into his flesh. He would become aware of this later, when he rubbed the sore spot on the back of his neck, blaming the pain on stress and fatigue. Cab was seated across from him, in the same chair that Kyle Price had occupied just a short time ago. The chair was still warm, giving credence to the term "hot seat." Cab looked at Jason, his shirt unbuttoned, his tie pulled down. He looked tired. He was unconsciously wringing his hands, like a suspect does when he nervously spins his lying tale of woe. His eyelids hung low, but he was not asleep, just lost in thought. One eye cocked toward Cab, and he spoke quietly.

"Well, my trusty partner, what do you think?"

"I think you have a suspect . . . a strong suspect. Look at the three components that point to a suspect; motive, opportunity, and ability. I think you have all three with Kyle Price. Reading between the lines, you can make an argument for motive. Maybe Amber was demanding too much of him, maybe pressuring him to make their relationship public. Hell, maybe she even demanded that he leave Christine, and threatened to tell her if Kyle didn't move out!"

"Really?" Jason asked.

"That's one of the oldest motives for murder in the book. Throw in Kyle's wealth, a portion of which he would certainly lose if Christine divorced him, and you have a compelling reason to believe he did it . . . it's classic. He certainly had many opportunities to kill her, Christ, he was fucking her regularly. Finally, he had the ability to kill her. Kyle is strong enough to control her while choking her to death. Remember, he's a weightlifter too, and although he's not in your league he does have enough strength to easily overpower someone Amber's size."

"So you think he did it then, huh?"

"Actually . . . no."

Jason cocked both eyebrows this time, and stared intently at his partner. He respected Cab more than the big man would ever know, and was acutely interested in his opinion.

"You don't?"

"No. I know what I just said, but I just don't think he has the ruthlessness to kill a woman he cares for cared for, in cold blood. If he did it, I think it would have been from a fit of uncontrollable rage. Something; a heated argument, or some sort of threat would have sparked this rage. It had to be serious too, Kyle's not particularly hot-headed. And if that were the case, it would have occurred at or near the scene of the argument. Amber was dressed to kill, forgive the pun. It looked like she was out for an evening of dining and dancing. I don't think Kyle would want to be seen with her around here, so that raises serious doubts in my mind about him killing her. But if he did, that leaves a few probable scenarios. He could have taken her to Philadelphia for a date, maybe had dinner and visited a club. That would still be shaky, given his notoriety, but he might still do it. And if he did, *and* if he killed her in Philly, why bring her back here? That's pretty risky, and serves no purpose. Why not just dump her body in some alley, wouldn't that be considered just another homicide in the big city?"

Cab waited for a reply, and hearing none, continued.

"Could he have killed her at her apartment? Maybe, but not likely. We found no signs of a struggle there when we searched it, and even if he cleaned it up, I think we'd have found something telltale. The coroner placed her death around eleven the night before she was found in the park, so it would be odd for Kyle to be just picking her up at that hour. And if they went to Philly and returned, eleven would seem too early. Besides, the FBI thinks Amber's murder might be one of a string of similar murders throughout the country. So we're also looking at the possibility of serial killer here, and if that were the case, Kyle would have to be living a double life. It just doesn't seem possible to me."

"It's happened before. Not all serial killers were seedy, grimy misfits."

"Yeah, but none that I can recall were pillars of their community, and had more money than God."

"Do we drop him as a suspect? Do we move on?"

"No, I don't think we can. He's not much, but he's the best link we have right now to Amber. He was her lover. He supported her financially. And despite what I think, he *could* be a stone cold murderer. He could be the FBI's man too. I think he has to stay in the forefront. Let's take some time and consider our next move. You okay with that?"

"Yes, Jason replied. "I'm okay with that."

Cab lifted his considerable bulk out of the chair, casting a shadow over Jason as he rose.

"And Jason, take some advice. Keep away from Kyle and those other party animals, at least until we have this killer behind bars."

Chapter 25

*The Park Deli was located on Park Boulevard, the main North-*South *route* through town. It had been a Highland Park mainstay for decades, although its reputation as the city's trendiest eatery had long been usurped by the newer chain restaurants and a few upscale places downtown. It remained a favorite of the cops, however, and the boys in blue could often be found having a meal at one of the booths or waiting around the counter for their take out order. The place was a combination corner grocery store and neighborhood diner. It contained six long rows of shelves, containing all the staples of life, as well as a small freezer case for frozen items. Mostly, it was a bread, milk, cigarettes, ice cream, and candy store. In addition, there were three rows of four-person booths along the northwest side of the deli. The seats were covered in vinyl, the tables were made of 60's Formica. There were wood partitions between each booth, providing a bit of privacy. Maybe that was why the cops liked the place so much. They hated the way people stared at them as they ate, so the relative privacy of the booths appealed to them.

Jason was driving back from the latest briefing with the FBI in Philadelphia and pulled over near the deli. He needed a break and could really use the extra surge of energy a cup of strong coffee would provide him. He had been thinking non-stop about the case, and about his friend Kyle Price. It was weighing heavy on his mind. It was still hard to believe that this man might be a cold-blooded killer, a man so depraved that he would track down innocent women and murder them in such a brutal fashion. Jason needed some down time, even though he really couldn't afford to take any time off right now. The pressure was on to make an arrest in this case.

The FBI, especially Devin Grey, had been hounding him for well over a week to bring charges against Kyle. She had even convinced her supervisors to make her part of the investigative task force and was temporarily assigned to the Philadelphia field office. She knew this could be a springboard for a meteoric rise through the FBI's support division. It may even lead to her appointment as a special agent. When she heard about the results of Kyle's interview, she went ballistic. She had called Jason three times since she'd been in town, but he didn't want to speak to her, fearing she had some personal interest in him also. Normally he would have jumped at the chance for a little sack time with the pretty analyst, but since he and Janet had gotten together, he no longer felt that urge. Nevertheless, he didn't want to test his newfound resolve, and was afraid if she pursued him hard enough, he might give in and revert to his old ways. Besides, she was making him angry by pushing this investigation so hard in one direction.

He wanted to keep an open mind and all this pressure was making it difficult. He just didn't have enough to prosecute. Something was missing. The motive was there, the ability and timing were there too. The most common motives for murder were love and money, and Kyle had an abundance of both. Police figured Amber was seeing more than one man, and Kyle could have become jealous. But jealous enough to kill? Unbalanced enough that one murder would trigger such a deep emotional response to cause him to seek out and kill other victims? Victims he apparently didn't even know before he somehow found and targeted them for a grisly death? Could Amber have been threatening him too? Maybe she *was* going to tell Christine, a revelation that Kyle had admitted would probably end their storybook marriage. Had she demanded money for her silence? Jason had not been able to establish any ironclad alibis for Kyle's whereabouts during the time of each murder.

Kyle's wealth certainly gave him the means to jet all over the country stalking his victims. He was smart enough to conceal his identity, and when his daughter had been kidnapped, he even learned some investigative police procedures that would help him avoid detection. Jason wondered if he had ever told Kyle anything about police methods that might be helping him as a murderer. The thought made him nauseous. There was no doubt Kyle had the savvy to pull off these crimes. The description supplied by Amber's dancer friend in Atlanta fit the general description of Kyle's height, weight and facial features. Although the composite created by the forensic artist was not very close, the killer was a master of disguises.

Not much was known about Price's past either. Both his parents had died at a relatively early age, and he had no siblings. The first place they had been able to uncover people who knew him well at all was during his college years, and nothing notable was found. Although the FBI had supplied a profile of the type of person who would be likely to commit such heinous crimes, nothing found in his adult life indicated that Kyle fit such a profile. But with his arrest on drug charges, it was known that he was capable of committing serious crimes. No one would have suspected that at all, so maybe Kyle was capable of even more mayhem. Maybe there was a darker side to him that was not yet discovered. Something even darker that the sexual escapades of which Jason had personal knowledge.

Perhaps he needed to dig deeper, uncover more hidden clues about this man he had started to grow close to before this all happened. On the other hand, there was no smoking gun. All of the evidence Jason had that implicated Kyle was circumstantial, and weak. Even if he wanted to press the matter, he didn't have enough probable cause for an arrest warrant. He had to search harder. He had to find something that would either indict the man, or clear him.

Jason got out of his parked car and started toward the deli for coffee. He spotted the Chief's car parked on a side street. He ate here regularly, enjoying the large portions despite the owner's obvious lack of attention to keeping the place clean. Jason had long ceased dining at the Park, ever since he'd looked up from his meal one day and saw a roach gingerly walking along the top of the wooden divider separating his booth from the next. The roach was taking its good old time crossing the span. It stopped in the middle, stood on its hind legs, and seemed to preen for Jason, it's ugly furry front legs pawing the air. Jason had left the rest of his meal untouched, put enough money on the table to cover the bill and tip, and left for good. He didn't go back for years, but then relented and occasionally picked up a coffee there. It was so damn convenient, and it didn't take an hour to get a simple cup of Java, unlike the local Starbucks. The popular coffee purveyor always had a line from here to eternity, plus a pimply faced kid behind the counter who didn't know the difference between Café Mocha and a glass of Jolt cola.

He spotted the Chief and the patrol Captain seated in one of the booths. There were mounds of food in front of them. Geez, some guys can't break a habit, no matter how disgusting it may be. Captain Kurtz caught sight of him and waved him over.

"Lieutenant, how about settling a dilemma the Chief and I are having?"

Jason glanced over at the chief, and he seemed to squirm a bit in his seat. Captain James T. Kurtz was a thirty-three year veteran of the force, and was definitely past his prime. He was an autocrat, meaning that when it came to business, it was his way or the highway. This type of thinking had gone out of vogue twenty years ago, but Captain Kurtz was a throwback. He still commanded by intimidation, causing young rookies to develop a fear of him during their all-important first year that they weren't able to conquer for at last five years afterwards. They would literally quake in their boots whenever the Captain came near them, and they'd likely shit themselves if he barked at them, always ending his tirade with a resounding "IS THAT CLEAR?" The unfortunate young officers were too petrified to even turn away from the spray of spittle coming from the Captain's blubbering lips.

Eventually however, their fear turned to loathing. It was then that they started to participate in the bastardization of Captain Kurtz's name. Even on official memos, jaded officers, protected by the civil service system, were fond of addressing their superior by his unofficial moniker, *Captain James T. Kirk,* commander of the starship HPD. Of course this infuriated the good Captain, not because he had anything against the real Captain Kirk, or the actor who played him, but because he hated those who dared poke fun at him. Knowing this of course, the officers found novel ways to continue the harassment.

Juvenile as the gags were, Jason still got a laugh when the Captain went storming into the chief's office, railing about the latest disgusting joke. The unwanted material included gift subscriptions of "Sophisticated Man" magazine and a host of homosexual oriented literature and free samples that were directed to his home, all addressed to Captain James T. Kirk.

Of course, the unwanted mailings were meant to trigger one of the Captain's other pet peeves, his hate for homosexuals. Together, these caused him to be constantly on edge, waiting for the next prank. Jason wondered what his blood pressure was, remembering how beet red his face and neck became whenever he went into one of his tirades. Some guys were easy prey, especially for cops bent on revenge. Kurtz was one of them.

Every morning at seven-thirty Captain Kurtz would head for the police department reception desk for a newspaper. The department received ten complimentary copies of the Highland Park News Herald, and they usually disappeared quickly, being carried into bathrooms, private offices, and squad cars. The Captain had a standing order that a copy be reserved exclusively for him. He could be seen at his desk with a cup of coffee and one jelly donut perusing the paper.

Unfortunately, there were quite a few times when an unknowing patrolman accidentally appropriated his reserved copy, and not having his morning news resulted in a very cantankerous Captain. It would just ruin his day. And he in turn wound up ruining the day for the Lieutenant and Sergeants who had the misfortune to be under his command on those mornings. Since cops were cops, they weren't going to take this lying down. Every once in awhile, some patrol officer took it upon himself to fuck with the Captain. It may have been because he had a bad day in court the day before, it may have been he just had a fight with his wife before coming in for dayshift, or it may have been because he was chewed out by his supervisor, and sought revenge by pissing off Captain Kurtz. No matter the reason, all of the police officers knew that when they pissed off the Captain, it was their supervisors who took the brunt of his wrath. Thank God for this chain of command stuff.

A favorite way to fuck with the Captain was to tamper with his newspaper. Regularly, a disgruntled cop would decide to mess up the Captain's day. They would approach the front desk in the lobby, where the newspapers were dropped off, and grab hold of the copy designated for Captain Kurtz. Then they would take out one of the sections, most often the part that contained local news, and in its place substitute a week old section they had saved just for this purpose. Then, a small group of officers would watch from a safe distance as the Captain sauntered up to the counter, picked up the paper, and shuffled it quickly, sizing up its heft and weight to make sure he had a complete copy. He then carried it back to his office, fixed himself a cup of coffee from his own coffeemaker, he didn't trust anyone else to prepare his brew, and sat down to enjoy his morning ritual.

Like Old Faithful, he would erupt, storming into the Desk Sergeant ranting and raving about his mutilated newspaper and threatening a full-scale inquiry to find those responsible. The Desk Sergeant always took a lot of abuse, since he was charged with preserving the order and flow of everything that went on in the front lobby, including walk-in complaints, telephone calls, and the general management of the flotsam and jetsam of life passing through these not-so-hallowed halls.

But despite the onslaughts, the Sergeants never dissuaded the officers from screwing with the newspaper. They were used to facing the heat on a regular basis, and disparaging remarks and foul language, even when directed their way, were repelled like water off a duck's back. The joy of seeing the Captain's day ruined far exceeded the inconvenience of one more chewing out. Just as long as he didn't see their hidden grins as he lambasted and insulted everyone from the Chief on down during these tirades. Best morale booster since the wearing of the hated uniform hat became optional.

Jason went over to the pair of aging cops, and slid into the booth next to the chief.

"Okay, I'll bite. What can I do for you guys?"

"Well," said the Captain, "we were talking about women officers. Specifically, about what they bring to the table, and whether they're worth their salt as cops."

Uh, oh, thought Jason, *no wonder the Chief is uneasy.* Kurtz is a sexist pig to boot. The Chief, although not enumerated with female officers himself, could ill afford to become involved in anything like sexual harassment. Jason saw that he was continually looking around the deli, making sure no one was within earshot.

"Anyway," Kurtz continued, "besides the fact that few can handle the job, we were talking about the distraction they cause the men trying to do real police work, what with all the affairs they cause and everything. They're a detriment to the married guys."

"I'm not sure Jason is interested in this right now, He may be in hurry, right Lieutenant?"

"No, I'm okay," Jason replied with a grin, enjoying the Chief's discomfort with this politically incorrect banter. "Lay it on me."

"I asked the Chief, purely hypothetical of course, which one of the women police officers did he think would be the best lay. Let's see, we have about 15 women, and although some of them are real pooches, there are some I wouldn't kick out of bed."

The Chief was really squirming now. Normally, he would have stepped in and ended this conversation, but Captain Kurtz was the only man of rank that was his senior on the force, and he had never really challenged him. Jason wondered what the purpose was in encouraging this farce. Everyone knew Kurtz had the hots for Sgt. Victoria Byers, a forty-four year old policewoman who had been one of the first females on the department, and was the senior woman officer. The Captain had taken some ribbing for this when he unwisely mentioned his fantasy at a staff meeting recently. Jason figured the Captain wanted to pin the others to a choice, which he would most certainly "leak" the minute they left the deli.

"I figure we'll do it this way. We each write down our selection on a napkin here, and on the count of three, we'll turn them over. This way, we won't be influenced by what each other says, and we'll see if any of us agree on our choice."

The Chief looked at Jason, and sighed with exasperation. The Chief knew that when Kurtz got onto something like this, it was easiest to humor him. Otherwise he would bug them forever.

"Okay, let's do it and get it over with. Hand me a clean napkin."

Jason was becoming more interested in this zany proposal. It was a great chance to get some fodder for gossip, should he need the opportunity to spread some juicy tidbits in the future. He grabbed a napkin from the tabletop dispenser and immediately jotted his answer on it, shielding it from the prying eyes of Captain Kurtz. The other men hastily scribbled their choice.

"Ready?" The Captain asked, almost salivating as he prepared to turn over his ballot.

"Ready." The Chief and Jason said in response.

"GO!"

The three men simultaneously turned their napkins over. Jason immediately looked at all three.

The Captain's napkin read "*Valerie Byers.*"

His read "*Fuck You.*"

The Chief's read "*Fuck You.*"

He and Chief Forestal burst out laughing, unable to contain their glee as the Captain's prank turned against him. Kurtz's face became redder than he ever saw it before, and bolstered by his part in this great victory over the evil Captain and the need to vent some of the pressure he was feeling, Jason remarked,

"Score one for the Klingons, Captain Kirk."

Jason hadn't been back in his office more than fifteen minutes when Trooper John Woodson knocked on the doorframe of his open door. Jason, his mood uplifted by the coffee and his encounter with Captain Kurtz, looked up from the report he was reading, and acknowledged the affable state police officer.

"Hey John, great to see you. What brings you to Highland Park? I thought you were in Missouri looking at the case there."

Jason could tell before the trooper even spoke that he had some important news. The man's face was beaming, and he looked like he would bust if he didn't talk to someone soon about his discovery.

"It's Sonja Peterson's computer," he said excitedly. "We found a virus in there. A virus unlike any I've encountered before. Complex in design, but simple in theory. It's simply brilliant in execution."

Jason listened intently, trying to follow the rapid pace of Woodson's explanation. He noted the irony of the term "execution" in describing what could be the killer's trademark. Woodson continued, barely drawing a breath.

"It enters the host computer, disguised as an innocuous advertisement. It's like a Trojan horse. When the user opens it up, the virus is released. But that's not the unique part." Woodson's words were tumbling out like marbles from a sack.

"It doesn't seek to destroy anything, it doesn't try to take over the computer; it just silently captures it."

"Whoa, John," Jason interrupted, holding up his hands in front of him to slow the trooper down. "You're going too fast. Remember that I'm basically an idiot when it comes to computer technology. I need the 'for dummies' version."

"Let me give you a little history. Commercial companies first used technology like this to target potential customers. When a web surfer would visit their site, certain companies would leave tiny files on the visitor's hard drive when they left. These are called cookies...very popular, even today. These cookies can track details such as the web browser you use, your log-in name, and even your shopping preferences and any other information you might divulge during your visits. They are effective even to the point of putting together your unique tastes by analyzing patterns they develop based on your activities online. Kind of scary, isn't it?"

"Big brother has really arrived, and in a fashion more subtle and sophisticated than envisioned by Orson Wells," Jason remarked.

"You bet. Some of these cookies disappear when you leave the web site, but most remain on your hard drive indefinitely, and update your records each and every time you visit the site that put them there. Your profile is then sent to the manufacturers and procurers of the types of things you're interested in, and you'll receive online email advertisements for a variety of goods and services. This is where the term "spamming" comes in. It refers to unsolicited advertisements. It's the computer version of junk mail and phone solicitation. You get spammed when these advertisers continually hawk their wares without your solicitation. A knowledgeable person can take a few simple steps to protect themselves against these unwanted cookies, but our boy is even more sophisticated. He does his thing not with a cookie, but with a very intelligent virus. One like this I've never seen before, and it tells me our killer is not your ordinary psychotic bumpkin."

"This virus doesn't do anything to the host computer once it invades, it just mirrors it. Every word, every transaction, each bit of electronic mail. This virus is much more invasive than a cookie. For instance, if you send me an email message, it not only comes to my address, it goes to the invader's address. In other words, he sees the same message I sent to you. The same duplication occurs when you shop on the web, send an instant message on your internet provider network, or when you visit any site at all on the internet. The invader is looking over your shoulder at your screen, seeing what you send, seeing what you receive."

"That *is* disturbing," Jason muttered. "Depending on the way a victim uses their computer, there could be a lot of private information intercepted. The killer would have access to all kinds of data about his intended victim long before he actually strikes."

"Exactly. But that's *still* not the unique part. We see the same technique used all the time in cases of identity theft. You know, where the crook uses intercepted online information to get credit card numbers, bank account data, and enough personal statistics to pull off dozens of fraudulent transactions before anyone catches on. It's a very profitable way to steal. I believe the average take for this type of identity theft is twenty-five thousand dollars. And that doesn't include the professionals. Even basic hackers and petty thieves are engaging in these frauds with impunity. There is no end to the number of ways people are ripped off using information stolen online."

He paused for a breath and Jason seized the opportunity to speak.

"Okay, I understand the part about mirroring the victim's computer. I see how our killer could get all this online information. That sounds pretty unique to me. Certainly it is something I've not encountered before in Highland Park. At least it hasn't been reported before, although I bet its happened here."

"You bet it has," Woodson continued, having caught his breath and ready for another filibuster. He had caught Jason's use of the term *our killer*, and was pleased that he was given some ownership of this case.

"I'm sure its happened hundreds of times. If you check with banks about fraudulent use of credit cards, you'll find many victims of such thievery. But because the perpetrators are so hard to catch, and it's so expensive to successfully conduct an investigation, no one bothers. The victim doesn't sustain much of a loss, only a fifty dollar maximum in most cases, sometimes nothing if they report the fraud right away."

"And the banks are making so much money on the interest they charge to cardholders that it's not worth it to them to pursue the great majority of these cases. The only ones they go after are the ones involving hundreds of thousands of dollars or those cases when the offender is handed to them on a silver platter, like when a suspicious person tips off the cops and they make a pinch. Then the bank investigators look into that offender for similar thefts. But most of these are just written off."

"I gotcha," Jason said. "But if this type of thing is so common, what's unique about our boy?"

"Ah," said Woodson, holding up his index finger for emphasis. For an instant he reminded Jason of a self-absorbed professor scolding an anxious student. "I'm coming to that."

It wasn't often he was asked to hypothesize in a homicide case, and he was relishing the moment. "Our boy isn't interested in just any old computer. He in only interested in those hosts that meet his stringent requirements."

"Yeah, that's right." Jason interrupted again, wishing the computer sleuth would get to the point. "He likes attractive women who are intelligent and have a sense of style and panache. He goes after women who are single, divorced, or separated. And obviously, from what you're telling me, he finds these women because of their online habits."

"You are correct. But to find these types of women, he would have to spend countless hours on the Internet. He would have to inject his virus into hundreds-maybe thousands-of computers before he found a victim to his liking. That would be a difficult assignment at best, and realistically, almost impossible to do on a regular basis. And if *our* killer didn't have the most recent information on a potential victim, his schemes would be risky. So, I worked for hours examining the virus's traits. I ran dozens of simulations, sending the virus into computers we set up to attract it. We used our host computers to send hundreds of email messages and to hit online sites similar to those frequently used by our victims. What I discovered was . . . "

Woodson paused for effect, noting that Jason had slid forward to the edge of his upholstered desk chair.

"Before attaching itself to a host computer, the virus runs loose in cyberspace. It busily scans thousands and thousands of data packets traveling between message switches, capturing and releasing the encrypted bits of messages, until it finds the words and phrases it is searching for coming from a potential host computer. At that point, the virus sends a signal back to the invader, and automatically generates a Trojan horse email to the unsuspecting target. Once open, the virus is deployed, completely invisible to the host. Now our killer has complete access to his future victim's cyber life, allowing him to carefully prepare for his next heinous sexual assault and murder."

"Damn, Woodson, that's frightening. I don't know how you were able to dissect that virus, but you've taken the biggest step so far in solving these crimes. It fits with the killer's actions in all of the murders we've been looking at, and ties a lot of the leads together." Jason thought about the possibilities opened up by this discovery. "The next question is; can we track this thing back to the man who sent it?"

"I think we can, but we've got to act quickly. This guy is smart, and he'll realize that if we have Sonja Peterson's computer, we have his scent. He may have already covered his tracks. It may be too late to trace the virus back to his home location. Besides, he's probably running his messages through a network of computers placed all over the country, masking the originating point."

"What do we have to do? Let's get moving. At least we have a chance."

"We're on it already, Lieutenant. My coworkers are trying to identify the source. They've found his ISP and have a search warrant for records that should give us the registered client. That's probably a fraud too, but it will help us discover the IP number of the message the virus was attached to, which is akin to a fingerprint. Every single packet of information has its own unique identifying number assigned to it by the ISP. At the very least, we will be able to find many of the messages he sent, and to whom he sent them. In other words, we should find more victims, and maybe, just maybe, we'll find a link that will lead us to his doorstep."

Once again Jason found himself in the Chief's office, pleading his case. This time it was an easy sell.

"We can't move quickly enough, Chief. This killer is no dummy. I'm convinced he realized his mistake at some point, knew he was vulnerable, and has already taken steps to cover his tracks. It's only because we have such great technical assistance and the cooperation of the Feds that we have even the slightest chance to locate this guy."

"I know. Move on it now, Jason. This is different than the drug case. Not only are we after a serial killer, but he probably has his next victim in his sights. Do what you need to do, don't worry about checking with me each step of the way, just keep me informed."

"Okay, Thanks. I'll let you know the minute something develops."

"Jason, one more thing. You're personally involved in this now, with Kyle being a suspect. I know that you two are friends. I *should* pull you off the case completely. In fact, everything I've been taught, and every instinct I have right now, is telling me to keep you away from this madman."

"Chief, I . . . " Jason knew the chief was right. He also knew that he had to stay involved, even if it meant suspension.

"I know Jason, I know. Against my better judgement, I'm leaving you on the case. Just don't fuck it up. Both our asses will be fried if you do."

Trooper Woodson almost creamed his jeans. He bolted from the chair he was seated on in his Harrisburg office, and was headed for the door before he realized he was talking on a regular phone, not a cell phone, and had run out of cord. The handset tumbled to the floor and rolled on the carpet. At the other end of the connection, Jason recoiled from the sudden banging noise and quickly pulled the receiver from his ear.

"Shit! What the hell was that?"

"Sorry Lieutenant. I dropped the phone. I've been waiting for this call for an eternity."

"I guess that means you're ready to go, heh? You have the anti-virus ready?"

"I like that term . . . anti-virus! But yeah, the trace is ready to go. In a few minutes, we'll be well on our way to finding this creep."

"The search warrant's signed. I'll fax you a copy. He could be anywhere in the world, more than likely he's in North America, but wherever he is, we're prepared to grab him. The FBI HRT is on stand by, and they are prepared to deploy immediately if he's anywhere in the States. They're also ready to contact their counterparts anywhere in the world to execute a high priority search. C'mon John, let's find this bastard."

Woodson went to work, and with a few dozen keystrokes, sent his masterpiece out into cyberspace. Woodson's anti-virus went to work sniffing and scratching until it found the trail it was programmed to detect. It worked its way through thousands of messages bearing telltale words and phrases and latched on to one that most assuredly was originated by Mirror Man's devious mind. The bait had worked, and the anti-virus took after the original like a bloodhound on the scent of an escaped convict. It tracked the virus all the way to the source, and pinpointed the ISP. The track only took thirty-seven minutes. Woodson's own creation also identified the ISP carrying the message, and quickly raided the electronic files of the ISP, a company called MagicTouch Internet, for the name and address of the account holder.

In no time at all, the address where the message originated flashed on the screen of Woodson's seventeen-inch screen. He read it over the phone to Jason.

"173 Fourth Street, Rockledge, Pennsylvania."

"Damn! That's Amber Mathieson's address. I was just talking to the old man that owns the building. He told me it's not rented out yet, that her brother gave him some money to keep her stuff there until he can get back up here and sort it out."

"Yeah, well there's something else too. There's someone signed onto the system right now."

"Fuck! He's in her apartment."

Jason refused to wait for HRT or anybody else. He literally grabbed Cab arms and hustled out to his car. Tires squealed as he exited the police station parking lot. Cab grabbed at the side of his door for a handhold as Jason put the car on two wheels several times as he sped toward Amber's apartment. As fast as he drove, his mind raced faster. He knew who would have easy access to Amber's place; Kyle Price. After all, he helped pay for it, and he probably had a spare key. Jason cursed himself for not realizing earlier what kind of monster this man must be and hoped that he could keep from beating him to a pulp when he and Cab burst through the apartment door.

Cab blanched when Jason swerved violently as he ran a red light, just missing a large gray Impala driven by an old man with a hat that had entered the intersection. The close call didn't faze Jason a bit, and he clamped down on the accelerator even more, causing the car to fishtail as he struggled to keep it on the road. Cab turned his head and looked to the rear, risking whiplash at this speed, hoping that the old man hadn't lost control and crashed into somebody's house or something. He saw that the man's car was stopped right in the middle of the street, and several other cars had come to a stop too, bringing the whole intersection to a standstill. Good, Cab thought, no one hurt . . . yet.

Another harrowing six minutes passed before Jason wheeled onto Fourth Street. He arrived on the scene the same time as a Rockledge police unit they had called for backup. Jason sprung from the unmarked car, flashing his badge and barking orders at the two wary Rockledge officers. Cab got out of the car tentatively, his legs wobbly. He noticed smoke pouring from the rear of their car, and hoped it was just burning rubber from the tires. He saw his partner directing the uniformed officers to cover the rear, and frantically motioned Cab to join him at the front door of the apartment.

It was a good thing the door to the common lobby was unlocked, because Jason put his full weight behind him as he shouldered it open. The door crashed against the inside wall, and he proceeded up the narrow stairway toward Amber's second floor apartment, with Cab right on his heels, gun drawn. Jason repeated his shoulder assault on Amber's door, and even though it was a solid core door, it caved in immediately, and the two detectives ran into the room, each facing a different side, scanning for occupants.

Knowing the layout, they swiftly worked their way into the bedroom, where Amber had kept her computer before she was murdered. They paused briefly in the closed doorway, and then Jason kicked hard at the door and went in low, crouching down as he looked quickly about the small room. There was no one there. However, on what used to be her bed, among an assortment of panties and bras, sat a laptop computer. There was no telltale phone cord attached, so Jason knew it was equipped with a wireless connection. He also knew the killer had been here, and deliberately set this scene up. He had purposely drawn them here. He must have anticipated that police would try to track him using the information they got from Sonja Peterson's computer. But how long ago had he been in this apartment? And why?

As he carefully approached the bed, on alert now for boobytraps or possible evidence, he glanced at the small, brightly-lit screen. He got his answer. *Fuck!* He was taunting them now. He was taking more risks, and that made him unpredictable and much more dangerous. He had gotten a taste of blood and his hunger was becoming insatiable. Cab, who had completed a search of the entire apartment, returned to the bedroom and saw Jason standing over the bed, mesmerized in thought. He leaned over Jason's shoulder to see what he was looking at. A slow steady scroll worked its way across the screen from right to left, the letters of a message undulating like a slithering snake.

I did Amber . . . I did Melina . . . I did them all . . . And I'm not done yet.

Chapter 26

Mirror Man had been following Jason carefully for a couple of days now. Most killers would not take such chances with a cop, but he was growing bolder and more confident in his ability to escape detection, and it was a rush to be so close to danger. He learned about Jason's relationship with Janet, and decided to watch them for awhile. What he saw angered him. The couple reminded him of he and Amber, the way they laughed so easily, the way she constantly reached out to stroke Jason's arm, or lightly lay her hand on top of his. She looked at him like he was the only man on earth, her eyes focused only on his, filtering out the swirls of activity that would distract others. Amber used to do the same things as they conversed over the din of music and voices inside the CatNipsU. He was building up resentment for the detective, and was growing ashamed of the pretty nurse for not seeing through this Lothario.

Doesn't she know he's just using her for a good fuck? Doesn't she know in a matter of months, if not a matter of weeks, the prick will dump her and move onto his next conquest? They're both a couple of horny idiots. She thinks she's found her Prince Charming, and he thinks he can milk this hot blooded bitch for all she's worth, having her attached to his arm like a walking trophy, only to cast her aside when he's tired of her no longer sweet pussy. *Maybe I should do them both.*

He followed them into the nooks. He took a table far enough away from them to be unobtrusive, but close enough to see them well. Janet looked divine this afternoon. She had just finished her workout, and a quick hot shower had left her with pink, glowing skin. Her hair had been blow-dried and styled in its usual way, and she had taken the time to apply fresh makeup. She had slipped into a short lavender skirt and a black scoop neck tank top. She looked relaxed, and Mirror Man could see her eyes twinkling as she conversed with Jason. He was fixated on her, blocking out Jason's visage completely.

He watched as she picked up her coffee cup with long slender fingers, her nails painted lavender to match her skirt. She raised the cup to her lips, and took a small sip. He saw the imprint of her lipstick on the rim of the cup as she set it back in the saucer, and immediately pictured her lips wrapped around his dick as he caressed her silky blond hair. He was growing excited, and became full of anticipation. This would be his most treasured memory ever, the seduction and murder of Janet Witherspoon, the lover of the man who was pursuing him. He watched her face as she spoke.

"Jason, I'm worried about Christine. With Kyle's arrest she has become very despondent. He was her entire world, and I'm not sure she can cope without him. She's hardly come out of the house since, and doesn't even take *my* calls. What can we do?"

Jason realized that Janet did not know Kyle was also a murder suspect. Although he felt bad not telling her, he knew it wouldn't be proper. He thought she might have heard it from Christine, but obviously Kyle's wife was not in a sharing mood. That suited him just fine for now.

"I don't know. It must be a real blow to her. Hell, it was a shock to all of us. I never imagined that Kyle would let himself be caught up in a drug operation. Even though it was just steroids, it was surprising that he could rationalize selling drugs illegally. It obviously wasn't a money thing, and doing something like that on principal seems contradictory to the Kyle we know."

"I know. And I never thought he'd keep anything from Christine. She always told me they shared everything, that they had no secrets. It was one of the things I admired about them. Not only are they married, they're the best of friends."

"Could be that's what hurts her the most," Jason said. "That he kept this dark secret from her. Maybe she feels betrayed. That's enough to send her into a tailspin."

Janet sighed. "I agree. I know she is also concerned about what will happen to him. Do you think we could meet with her, and you could talk to her about his case, what the results could be . . . what kind of sentence he could get?"

"I really can't. I'm involved with the prosecution. It would be unethical, as well as a violation of my department's policies. They have competent attorneys. I'm sure they have already laid out all the options and possibilities."

"Yes, but coming from you, a trusted friend, I think it would comfort them a bit."

"I really wish I could," Jason replied earnestly. He looked deep into her eyes. "You know if I could . . . " His voice trailed off. " I would do anything I could for them . . . for you. But this is something I can't do. It wouldn't be right."

"Christ, Jason, I just don't understand this attitude."

Janet had raised her voice, and her usually sultry tone had taken on a hard edge. She leaned toward him, her eyes burning into his like twin laser beams.

"It's not like he's a stranger, or even a casual friend. My God, we've all fucked together. I . . . he's . . . well, there's a long history with him Christine and me. We've got to stick together. I would think you could stretch the rules for him . . . and me. He's a good man, just got himself caught up in this. How can you stand by and not do anything to help him?"

Jason was stunned. It was not just her words that surprised him, he was used to fielding such tirades from people. It was part of his job. It was the sudden change that swept over her. He could see by Janet's eyes that she was passionate about this. She was as intense as he'd ever seen her. He wasn't sure what to say next. It was if storm clouds had suddenly rolled in and spoiled a great day at the beach.

"I'm . . . sorry, Janet. I'm a cop. There is no flexibility here. I will make sure he's treated . . . "

"You're a real hypocrite. You had no ethical problem asking me to get you medical records for your investigation, did you? But now you're on your high horse. I don't understand the difference."

"There *is* a difference. The reason . . . "

"Fuck the speech, Jason. Just fuck it. I can't handle it right now. Don't say anything more, just think about this, will you? Think about *us*, the future. It could be so good. Don't let anything fuck that up. Okay?"

"Are you sure there's not some other reason that you feel so strongly about this?"

"What exactly do you mean?"

He was thinking about her and Kyle. Maybe it was more than friendship she had with him. He could have been a former lover. Maybe Christine was even involved in some sort of three-way. It wasn't a big leap to make, after the behavior he'd witnessed. But on the other hand, if it happened before they met, it wasn't any of his business.

"Ah, nothing. Let's forget it."

They sat in silence, Jason looking down, mindlessly ripping at some empty sugar packets, tearing them into strips and rolling them up with his fingers. Janet was staring at him, waiting for an answer.

"I can't leave it be, Jason. Will you try and think of some way out of this for Kyle and Christine?"

He tried reason . . . and the truth. He would not allow himself to be compromised again.

"There's nothing to think about, sweetheart. There's just no room for any other option. I want to help him, and Christine too, but I've got to stay out of it. He has great attorneys. They'll figure out something. Don't you understand the position I'm in, I'm already walking on eggshells because of things we've done together. Damn, I could be fired if that shit ever came out."

As quickly as it formed, the storm cloud passed from her face. She sighed, and took his hand, squeezing it gently.

"Believe me, I know what this is doing to you. I do understand. Just think about it before you decide what to do. I know you'll come up with some way to make this right. I know you have some hidden talents, things you don't even tell me. You pretend you're not smart about certain things, but I know you are. You'll find a solution to this too. Right *Jayman*?"

She emphasized the last word, watching his face for a telltale sign. Nothing. If he picked up what she said, he was really good at not letting her see any sign of recognition. Well, maybe he just didn't hear. She hoped he'd got her message. He just had to do something. Let's switch gears a bit, she thought.

"I have a feeling it will be a long, busy shift, and I could use a little R&R afterwards." She gave him a sly wink to accentuate her meaning. "Will I see you tonight?"

Jason exhaled sharply, wondering how she would feel about him if she knew he was holding back information about Kyle's involvement with Amber and the fact that he was a murder suspect. This whole mess was going to get worse before it got better.

"I don't know. It depends on what goes on tonight. I'll call you later." He leaned over and kissed Janet briefly. It was a gentle brush of the lips reminiscent of a long married couple bidding each other goodbye before work rather than red-hot lovers preparing for a sensuous interlude. She gave no outward sign, but was quite perturbed by his lack of ardor, and rose to leave.

"Come on Jayman, let's go. I'll walk you to your car."

The Mirror Man, in one of his best disguises, watched as they rose and walked out of the nooks. He was pleased to see that there was some sort of conflict going on between them. Jason put his arm around her waist as they left the room, but Janet twisted away from his grasp. Mirror Man also rose, moving swiftly to the table where they had been seated. He paused, looking at the remains of their breakfast. He picked up the delicate coffee cup Janet had been using, seeing the waxy impression of her lower lip still remaining on the rim. He wiped the lipstick off with his thumb, and then rubbed it over his pursed lips, smelling and tasting her essence as his tongue licked at the faint smear.

She *is* pretty sweet, he thought. Too sweet for the cop. He didn't like this at all. The four of them, the cop, the rich guy, and their fawning women, they all disgusted him. He thought about his options. Maybe this could be the end, a way to bring this spree full circle. Amber was the first, right here in Highland Park. He could finish it here. It would be a fitting end, and anyone could make sense of it all as they put together the pieces of the puzzle he had so carefully constructed. Even the dullards who were trying to catch him could figure it all out. He never killed a man before, but maybe it was time. After all, they were a part of his problems too.

He remembered Jack, flashbacks of his childhood "buddy" invading his memory now as they did so often. He could fix it so that memories of *him* could torture others like he had been tortured for so long. He had a few options to choose from. Should he kill all or some? Which would cause the most immediate pain? Which deaths would cause the most long-lasting grief? In what order should he kill them? The police would like this, he thought. They would say he's becoming an "organized killer."

He was a worthy adversary. He was sure he had the respect of the FBI, and this local cop, Jason Coulter. They'll learn a great deal from him, maybe even write a book about the case. The thought brought a twisted smile to his face. He made up his mind. He was nothing if not decisive. He'd have to work quickly now. He had a plan to put in motion, no time to waste. The end was near.

Christine was sitting in the study, reading a report from the investigator hired by Kyle's attorney. She and Kyle had just finished one of their worst fights ever, and she was feeling such a range of emotions, from anger, to fear, to depression. Finally fatigue set in, and she had absentmindedly picked up the documents for something to do, something to take her mind off the thoughts she could no longer bear to think. She had attacked him as soon as he told her about Amber, and that the police believed that Kyle had killed her. Momentarily, the horrendous realization that her husband and lover was the focus of a murder investigation escaped her completely. She was shocked to learn that her husband had been cheating on her. She felt totally betrayed, as she had grown to trust him completely once again, the ravages of his last affair long suppressed from her conscious memory.

Now both images, once and again, came flooding into the present, and hit her so hard that she was in physical pain, her stomach wrenching as she fought the nausea that threatened to overcome her. She had thrown a vase against the wall, leaving a deep gouge and shattering the expensive heirloom into a thousand pieces. She had pounded her fists against his chest, and he had stood against her taking the blows in silence, arms at his sides. Through vision made misty by her crying, she saw the tears run from his eyes also. Finally spent, she collapsed onto the sofa, and buried her head in the large, soft pillows that rimmed one of her favorite pieces of furniture. Kyle had left silently, knowing there was nothing he could or should say that would make any difference. That was hours ago, and she was calmer now, and although she would not admit it to herself, she still loved him and couldn't imagine life without him.

She turned her attention to the report. The P.I. believed they had a strong case against him for selling steroids, as the cops had computer evidence linking him to the website and information from Apex gym members that implicated Kyle. This was a felony, but would be treated more like a crime of illegal commerce than a violation of the controlled substance act. The attorneys had told her that her husband, if found guilty, would probably face only a fraction of the maximum five years. They thought he would get a lenient sentence due to his reputation in the community, his work for and funding of many charities, and the fact that this was his first offense. Still, with the zero-tolerance on drug dealing of any kind that was prevalent in Montgomery County, he could expect some jail time. They thought Kyle could get a deal, maybe less than a year, to be served in the federal prison in Lewisburg.

The report also contained the investigator's findings regarding the murder accusations. Christine was relieved that the private investigator found no evidence, no supporting facts, for the police to suspect her husband killed Amber Mathieson. In his opinion, the police were being pressured into developing a suspect and Kyle's entanglement with the victim and his present indictment for drug violations was fueling this current probe against him. The conclusion of the investigator was that Kyle would be vindicated of this killing, and that the defeated accusation would make the police look incompetent, and would bode well for the ability of Kyle's attorney to mitigate the sentence in the drug case. If they got the right jury, the investigator wrote, they could even get an acquittal. But still, a decision to fight the charges all the way to the end was risky. More likely, the District Attorney and the U.S. Attorney would offer a plea bargain, a deal of sorts. They would make sure that Kyle expressed guilt for the acts he committed, while offering a significant compromise on sentencing.

Although she didn't understand the nuances of the report, Christine knew enough to realize that her husband might come out of all this pretty much intact. He'd been through tough times before, they both had. She thought they would both fall apart when Natalie had been kidnapped, and likely would have if his daughter had been killed or seriously injured. But the experience had made them stronger, and had also taught them that life and love are fragile, and must be nurtured and cherished. That was how she and Kyle had determined that they would live their lives, and for the most part, were successful. These events would test their love and commitment, but she was beginning to believe they could see their way through both trials; the legal one, and the emotional one caused by Kyle's infidelity.

Although still sluggish, Christine was starting to feel a little better, and shook her head to clear the cobwebs. She needed a workout. She needed to clear her mind and push her body to the limit, sweat out the toxins that were heavy in her system right now. A workout always helped raise her spirits, and that was something she needed now more than ever. She rose and walked to the bedroom, throwing a few items in her gym bag. A quick visit to the bathroom to splash water on her face and touch up her makeup and she was out the door, heading for the Apex.

It was well after closing as she finished up her workout. The gym was quiet. Deathly quiet. The only sounds were her sometimes-labored breathing and the steady clank-clank-clank of the lateral pectoral machine's metal plates banging together as she rhythmically contracted her arm and chest muscles. She counted to twenty and let the padded levers fall to rest. She could feel a slight numbness in her pecs, and knew she had worked them to the point of failure. Her skin glistened with perspiration, and she wiped her face and neck with a towel, draping it around her shoulders when she was done. That was all for tonight. A quick sauna to purge the body of any remaining toxins, and a nice hot, comfortable shower would complete her night. Too bad neither Maxine nor Antonio were still on duty. A rubdown by one the Apex's talented and certified massage therapists would really have topped off this workout.

It wasn't often she had the opportunity to have the whole place to herself, but it wasn't rare either. Nonetheless, these nights were valued for their solitude as well as the chance to have exclusive use of the facilities. She headed toward the locker rooms, pausing in front of one of the many full-length mirrors to check herself out. Not bad, she thought, as she looked at her image head to toe. She turned around to check her caboose. She always thought her ass was one of her best attributes. Not too small, but well rounded and firm. Still thong-worthy. There was a time when looking at her reflection caused her much consternation. She had been very critical of her body. But now she was much more relaxed, more accepting. As her husband might say, she was close to self-actualization, the top rung of Maslow's hierarchy of needs. She remembered the philosophical kick he'd been on during his MBA studies, and inwardly smiled. He had been so much like a boy then, but there was a hint of the success and worldliness that would follow.

As she entered the locker room she heard a muffled noise. Again. It was coming from the spa area located between the women and men's locker rooms.

She walked toward that section of the gym that contained the pool, two large Jacuzzis, the sauna, and the massage room. As she got closer she heard low moans. She stopped . . . hesitated . . . listened. The moans continued. Sounds of water. Breathing noises. She was not scared, expecting to find a couple of adventurous lovers in the midst of a wet and wild tryst.

Maybe Deter, the gym's manager, and Marjo. Maybe one of the young fitness trainers and his latest bombshell protégé. She crept closer, taking care not to make a sound as she padded along the tile floor. She reached the opening and peeked out. *Jesus! No!* In an instant, her relaxed body went from zero to sixty. Her heartbeat raced and her head pounded, ready to explode. *Not him! Not him!* She lost control of her body, and slid down the wall to the floor in a crumpled heap, her stomach retching, her lungs fighting to breathe. Her world had just fallen apart.

The water had turned completely pink. It bubbled incessantly, causing frothy pink suds to rise to the surface of the Apex's twelve-person Jacuzzi. The spa had the effervescence of champagne being poured into a crystal flute, and occasionally a whirling bubble would break free from the foam and drift erratically toward the vaulted ceiling. Jason watched them drift aimlessly, riding currents of air stirred by huge electric fans that hung like chandeliers from the top of the two-story high roof. Even from the ground, the blades of the fans seemed as large as helicopter rotors. Despite the size of the room and the attempts to keep air circulating effectively, there was a feeling of clammy closeness, the kind of watery sheen left by the air as it contacts your bare skin. A heavy odor of chlorine hung in the mist too, which was one of the reasons he never enjoyed hot tubbing at the Apex or any other open-to-the-public facility. Intimacy was the other reason. If he was going to put his body in a hot, steamy bath with almost a dozen other people, they better be current or former lovers. Spending time in a swirling Jacuzzi was akin to rolling around on a plastic mattress with other drooling, sweaty, naked people. Jason wasn't going to do that with just anyone. He looked at the churning water again. *Imagine what swirls around in there on a daily basis!*

Of course, there was another item in this particular Jacuzzi that made matters worse. Floating in the middle of the circular pool, kept in perpetual motion by the rotating action of the water jets, was the lifeless, mutilated body of Kyle Price. The coroner would have no trouble determining the manner and cause of death of this one. Kyle's throat had been cut from ear to ear, and the wound was so deep and so wide that his throat had become waterlogged and had sunk below the surface, causing his head to rise up and down like a cork bob on the end of a fishing line. There was still fresh blood oozing from the wound, thick and gooey as it was squeezed from the neck with each downward bobbing of the head, changing into thin rivulets as it was sucked into the whirlpool and finally beat into rich pink foam. It was a gory sight, and the fact that the dead man was Jason's friend made matters worse.

An investigator with Jason's time and experience sees a lot of bloody sights, and it took a lot to disturb him. Sometimes, in fact, he felt he was too callous, not feeling the slightest anguish over the most brutal scenes anyone could imagine. But this one bothered him. He fought the urge to spill his guts, and concentrated on the crime scene. As usual, Cab arrived at the Apex a few minutes after him, and knowing who the victim was, bypassed his usual first look at the body. He made none of his trademark wisecracks as he made his way past the patrol officers to where his partner was standing, looking lost and unsure. Jason was turned away from the Jacuzzi, staring toward the ceiling. This was very uncharacteristic of Jason, and Cab didn't hesitate to step in and help his boss.

"I'm sorry, Jason. Really I am." Cab could see his partner was in anguish, a rare state for the usually cool, brusque mannered detective.

"Listen, there's no need for you to handle this. Let me do it. Why don't you get some fresh air? I'll keep you posted. Do you know if Christine has been called yet?"

"Oh, shit. Christine. She's the one who found him. She collapsed after making the call to 911. The paramedics took her into the training room to check her out. I think she's okay physically, but seeing him like this was too much for her. She went nuts. She was still wailing when I got here. I should check on her."

"Good idea, but don't question her yourself. Just be her friend, she'll need that. I'll talk to her when she's able. Do you know if she saw anything? Did she see who did this? Was she talking at all to the first responding officers before she lost it? This is a fresh one, Jason, we've got to get some information quickly. The killer can't be far."

Jason smiled weakly. "You're beginning to sound like me. No, she didn't say anything useful. She thought she heard moans, but the way his throat was cut, it could have been gurgling sounds mixed with the sound of the water jets."

"Or, it could have been Kyle groaning before he was cut. Maybe he sustained other wounds before his throat was slashed. That would mean the killer was here just before Christine found him."

"Yeah, maybe." Jason looked over at his dead friend, still bobbing in the water. "Can you please get them to take some quick photographs and get him the fuck outta there. We could be losing fucking evidence, trace evidence that will be sucked out and treated by the filtration system."

Cab signaled a Highland Park detective who was standing on the other side of the Jacuzzi. He relayed his boss's instructions, cutting the man off before he could finish his sentence about waiting for the county forensic team. Satisfied that his order would be carried out, Cab went to the training room. Christine was sitting on one of the wooden benches near the training tables, her face in her hands. The paramedics had placed a blanket over her shoulders, trying to keep her warm and fend off shock. One of them was kneeling on the floor, whispering to her softly in a vain attempt to console her. The other was going through his gear that had been placed on a training table. He was rummaging through a large nylon bag, maybe looking for something to help his partner, or maybe just trying to look busy.

The man on the floor saw the burly detective approaching, and was only too willing to give up his spot. He rose quickly and stepped aside, nodding to Cab as he did, figuratively handing off the baton. Cab knelt beside Christine, close enough to hear her low sobbing, a deep guttural cry that comes only when a person has expended all of the energy to grieve, yet are still unable to gain control of their emotions. Cab had witnessed it before, but it never got any easier. No wonder the paramedics were quick to turn over the scene. She needed life support for her mind, not her body, and they felt pretty useless just standing around.

Cab placed one of his huge hands on her shoulder, squeezing as gently as he could. Even so, his vise-like grip would probably leave a bruise on her sensitive skin.

"Christine honey, it's Cab. You're okay, you're safe. Jason and I are here with you, and we're going to make sure you get through this. I promise you that."

She stirred and lowered her hands from her face. Her usually perfect makeup was smeared and running, and she had the deer-caught-in-the–headlights look of a person totally disoriented. Cab tried to smile, but his mouth wouldn't cooperate. Instead, he had a pained, twisted look that caused Christine to instinctively feel sorry for him. Momentarily, roles were switched as she mistook his expression for sorrow and reached to comfort him, and then wrapped her arms tightly around his bulk. She buried her head on his thick shoulder. The paramedics looked at each other in awe, amazed that the detective could effect such a dramatic reaction in a few seconds, especially since they tried unsuccessfully to get any sort of response.

Christine insisted on going home. Cab had tried to convince her to go to the hospital with the paramedics and be checked out for shock, but she shook her head vehemently. He kept at her, and only relented when she agreed to let him call Janet, and have Janet meet her at her house. He did so, and the nurse at the duty station told him she would page Janet and give her the message to go immediately to Christine's home, and to give Detective Calloway a call as soon as she arrived. Cab made her repeat the message twice, which made him feel a lot like his boss. *Damn! I'm getting just as anal as Jason.* Cab shook his head at the thought. He would have even insisted the nurse fetch Janet so that he could talk to her himself had he not been in the middle of a homicide scene.

Chapter 27

He waited for her outside. It would be at least another hour until she appeared, and that was if she didn't have to work overtime. He was driving a burgundy Ford panel van that he rented yesterday. Inside the empty cargo area he had carefully spread heavy gauge plastic over the floor. He had punched some holes in each corner and a couple on each side and installed grommets to prevent tearing when he tied it down. He tested it with his own twisting and turning body to make sure the plastic wouldn't slide under pressure. In his knapsack lying on the front passenger seat he had packed plastic wire binders, similar to police flexcuffs, that he would use to secure her hands and feet. He bought some bungee cords to help secure her body and prevent her from wiggling around too much. He would secure the cords to the frame since there were numerous cutouts designed to secure loads in the back of the van. He also had a fresh roll of duct tape along with the usual accoutrements of his calling, including his razor, lock picks, pry tools, lengths of rope, and some rags and cleaning solvents.

He was still fuming about the run-in he had with the clerk at Avis. He wanted a red van and the sniveling clerk gave him a hard time about it. The customer is always right *except* when they want something that takes a little extra effort. The clerk was a real dick, wanting to know what the big deal was and reminding him that these type vans were for work, not show. He had a hard time controlling his temper, but knew any outburst would make him a more memorable customer than he wanted to be, and of course, there was always the chance the pussy clerk might call the cops. Nevertheless, it was important that he get a color as close to blood red as he could. Not that he was anticipating any problems like he had with Sonja, but that incident proved he could never be too careful. He wanted to be ready just in case. If he did have to cut her, at least any blood that he missed during cleanup would be hard to discern with the naked eye when he returned the van. Of course, if things got screwed up and the van got

WILLIAM M. HEIM

damaged too much, he would just torch it. After all, he used another bogus credit card, so he needn't be too worried about it.

He knew exactly what door she would come out of at the end of her shift, and where she had parked her car. It had been so easy to find out her schedule. He just called the hospital and said he wanted to bring her a little gift for taking such good care of his wife, and could they tell him when she was working next please? He had followed her home the previous two days, so he knew the route she took. He scoped out the route carefully, choosing the most remote section of highway to confront her. Since she was working the 3-11 shift, and often had to stay late, it would be a least 11:15 and as late as midnight before she left the parking lot. It would be another ten minutes before they reached the spot he had chosen to take her. He waited patiently, continually rehearsing in his mind and throwing in some surprises to work out in advance to prevent the panic he experienced when Sonja reacted so violently. He still shuddered when he recalled how close he'd come to failure . . . and discovery.

Sometimes he felt like the end was coming and that he couldn't keep this up for too much longer. His mother's face flashed into his mind's eye and scenes from his childhood, his relationship with Carol, and several of his killings flooded his conscious memory. One day, he always knew, it must stop. There was a time when he thought the urges would go away, and he would be finished with this and resume a normal life. Why couldn't he have a life like Kyle Price, or even Jason Coulter. These men were admired by most, especially women. They were not better looking than he was. They were certainly not as smart or skilled as he was.

He had clearly demonstrated his superiority in every way. What was it then that kept him from becoming as prominent and popular as those men. He should be, no . . . he was their equal. If he could have just repressed these feelings that drove him to stalk and kill, he may have been able to lead a legitimate life. He too could have taken his rightful place as a mover and shaker in some upscale community, somewhere like Columbia, and enjoy being *someone* for once in his life. But now there was no turning back. At least he would control his own destiny. No one would write the final scene but him.

These thoughts faded as quickly as they had appeared when he caught sight of Janet leaving the hospital. She was early. As usual, she looked radiant. Even after a full shift of tending to the needs of others, she looked fresh and alert. He watched her as she started to walk across the parking lot, her long blond hair tossing about with each step. Her fingers brushed it back as it fell over her face, one of the unconscious habits he loved about her. He imagined her sitting across from him, smiling as she reached for some errant strands of her fine blond hair and swept them back from her lovely face. He must have pictured that simple scene a thousand times, and every time it aroused him greatly. Her hair and her penetrating blue eyes mesmerized him. *But something was wrong.*

Her pace was too quick, her strides too purposeful. He saw her unconsciously scan the lot for movement, a habit she had gotten into years ago while taking a self-defense class for women. As a nurse, Janet often worked late into the evening and she and many of her peers took such classes to increase their confidence about traveling home so late. She quickened her pace even more, almost breaking into a run. She had her keys out and ready and he saw her point her remote toward her car and unlock the door. *She knows.* Either she knows about him, somehow determined that she was about to become a victim, or she knows about Kyle. Maybe they found his body already, and called her at the hospital. That would explain her leaving so early. Regardless, he would proceed with his plan. It was too late for anyone to stop him now. He started his car, and prepared for the chase.

He watched her pull out onto Highland Drive and head south, just as expected. She made a right turn on Primrose, and another right on Oak. She would be on Oak Street for four minutes, make a left turn onto Johnson Way, and exactly one mile later, at a dark, remote intersection she would slow for a stop sign. It was then he would strike her. Everything went according to plan, and his confidence was growing. But wait . . . she was turning onto Preston Avenue. This isn't her way home. *Shit!* He felt a surge of panic, and shook his head violently in an attempt to ward off the feeling. *Damn! Why was this happening now? It was so close to the end, why did she have to change now?*

He was sure now that she knew something was wrong. By the way she was driving, at least fifteen miles over the speed limit, he figured that the cops had found Kyle, and that Jason or one of his cops had called her at the hospital to tell her. He didn't know Highland Park all that well, but it appeared the route she was taking did not lead to the police station. He had no clue where she was headed. In another minute, she would reach the main road, and traffic would be heavy, precluding his attempts to stop her. They were approaching a stop sign, maybe the last one before she hit the main road. There were houses around, and the intersection was well lighted. But it was now or never. He forced his racing thoughts to slow down, and in the few remaining seconds before he had to make his move, he reviewed his plan of action.

She was coming to the intersection, and he saw her brake lights flash. He quickly closed the gap between their vehicles, until he was only a couple of feet behind her. At precisely the right moment, he bumped the rear of Janet's car with his own, not hard, but enough to cause a jolt without causing damage. He allowed her to exit her car first, and she was grimacing as she walked back to inspect her vehicle for damage. He tried to look flustered, and got out of his car to meet her, apologizing profusely.

"Oh shit, I am so sorry. Are you alright?"

"Yeah, I think so." She was rubbing the back of her neck. "What happened?"

"I just wasn't paying attention, I looked away for a moment, and you were stopped in front of me. I didn't even have time to hit my brake. Is there any damage?"

"I can't see any, but your headlights don't throw enough light to really see. Let me get a flashlight from my car."

As she was speaking, he put one of his hands in his pocket, fingering a length of thick rope he knew he would need very soon. As she turned, he took out the rope and quickly looped it over her head and pulled, jerking her head back violently. Her hands instinctively went to her neck and her fingers encircled the rope, trying to ease the tension it was already placing on her windpipe. He pulled harder, twisting the short rope around his left wrist and causing it to bite further into the soft tissue of her neck. It effectively cut off her airway. At the same time he used his leg to sweep hers from under her, and she fell into him. Holding the twisted rope with one hand and grabbing her around the waist with the other, he walked backward toward the rear of the van. She struggled at first, but then began to lose consciousness. He eased up a bit so she would not pass out and become dead weight. As it was, her feet were moving backwards with his in an eerie, disjointed dance.

When they reached the back doors of he van, he opened them quickly and threw her inside. He climbed on top of her and reached for his bag, taking out the cords and other tools he needed to secure his prey. He tied down her hands and feet, and ripped a piece of duct tape from the roll with his teeth. He took a washcloth and jammed it into her mouth, and then secured it by pasting the tape across her lips. With this done, he released his grip on the rope around her neck, and she inhaled sharply through her nose, her body aching for air. Once he was assured she was immobilized, he climbed out and walked to her car, still running at the edge of the intersection. He got in and pulled it over to the curb. He parked her car legally knowing this would bide time. It should be hours, maybe days, before anyone noticed she was missing and became suspicious. He reentered his van and drove away, headed for a secluded park where he would take care of business.

Still in a state of panic and shock, Janet tried to shake off the horrible feeling of doom as she lay in the back of the van. She'd been taken completely by surprise, and was overwhelmed before she could even think about fighting off her attacker. Her scalp hurt where he had pulled her hair, and it felt as if he ripped large clumps out as he pulled her along the street. She tested her restraints, twisting her wrists and craning her neck to see how she was secured to the sides of the van. She felt a sharp pain in her shoulder as she turned, and figured it was dislocated. It had probably been ripped out of its socket during his struggle to throw her into the van. She needed to calm down, to be rational.

She then started to assess her overall physical condition. She felt okay, nothing wrong with her senses. She couldn't find any bleeding, except for her lip, where she had accidentally bitten it when he first attacked her. Her head throbbed a bit, but she could still think clearly. She wasn't sure whether that was a blessing or a curse, based on what she may face in the near future. Her restraints were tight, and wouldn't give even a bit with all her twisting and turning.

As her eyes adjusted to the darkness, she looked backward toward the front of the vehicle to try and see her captor. The pain was too great, and she didn't think she could crane her neck enough to see anyway, so she stopped trying. She tried to remember what Jason had told her during one of their early dates, when he was trying to impress her with his prowess as a cop. He told her that if she was ever in a situation where she might be a victim that she should never give up looking for a way out. She should concentrate on trying to find a means of escape or attack. Run a hundred scenarios through your mind, he said. Picture the guy doing one thing and picture yourself doing something to thwart him. If you do it enough, something will develop that you can use. Maybe not the same situation as you imagined, but something similar, and you'll be ready to move.

She'd never thought she would have to rely on this advice, but was now trying to do what he said. She began to think about escaping, waiting for the van to stop and for her attacker to come for her. Terror was just beneath the surface, but for now she was okay, she had control of her faculties and she had hope. All of a sudden it came to her. She also had her cell phone. Her phone should be on. If she could reach it, hit one of the buttons, she could at least connect to someone and signal her whereabouts. She knew that cell phones were now included in the county 911 system, and a call to the emergency center would pinpoint her location within a few hundred yards. The signal would also register at the Price house, and maybe someone would pick it up. Something was up at the Price's house too. She had been told to go there right away, some kind of emergency...but no one answered when she tried to call. Then this happened. The phone was in the pocket of the hip length lab coat she wore over her blouse.

She liked the deep pockets in the coat, where she could stuff her stethoscope, and the variety of instruments she used during her rounds. It was in her right pocket, and although her hands were tied, she was able to get her hand close enough to reach the number pad. She felt for the location of the numbers, and pressed what she thought was the key for speed dial, and then the number one. Please, she prayed, please work.

Christine's eyes were sore from non-stop crying. The sharp ring of the telephone interrupted her thoughts. She reached over for the portable phone on the table next to where she was seated in the study, and clicked it on.

"Hello? Hello?" There was no answer. Christine listened hard, and could hear nothing but some background noise. Some sort of hum, or maybe machinery running. No voices. The caller stayed on the line, even when Christine said, "Who's there" a few more times. She got up and carried the phone to the main unit, and inserted in into the machine's phone cradle. She hit the identifier button like Kyle had shown her. Immediately, the built-in screen lit up, showing a map of the Highland Park area and pinpointing the source of the call. It was coming from the cell phone she'd lent to Janet, and the call was coming from the area of Bronson Road, a street leading into Mulligan Park.

"Janet . . . Janet? Can you hear me. Are you okay? Say something Janet." Nothing. Only the same steady hum as before. She watched the screen, hit the update icon, and the blip changed location. It was headed to the park. *Shit! Something's wrong.* She left the line open, retrieved her own cell phone, and dialed the Highland Park Police Department Detective Division.

Jason was just starting to pack up to leave his office when the phone rang. He had a nightly ritual at the end of his tour, which included surveying all of the calls he didn't yet return, all of the cases he still needed to review, and all of the reports he was working on himself. He organized them into three neat piles in the center of his desk, by priority of course, and then weighted them down with three unique paperweights. One paperweight was a brightly colored tropical fish made out of glass. He had bought this the first time he vacationed in the Caribbean. The second paperweight was a crudely made ashtray, the product of Cab's son's kindergarten class several years ago. Marcus had given him this treasure during one of his visits to Cab's, when he had played catch with the boy. The third was a small rectangular sign given to him by his father before his untimely death of a heart attack. It was from his father's desk, and contained the early slogan of the IBM Corporation, back when a single computer took up a whole room. The sign consisted of a white background with black lettering framed in wood. It had a weighted base for stability, and it looked like a miniature billboard. The message was simple: THINK. For Jason, this was a link to his past, to his father's rock solid values and always, calm demeanor. It gave him pause, and during his most hectic or exasperating days served as a silent advisor, urging him to take the time to reflect. Slow down, take a minute, think about it. He picked up the receiver.

"Detectives, Lieutenant Coulter."

His body stiffened as he strained to listen to the harried voice on the other end of the phone. He wasn't ready for the message he was getting. He felt himself panicking, and took several deep breaths to slow down his body's reaction. He jotted down a couple of notes, ripped the sheet from his pad, and ran from his office.

Mirror Man pulled the van into the secluded park he'd selected for just this purpose. It had three ways in and out, which was appealing to him. He found a spot where he could observe the road leading to where he would position the van without being seen himself. Mulligan Park was just a couple of miles outside the city limits, in a more remote part of the county where there were no full time police officers. The chance of discovery would be very slim, well within his acceptable range. Actually that mattered very little to him now, as long as he had enough time to complete the deed. He looked over his shoulder at Janet, still struggling against her bonds, twisting her head forcefully in an attempt to work the gag out of her mouth. He stopped at the chosen point and backed the van into a small clearing shrouded by thick underbrush. He got out and walked to the roadway, making sure the van could not be seen by a passing car. Not too bad, he thought. Unless someone is really looking for it, it is practically invisible.

He returned to the van and got into the back with Janet. Her fear was already escalating, and he could see the wild desperation in her eyes and smell the sweat induced by her terror. With his finger, he gently brushed back her hair, and looked at her with his piercing eyes and crooked grin. *This was going to be really good.* Perhaps his swan song, his final act of violence. He may never have to kill again, this could certainly satisfy his urges. Soon he would return to a normal life, and work toward becoming the man he'd always dreamed he could be. The spectra of his mother and the rubber man, Carol, Jack, and all the other visions that would seize hold of his thoughts would at last vanish. He took out his razor, the one he'd used to cut Sonja, and began slicing the front of her Janet's nurse uniform. His eyes never left hers as he slipped the blade under her blouse, cutting the buttons off one by one. He smelled urine as she lost control of her bladder.

Shit! I can't do this by myself, Jason thought as he sped away from the police station. I need to call it in, to get some backup. He reached for the police radio microphone, and then hesitated. The killer might have a scanner, he might hear if a call for help is broadcast over the police frequency. This could lead him to kill Janet quickly and flee. He reached for the cell phone on his belt, and dialed headquarters. He gave instructions to the officer who answered, and continued to speed toward Mulligan Park.

He figured there was no time to get the state police for assistance, so he had directed the desk officer to contact three on-duty Highland Park patrol units by phone to respond.

"Have everyone stay off the radio," Jason barked.

He knew they would be a couple of minutes behind him, and also left orders that the units cut off emergency lights and sirens well before they got to the park, and not enter the area until they heard from him. He thought it best if he could locate the killer first, then have the units come in. He was afraid that if the killer heard any of them coming, he would finish off Janet before they could get close. He worked on a plan as he drove, and tried to picture the layout of the park, wondering where the killer would take her. He drove like a man possessed, and a couple of times almost lost control of the unmarked cruiser rounding a curve at over sixty. Where would the killer go? He would obviously try to get off the beaten path, foregoing any of the paved or graveled parking areas. He would stay away from open areas, like the ball field or bandshell. Where were the most secluded areas, those shielded by trees and thick underbrush, but still accessible by vehicle? Would he pull her from the van and drag her deep into the forest? As Jason drove, he rummaged around his car for some equipment.

Opening the glove compartment, he reached for his ASP, an expandable metal baton that was issued to the officers, kind of a modern day nightstick. He also made a mental note to grab a flashbang from the trunk. He had "procured" a couple of them from the SWAT team just for a situation like this. He knew the chief would probably suspend him for using it without authorization, but he also knew the loud roar and blinding flash the device emitted when triggered would provide the distraction that could save Janet's life.

It only took him ten minutes to reach the park's west entrance. He dialed Christine's cell phone, and she picked up on the first ring.

"Where is she," he asked, his voice raised a bit by his anxiety.

"Mulligan Park. The signal hasn't moved for a couple minutes. I've been updating it every thirty seconds or so."

"Can you pinpoint which section of the park? Is there any detail to the map?"

"Yes, I zeroed in on the area. The whole park is laid out here, although not in detail. It looks like she's close to where Arbor Drive intersects with Bandshell Way, maybe halfway between the intersection and the west park entrance."

Bingo.

"Okay, I know where that is. Keep that line open as long as you can, and call me only if the signal moves. Understand? I'll be out of the car soon, and probably won't be able to respond easily."

Jason veered into the west drive, almost missing it, not realizing how fast he was going. He grimaced as the rear wheels slid and squealed and he fought to regain control of the vehicle. *Damn, Jason, you'll blow this if you don't get yourself under control.* He slowed down as he straightened out the cruiser, and headed for the spot Christine described.

He shut off the car lights and poked his flashlight out the side window, illuminating the roadway as little as possible, just enough to keep from sliding off the asphalt. Well before he reached the halfway point, Jason stopped the car. He popped the trunk and removed two flashbangs and his portable radio. He walked as quietly as he could along the side of the road, moving swiftly but cautiously, peering into the underbrush as he went. He'd underestimated the distance he needed to go, and had walked for more than a half mile. He was getting out of breath, and considered calling in his backup, which must have arrived at the park entrances by now. But he continued on. Less than two hundreds yards later, he caught a glimpse of metal reflected by the moonlight. He moved in slowly and deliberately. It was the van. He watched and listened for a few seconds, and moved closer. As he approached, he heard sounds inside, shuffling . . . muffled voices.

The van was shaking slightly. Images of Janet being strangled or sliced to death by the madman flashed through his brain. He could feel the beating of his heart and hear his breathing become more labored as he reacted to the sights and sounds, both real and imagined. He could sense it . . . not much time left.

Chapter 28

He bit down hard on her nipple. She let out a horrific cry, a terrible guttural noise that would have chilled most to the bone if it had not been stifled by the wad of cloth he'd shoved far down her throat. Opening her mouth like that will only cause her to choke faster, he thought. As he raised his head from her chest, a trickle of fresh blood ran down his lower lip. He smiled at her in the darkness, hoping she could see his pearly whites before she drifted off into unconsciousness. He still had the razor in his right hand, and lowered it to her cotton nurse's pants, slipping it under the waistband and slicing downward, cutting toward her crotch. He didn't take his eyes off hers as his hand moved, wanting to see the fear in her eyes if she was still awake. Suddenly, he felt her body stiffen, and a second later felt the thick, sticky ooze of blood on his hand. He had cut her with the razor as he was slicing through the fabric of her pants.

What's that! That sound. It took a second for him to process it, but he knew then that it was the squeal of tires. He sat up, ears straining to hear another indication of an intruder. None came, but the hairs on the back of his neck were standing up, and his instincts told him to flee. He looked down at Janet, and saw her body was still and lifeless, her eyes shut, and in the darkness he could not see her chest rising. He was finished here.

Jason flattened himself against the side of the van. He struggled to calm down, his pulse raging and his mind spinning in a hundred different directions. He thought of the sign on his desk, the one from his father; *Think.* He reached for one of the flashbangs and tucked it under his arm. With a flick of his wrist, the expandable baton slid open and was ready to use. After smashing the window, he would throw in the flashbang. Immediately, he would go in from the passenger side, pull himself into the front seat, and confront whoever was inside. The explosion *should* disorient the killer, and Jason would be on him before he could react. It was a big *should.*

234

She lay quietly in the dark, wanting to sob, but holding herself back. She dared not move, dared hardly to breathe. The attack stopped as quickly as it had started. It had been brutal, and she thought several times that she would pass out from the pain. The only thing that kept her from doing so was her thoughts of escape, looking for some way to get out, to make him stop, to make him go away. She knew if she lost consciousness she would be done, totally left to his mercy, which was nonexistent. He was cutting her down there, she felt the sharp pain and flow of blood as the razor severed her flesh. She grit her teeth to keep from crying out. But then, she suddenly felt his weight off her. She thought maybe he was gone, but was too scared to even open an eye to check. The rag in her throat was stifling, but she was able to breathe through her nose. After being motionless for at least a full minute, and hearing nothing, she opened her eyes. She saw only blackness. There was nothing, nobody near her. She craned her neck and looked around the van as best she could. She could not see him. She grew bolder and began to struggle once again against her bonds, trying to kick and twist and turn in hopes of breaking free. After a couple of minutes she was exhausted, and again lay motionless, panting hard. *What now?*

Ah, yes. It was a game of cat and mouse. This was the end, he was sure of it. He wanted to win, he *would* win. He had conquered his demons, had committed his last vengeful act to even the score with those in his past. He would vanquish this last foe, and be off. If he got captured by others, it did not matter, because they were not part of the game now, the game was finished, He was not caught during the game. He was not outsmarted, the cops had not even come close. Shit, the closest anyone came was Sonja, that chubby bitch from Missouri, who had put up such a fight before he'd cut her up. He watched Jason from the thicket in which he had concealed himself. The detective moved slowly and noiselessly to the vehicle's passenger window, crouching with gun drawn, and a collapsible baton at the ready. He saw him up against the van, suddenly thrusting his arm downward. The baton expanded with a metallic clank. The detective holstered the gun, and reached for a larger object fastened to his belt. Jason seemed to hesitate for a second, like he was making up his mind about something, and then he swung into action.

She heard the glass shatter, and a split second later the interior of the van exploded in a burst of sound and light. She was deafened by the noise, and an intense flash of light burned her eyes, a hundred times stronger than a flashbulb popping at point blank range. She was disoriented and very, very frightened.

Mirror Man saw Jason swing the baton at the window with all his might, and the glass shattered with a bang. Next, an explosion, so loud it seemed to rock the van, and shards of light came streaming out of the back windows like starbursts as they too shattered from the blast.

Jason was pulling himself into the opening where there had been a window only seconds before. He was inside the van quickly, ignorant of the cuts on his arms and torso inflicted by sharp pieces of glass still hanging along the bottom of the window frame. He saw that the front seat was clear, and thrust himself over it into the cargo area. His eyes, although he had shielded them from the blast, were not yet focused. He swept the baton around in a circle near the top of the van, figuring that the killer would be on top of Janet, or raising himself up to strike Jason. He did not connect. As his eyes adjusted to the ambient light he saw her, lying still on the floor. At first, he feared he was too late, that she was gone. Then he saw she was shaking, probably out of sheer terror.

He talked to her quietly, almost in a whisper, trying to calm her fears and let her know she was safe in his arms. He himself was doubtful of that fact, and was uneasy that her attacker was not here. He had to be lurking somewhere close, maybe right outside the doors of the van, maybe even hidden somewhere inside, waiting to ambush Jason. He mustn't let his guard down now, but it was hard to take his attention from Janet. She was shaking like a child caught outside in a bitter cold snowstorm, and he was afraid she was going into shock, a condition that left untreated could result in death. Using a pocketknife, he swiftly cut the bonds holding her arms and legs, and removed the tape and rag from her mouth, holding a finger to his lips to keep her silent. She understood, and kept as silent as she could. She was making soft whimpering sounds that made his heart melt.

He took off his jacket and wrapped it around her. He was suddenly overcome with a strange combination of rage and nausea when he saw the blood trickling from the bite on her exposed nipple. Fighting to keep himself under control, he told her not to move until he came back, and gave her the baton. He was going to give her his gun, but reconsidered. She was in no condition to use it, even if she had the chance. He checked the inside of the dark vehicle thoroughly, feeling around for false compartments or modifications that might somehow hide a body. The killer was not here. He secured the rear doors with the cords that were used to tie up Janet so they could not be opened from the outside.

He instructed Janet to call 911, and tell them he was out on foot after the killer. He motioned for her sit near the rear doors, where she could feel somewhat secure from a surprise attack. Then he climbed into the passenger compartment and quickly exited the van.

He was no sooner out the door when he was attacked, the assailant slicing at his face with the razor. The first strike caught him high on his left cheek, causing his flesh to burn as the sharp blade opened a three-inch gash. He blocked the second slash with his forearm, but felt the burning sensation again. He tumbled to the ground, rolling away from the dark figure pursuing him, trying to put some distance between himself and the lethal blade of the razor. He felt fear and panic, realizing he could be cut to shreds in the next few seconds. But the vision of Janet lying in the van flashed through his mind, and the vision of a young helpless girl lying on the floor of an office building bathroom followed, replacing his fear with rage, and giving him the will to survive. His instincts kicked in.

He reached for his holster as he rolled, trying to find his .40 caliber semi-automatic in its familiar place. His hands closed around the grip of the weapon and he pulled it from the holster, struggling to get back on his feet as the killer came closer, swinging the blade from side to side. Another slash, and Jason's neck was warm with blood. He thrust the gun toward his attacker, and fired once, twice, three times. The third bullet hit home, and Mirror Man went reeling back. He was hit but not down. He started to recover. The man was a monster, and like a second rate horror film, he didn't know when to die. Jason fired two more times, this time almost point blank into his attacker's chest. Finally, his assailant collapsed in a heap. Jason also dropped to the ground, overcome by his injuries and the sudden realization that he'd narrowly avoided death.

He struggled to remain conscious, casting a wary eye on the still figure that lay only a few feet from him. He was relieved to hear the sound of approaching sirens, getting louder by the second. As the sounds grew stronger, he let himself go, drifting off into a coma-like state. He could hear the cacophony of his rescue, the shrieking of tires, the raised voices shouting orders, and the noisy hustle and bustle of men and equipment. Police, paramedics, and even firefighters poured onto the scene, with the jaws of life ready, just in case. He heard it all, but it seemed like it was happening far, far away. Finally, he heard the voice of his partner, so close he could feel Cab's breath on his ear.

"I'm here, Jason, I'm here. We got Janet. She'll be okay. Hang in there now, it's going to be fine . . . "

Chapter 29

He watched her sleeping. She seemed to be resting well, her breathing regular and rhythmic. She was curled up like a child cuddling her small well-worn blankie, dreaming unconsciously in the middle of the night. She was beautiful despite the freshly treated cuts and bruises on her face, and as he watched her chest gently rise and fall, he was amazed at the deep feelings he felt for her. He carefully brushed some strands of hair covering her right eye. He winced at the sight of a red and purple raw welt just below, and hoped it didn't feel as bad as it looked. He had forgotten his own pain, his arm still throbbing from the knife slash which left a deep six inch long cut. The wound on his neck did not hurt much now, but if had been an inch to the right he would not have made it to the hospital. Actually, he felt much better than he thought he would after his fight with the killer, and he was convinced Janet was the reason.

For the first time in many years, he had that feeling of awe and wonder. *Soulmate.* It was only the second time he felt so strongly about a woman. *Soulmate.* He knew that many people never got to experience it once, never got to have what Cab and Shawna have and what he so badly wanted in his own life. Someone to complete him. He never thought he'd get another chance to feel the pure elation and head-in-the-clouds euphoria that finding your soul mate brings to the human spirit. Once you felt it, you never forget. It leaves an imprint on your psyche no less than that of the love of your parents. It defines the rest of your existence. And here, right now, despite the odds against it, he had another chance. But once again, he felt some reservation, a gut feeling that something was not quite right. It wasn't a strong feeling, and he couldn't rationalize it at the moment, but it was there, gnawing at him in such a way that it kept him on edge. What should have been a peaceful, comfortable feeling was instead disquieting and restless.

It was probably just nerves, realizing that the end of his devil-may-care days of flitting from one woman to the next would soon be over. It was the big "C" that career bachelors never talked about; although they thought about it incessantly, more than women ever suspected. Surely it would pass, like cold feet before a marriage ceremony. He tried to dismiss the gnawing, but it wouldn't subside. It was like the dull ache of his sore muscles and joints brought on by the fight and fatigue of the last twenty-four hours. He could ignore the sore muscles and the nagging emotions for awhile, but they would remind him periodically that he needed to attend to them sooner or later.

Janet stirred, but did not awaken. She sighed and moved her arm, and only then did Jason realize that he had unconsciously placed his hand over hers. She was warm, and her skin was moist with perspiration. He thought perhaps she was getting too hot under the hospital sheets, and fluffed them up, taking care to fold them neatly around her shoulders. He knew that her doctors had sedated her. The heinous assault and the emotional roller coaster of not knowing if she would live or die had taken a heavy toll on her body and her mind. Compared to the trauma *she* had endured, Jason thought his problems were nothing. He derided himself for making such a big thing of them. It would work out, he was sure of it. He pushed a call button for the nurse. Maybe they could make her more comfortable.

The debriefing was an upbeat affair. The ceremonial conference room in the FBI's Philadelphia field office was packed with the detectives who worked the case, their bosses who were looking for some of the credit, and of course the politicians whose public life thrived on the limelight. Jason and Cab found seats around the outer wall of the room. The chairs arranged around the conference table were already filled, and Jason saw that one of the amply cushioned armchairs was occupied by none other than Devin Gray, crime analyst and soon-to-be FBI special agent.

She was resplendent in her navy blue Anne Taylor suit, which was neatly complimented by a double stranded silver chain. A matching bracelet adorned her slim wrist. She was engaged in an animated conversation with a man Jason recognized as the special agent-in-charge of the local FBI office. Jason had met him once when he had visited Chief Forester in Highland Park one day and told the Chief that the FBI was here to help local police agencies in any way possible. They never saw him again until today. He was about the same age as the Chief, but looked at least ten years younger, with a fifty-dollar haircut and a suit that cost twenty times that. Devin smiled more in those few minutes of conversation than Jason had seen her do the whole time he was with her in Quantico. She looked pretty when she did, her flawless white teeth framed by full pink lips that Jason noticed for the first time. Her upper lip had that exaggerated heart shaped split in the middle, and he wondered why he didn't see this before. Maybe it was a new lipstick or lip liner. Whatever is was, it looked good on her.

Supervisory Special Agent Thomas Parsons was there too, along with Lt. Ramos, and a few of the Mirror Man task force members from the Columbia and Albuquerque police departments. There were also two investigators present from the Carbon County Sheriff's Department, where police learned the killer had committed his first murder a few years ago...that of his college girlfriend. That murder went unsolved until the FBI raided Mirror Man's apartment and found letters and notes implicating him in the stalking and murder of Carol Snively. They had found her body in suburban Atlanta three years after she had graduated from the University of Georgia in Athens. Her throat had been cut with a razor, and at the time police attributed the death to a serial rapist who was terrorizing young women in the Atlanta metro area. The rapist was captured, but police only had enough evidence to convict him of one out of the four murders they attributed to him. If he *did* kill others, they now knew Carol Snively was not one of his victims. The task force members meandered around the room, slapping backs and exchanging handshakes, their version of exchanging high fives after a big game. Jason, normally eager to join in such celebrations, was uncharacteristically subdued. Cab followed his lead, and the Highland Park detectives remained aloof, quite different from their performance during the first meeting in Quantico.

At one point, Jason caught Devin looking his way, and when their eyes met, she smiled demurely. He smiled too, but broke eye contact quickly. She was looking hot, but one thing he didn't need now was temptation. She started to make her way around the room to where he and Cab were seated, but was interrupted by the sound of a gavel banging on the podium, and Agent Parsons called the meeting to order. He pointed to Devin as he introduced her, generously crediting her with discovering the link between the murders and bringing the matter to the attention of the proper authorities. She made her way to the podium when requested by Parsons and once again Jason found himself listening to the attractive and beguiling analyst talk about the grisly subject of murder.

"Thank you Agent Parsons. I am pleased to be here today, and am glad to be able to tell you that together we have solved four murders and an attempted murder. One Theodore Robert Sykes committed all of these, age 26, originally from Decatur, Georgia. Before I get into the details, I would like to extend my congratulations to all of you in this room, especially Detective Lieutenant Jason Coulter from the Highland Park Police Department." Devin looked in his direction as she spoke.

"Lieutenant Coulter caught Sykes after he had kidnapped a woman in his city and took her to a remote area of a county park, intending to sexually assault and kill her. Although she sustained serious injuries, Lt. Coulter no doubt saved her life, and put a stop to this killer's rampage."

Jason shifted uneasily in his chair. Usually he loved such accolades, but this was different. That woman she was referring to was his lover, and another of the victims had been his friend, Kyle Price. This whole mess was too close for comfort. He smiled weakly and nodded as he acknowledged a brief round of applause from the other detectives.

"This is what we know. Ted Sykes was an abused child. Records from Children and Youth Services show that his mother and he came into contact with them on several occasions, but nothing major could be substantiated and he was never taken from his home. As far as we know, his father was never in the picture. Sykes was generally a misfit, but somehow developed the ability to use social skills he learned from watching others to his advantage, even though everything indicates he was a sociopath. He was also extremely intelligent, and his knowledge and skill with a computer was simply amazing.

"As an adult," Devin continued, "he was able to blend in with everyone else, and his computer skills enabled him to get good jobs, high paying jobs at that. Usually however, he didn't stay long, often getting into arguments with his boss or another male authority figure. He was a fairly attractive man, but as we know, had a deep hatred for women. He could never sustain any type of relationship. When he was twenty-three, he killed his former girlfriend, who had left him almost two years earlier."

Devin paused for effect. "Think about that. Sykes hated her enough to want to kill her, but he was patient enough to wait a long time and plan very carefully before he acted on his urges. We actually think he acted when he did because of the other rape-homicides occurring in the area where she lived. He was smart enough to copycat the crime, and knew that if the other killer got caught, chances were he would be free and clear, that police would stop looking. And he was right. This man liked to be in control of himself . . . and others. There's no doubt that he had a way with women that belied his true nature, but when they discovered what he was really like, they ran as fast as they could."

Jason started to make a smart-ass comment, but stopped, coughing to cover up his interruption. Devin didn't flinch.

"Sometime in his early twenties, he developed some semblance of social graces and was able to attract women using a variety of wiles and ruses. He made good use of these same skills as he lured his victims into position, both on the Internet and when he stalked them in person. He didn't take trophies like many serial killers, but he did have an interesting quirk. He always made some face-to-face contact with his intended victims a short time before he struck. We think it helped to excite him, helped to build his desire into a crescendo that he couldn't resist, and thus he wouldn't back down, even if a little bit of reason invaded his sick, twisted mind."

She stopped briefly to sip from a glass of water, her lips moist as she set the glass back on the table. She glanced at Jason, and he swallowed hard.

"Actually, Ted Sykes left us quite a bit of information about himself and his gruesome activities. He left a kind of journal on his personal computer. It was not secured or coded at all, and it seems that he consciously left it for police to find in the event of his capture…or his death. It appears that he made entries into this file while he was trolling the Internet for future victims. While his virus sought out potential targets, he occupied himself by writing about his pursuits." She held up a transcript of his computer diary.

"Most of it is the stream-of-consciousness ramblings of a disturbed person, but some of it is quite lucid, and quite descriptive. It would have been damning evidence in a criminal trial, and even though he's dead, his journal will help our profilers learn more about the criminal mind. He obviously wasn't afraid of us finding this stuff. He knew that by the time we discovered his lair, before we could take custody of his computer and learn all this about him, he would have accomplished what he set out to do, and as his journal makes perfectly clear, would probably be dead."

"All of which fits the standard profile of an organized killer," Agent Parsons chimed in. "He was methodical in all of the killings and the attempted murder of Ms. Peterson. Each of them was carefully planned, and he had the patience to wait for the right moment before striking. Like most organized serial killers, he stalked his prey as the last step before carrying out the murder.

"Most serial killers also have a signature, like arranging the bodies of their victims in certain poses or leaving some accoutrements on or near the body that have some special significance to the killer. As Ms. Gray said, some of them take a part of the victim with them as a trophy, a lock of hair, a piece of clothing . . . whatever their particular desire or perversion dictates. In this case, Sykes' signature was the type of murder, strangulation by shoving a cloth down the victim's throat, and the ritualistic personal contact he made with each of the victims before the murder."

"That's right sir. And the other signature of his was of course, his use of the Internet to select his victims. That, unfortunately, is something we are bound to see more of in the future."

"You bet!" Jason put in his two cents for the first time since the meeting started. "And did you see this morning's headlines? '*Police Shatter Mirror Man Case.*' This guy called himself Mirror Man. A catchy nickname don't you think? I wonder what brainiac leaked that information to the press? Did someone release this maniac's entire journal? I'm sure this moniker will be very appealing to his fellow psychotics. Every two bit pervert with a personal computer and access to an ISP will be out there combing the world wide web for some unsuspecting mama or child to take advantage of. Once they know the technology exists, even if they don't know jackshit about it themselves, they'll find some other pervert to replicate what our guy did and we'll have hundreds of copycat killers on our hands. Isn't technology wonderful?"

"The media monitors all our unscrambled police channels," answered Parsons. "Someone probably let it slip. They would have gotten it eventually anyway, might as well get it over with now. There's no trial so it will soon blow over."

Let it slip, my ass, Jason thought. He would bet the mortgage that Parsons himself gave that juicy tidbit to the media. What better way to help rebuild the sagging image of the FBI than to romanticize this fiend, give him a personality…and then make sure the Bureau was featured prominently in all the newspaper and TV coverage. Hell, this might even wind up as a movie of the week.

One of the officers from Columbia spoke up next. "Sykes killed or tried to kill only women, except for Kyle Price. Why him?"

Devin Gray answered. "That's in his writing too. Price was sleeping with Amber Mathieson, and this launched Sykes into a jealous rage. In Sykes' case, he was able to control his hatred, and managed to play out his game until he was ready for the final hand. He had it in mind the whole time to take Price out, but wanted to wait until it would have the most impact. He even got a job in Price's organization, and was highly regarded for his computer skills, and his sadistic ability to inflict pain. It seems he became involved in the gruesome disciplining of plant employees suspected of theft. It was obvious that toward the end, Sykes was losing control, and was starting to escalate his killings. He may have soon reached the point where he would have even gone after his pursuers." She glanced at Jason as she spoke. "I'm relieved it didn't come to that."

"I think we all echo that sentiment," Agent Parsons said. "And on that note, we'll conclude this briefing. Chief Forestall and I have to prepare for another media conference." He bent over to whisper to the Chief, "I heard CNN is out in the hall waiting."

Chapter 30

Jason sat on a bench at the edge of Arbor Pond, one of two large man-made ponds in Mulligan Park. It was a beautifully landscaped portion of this popular community park. The landscape surrounding the pond was framed by tall evergreens and the pond itself featured a natural stone fountain that cascaded an endless stream of clear cool water ten feet above the rippling surface. It was the centerpiece for this tranquil milieu. It was early in the morning, and Jason was the only person in the park, save for an occasional jogger who passed by, following a path that wandered through the entire park. The occasional muffled footfalls of passing joggers did nothing to interrupt the sweet soundtrack of nature. The tweets and warbles of birds singing proudly on high branches blended freely with the steady pitter-patter of the fountain spray, sounding like the symphony of an exotic rain forest.

Nature was in-sync. Not so with the life and love of the man who sat on the rough-hewn bench below the lush forest canopy. The idyllic setting was wasted on Jason. He was too lost in thought to notice. *Another chapter finished.* It ended abruptly, which was quite a contrast considering the slow beginning to their love affair. Jason remembered how intimidated he was about approaching her. She was beautiful, high brow, and seemingly unattainable for a mere cop. He had imagined her type to be more Wall Street, with slicked back hair and thousand dollar suits driving a Mercedes. Or maybe preppy tousled hair, Docksiders, a Rolex, and a Porsche. Whichever one attracted her, he had figured it wasn't a sports coat from Boscov's, brown wing tips, and a Bianci .40 caliber holster, tooling around in a plain Crown Victoria. But he was wrong. She did go for him, and in a big way.

They had spent some torrid nights together, nights that left him drained; with unsteady legs and a full heart. More important for a long-term relationship, they whiled away many a day having spontaneous, inane fun or immersed in deep philosophic discussions. Everything seemed good. Despite their busy schedules and stressful occupations, they had managed to forge some pretty strong bonds. They always made the most of their time together. He had gone so far as to look at engagement rings one day at Jewelers Row. He had swallowed hard when he saw the sign hanging at one of the many stores that populated this part of Sansom Street in Philadelphia. *Two Months Salary for a Lifetime of Happiness.* Jesus, that was a fortune to spend on a diamond, even when calculated at a cop's salary.

She called him after she had gotten home from the hospital, saying she needed to see him soon. Her voice was melancholy, but he attributed that to the ordeal she'd been through, and the few days lying in the hospital. She had too much time to remember what had occurred the night she was hurt. It was hard not to relive the horror and the pain, as she lay alone in the stark hospital room with no one to comfort or even distract her from these harmful thoughts. There was also the realization that her model-beautiful face was scarred.

It was a temporary condition the surgeon had assured her, but still a depressing sight for Janet as she looked at the blotchy purplish lumps and crisscross stitching that marred her image in the small mirror she had insisted the nurses bring her. Her coworkers had resisted her request for a mirror, telling her she looked fine, and to give it some time. But the more they stalled, the more adamant she had become about having it. In the end, the psychiatrist on staff had sided with Janet, saying that the longer she's allowed to imagine how badly her face was disfigured, the longer it would take her to recover and move on. It might result in her never being able to accept the tiniest of scars remaining from the brutal attack.

When she called, Jason told her that he would be right over, but she cut him off, suggesting that they meet somewhere, maybe Pompano's. That was his first clue that something was wrong, and he felt the first twinges of uneasiness in his gut. He agreed to meet her.

She had looked radiant despite the extra makeup she wore to dull the still visible scars. She had that sparkle back in her eyes, but it had been immediately apparent to Jason that she was also very, very, troubled. At first he thought it might have something to do with Christine, who was taking Kyle's death real hard, or maybe it had something to do with her own recovery. After all, the trauma she'd experienced could take a severe toll on her psyche. It was common for depression to set in, and for self-doubt and confusion to temporarily alter a victim's personality. But as soon as he looked into her eyes he knew it wasn't either of those things, or anything other than his greatest fear. *They were done.*

She told him quickly, seeing the pain in his face and recognizing and acknowledging what he already knew. It had been a long time since he hurt this bad. The wounds he sustained in his fight with Ted didn't hurt nearly as much as

245

the deep gut-wrenching pain he felt now. She had left the restaurant right after she told him, holding back tears as she let the words flow just as she rehearsed. He remembered only bits and pieces . . . *we look at life differently, want different things, have different values. You know what you want, I don't,* she said . . . and that much was true. He did know what he wanted, in life maybe not, but in love, he knew. Never more than now, he knew what he wanted.

As she walked out of the room, the very place where their love had first bloomed, he resisted the urge to follow. He wouldn't even turn his head to follow her, but held his breath and listened to her leave. He hoped he would hear her footsteps change direction. He hoped that she would return and stand next to his chair and smile down at him in that slightly quizzical way that he found so seductive. He waited, but too many seconds passed and the sound of her footsteps faded. The waiter came by and started to remove their untouched drinks. Barely audible, he heard Jason talking, mumbling to himself.

"You know what you want too and it's just not me . . . at least for now."

He finished crying, his body shuddering with the last vestiges of unbridled grief. He had let himself go for a long time, knowing it was going to happen sooner or later, and preferring to let it out here…in Mulligan Park, a place that would always hold some special meaning for him now. He looked up at the treetops, hearing for the first time the warbling of a lone finch. Using a cupped hand to shield his eyes from the dappled rays of sunlight breaking through gaps in the boughs of the thick trees overhead, he searched for the bird. He became aware of the gentle gurgling of the water, stirred by the never-ending pulse of the fountain's cascade. He spotted a jogger coming through the woods, reminding him it had been a long time since he had a really good workout.

He watched as a young woman, about Sonja Peterson's age, ran along the path, her breathing measured and her gaze focused on the route ahead. Her arms and legs moved in unison, with a natural beauty not unlike a big cat moving effortlessly through the jungle. She was absorbed in her run, and gave no indication that she was aware of the horror that had taken place in this serene park only a few short days ago. It was a beautiful morning, and she was taking full advantage of it. A voice inside reminded Jason that he had a role insuring that such order and beauty continue.

He watched the young woman until her form blended with the greens, browns, and yellows of the well-manicured foliage that lined the pathway. The colors of autumn. He rose, and walked slowly toward the parking lot where he had left his car. He reached for the cell phone hanging from his belt, and hit the number "1" on his speed dial.

"Highland Park Police, Officer Michaels."

"Lt. Coulter here. Anything going on?"

"Hey Boss, watcha doin'? Nothing here. They tell me it was a quiet night. Guess that's alright with you for a change, eh?"

"Yeah, Michaels. That's alright with me."